WHISTLEBLOWER

Also By Kate Marchant

WHISTLEBLOWER

kate marchant

wattpad books

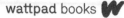

An imprint of Wattpad WEBTOON Book Group
Content warning: sexual assault, misogyny, bullying, rape, date rape

Published in Canada by Wattpad WEBTOON Book Group, a division of
Wattpad Corp.

36 Wellington Street E., Suite 200, Toronto, ON M5E 1C7 Canada

www.wattpad.com
First Wattpad Books edition: March 2023

ISBN 978-1-98936-508-3 (Trade Paper edition)
ISBN 978-1-98936-509-0 (eBook edition)

Library and Archives Canada Cataloguing in Publication information is
available upon request.

Printed and bound in Canada

1 3 5 7 9 10 8 6 4 2

Cover design by Lesley Worrell
Images © JoyCrew via Shutterstock

For my sister, Elizabeth,
and for anyone else who wants to burn it all down.

chapter 1

I wish I could say it was the first time I'd put off an assignment until the day it was due, but my parents didn't raise a liar.

It was only the first week of the semester. Hanna and I still hadn't finished unpacking in our new off-campus apartment, and somehow I'd already managed to spend fifty-eight dollars on carne asada tacos and avoid all academic responsibility. But this morning, I'd had hope. I'd thought I'd pulled off another successful feat of procrastination—another last-minute lunge across the finish line. I hadn't accounted for the rain.

Garland, California (population thirty thousand during the school year and half that in the summer), was an hour east of downtown Los Angeles. We were used to droughts. But by the time I'd made it to Buchanan, the main library on campus, I was soaked from the crown of my head to the chipped nail polish on my toes. I'd worn a sundress. I looked like an idiot. A very damp idiot. And as I stood there, wrestling my USB drive into the slot on an ancient copy machine and dripping a puddle onto the baby poop–green carpet, my phone started to vibrate somewhere in the depths of my backpack.

I groaned and dropped it to the floor to begin a search and rescue mission. There were only four people who could realistically be calling me—Andre Shepherd, Hanna Pham, and either of my parents. It was Hanna.

"Why are there granola bars all over the bathroom floor?" she demanded in lieu of a greeting.

"I'm sorry. The bottom of the box gave out. I was in a rush."

"Are you in class right now?"

"No, I'm at Buchanan. I have to print out my pitch."

It was Thursday morning, and the editor in chief of Garland University's school paper wanted a hard copy turned in to a box on her desk by noon. *Joke's on her*, I thought. My pitch was going to suck no matter what format it was in. The abomination in question had started chugging out of the printer at a speed of approximately two lines an hour.

"Actually, never mind. I think I'm in hell."

"At least you finished it, right?" Hanna said. "Ellison's got to respect the bare minimum. And you did your best! That's what counts."

I barked out a bitter laugh. "I would hardly call this my best."

"Don't be modest. It's gross."

"I'm not being modest, Han. This might be the worst thing I've ever written." And I'd authored One Direction fan

2

fiction back in middle school, so the standards of judgment were pretty low. "And you know what? I'm mad at myself. This story had so much potential. I should've started drafting it last week—"

"Yeah, but you spent half the summer in Mexico City. I think you get a free pass on this one. Visiting family is more important than a fluff piece about the football team."

Except it'd turned out more like a celebrity gossip column than a fluff piece. I hadn't started brainstorming until last weekend, when Hanna and I had arrived at our new place and I was forced to accept that school is an inevitable evil with which I must grapple for two more years. Speaking of—I had class in four and a half minutes. My article and I were both going to be late.

"Just push all the granola bars against the bathtub and I'll take care of them after I get back from Intro to Dick Jokes," I told Hanna.

It was the name Andre had given to the class we were taking. Human Sexuality—more commonly referred to as BIO 108 by kids relaying the details of their semester schedules to their parents—fulfilled the core requirement for a science-based course despite involving very little science other than reproductive anatomy. The roster was full of seniors and athletes who got to pick their classes before the rest of the student body, but I'd been lucky enough (or, rather, vigilant enough) to get a spot when someone dropped it less than twenty-four hours before the first lecture.

"Take your time," Hanna told me. "I'll be at figure drawing for a while."

"Enjoy the penises."

"You too."

I shoved my phone into the pocket of my sundress—the one redeeming value of an otherwise useless garment—as a pair of footsteps thundered up the stairs. A girl with headphones shoved on over a mass of thick, dark curls stomped around the corner. I recognized her. Mehri Rajavi was another writer at the *Daily*—a junior, like me. She was also having about as great a morning as I was, if the way she was spitting out curses under her breath was any indication.

"Hi, Mehri," I greeted her as she jammed a button on the copy machine next to mine.

She squinted hard at me, then said, "Hey, girl."

She didn't recognize me. It was fine. We'd only had that IR class together. And intermediate nonfiction. And a freshman seminar on journalism in the Middle East. Then, of course, there was the fact that she was friends with Hanna, so I'd once tagged along to Mehri's art show and spent an hour staring at a collection of enormous watercolor flowers that blatantly resembled female genitalia.

"Guess this is what we get for waiting until the last minute to print," I quipped, powering through the discomfort of having someone I'd met multiple times totally blank on my name. "Ellison's going to drop-kick me across the student union."

Mehri humored me with the kind of tight, toothless smile one offers a relative when they've made a tasteless political joke and you're not in the mood to start World War III at the dinner table. I smacked the side of my printer, willing it to have mercy on me. The third sheet of my rambling four-page pitch slid into the tray right as my phone buzzed with a text.

It was from Andre: *Did u die?*

4

I replied, *I wish!!!*

The printer took pity on me and spat out the last page of my pitch. I snatched it, crinkling one corner by accident—usually I would've taken the time to reprint, but it wasn't like I had a piece of groundbreaking journalism in my hands—and did a dorky jog toward the stairs, sandals squelching as I went.

"Good luck, Mehri!" I called over my shoulder, already knowing that our entire interaction was going to haunt me when I tried to fall asleep that night.

"Oh, thanks," she replied, a bit bemused. "Hey, wait, do you—"

I was already too far to turn back. I hustled down the stairs—half expecting to slip and eat shit, because that seemed like it would fit in thematically with the rest of my morning—and comforted myself with the knowledge that Mehri probably wouldn't remember our conversation by tomorrow.

I was forgettable. It was something I tried to think of as a party trick rather than a heroic flaw.

—

Outside of Buchanan, I tucked the pages of my pitch close to my chest and made a run for it through the rain. The tree-lined parkway that ran down the middle of campus was slick with puddles, and green and white confetti from orientation week floated among clumps of dead leaves. Most of Garland's campus was composed of manicured rosebushes, paved walkways, and redbrick buildings, but the trio of newer constructions on the far edge of campus were modern steel and concrete monstrosities. I stumbled into the lobby of the nearest one. The stairs at that end of the building were caution-taped off and reeked of fresh paint, so I headed for the elevator, slipping and sliding in my sandals and breathing harder than I probably should've been after such mild exertion.

I smacked the call button before checking my phone again.

Professor's here, Andre had texted two minutes ago. Then, a minute later: *He's calling attendance pls move ur ass.*

I paced, leaving a trail of wet footprints in my wake as I cursed my last name, Cates, for beginning with the third letter of the alphabet.

The elevator was tucked away in a dim little alcove that someone had tried to make less like a scene out of a horror movie by sticking a potted shrub in the corner and hanging a corkboard on the wall. There were only two things pinned up: a torn scrap of paper advertising the sale of a used futon and a glossy green poster listing the dates of this season's home football games. There were three faces on the poster. On the right was Kyle Fogarty, our star tight end. He and his blond undercut were shooting the camera an easy, confident smirk. On the left was our quarterback, Bodie St. James, who could launch a football fifty yards down the field with pinpoint accuracy and shrug off guys who were built like boulders. It was a great photo of him. He looked like a stoic, fearsome gladiator. I'd heard his friends thought he was more like a puppy.

Bodie and I had never spoken, but from what I'd gathered, he was a very nice person—polite to a fault, respectful of his elders, recycled his plastic bottles. The kind of nice that didn't make a big deal about itself.

Between Fogarty and St. James was head coach Truman Vaughn, the father figure of Garland's multimillion-dollar behemoth of a football program. I stuck my tongue out at his photo.

It was a well-known fact that Vaughn had been to rehab sometime in the '90s for alcoholism. His comeback had been a huge deal. He'd convinced the president and board of trustees that his days of partying were over and he was ready to give his all to the program. As it turned out, *that* was a load of shit. The pitch in my hands contained several firsthand accounts of a wild night out Vaughn had been spotted having over the summer break. It was the most scandalous story I'd ever attempted for the *Daily*. Half of me had hope that Ellison would recognize my growth and see that I'd tried to push myself out on a limb. The other half of me knew the quality was lacking and hoped she'd be so busy sorting through that week's batch of pitches that she wouldn't even glance at my name on the top—she'd just toss the thing in the trash and be done with it.

And no one else will ever know, I thought regretfully, *that Vaughn's lying about his sobriety.*

The elevator arrived, announcing itself with a cheery *ding* that sounded borderline mocking. I threw myself inside and sighed with relief, now that I was, as Andre had so eloquently suggested, moving my ass.

"Hold the door!" someone called.

Any other morning, I would've.

"Sorry, buddy," I muttered under my breath.

I was hidden in the corner of the elevator, so whoever was jogging down the hall couldn't see the guilt on my face as I pressed the Close Doors button. But before they could shut, a hand appeared between them. A very large hand. I had just enough time to yank my arm back from the button panel and stand bolt upright before the doors bounced open again, revealing a face I'd seen not ten seconds earlier.

Dark, damp hair. Pink cheeks. Eyes dark as thunderclouds.

Puta madre, I thought.

"Going down?" Bodie St. James asked.

He didn't look like the golden retriever his friends described. He looked like some kind of primordial warrior who could snap my arm in half with his bare hands. Of course, I'd just tried to close the doors in his face, so I was likely projecting.

"Are you going down?" Bodie repeated when all I did was stare at him.

His short, dark hair was dripping onto the wide shoulders of a matte black Nike jacket with a metallic Garland Lions logo on the left breast. The school bought the football team new ones every season. This year's model appeared to be waterproof.

I nodded and said, "Basement."

He's so tall up close was the only coherent thought my brain seemed capable of composing as he stepped into the elevator. Then the doors slid shut, and we were alone. A part of me wanted desperately to apologize—to explain myself, and why I was in such a rush—but pinching my mouth shut and frowning down at my phone felt so much more comfortable.

The elevator began its descent to the basement. The agonizing quiet seemed to drag on for a small eternity.

And then, abruptly, Bodie spoke.

"Weather's nice today, huh?"

It took me a moment to accept that I was the only person

he could possibly be talking to, and that I should therefore look up and acknowledge him. I'd never been very comfortable bearing the weight of someone's full attention, but making eye contact with Bodie made my stomach twist in a way it hadn't since I'd been forced to take the stage at my third-grade talent show.

Oh my god, I thought. *He's trying to make small talk.*

"Yeah, it's lovely," I said, like I wasn't tragically underdressed and dripping wet. The corner of Bodie's mouth twitched.

"Essay due already?" he asked.

"It's for the school paper, actually."

"You're a writer?"

"Only on a deadline," I said.

Maybe he was just indulging me, but Bodie smiled. He had a sharp, sullen face—high cheekbones, pointy nose—but an honest, boyish smile. He opened his mouth to speak again, but the elevator lurched to a stop and the electronic display over the doors flickered to B before he could.

The doors dinged and slid open, catapulting me back into reality.

"Stay dry out there," I advised, sounding startlingly like my nana.

I turned and skittered into the hall, fleeing the scene of the second failed social interaction I'd had that morning. And then it got worse. So much worse—because the sounds of my tiny, wet footsteps were echoed by a heavier, steadier pair.

Bodie St. James and I were heading in the same direction.

I was acutely aware of my dress sticking to my legs as I approached the nearest of two sets of double doors that led into the lecture hall. It occurred to me that I was about to walk into a crowded room both late and dripping wet, which meant that people were going to stare. I paused to pull my hair over one shoulder and fidget with my backpack straps. And, because the morning *could* in fact get worse, Bodie stopped at my side.

"You in this class too?" he asked.

I nodded in defeat.

Bodie smiled like we had some kind of inside joke.

"C'mon," he told me conspiratorially, "we'll go together."

Before I could respond, he'd shouldered open the classroom door and marched in with all the confidence of someone who was either blissfully dumb or very fond of being the center of attention. I hesitated for a moment before following him, my shoulders hunched and my heart hammering.

But nobody was looking at me. They were all watching Bodie.

On stage at the front of the lecture hall, standing behind a podium under dual projection screens, our professor glanced up from the stack of papers he was shuffling through.

Nick, who'd insisted during Tuesday's class that we all call him exclusively by his first name, was the type of guy who prided himself on being cool: midthirties, wore graphic tees under blazers, read a lot of classic literature, and made a point of quoting it so you'd know. He had trendy grandpa-style glasses perched on the end of his hooked nose, and his hair was just long enough to fit in a tiny ponytail.

His stern frown softened when he recognized Garland's starting quarterback.

"I'm so sorry, Nick," Bodie said, sounding genuinely

apologetic. "I sprinted here, I swear. Did you call attendance already?"

Nick reshuffled the papers on his podium.

"Don't worry about it, Bodie," he said, smiling as he checked *St. James* off on the list. "I'm still setting up the PowerPoint. You didn't really miss anything, technically, so I'll mark you present. Excited to have you in our class—I'm glad your schedule moved around."

It was like watching a guy pull a dove out of a hat. Bodie just had to smile in that humble, slightly self-deprecating way of his and people tripped over themselves to do favors for him.

"Thanks so much, Nick," he said, beaming. "Happy to be here."

Then, still facing the podium, Bodie reached his hand behind his back and curled his fingers as if to say *Come here*. It took me a second to realize he was signaling me. I was still standing a good two thirds of the way up the aisle, so I saw people turn in their chairs out of the corner of my eye as I hurried down to the stage.

Nick's face dropped when he noticed me, and I realized what Bodie had just orchestrated. Nick couldn't play favorites now. Not when the whole class was watching. He'd marked Bodie present, and he'd have to mark me the same.

"Hey there," Nick said, his smile tight. "Your name?"

"Laurel Cates," I answered, my voice high-pitched in that way it always seemed to get when I was trying to be polite.

Nick shuffled through the pages and jotted down another check mark.

"I'll let it slide this time," he told me.

"Thank you," I gushed.

Nick nodded and went back to his laptop.

I spun around and flinched a little at the sight of the crowded auditorium. There were so many people. Granted, most of them were staring down at their phones in their laps or scribbling mindlessly in notebooks, but still. I turned to Bodie, knowing I should say thank you but a little horrified that I might blurt out something either offensive or too affectionate by accident. But before I could even open my mouth, he tucked his thumb under the strap of his backpack and gave me a knowing smile.

"Aren't you glad you didn't close the doors on me?" he asked.

And then he winked.

It was so utterly *charming*—devoid of any bitterness or passive aggression—that I almost didn't catch the flicker of triumph in his eyes before he turned and marched up the aisle to find a seat.

chapter 2

It took me a moment to remember that I was standing on stage in front of almost a hundred people with what had to be a shell-shocked expression on my face.

I snapped my mouth shut and scanned the crowd for Andre. He was sitting three rows from the back and two chairs in from the aisle, where he'd saved me a seat with his backpack. His hair was easy to spot—tall on top, fade on the sides, with twin racing stripes buzzed over each of his ears. It helped, of course, that he was six foot four and wearing the same black Nike jacket as all the other football players.

He watched me with one eyebrow raised as I hurried up the aisle and dropped into the seat beside him, sighing in relief.

"The fuck did you do?" he whisper-hissed. "Swim here?"

"Funny," I grumbled, shaking a little as I tugged my backpack off.

Andre must've notice I was flustered, because he shut up and let me unpack. I slapped the loose pages of my pitch onto the uselessly small swiveling desk built onto my chair and sat back.

"Is that your pitch?" Andre asked. "I thought you were turning it in this morning."

"I'm going to the student union right after this. Printing in Buchanan was a *nightmare*."

"You should hit up the architecture library. They got new printers this summer. Nice ones. I'll swipe you in."

I sighed and scrubbed my hands over my face. Why was I like this? Why was I incapable of starting assignments I cared about until the day they were due?

Up on stage, Nick was connecting his laptop to the projector. Three rows down, Bodie squeezed past people's knees to get to a clump of football players sitting together.

"Holy shit," said Kyle Fogarty. "Coach shakes down the professor to get you into the class, and then you show up *late*? What a fucking power move."

Bodie grimaced, so quick I could've blinked and missed it. "Wasn't on purpose," he said. "Coach asked me to grab breakfast with him this morning. We had to talk strategy for next weekend."

I'm not sure why the knowledge that Vaughn had gotten Bodie a spot in a class with a full roster came as such a surprise. A football player getting preferential treatment at Garland was far from a novelty. While the *Daily* had to print in black-and-white because the university couldn't find it in the budget to give us color printing, the football team got free soft-serve ice cream and massages at their brand-new training facility. Every fall, the town of Garland rejoiced in the almighty glory of collegiate football and kissed the team's collective ass.

The rest of the players welcomed Bodie with a ritualistic series of handshakes and pats on the back. I watched them with detached fascination, wincing when Scott Quinton—an offensive tackle who had the neck of a sea lion—clapped Bodie on the shoulder so hard I felt a phantom ache in my own arm.

"Boys are so dumb," I murmured. "Doesn't that *hurt*?"

Andre looked up from his laptop and gave me a withering stare. "You and Hanna tweeze each other's eyebrows."

"Fair," I conceded. "Shouldn't you be down there? With the team?"

"Nah," he said, even though I could tell it had something to do with the fact that he was second string and the guys sitting up in front of us were starters. "You're way better company. Plus, I need your advice. Which font looks better?"

He tipped his laptop screen so I could see what he was working on—something bright and geometric and beautiful, like all the graphic art he made, with the words *Garland Black Student Union* across the top.

"Second one," I said after he clicked between a few options.

"Futura." Andre hummed thoughtfully. "Keeping it classic. I like it."

"Nerd."

I wasn't sure how Andre ever found time to sleep. He always seemed to be bouncing between places—the studio, football practice, BSU meetings—and would show up at the apartment Hanna and I shared at odd hours of the day to riffle through our kitchen, eating handfuls of breakfast cereal and pistachios until Hanna's oldest-sibling instinct finally took over and she cooked him something more substantial. I'd call him a moocher, but that didn't seem fair. He simply needed to consume more calories a day than I did in a week (which was why I really needed to stop going taco for taco with him at Pepito's).

I turned my attention back to the display of camaraderie a few rows down. Fogarty and his blond faux hawk—which he'd undoubtedly dye green again next weekend, as he did for every opening home game—were so loud. The other boys fed off of his rowdy energy, laughing and shouting to be heard over each other, until half the room was chuckling along with their jokes and insults.

And then Bodie tapped the shoulder of the guy beside him and pressed one finger to his lips, smiling in a way that was too friendly to be authoritative. The whole group quieted instantly.

"How's St. James looking?" Andre whispered.

"I'm not—" I began, then huffed. "I'm just *thinking*."

It wasn't that I liked Bodie now, because I didn't. Just because a conventionally attractive white boy with a charming smile and the body of an Olympian had been nice to me didn't mean I had to spontaneously develop an infatuation. And if what Kyle Fogarty had said was true—if Coach Vaughn had reached out to Nick to secure a spot for Bodie in one of the most popular classes at Garland—then that was a gross misconduct I couldn't forgive. The cherry on top of a pile of privilege.

So, no. I didn't have a crush on Bodie St. James. I just thought he was fun to look at.

"Do you think he knows?" I asked Andre.

"Knows what?"

I tapped a finger on the pitch on my desk. Andre was the first person I'd texted about the scoop. He'd been unsurprised, since everyone at Garland knew the stories about the coach's struggle with substance abuse, but disappointed—not so much because he liked Vaughn (he was, in Andre's words, *actually kind of a huge dick*) but because the season was shaping up to be Garland's best of the decade.

"About the drinking? Probably, but I'm not gonna be the one to bring it up. We aren't tight like that."

"I thought you talked to him."

"I mean, sometimes. He's run drills with me before and he invited me out to lunch once. But he's nice to everyone on the team, you know?"

"Right," I murmured.

I was staring at the curve of Bodie's jaw, thinking that he must've shaved that morning because the skin there was clean and smooth, when the words *Unit One: Evolution and Sexual Anatomy* suddenly appeared on the dual projector screens, bright red and menacing. The lecture hall erupted with snickers and nervous laughter. Nick, bless his heart, hadn't realized that the class was full of student athletes who were more interested in the prospect of watching adult films than in learning about the sociology of fetishes and romantic attraction. He dove into his lecture without flinching.

I sighed and tried to forget about the damp, crumpled pitch on my desk.

—

The assault of genitalia diagrams was seemingly endless. When Nick finally clicked off the projector, turned on the lights, and told us to have a good weekend—but not *too* good a weekend, because we had reading due Tuesday—I was the first person in the room to lurch out of my seat. I hugged my notebook to my chest, the loose sheets of my pitch shoved inside for safekeeping, and shuffled backward into the aisle.

"You want to grab lunch after I turn this in?" I asked Andre over the cacophony of chatter and zippers while everyone packed up.

"What kind of a question is that? Of course I want lunch. I'm going to meet up with Hanna at the Art House. You can pick us up when you're ready."

"Please don't tell me you're starting Thirsty Thursday this early," I begged.

"Blackout Thursday," Andre corrected. "And it's never too early to pregame. Don't give me that look! We're just going to play a round of beer pong. Relax. We're saving the Fireball for tonight."

I scrunched my nose and shivered with disgust.

"Do you *hate* yourselves?"

"Go turn in your damn article!" Andre said, shooing me off with a wave of his hand.

Before I turned to leave, I allowed myself one glance across the room. Bodie St. James stood with his fingers laced behind his head as he stretched his elbows out and arched his back. He turned to Kyle Fogarty and said something that made him laugh, then slung his backpack over his shoulder and stepped into the opposite aisle.

He didn't so much as look back in my direction. There

was no good reason for me to feel disappointed. I'd known damn well he wouldn't.

Outside, the rain clouds had thinned so streaks of golden sunlight were pouring through. While very picturesque, this meant the air was both damp *and* warm. My thick, heavy hair had never done well in humidity. It crackled as I trudged across campus.

The student union was a massive horseshoe-shaped building at the far end of a quad that housed the enormous oval fountain where the bravest of the seniors always went skinny-dipping the week before graduation. It was a perpetually crowded part of campus, even with the grass soaked and the skies still half gray. There were people studying on beach towels and a pair of guys tossing a football back and forth, both of them wearing bro tanks and board shorts.

The media center on the top floor buzzed with noise and smelled vaguely of stale coffee and warm printer ink. *Daily* headquarters hadn't been updated in at least five years. I was sure the aggressively yellow walls and overabundance of bean-bag chairs (all of which were eternally leaking pellets of foam stuffing) had once been the cutting edge of interior design, but now the whole place felt like a giant throwback. Although the open concept was nice, at least.

At any given time there were minimum thirty people in the media center, scattered across the seating areas and desktop-armed tables, some of them collaborating with teammates and some of them staring vacantly at the sunflower-yellow walls while they squished beanbag foam pellets between their fingers.

I spotted our editor in chief immediately. She was hard to miss.

Ellison Michaels was six feet tall and walked with the authority of an industrial-grade steamroller. She had a travel mug in one hand and a stack of papers in the other. Trailing one step behind her was a wide-eyed kid with AirPods in both ears and half-moons of sweats staining the armpits of his Garland-green polo shirt.

AirPods Boy was talking fast. Ellison was nodding every few seconds, listening intently but not looking at him. Wherever she went, rooms orbited around her. Ellison was simultaneously a supermassive black hole—unmovable and terrifying—and a supernova, blindingly bright and capable of titanic explosions that could vaporize everything in her wake. And her hair was always perfect.

A lot of people talked a lot of shit about Ellison for being so authoritarian, but I liked her. Freshman year, when I'd drafted my first article for the *Daily*, she was the sophomore editor assigned to my work. Her infamous red-ink revisions had been so scathing that I'd sat down and cried at a table in the student union. That night, I'd opened my laptop to change my major, but stopped when I saw an email from the editor in chief at the time (a senior who'd gone on to work at the *Washington Post*). He'd said Ellison had told him I showed enormous potential. He'd invited me to sit in on one of the closed-door weekly meetings with all the senior writers. I'd been the only freshman there—wide-eyed and incapable of not smiling.

Maybe I was biased, because to me, Ellison Michaels was pretty cool. But she also scared the living daylights out of me. And it didn't help that I was holding a very half-assed story pitch I knew she'd have to read.

Just get it over with. I darted between beanbag chairs to intercept her.

"Ellison?"

"Your pitch is late." She greeted me, blunt and no-nonsense. She hadn't stopped moving, so I had no choice but to scramble along beside her, falling into step with AirPods Boy, whose face was pinched in a way that told me I'd interrupted him midsentence. My grip on the notebook clutched to my chest tightened as I fortified myself to say something.

Um is what came out.

Ellison expected hard-hitting expository journalism. Something cutting-edge. Something that upheld her original assessment of me as having *great potential.* Instead, I was going to hand her what was basically glorified gossip about the head coach of Garland's football team, and she was going to uncap her trademark red pen and stab me in the eye.

AirPods Boy cleared his throat impatiently.

"Like I was saying," he resumed, "President Sterling wants coverage of the alumni fundraiser this weekend. They're doing a reception luncheon in Buchanan, campus tours, professor talks in Cannon Hall."

"Assign a sophomore," Ellison said then to me: "Do you have it?"

I fumbled with my notebook.

"Yes! Yes, right here. But I was wondering if I could explain where I was going with it."

Ellison plucked my pitch out of my hand, unmoved by the wrinkles and smudges of ink where rain had blotted the paper, and slapped it onto the top of the stack in her arm. Then she held up a finger, silencing me, and scanned the first page. And, oh god, she was actually going to read it in front of me.

"You work at the Garland Country Club?" she asked, not looking up.

"I do. I'm mostly part of the waitstaff, but sometimes I'm ball girl for—"

"Cheryl and Tori Lasseter, Jessica Kaufman, and Diana Cabrera."

My favorite co-worker and I referred to them as the Real Housewives of Garland. Their hobbies included group vacations, chugging white wine spritzers, and talking trash about their mutual acquaintances and ex-husbands over semifriendly tennis matches that often ended in tears, tirades, and promises to take it easier on each other next time.

"They're members," I said. "They told me they were on a ladies' trip in San Diego this August when they saw Truman Vaughn out at some upscale bar."

"As in Vaughn, the head coach of the football team, Vaughn?" I nodded.

"'He invited them onto his yacht,'" Ellison read with an arched eyebrow. "'They reported he was visibly drunk and smelled of alcohol,'" she read on. "'He bought them a round of drinks and invited them back to his hotel room at the Alvarado Resort.'" Ellison stopped, turned the page over, and frowned when she found it blank. "Did they go or not?"

"No, they said they ended up going out to this club they were dying to see. Diana—she's the ringleader of their friend group—read on Yelp that there'd be male cage dancers, which I guess is a selling point. But Vaughn gave them his number and told them to text him if they changed their minds."

"And that's it?"

"Just about, yeah."

Ellison sighed and passed my crumpled stack of papers back to me.

"I can't print this," she said.

"I can make it better."

"It's nothing personal, Laurel," she insisted, her face softening with a gentle smile at my obvious humiliation. "I can't run a story about Vaughn having a vacation. Not on the university's dime—that's why we've got a faculty advisor who would veto this in a heartbeat. Someone has to keep us from totally devolving into TMZ."

"But isn't it concerning? I mean, he had an addiction—"

"*Had*," Ellison repeated. "That was almost a decade ago. Just because he was drinking on vacation doesn't mean he's relapsed. And as long as whatever he's doing in his personal time isn't affecting the school, printing something like this is tacky."

"I understand," I conceded. "But I really think there's more here—"

"Write me something like that feature you did on the guys who run the taco stand on Cerezo Street. That was a solid piece, Cates."

It was the article that'd convinced her I had potential. That I had a voice.

AirPods Boy cleared his throat and flashed Ellison the time on his phone.

"Shit, already?" she said. "I've got a budget meeting I need to get to. Look, if you really want to write about Vaughn, why don't you cover the football game next weekend? His foundation is giving away a bunch of sports equipment to elementary schools in Orange County. You're good at profiles. You're good at telling stories about people, getting right to the heart of them. I know you can absolutely kill something like that. Chin up, okay?"

And then she was gone, turning the corner to her office and marching down the hallway, the rubber soles of AirPods Boy's sneakers squealing against the tiled floor as he stumbled after her.

chapter 3

There were no sororities or fraternities at Garland, but a lack of Greek infrastructure had never stopped our student body from finding ways to party like the world was ending. It was the first Thursday of the semester, which meant that all day long there'd be parties up and down the Rodeo—a street a few blocks north of campus that was lined with twelve historic Victorian houses that'd all been rented out to different student interest groups and sports teams.

The house rented out by the art club was perhaps the oldest of the bunch: an enormous brown-shingled monstrosity with peeling paisley wallpaper and warped wood flooring in every tiny, cramped room. Their parties, while infrequent, had a cool, intellectual vibe. Music I hadn't heard, discussions of poetry I hadn't read. It wasn't really my scene, aside from the boxed wine, but I'd been there enough to know how to blend in.

I knocked on the front door and was let in by a pair of boys in denim jackets and beanies—ridiculous, in this heat—who were arguing in the front hall.

"No, dude, that's the thing," one said to the other. "If Banksy was just one guy, we'd have caught him by now. It's got to be more than one guy—"

Darting between them, I made my way to the cramped kitchen, where Hanna and Andre were setting up empty red cups at either end of a table that looked like it been handcrafted by a freshman who'd accidentally enrolled in a woodshop class and decided to roll with it.

I cleared my throat pointedly and said, "It's not even noon—"

"—and I've already beaten him twice," Hanna finished with a triumphant smile.

Her pin-straight black hair—which she'd chopped off over the summer so it fell two inches shy of touching her shoulders—was impeccably neat, but her face had that red tint that it inevitably took on whenever she drank so much as a sip of something alcoholic.

"Please tell me you're not playing with Natty Light," I said, eyeing the cardboard case on the kitchen counter amid a small army of empty liquor and kombucha bottles.

"Why? You want some?"

"No. But if you've got that Fireball on hand, I'd like to chug it."

"Did the pitch go over all right?" Andre asked worriedly.

I deflated and slumped against the fridge.

"She hated it. She wants me to cover next weekend's football game instead. I guess Vaughn's charity is going to give a bunch of sports equipment to public schools every time Garland scores a touchdown or something. She wants me to do a profile on him."

"That's good, right?" Hanna offered. "Ellison didn't shut you down. She just, you know, redirected you."

"I guess. I'm just upset with myself. I feel like I'm supposed to be better at this. Writing's my *thing*. I know I'm not brilliant or gifted, but I'm also not, you know, fanatically incompetent. I'm just"—I pinched one eye shut and sliced my hand through the air—"right smack in the middle."

And my articles always wound up buried five pages deep in the *Daily*, where no one would read them, because they were too decent to be tossed but they weren't exciting enough to warrant a spot on the front page, which was all most people bothered to read anyway. Sometimes I felt like I was an extra in a movie. Like somehow the role I'd been given in life wasn't a speaking one.

"Obviously I'm biased," Hanna said, "but I think everything you come up with is pure, untainted genius."

Her optimism, while appreciated, was exhausting.

"Are we getting lunch, or what?" I asked.

"One more round of BP! Just one. Please?"

"Fine," I relented. "But I'm just watching."

Hanna grinned and shouted, "Andre!"

Andre, who was standing directly behind her, put his hand on top of her head. She flinched and spun around to face him, her hair mussing under the weight of his palm.

"Don't *startle* me like that. I could hurt you."

27

This coming from a girl who was a full foot shorter than him.

"Are we going round three?" Andre asked.

"Laurel," Hanna said, "get the Natty Light."

I scoffed in disgust but helped Andre distribute a bit of watery, room-temperature beer into every cup. While I chugged the leftover half of one can against my better judgment, Hanna made a show of stretching.

"Is this really necessary?" I asked as she bent over to touch her toes.

"You're just mad," she said, nose to her knees, "that you have the flexibility of uncooked spaghetti."

"I'd challenge you on that, but this dress is too short."

Hanna rolled her eyes then popped up and took her position at the opposite end of the table. She and Andre held each other's eyes as they tossed Ping-Pong balls to decide who got first throw. I leaned against the wall and watched, wondering how I was supposed to convince Ellison that Truman Vaughn's breach of sobriety warranted just as much attention as his charity endeavors.

I sighed. Being overdramatic helped me think.

"I hear moping," Hanna accused me without tearing her eyes from Andre's. They tossed their Ping-Pong balls simultaneously. Both missed. "No moping."

"I'm not moping," I mumbled, like a liar.

Hanna sank the first shot. She whooped a cheer, then stepped up to me and pressed her palms to my cheeks. The look she leveled me with was devastatingly maternal.

"Your pitch sucked," she said. "There. Happy? You procrastinated, and you blew it. But just because you screwed up a deadline doesn't mean you have to give up on the story. Your instincts about people are scary good, Laurel. You knew my ex was trash six months before I did. I don't give a shit what Ellison says. Write *your* article. And stop pouting. I need you to help catch Andre's missed shots."

"Excuse me," he said with a scoff. "What about all the missed shots on *my* side?"

Hanna tossed her head back and laughed. Then, with a flick of her wrist, she sent a Ping-Pong ball soaring into the center cup at the other end of the table.

"Good one," she told Andre. "Drink up."

Within fifteen minutes, Hanna had proven triumphant. Andre drained the last of his beer in defeat, shouted "Kobe!" and chucked his empty cup at the trash can eight feet away, missing spectacularly. And, at long last, we were off to lunch.

Outside the Art House, the afternoon air was warm and full of noise. The Rodeo always made for great people watching, but the first weekend of the semester was a special treat. A pair of boys in identical salmon-pink shorts strolled by on the sidewalk, loudly debating our football team's odds of making the NCAA Championship this year. Across the street, outside the Engineering House, a girl in Birkenstocks was aggressively flirting with a boy who was trying to chain his bike to a tree while simultaneously holding back the hair of her friend, who was puking into a hedge—another casualty of Blackout Thursday.

Hanna, Andre, and I fell into step beside each other as we headed down the Rodeo toward Cerezo Street, the main road in Garland. The two of them almost immediately started up a discussion about beer pong strategies, and since I'd never been anywhere near good at drinking games, I let my mind wander.

Ellison hadn't called me to tell me I was kicked off the *Daily* team, so that was a good sign. But still. I couldn't shake the weight of her disappointment. Her insistence that I write something safe. Something easy.

I wasn't paying any attention to where I was walking, since my need for constant positive feedback and validation had taken over my thoughts, so I was only mildly surprised when the toe of my white canvas sneaker caught a ledge in the pavement and I stumbled.

Hanna, ever the supportive friend, threw back her head and cackled.

"I meant to do that."

"Whatever you say," she said, looping her arm through mine.

Up ahead, smack in the middle of the two-block span the Rodeo covered, the Baseball House was blasting their usual brand of rap music—something Post Malone, with the bass boosted. If the houses on the Rodeo had been fraternities and sororities, then the Baseball House would've been the frat full of gorgeous, empty-headed boys with muscular arms and rich parents. The wraparound porch was packed with beautiful, laughing people.

I spotted Bodie St. James before I realized I was looking for him.

He was leaning against the porch railing, a smile on his face and a bottle of what looked like orange juice in his hand. His jeans were dark wash and his T-shirt was black, the sleeves rolled up a little to show off his biceps, which were, admittedly, very aesthetically pleasing. But it wasn't his arms that struck me—it was the crowd of people gathered around him who seemed to hang on his every word when he was speaking and glance at him for approval when he wasn't.

I wondered, briefly, what it felt like to be that adored. In high school, I'd kept to myself. I'd had friends in my classes, sure, but we never hung out after the final bell. We knew our friendships were built out of sheer self-preservation. I didn't have any siblings, and all three of my cousins lived in Mexico and were under the age of sixteen. For most of my life, my parents had been—without a doubt—the most important people in my life.

It'd been hard to leave for Garland, even though it was only a two-hour drive from Bakersfield. And I'd been so lucky to find Hanna and Andre. They were enough. They were *everything*. But sometimes I wondered what it would feel like to walk into a crowded house party and have people climbing over each other to snag a high five.

Hanna gave my arm a squeeze.

"I'm fine," I blurted.

"I know you are. But let's eat our feelings anyway."

I squeezed her arm back.

Before we passed the Baseball House, I looked again. Bodie was clapping friends on their shoulders, nodding and tipping his head in a way that seemed to say, *I'm gonna head out.* He turned to come down the porch stairs just as we were passing by on the sidewalk. I ducked my head like the coward I was.

The Rodeo ended at Cerezo Street, which ran along the west side of campus and was home to the best taco stand in Garland. Pepito's was, in essence, a food truck without wheels. The tiny building was compact and sturdy, with a red terra-cotta tiled roof that held large marquee letters spelling out *P-E-P-I-T-O-S*. On the adobe wall over the order window, painted in loopy red script, were some of their primary menu options—burritos, tacos, enchiladas—and off to the side, between the stand and a small parking lot, were some tables and benches. There were a few students here for lunch, but come tonight, the place would be packed with drunk kids.

Pedro was at the grill, Joaquín was handling condiments, and Oscar was manning the register. He grinned under his wiry mustache when Andre and I stepped up to the counter to order.

"Back already?" he asked.

"Por supuesto."

Andre and I had accidentally become regulars during sophomore year. The guys had taken to calling him Tigre because of the stripes buzzed into his hair and his voracious appetite.

"¿El regular?" Oscar asked.

"Y un chile relleno para mi amiga."

Everyone winces the first time they hear me speak Spanish. There are plenty of traces of my mom in me, but my accent is my father's. It doesn't help that my vocabulary is limited to the basics—just enough to survive family visits to Mexico City and phone calls with my *abuelita*—and some bits and pieces collected from telenovelas, song lyrics, and my cousins (who howl with laughter when I sound out the swear words they teach me). Whatever I speak, it's not the language that my mom and her family speak. But the staff at Pepito's never make fun of me for that.

"Un chile relleno, tres tacos de carne asada," Oscar read off

as he punched our order into the register. *"Y para Tigre, un super burrito con todo."*

Andre slapped his debit card onto the counter.

"I got this one," he told me. I wanted to protest, since Andre had a bad habit of paying for my stuff, but I knew my taco addiction was bleeding my bank account dry.

Hanna and I found an empty table. The metal benches were cool beneath my bare thighs, and the breeze that carried down Cerezo Street was a welcome relief from the hot sun. Andre joined us when he was finished paying and informed us we were order number eighty-six.

Then the three of us sat and waited, venting our fall semester frustrations. Andre was bummed because he'd been doing well in practice—he'd worked out all summer to try to put on some more weight—but Kyle Fogarty, the first-string tight end, was still Coach Vaughn's clear favorite. Hanna was already struggling in her figure drawing class. She'd accidentally included an extra knuckle while sketching a hand during warm-up exercises, and her professor had pulled her aside to check if Hanna was in the right class. And I'd gotten my pitch eviscerated by Ellison, so all three of us could agree that junior year was already crashing and burning.

Andre's phone buzzed loudly on the metal table. He looked at the screen for a moment before his eyebrows pinched.

"What's up?" I asked.

"Nothing. St. James texted me."

Hanna quirked an eyebrow and asked, "In the team group chat?"

Andre shook his head. "No, just me."

"What'd he say?" I asked, attempting to sound uninterested.

"He wants me to come by the Baseball House," Andre said with a shrug. "He says a bunch of the guys are there hanging out. It's a good time. Bunch of free pizza left over. They've got beer pong. I should bring some friends."

I tapped my fingertips against my cheek. "He said that?"

Andre nodded.

It was hard not to let my mind roll out the corkboard and start pinning strings between photographs and news clippings, like some kind of television detective.

It'd looked like Bodie was leaving the Baseball House when we passed. Maybe he'd just been running out to get something—more beer, more snacks, more girls. Maybe he'd left then changed his mind and gone back. Maybe he'd seen Andre walk by and thought to invite him. Maybe he'd just sent out a mass text to all the players who weren't there.

Or, the part me that'd chugged half a Natty Light proposed, *maybe he saw me walking with Andre and recognized me from the elevator.*

"You have to go!" I said, giving Andre's arm an encouraging shove that might've been a bit too aggressive. "It's team bonding. And Hanna and I will come with you, if you want some backup."

"I, for one," Hanna piped up, "would *love* to kick St. James's ass at beer pong."

Andre still looked unsure.

"Order eighty-six!" Joaquín bellowed from the pickup window.

"You text St. James back," Hanna told Andre, "and we'll grab the food."

"But—" he began.

"Do it," I said.

I felt jittery and light on my feet as Hanna and I walked up to the pickup window. It was embarrassing, really. I didn't know why I had to get all excited at the prospect of seeing Bodie St. James again. It wasn't like he'd recognize me.

"That was nice of Bodie," I murmured. "To include Andre, I mean."

"It's about damn time the first string got their heads out of their asses," Hanna grumbled. "I swear, it makes me so *mad* that some of those guys hang out in like—like these little, exclusive groups. They think they're too cool to be seen with the nonstarters."

"Because they're oversized children."

Hanna hummed in agreement, then turned to me with her eyebrows pinched in thought.

"Do you think St. James is *nice*, or do you think he's, like, genuinely a good person?"

I frowned. "What do you mean?"

"Nice people care about other people's feelings. Good people care about what's right and what's wrong. It's an important distinction, right?"

Joaquín interrupted our surprisingly philosophical linguistics debate by shoving two greasy paper bags across the counter. I asked him for extra hot sauce. He nodded, shouted to Oscar for assistance since nobody else was in line to order, and ducked around Pedro, their movements a well-rehearsed dance that allowed them to avoid bumping into either each other or the hot grills in the compact space. The stand was too small to accommodate anything more than three men, an industrial fridge, the grills, and a condiment station. I might've called it a *small operation* if I hadn't written an article about how the three friends who owned and operated Pepito's had graduated culinary school, gotten their MBAs together, and made enough revenue in the stand's first three years to pay off all their student loans combined.

"Talk to me," Hanna said. "What's your next move for this Vaughn story?"

"The first game of the season is—"

"No, I mean *your* story. The real one."

I shot her a look. She shot one back.

"Okay, so, the women I talked to at the country club said Vaughn was *drunk*. Like, stumbling and slurring drunk. And if he's relapsed or something, he might need help, so it's probably better that I keep digging. For Vaughn's sake."

"That's fair," Hanna said.

"I can ask the Real Housewives for another interview. A formal one. And maybe, if it comes down to it, I can drive down to San Diego this weekend and see if anyone who works at the Alvarado Resort remembers seeing—oh, gracias."

Joaquín, who'd reappeared at the pickup window with a tiny lidded plastic cup of homemade hot sauce, was frowning.

"The Alvarado Resort?" he repeated, his voice gruff.

"Yeah. Have you been?"

Joaquín shook his head sharply and said, "Don't go."

Hanna and I exchanged startled looks.

"Why not?"

"My cousin's friend got assaulted there this summer."

My heart did a belly flop and landed in my stomach.

"See," Hanna said, smacking my arm. "*Instinct.* I'm telling you, Laurel, your gut knows what's up. That place sounds shady as fuck if people are going around—oh, *hell* yes, come to mama."

Joaquín slid the third bag onto the counter and into Hanna's waiting arms. I murmured my thanks as Hanna riffled through the bags, identifying which two contained her chile relleno and Andre's burrito. She grabbed one in either hand and started back to the table.

"Aight," Andre called. "St. James said we're good to go. He's on for BP."

Hanna whooped and smacked the side of her bag.

"Son of a bitch doesn't know what's coming," she said, cackling.

Bodie was still at the party. The flicker of excitement I felt was brief, since my mind immediately went to his coach.

"C'mon, Laurel," Andre called.

He and Hanna were waiting for me at the crosswalk, both of them practically bouncing from the twin excitement of hot food and social acceptance. I told myself I'd be quick—a few minutes of digging and I was sure I'd find a dead end and be able to renounce my pitch. I'd be able to write Ellison's fluffy charity piece without any lingering doubts about Vaughn. But until I knew for sure that there was no connection between Joaquín's cousin's friend and the head coach of our football team, I was in no mood to party.

"You guys go ahead," I said. "I'm going to ask Joaquín a few questions."

Hanna smiled in delighted surprise.

"That's my girl," she said, reaching out to pat my cheek.

"Do you want us to wait for you?" Andre offered, sounding a little too eager to hang back. But I didn't want to keep him from bonding with his team, and without Hanna as a wingwoman, he'd probably chicken out before he made it halfway to the Baseball House.

So I said, "No, go have fun. I'll meet up with you when I'm done."

Hanna grabbed Andre by the sleeve of his shirt and towed him away before he could come up with any other excuses. I watched them until they'd made it to the opposite side of Cerezo Street, then took a bolstering breath and turned back to the taco stand. Forget Ellison. I was trusting my gut.

chapter 4

I'd interviewed Joaquín before for my profile on Pepito's, so he knew the drill. He ducked out of the stand and met me at the table that Hanna and Andre had vacated, offering me a pen and a clean paper bag to take notes on when I sheepishly informed him that my phone was at 7 percent battery.

"Thank you so much for this," I told him as I jotted down the date.

Joaquín rubbed a palm against the back of his neck and said, "I don't know if I'm going to be any help. All I know is that Gabi went to that resort this summer and shit went bad. She didn't tell me much either. I heard most of it from my *tía*."

"Is Gabi the one who goes to that crazy expensive boarding school in Santo Domingo?"

Joaquín smiled, pleased I'd held on to this detail over the

years. "No, that's my other cousin, Marife. Gabi's a senior at UC San Diego. She and some of her friends moved into a place together—*como que* one of those university apartments—and their lease started the first of August. Classes don't start for another month, right? So they were going out to all the bars, all the clubs, all these places."

"And they went to the Alvarado Resort?"

He nodded.

"Do you know exactly which night they were there?" I asked.

Joaquín cast his eyes skyward in thought. "Uh, I think it was a Friday? But *ya no recuerdo*."

"What happened?"

"They got separated, I guess. Her friend disappeared and texted them something like, *Hey, I met this guy, he says there's a party on this yacht and I'm going to go with him.*"

"A yacht?" I repeated, my hand going slack around my borrowed pen and the hair on the back of my neck prickling. "Someone invited her onto a yacht? Do you know who this guy was? Or—or what he looked like? Or what the name of the boat was?"

"*No sé*," Joaquín said with an apologetic shake of his head. "Gabi might remember, though."

"Did she go to this party?"

"No. No, it was just her friend Josefina. Gabi and the others went to pick her up the next morning and took her to the hospital."

I had too many questions to sort through, but it was clear that Joaquín had supplied all he knew. I needed another source—preferably a primary one. So Joaquín gave me his cousin's full name, phone number, school email, and, for good measure, Instagram handle. We stood by the order window together so I could pull up her account on my phone while I used Oscar's charger. Gabi de Hostos's page was set to public. Among the artistic shots of sunsets and acai bowls, I spotted a picture crowded with girls, all of them midlaugh and wearing standard college party attire (skinny jeans, skimpy shirt, sneakers you didn't mind getting ruined).

"Ay, I think that's her," Joaquín said, reaching across me to tap the girl on the far right of the screen. "That's Josefina."

"Joaquín!" Oscar called. "We need hands on deck."

A small line had formed at the order window.

"I should let you go," I told Joaquín.

"You sure? You need anything else?"

"No, this is—this is all great. Thank you so much."

Joaquín nodded and ducked back into the stand. I turned my undivided attention to social media sleuthing. Josefina's account was set to private, but after a few tries, I was able to pull open one of the other girls' profiles. I scrolled through her most recent posts and found a dimly lit photo of her and Gabi, both of them beaming and clutching half-drunk piña coladas in front of a wood-paneled wall decorated with framed pictures of a crowded harbor. The geotag read *The Alvarado Resort, San Diego.*

The picture had been posted three weeks ago—the same week the Real Housewives had taken their girls' trip to San Diego.

I closed Instagram, fully intent on texting Hanna that she'd been right—that *I'd* been right—when my eyes caught the little red bubble above my email icon. I hoped it was spam—*prayed* for a five dollar–off coupon to some store I'd naively given my student email to in hopes of landing discounts. But, of course, the cosmic misfortune had to continue. Half an hour ago, Ellison Michaels had sent me a calendar request for an untitled meeting.

A meeting that was set to start in three minutes.

I swore, tucked my bag of tacos to my chest, and started off toward the student union at a brisk jog.

—

The media center was predictably quiet, given that it was almost two in the afternoon on Thirsty Thursday. There were a handful of stragglers seated in leaky beanbag chairs, frowning down at their laptops in stoic silence, and one cluster of guys who'd convened around one of the monitors on the desks to watch gaming videos on YouTube.

Nobody looked up when I spilled out of the elevator— panting, underarms and hairline damp with sweat, legs shaking like one of those marathon runners whose body begins to give out with the finish line in sight. It was pretty anticlimactic when I knocked on Ellison's door and got no response. I clutched the stitch in my side and tugged out my phone to double-check the location on her calendar invite. *Student Union.* That didn't help, did it? Ellison and I had only ever met in her office, but the gap between the bottom of her door and the carpet was dark, and when I pressed my ear to the wood, it was silent save for the gentle hum of air conditioning.

"Cates."

I jerked back from the door. Ellison had appeared in the

hallway behind me, a notebook and stack of folders balanced in one arm as she tugged out a key ring—complete with a USB drive shaped like a killer whale and a miniature blue flashlight bearing the LA Dodgers emblem—to unlock her door.

"Hey," she said, giving me a once-over.

"Hey," I parroted, trying not to look like I was on the brink of passing out as she shouldered open her office door and I trailed her inside.

"Ignore the mess."

By this she meant a tailored black blazer tossed over the back of her seat (instead of hung on the hook mounted on the back of the door) and a few piles of papers that she hadn't yet alphabetized. The place was otherwise impeccably organized—a tiny closet of a room that smelled of tasteful scented candles and was dominated by an IKEA desk and a row of silver file cabinets. If this was a mess, I hated to think what Ellison Michaels might say about my bedroom.

"Sorry I didn't respond right away," I blurted. "I was getting lunch."

"You're fine," Ellison said, rubbing her temples. "I'm technically late too. My meeting ran longer than I thought it would. Owens and I had to go through this year's budget, and—yeah. But we're both here now. So let's—*shit*." She'd picked up a mug on her desk. "I need to nuke this in the microwave. Can you grab a conference room so we have some space?"

While Ellison whisked her lukewarm herbal tea to the break room, I slipped into the first empty conference room along the hall. I took a seat in one of the twenty or so swiveling chairs around the long table and twisted back and forth, my bag of room-temperature tacos in my lap and my stomach in knots.

What was this meeting even about? Why did we need *space*? Was this a roast? Was Ellison going to call in all the other reporters and make an example of me and my half-assed pitch?

The conference room door swung open again.

But it wasn't the editor in chief of Garland's paper who stood in the doorway—it was Mehri Rajavi. She had an over-stuffed plastic binder tucked under one arm.

"Laurel," she said. "Good, you're here."

"Ellison and I have a meeting," I blurted, because I didn't want to look like the kind of jerk who monopolized a conference room to use as their own personal office space. "She'll be right back. She had to heat up her tea."

"I know," Mehri said, grabbing a swivel chair. "I asked her to call you in."

I opened my mouth, then snapped it shut. Mehri—who apparently knew my name now, despite not recognizing me a few hours ago—deposited her backpack on the floor and sat down across the table from me.

"You asked her to what?"

"Look," Mehri said, her voice lowered, "before Ellison gets here, I need to tell you something. Okay? So, this morning, right? I think you accidentally printed two copies of your pitch. And I was going to chuck it in the recycling bin, but—" She shrugged, unembarrassed. "I read it."

My body froze in a moment of blinding, suffocating panic as I pictured a copy of my pitch sitting unaccompanied in a printer tray in Buchanan.

"You—"

Before I could properly articulate just how mortifying this was and beg Mehri to have mercy on my chronically stupid soul, Ellison burst into the room in a flurry of blond hair and muttered curses.

"All right," she said, smacking her steaming mug onto the table. "Mehri, want to start us off?"

My chest tightened. She was going to shove me under the bus. Mehri was going to flay me alive and lay all my journalistic sins on the table for Ellison to pick over, for the two of them to poke at and criticize, and it would be a blow of humiliation I might never recover from.

"Laurel sent me her pitch this morning to proofread."

It took my frantic, catastrophizing brain a moment to register that Mehri Rajavi had just lied through her teeth.

"You proofread it?" Ellison repeated. I could tell from the way her lips quirked that she was biting back a comment about Mehri needing a referral for an optician, because my pitch had definitely been an apocalyptic wasteland of run-on sentences that you'd have to be blind to stumble through unscathed.

But Mehri doubled down.

"I did. And it really got me thinking, so I decided to do some digging."

She smacked the binder onto the table with the kind of dramatic flair that suggested this specific binder was a big deal. I glanced at Ellison. She was blowing on her tea with her forehead scrunched, but otherwise gave nothing away.

"What's in the binder?" I asked, feeling very out of the loop.

"This," Mehri said, giving the front cover an open-palmed

pat, "is Pandora's box. The *Daily* gets hundreds of tips a year. We used to only do paper tips, and we let people submit them anonymously, so a lot of them are petty or a total waste of time and just got shoved away in binders. You know, kids who failed a class they never showed up to and want to throw wild accusations at the professor to get their grades reevaluated. Stuff like—hold on—this one."

She flipped to a dog-eared page and swung it around so I could see.

I read the tip aloud.

"'Professor Jones taught us false information about the United States moon landing of 1969. He then gave me an F on my final paper when I challenged him. I believe he's working with the Kennedys to silence me.'"

"I don't think we followed up on that one," Ellison quipped, sipping her tea. "That whole binder's a mess. College kids are heathens."

I watched, increasingly wary, as Mehri flipped to another page she'd dog-eared and slid the binder across the table.

"Okay, but read that one."

Ellison and I leaned over the table. It was an old tip, dated almost seven years ago and handwritten on an old paper form from before we'd gone totally electronic. There was no personal information—no name, no phone number, no email address. Just a lonely pair of initials: SP.

I was working an event for the athletics department three weeks ago and Truman Vaughn called me a frigid bitch for not filling up his water. Then he grabbed my ass. I don't think anyone else saw and I don't know if I'm supposed to tell campus police or what. Is it even serious enough for police? Please advise.

Ellison's face had gone pale.

"Nobody followed up with this one either," I guessed quietly.

"Truman Vaughn is the patron saint of our athletic program," Mehri said. "I don't think anyone wanted to find—you know. And then there's the fact that the *Daily* is funded by the university, so when you think about it, we have zero autonomy."

I looked at Ellison.

"Professor Owens can pull the plug on anything he thinks breaches our institutional loyalty," she said.

"Isn't that censorship?" I asked.

Ellison opened her mouth to argue.

Mehri cut her off with "Yeah, it is."

I looked down at the binder again. "And isn't *this* harassment?"

"It is," Mehri said again. "And it isn't even the only tip I found."

She flipped the binder open to a new page, and another, and another. Three additional accounts of Truman Vaughn saying nasty things and putting a hand where it didn't belong. Mehri Rajavi had scooped me. She'd swept in and took over my investigation, and it was entirely my own fault—but at the moment, I couldn't find it in me to be upset. Because this was big. This was really, *really* big.

"There are four different tips about Vaughn," Mehri said, looking as nauseated and angry as I felt. "This is the last binder of paper tips we have before we moved everything online. I looked at our electronic records. There's nothing with Vaughn in it. Not a single tip."

"President Sterling instated a new faculty advisor when we went electronic," I said.

Ellison nodded sharply.

"Oh my god," I said. "They're covering it up."

"Exactly," Mehri said, her dark eyes alight. She was relieved, I realized. It was a relief to uncover something that bothered you, to share it with others, and to be told that you had a right to be bothered.

It was a relief to have someone on your side.

"You know how the women I interviewed at the country club said Vaughn invited them to party on his yacht?" I asked. Mehri nodded. She'd read my pitch, after all. "I just talked to one of the guys who works at Pepito's, that taco stand off campus, and he said his cousin's friend got assaulted during a yacht party at the same resort."

"San Diego is on the water," Ellison pointed out. "There have to be thousands of yachts in the harbor at any given time."

"But how many of those yachts are owned by men inviting drunk women to come party on them?"

Ellison shook her head grimly.

"That's a big jump, Laurel," she warned.

"Which is why we need to investigate," I said, thinking of Hanna. She'd believed in me. I just needed someone like Ellison to believe in me too—someone whose support would do more than just boost my morale. "Maybe we won't find anything, but we're journalists. This is what we do."

Ellison took a deep breath and scrubbed her hands over

her face, looking suddenly young and tired. I kept forgetting that she was a college student, like us, and not some supernatural, immortal entity fueled by caffeine and an unrelenting desire to rip lousy journalism to shreds.

"Starting in October, we're only going to print once a month," she said. "We'll be redirecting our efforts to the Facebook page and the website."

"What the fuck?" Mehri cried, voicing my own thoughts verbatim.

"Owens told me the school's cutting our budget. They want to reallocate funds toward other student groups. And that's why I'm telling you guys"—Ellison leaned across the table and looked between Mehri and me, imploring—"if we write about Vaughn's charity and Sterling's fundraising efforts, I think the university might be more willing to renegotiate the budget in our favor. I'm trying to keep us alive."

"You're saying no to protect your own ass," Mehri accused her.

Ellison narrowed her eyes. "That's not what—"

"It's exactly what you're doing. You want to kiss up to the people in charge because you know you'll end up with a cush job after graduation if you do what they want you to."

"I am *not* going to be the one who lets this place crash and burn," Ellison said, jabbing a finger against the table. "I'm the first female editor in chief the *Daily's* had in thirty years. Three fucking decades, Mehri. I had to work my ass off for this, and I *still* have people whispering behind my back because they think I only got this position so the school can brag about having a woman in this office. I'm not stupid. If this paper tanks, *I'm* the one who's getting blamed."

"You want to pull the feminism card?" Mehri shot back. "What about the women who wrote these tips? They just have to take one for the team? I think that's a pretty fucking privileged thing to decide for them."

"I am *not* letting this paper collapse," Ellison said through her teeth. "Not when the work we do as journalists is so important."

"But *this* is important," I said.

Mehri and Ellison turned to me. My face grew hot, but I powered on. "What's the point of trying to save the paper if all we do is print propaganda? Look, I have reason to believe Vaughn was at the Alvarado Resort the same week this girl was assaulted. And maybe it's just a coincidence—maybe Vaughn really was just there on vacation, and some other guy on some other boat did it—but . . ." I trailed off, staring across the scratched wood surface of the table between us. "I have to know."

Ellison lifted her mug of tea to her lips, her eyes unfocused as they stared into oblivion through the haze of steam. She was thinking. Hearing me out. I held my breath and waited for her decision.

"Next Monday," Ellison finally said, "I want to run a profile about Vaughn's charity."

My heart sank.

"That's bullshit," Mehri said. "Are we supposed to ignore—"

"We're not ignoring anything," Ellison interrupted her. "I'm not saying we can't look into this. All of it. But what we can't do is print these tips and throw our hands up and hope they're true. We have to figure out who sent them and get in contact before anyone else knows they exist, or we compromise everything. We have to do this right."

Mehri picked at the plastic coating on the binder on the table, peeling away tiny, jagged ribbons. I couldn't blame her for being impatient and frustrated. I had the same pit of unrest in my stomach.

But I trusted Ellison.

So I said, "Okay. We'll do a profile."

Mehri ground her teeth as we sat in tense silence for a long moment. It was Ellison who broke it.

"I have to go to class," she announced. "But we'll circle back to this, okay?"

Ellison stood, mug in hand, and shuffled to the door. I watched until it clicked shut behind her. Then I spun in my chair to face Mehri.

"What if we work something into the charity profile?" I blurted.

She blinked at me.

"Like what?"

"Something about Vaughn. The way he talks to his team, the way he talks to reporters. We could go subtle. Just—just something to spark a conversation. I have a friend on the team. Andre Shepherd. He could be a source."

Mehri arched an eyebrow thoughtfully.

"Has he ever said anything about Vaughn being a sexist dick in the locker room? Or harassing reporters, staff, anybody?"

"He's mentioned Vaughn tells dirty jokes. Nothing specific, though. But I can ask."

"Okay," Mehri said, one corner of her mouth finally quirking up in a smile. "Okay, good."

She collected her binder and backpack and started toward the conference room door. I stood from my seat, my knees wobbling, and gathered my things. Cell phone. Bag of room-temperature tacos. Check and check.

"Hey, Mehri," I called after her, wanting to ask why she'd invited me into this meeting instead of scooping me but too mortified to vocalize it. "Thank you."

"I got your back, you got mine," she said.

—

I waited until I'd plopped down on the wall of the fountain in the courtyard outside the student union to check my phone again. I had three notifications from Andre. The first was a text that read *Come to based bull hose so much free beet.* The second was a Snapchat—a blurry picture of Hanna, grinning and flipping off the camera with both hands in what looked like a very modern and recently updated kitchen, captioned *She brat St Jamed!!! Pong queen of three year!!! Where art you???* The third was a text he'd sent ten minutes ago: *Were gong home.*

Comforted by the knowledge that my friends had ended up having a great time despite my unplanned absence, I tore open my bag of tacos and did what I always did when I felt stressed: turn to culinary comforts.

A part of me was upset that my afternoon had taken such a turn. I'd daydreamed about going to parties at the Baseball House, but I'd never actually been inside. It was a little difficult to picture what it would look like as I sat in some corner, eating my tacos, until Bodie St. James spotted me from across the room, recognized me, and came over to—I don't know, say hey? Ask me not to spill carne asada on the carpet? My imagination was a bit pessimistic.

My phone lit up with another text right as a huge chunk of pico de gallo tumbled out of my taco and landed on my leg. It was from my mom.

How did the pitch go? TQM

I brushed cilantro off my thigh and typed out a response. *Great!* Lie. *My editor asked me to write a profile on the football coach. Just had lunch with Andre and Hanna. Headed home to study. TQM.*

Half of me was terrified that I'd just convinced Mehri and Ellison that we should dive headfirst into an investigation that might end up being a very shallow pool, and that the three of us would crack our heads open on the bottom of it. The other half of me feared that there was no bottom—just a deep, dark pit of things better left unseen.

I pulled up Gabi de Hostos's Instagram profile again. Before I could second-guess myself, I clicked to message her.

Hey Gabi! My name is Laurel, and I'm a student journalist for Garland University's paper. Your cousin Joaquín mentioned you visited the Alvarado Resort this summer. I was wondering if you'd be willing to speak to me about your experience there

I pressed Send, put my phone facedown on the bench, and inhaled all three of my tacos. It probably took me all of two minutes. When I was done, I brushed a few chunks of pico de gallo off my lap, stood, and headed home.

The apartment Hanna and I rented was not glamorous. Between the two of us, we'd had just enough cash to afford a place three blocks east of the Rodeo, where things got as sketchy as they could possibly get in a town as wealthy and sleepy as Garland. The building was two stories, with one wide hallway down the middle. All the windows on the first floor had bars over them, the intercom had been broken for years, and there was a wasp infestation in the laundry room. Our apartment on the second floor overlooked a gas station and had a busted air conditioning unit that rattled and groaned like a dying animal. But it was ours, and we loved it.

I heard Andre and Hanna before I even made it to our door. Their voices carried through the paper-thin walls, loud and a little slurred.

"It says *two* eggs." Andre was shouting.

"Well, I can't take an egg out now, so we're going with it."

I waited a moment, smiling to myself as I listened to them bicker, before I tugged out my keys. Andre shouted my name as I stepped through the door. He was sitting in one of the short, little IKEA chairs around our rickety dining table, his knees tucked up almost to his chest and a crushed cardboard box of cake mix in his hands, the back of which he was consulting as if it were a sacred text.

Hanna stood over the counter in our kitchenette, a spatula in her hand and a wreath of Ping-Pong balls that someone had hot glued together perched on her head like a crown.

"Where did you get *that*?" I asked her.

She flicked her spatula, splattering one large glob of cake batter onto the linoleum floor, and held her chin high.

"I won it."

"You should've seen it," Andre said. "She beat half the team."

"And then Kyle Fogarty—who is fine as *hell*, by the way— bestowed upon me this crown"—Hanna paused to take on perhaps the worst British accent I'd ever heard—"which I shall be wearing to all social functions henceforth."

Andre made a show of rolling his eyes.

"Sorry we didn't wait for you," he told me. "You were gone for, like, two hours, though. How'd the investigating go?"

I pulled out the seat beside him and plopped down.

"Would you say Vaughn is, like, *sexist?*"

"Like how sexist are we talking?" Andre asked.

"Enough to call women bitches."

"Oh, definitely."

"Or grab their asses."

Andre reared back. "Damn. I mean, I don't know. He's an asshole, but that seems . . . I guess?"

"What do you mean?" I pressed.

"I mean, he's a good coach and he seems like a nice enough guy, but . . . he *says* shit. Sexist shit. Nothing awful, but—okay, like, there's this one ESPN reporter who always gave him hardball questions, right? He *hated* her. And he used to come into the locker room after games and say shit like *She just needs a good dicking down.* Just some gross, antiquated bullshit like that."

"Andre, that's fucked up," Hanna snapped. "Did you say anything?"

Andre shrank down in his already-small chair and I felt a fierce burst of frustration—not *at* Andre, but *for* him. He was second string. He wasn't in a position to stand up to the head coach, not when he could count his minutes of playing time on one hand.

"What about the starters?" I asked.

"I don't know. They don't really say anything, but I think

sometimes you just let things go because . . ." He trailed off.

Because it's Coach Vaughn. The man who has former play-ers on nearly every NFL team. The man who's family friends with state senators, B-list actors, and CFOs from Fortune 500 companies. The man who makes dreams come true for the players who serve him like brave knights serve a king.

"Would you be comfortable giving us some quotes for our article?" I asked.

"Yes, ma'am," Andre said with a stifled hiccup. "I'd be honored."

"Awesome. Remind me to ask again when you're sober."

"Look, no lie, I'll do it," he said, swiveling in our IKEA chair to face me head-on, so I'd understand how serious he was being. "You know I'll do it. But you know who you *really* got to talk to?"

I did, unfortunately, know who Andre was referring to.

Bodie St. James.

chapter 5

Wednesday came before I was ready for it. I hunched my back against the morning breeze and clutched my paper cup of coffee for warmth, staring out at the training field and doing my best not to succumb to panic. There was a clipboard tucked between my butt and the bleachers. It held a single page of questions I'd drafted. I'd consulted Mehri for advice, but she'd just shrugged and told me to "follow my instincts." My instincts were telling me to sprint home and throw myself back into bed, but I didn't think that was what she'd meant.

My right knee bounced as I exhaled, breath visible in the morning air. I checked my phone again. Seven fifty-eight. Practice was almost over. The football team had been here for over two hours already. I'd arrived at seven to give myself plenty of time to gather my courage and gulp down a black coffee (which I'd thought would make me feel very mature and put together, but which just left me with a stomachache).

My phone lit up with a pair of texts from Hanna.

You are a strong confident kickass journalist and I believe in you

Also we need more toilet paper can you steal some from campus?

I finished the last third of my coffee in one gulp and peered out across the field. The team had been scrimmaging for the last fifteen minutes, but Andre kept glancing over between plays and waving at me with the abandon of a five-year-old who'd spotted his best friend at the grocery store. Each time, a few of the other players turned and narrowed their eyes at me, trying to figure out if the girl with the clipboard was some kind of undercover NFL scout.

Andre was in a dark-green practice jersey, so I deduced that the guys in white were the starters. Like Bodie. The sight of him made my already-tender stomach twist into knots, so I tried to keep my eyes locked on Andre. Then Coach Vaughn pulled Andre to the side to talk him through a play, and I had to resort to examining a microscopic hangnail on my left thumb. Soon the shrill sound of a whistle cut through the air and made my eardrums wobble. Eight o'clock. Go time. I collected my empty coffee cup and tugged my clipboard from underneath me. Then I climbed over two rows of bleachers and hopped to the ground, feeling like perhaps the least athletic being to ever take the field.

I trudged across the grass to the huddle of players and coaching staff like a member of the French aristocracy on her way to the guillotine. Truman Vaughn's voice carried across the field. He was my height—about five eight—but built like a panther, with lithe muscle and a cutting stare. His lips were narrow and his dark hair was speckled gray around the temples. Beside him stood the assistant coach, Chester Gordon, a big-eared redhead whose eyebrows were practically translucent. The players stood in a semicircle before them, a patient audience to their pep talk.

"—we'll run it again tomorrow, bright and early. Lions on three."

The boys erupted in a single, unified "One-two-three-Lions!"

I took a deep breath and scolded myself for feeling so nervous. I'd interviewed people before. I knew how to do this. Besides, Bodie and I had already met—briefly and awkwardly, but that still counted. And it wasn't like I was going on a first date with the guy. I was just trying to figure out if his head coach was a scumbag.

Half the players took off for the locker room. The other half hovered around the field, packing up their gear and talking among themselves and with the coaching staff. I kept my eyes on Bodie's back as Andre jogged over to meet me a few yards out from the bench.

"Detective Cates," he greeted me.

I pressed a hand to my stomach and shook my head. "I drank so much coffee, Andre. I'm going to be sick."

He grimaced and plucked my coffee cup out of my hand. "Maybe I should—wow, damn. You really killed it. Is this a venti?"

It was. I was a fool. An overcaffeinated fool.

"Hey," Andre said, as sternly as Andre could. "You've got

this. St. James is honest to goodness one of the nicest guys I know. He won't give you trouble. Just do your thing."

He gave me a quick thumbs-up as I trudged closer to the bench, where the aforementioned *nicest guy* had shed his jersey and pads, so he was down to just a black, sleeveless Under Armour shirt that was so tight I could see the muscles in his shoulders working.

Madre de dios, please keep your shirt on, I thought. *This will be so much easier if you keep your shirt on.*

I squeezed around a clump of large, damp, smelly bodies—and then I was standing *right there*, close enough that I could see the rivulets of sweat running down the back of his flushed neck.

"Bodie?" I asked.

I had only a split second to scrub my sweaty palm against the side of my leggings as furtively as I could before he turned around, eyebrows pinched in question and a Gatorade squeeze bottle held halfway to his mouth.

"Hi," I croaked. "Could I borrow you for a sec?"

Bodie's fingers clenched and his water bottle spurted out a cloud of mist. He reared back.

"I'm with the *Daily* and we're—"

"St. James!" someone shouted, loudly and directly adjacent to my head. Kyle Fogarty stepped around me, his faux hawk glistening artificial green in the sunlight, and smacked Bodie on the arm. "Baseball House has leftover pizza. Let's go."

I stepped to the side, feeling entirely invisible.

"I'll catch up with you," Bodie said. "I've got to do something quick for . . ."

He trailed off and tipped his chin in my direction. Fogarty turned and looked surprised. He hadn't noticed me. Predictable.

"For who?"

Fogarty directed the question at Bodie, as if I wasn't capable of introducing myself. But whatever outrage I felt at the slight turned into unexpected despondency as Bodie remained silent. He didn't remember me. It was fine—I'd grown numb to the sting of people forgetting my name, my face, where they'd seen me before. And I couldn't blame Bodie. It'd been nearly a week since we caught the same elevator, and he'd been standing a few feet away when I'd told Nick who I was. He probably hadn't heard me anyway.

I plastered on a smile and held out a hand, channeling Ellison's confidence and professionalism as I faced Fogarty and said, "Laurel Cates, for the *Daily*."

Fogarty shook my outstretched hand. He was, objectively speaking, a ridiculously attractive human being. Flawless skin, shiny hair, arrestingly symmetrical features. If you gave a hundred people a photo of him and a photo of Bodie, my guess was that almost every one of them would pick out Fogarty as the objectively hotter of the two. But there was something in Bodie's eyes that wasn't in Fogarty's. An alertness. A kindness.

But I did *not* have a crush.

"You writing an article on my boy here?" Fogarty asked me, grabbing Bodie by the back of the neck and jostling him.

"Well, actually, it's—"

"You should mention how big his dick is."

I choked on the rest of my sentence.

"Fuck off," Bodie said, giving Fogarty a shove. "I'll text you."

Fogarty laughed like a teenager who'd just executed a *that's what she said* joke he was immensely proud of. I watched him sprint off to catch up with a group of his teammates on their way to the locker room and wondered why boys thought it was funny to say wildly inappropriate things to girls just to make them uncomfortable.

"Sorry about him," Bodie said, cheeks splotchy pink with what could've been a sunburn but was more likely embarrassment. "Uh, what'd you need me for, exactly?"

He lifted a hand to wipe the sweat from his forehead, and my eyes shifted—against my will—to the pale underside of his biceps.

"Do you have some time for an interview? I just have a few questions"—I held up my clipboard and hoped he couldn't tell that my entire body was vibrating with caffeine and terror—"for a profile we're doing on Coach Vaughn."

"I have class at nine thirty. Could we do it right now?"

"Yeah, this shouldn't take more than twenty minutes. We can go sit down at the library or Starbucks or somewhere quiet."

"I actually need to grab some food. Is the campus center okay?"

I nodded and opened my mouth to say something absurdly unprofessional, like okey dokey, when Bodie spoke again.

"Let me just get dressed and I'll meet you out front?"

"Yeah! Yes. Definitely. Hit the showers, or whatever."

I spent the next fifteen minutes sitting by myself on the front steps of the training center and reliving every awkward second of our interaction in my head. When Bodie finally reappeared, his hair damp and a backpack slung over one shoulder, it occurred to me that I should've been using my alone time to prep some small talk for the short walk to the campus center. But it soon became clear that even if I'd thought of a great anecdote to share or a handful of softball questions to get my source loosened up, I wouldn't have had time to get a word in.

Bodie couldn't make it twenty steps across campus without someone reaching out to him. Hand slaps, those little bro hugs with lots of back patting, shouted greetings from across entire quads. It was an unrelenting siege of camaraderie and networking. Nobody paid me much attention, since the clipboard tucked to my chest made it clear that Bodie and I weren't just hanging out, so I just hovered in wide-eyed shock and experienced, secondhand, what it was like to be recognized. To be known.

Thankfully, the breakfast crowd at the food court on the first floor of the campus center was calm. Bodie marched straight past Panda Express and Five Guys to get in line at the little booth tucked in the back corner—a less popular chain known for their overpriced artisanal soups and salads. I fell into line with him, figuring a little food might help soak up all the caffeine currently burning holes in my delicate stomach lining. Bodie ordered the salmon, which came with a scoop of quinoa and a side of steamed broccoli. I asked for the same. I wish I could say this was a mirroring technique to make my source more comfortable around me, but really I'd just panicked when the girl behind the register asked what I wanted.

While Bodie got caught by a really tall kid wearing a Garland volleyball T-shirt who wanted to know if he'd also thought that the econ homework was stupid, I grabbed a tiny table in the corner and tried to stop myself from fidgeting with my hair. It didn't feel like an interview. It felt unnervingly like a first date, if it was socially acceptable to bring a clipboard of prepared questions and record the conversation for later analysis.

I reached for my biodegradable fork, eager for a distraction. The first mouthful of salmon nearly made me choke.

"You good?" Bodie asked as he set his tray down across from mine.

I shot him a thumbs-up and discreetly scanned the tables around us in search of salt and pepper shakers, or soy sauce, or ketchup, or *something* with some semblance of flavor.

"Not a fan?"

"No, it's good!" I cried, wide-eyed with embarrassment. "It's great, it's really—"

"Bland. You can say it."

His eyes twinkled with humor, but I still felt like a wimp. My mother hadn't raised me to be a picky eater. She'd fed me the entire spectrum of human cuisine—from cottage cheese to habanero peppers—before I'd started kindergarten. I was stronger than this slab of unseasoned fish. I skewered another bite on my fork, committed to proving I could handle the diet of a Division I athlete. Bodie took mercy on me and tossed a pair of tiny packets of sriracha onto the table.

"Oh, god, thank you."

He snorted and dropped into the seat across from me while I tore open a packet of sriracha with my teeth and smeared it over my salmon. Which, now that I thought about it, was a weird thing to be enjoying at nine o'clock in the morning.

"Is this the kind of stuff you usually eat after practice?"

Bodie nodded. "Every day. It's got lean protein, whole grains." He sounded like he was trying to talk himself into it. "Good fuel."

The idea that food was just gas for the engine—not an art form, not an expression of self and community—was, frankly, laughable.

"Don't you guys burn thousands of calories?" I asked. "If I worked out that much, I'd have the most self-indulgent breakfast I could think of. Like half a chocolate cake."

"Breakfast burrito."

"Hm?"

Bodie's cheeks pinked. "Most decadent breakfast I can think of. My dad made me breakfast burritos in high school when we had morning conditioning, and they were so over the top. I mean, scrambled eggs, hash browns, hot sauce. Way too much cheese."

"No such thing," I chided. "My mom does these chile rellenos with about ten pounds of queso fresco on them. I could eat my body weight."

Bodie smiled and ducked his head. "Yeah, that was me with the breakfast burritos. I had to cut myself off when I started getting serious about football."

"When was that?"

"Summer before senior year. That's when Coach Vaughn first reached out to me, said Garland was seriously considering me." Bodie cleared his throat. "So you guys are running a profile on him?"

"Oh, yeah. We're—oh, wait, sorry." I fumbled for my cell phone. "I'll be recording our conversation, if that's all right with you. I'm probably the only person who will ever listen to it, so it's okay if you're chewing and stuff."

"Do what you need to do."

The full brunt of Bodie's smile was blinding. I looked down at my phone, glad for the excuse to avoid eye contact, and started an audio recording. Then I cleared my throat and read off the first question that Mehri and I had co-authored.

"How has Vaughn influenced you as a player and as a man?"

Bodie let out a low whistle. "Right to the heavy stuff, huh? Um, I think Vaughn's just—he's a good leader. He knows the game really well, and he's really good at passing on what he knows."

"Mm-hmm."

"Sorry," Bodie said sheepishly. "I feel like I'm using the same three words over and over."

"It's all right. I'll redact all the *ums*."

He beamed at me. I had to look down at my clipboard again.

"Is Vaughn optimistic about this season?"

"We're looking really strong this year," Bodie said, his eyes drifting off to the side, like an invisible teleprompter had appeared somewhere beyond my shoulder. "Our offensive line has been working really hard to pick up some of the slack we saw last season, and we've developed a lot of new plays that I think are going to put our strongest players—Fogarty, Torres, McGrady—in a position to do what they do best. I think we're championship contenders this season, for sure."

Ugh. He was giving me the typical media spiel. Someone had trained him well.

"Yeah, I saw you guys practicing," I said, trying not to betray my disappointment. "You looked good. I mean, like, the whole team looked—the team looks really talented. Have there been any hiccups yet? Any drama in the locker room?"

"No. We argue sometimes, but"—he shrugged—"brothers argue, I guess."

This was going nowhere. Bodie seemed so stilted, which was odd, given that he probably did interviews all the time. Maybe I'd thrown him off with too heavy of an opening question. Or maybe my anxiety was transferring via osmosis, not that I would know. I wasn't a chemistry major.

I looked down at my list of questions again—bland, predictable questions about performance and coaching strategies that would inevitably lead to more stilted responses. With one swipe of my hand, I shoved my clipboard to the side.

"What's Vaughn's favorite snack?"

Bodie blinked, bemused. "What?"

I propped my elbows on the table. "Favorite snack. Go. Quick-fire round."

"Uh, I guess celery sticks and peanut butter."

"Favorite drink?"

Bodie shook his head. "He's sober."

"I know," I said, mortified. "Oh god, I didn't mean—"

Bodie's face flushed. "Gatorade. The red one."

"I'm so sorry. I wasn't trying to—"

"No, no, you're fine. That was my bad," Bodie insisted, reaching for his fork again and stabbing at his quinoa. "I'm just used to reporters asking about his sobriety and how it affects his coaching. A lot of people like to drag up his past."

I nodded, because I *did* know about that.

"Favorite movie?" I asked, eager to get us back on steadier ground.

"Oh, easy," Bodie said with a relieved smile. "*The Godfather*. He loves those movies. Like, to an embarrassing degree. Quotes them all the time—you know, 'I'm going to make him an offer he can't refuse.'"

I snorted, surprised he'd gone for the full impression.

"What's wrong with my Sicilian accent?" Bodie demanded, sitting back and folding his arms over his chest. I knew, logically, that he wasn't flexing on purpose, but my eyes snapped to his biceps anyway.

I arched an eyebrow. "Is that what that was?"

"Now you're just being unprofessional."

"My sincerest apologies, Mr. St. James."

The corners of Bodie's mouth twitched up. It was an easy thing to give him shit, like I was joking around with Andre or Hanna. I got it then—why everyone adored him. He made you feel like you were his friend. Like you were in on the joke together.

"What does he see in those movies anyway?" I asked. "I mean, I know one of them won the Oscar for best picture, but they're so violent and—I don't know. *Macho*."

Bodie shrugged. "I guess he likes the whole brotherhood thing. I'm not saying that a football team is, like, the *Mafia*, but I think there's something there about loyalty and watching out for each other. And he thinks that main guy is badass. Vaughn actually goes sailing a lot, so he bought this boat last year and named it after—you know, what's his name—the guy, the Godfather?"

"Vito Corleone," I offered.

"That's it, yeah. Sorry. I'm bad with names."

He sounded highly apologetic for such a small blip in trivia. His eyes lingered on mine for a second longer than was strictly necessary, and it struck me that he was explaining himself. He hadn't forgotten me from the elevator. Just my name.

Heat bloomed in my chest. I tried, fervently, not to grin like an absolute moron.

"What kind of speeches does Vaughn give in the locker room?" I asked. "Does he ever whip out the Sicilian accent?"

Bodie laughed—a full, stomach-deep laugh. The fact that I'd been the cause made pride bloom in my chest.

"Actually, yeah." He straightened in his chair, suddenly inspired. "That's one of the best things Vaughn does as a coach. I know people say he's a stone-cold asshole on the sidelines, but that's his game face. He's really animated in the locker room. And the speeches he gives are just—" Bodie shook his head. "He can be pretty funny."

"Why do you think he's different when the cameras aren't around?"

"I don't think he's a big fan of the media," Bodie said, shooting me an apologetic glance. "It's not that you guys aren't great and really important to the program. I think he just feels more comfortable when it's just the team. And he definitely says some stuff I don't think female reporters should hear."

And there it was—the sexism Andre had mentioned. The same sexism Mehri had uncovered in our binder of tips.

I tried to sound casual as I asked, "Really? What kind of stuff?"

"Just dumb shit."

"Sexist shit?" I pressed.

Bodie winced and shifted in his seat. "It's not like—it's just stupid. Outdated jokes. It's nothing genuinely awful, I promise. We've all had consent and harassment training. The school sends in someone during the first week of classes to talk to us and make us take this quiz, and everybody does it. Coaching staff too. Vaughn flew back a day early from his charity trip to San Diego just to make it this year. He was sunburned as *shit*."

My stomach lurched. "What kind of charity trip?"

"For the Vaughn Foundation. They do a lot of fundraising for high school athletics all over Orange County, so they were down there to meet with some prospective donors."

"Did anyone else on the team go with him?" I asked. "Or coaching staff? Anyone affiliated with the university?"

"I'm not sure," Bodie said. "I'd have to ask him."

I waited a moment, hoping he'd elaborate, but he didn't. Instead, he picked up my unused sriracha packet and worked it between his fingers, like it was suddenly his life mission to smooth every crease in the plastic.

"And the Vaughn Foundation," I said, narrowing my eyes at Bodie's fidgeting hands, "when they're networking, what kind of events do they usually do? Auctions? Dinner parties? Cocktail hours?"

Or bar crawls, because clearly Vaughn had penciled in time between fundraising functions to stop by the Alvarado Resort and get plastered. Bodie pressed his lips together and glanced between me, the people eating a few tables away, and my phone where it sat between us.

"Is something wrong?" I asked.

"No. But could we—" he began, then cut himself off with a huff.

I didn't think. I just reached over the table and tapped my screen, ending the recording.

"We can talk off the record," I said.

The tension in Bodie's shoulders eased fractionally, but it was a long moment before he leaned over the table and spoke again.

"I helped out at Vaughn's charity over the summer."

"What kind of work did you do? I didn't—" *See that on your LinkedIn profile.* I'd done my research, of course, but I didn't want to be too creepy about it. Although Bodie's résumé looked like just about every other business major's at Garland, so it wasn't like I'd uncovered anything secret or deeply personal. "I didn't know they hired students."

"I was just doing paperwork and other administrative stuff. I was just an intern. But they had me helping with the books, and I—" He cut himself off with a grimace. "Off the record means you won't run it in an article, right?"

"No, you're good," I said quickly. "This is *totally* between us."

My hands were shaking. I sandwiched them between my thighs. Bodie was quiet for a long moment, during which I dreamed up about a thousand reasons why he would want to speak off the record about anything.

"There were discrepancies in the books."

"What kind?" I asked, hunching over the table. We were insulated at our little table in the corner, sheltered from prying eyes and ears by a structural column and a trash station, but this felt like the kind of conversation that called for a lot more privacy than a college food court could offer.

"So, in July, for example, we received about eighty-five thousand dollars in donations. Most of that went straight to buying wholesale sports equipment and shipping it to schools, but sometimes we have to cover fundraising expenses. I was batching up all our receipts for that, and like ten grand was unaccounted for."

I really wished I'd taken the business class Hanna had tried to rope me into last year.

"*Unaccounted for* like you didn't have the receipts or like it went missing?"

"We didn't have any receipts. I asked my supervisor, and he sent me this invoice for some LLC I'd never heard of. I couldn't find any info about them online."

I lowered my voice to a near whisper. "Do you think someone might be embezzling? Because if you do, you should talk to the police."

Bodie sat up straight, whiplashed by my sudden sense of urgency. "I have to get to class," he announced, popping the lid onto his half-eaten salmon. He stood, pulling his backpack onto one shoulder as he went. "Sorry. Did you get everything you need?"

"I think so." Hard to say when I was still clawing my way out of the avalanche of information he'd just dumped on me. Bodie turned to go. "St. James?" He stopped reluctantly, and met my eyes. "It was off the record, okay. I'm not repeating what you told me to anyone."

He offered me one last smile, clearly grateful but not entirely comforted.

"It was nice talking to you, Laurel."

Then he turned and was gone, a mountain of a boy weaving through the growing prelunch crowd with surprising agility. He was, as Andre had phrased it, *the nicest guy.*

And maybe a good one too.

chapter 6

On Saturday morning, before it was even light outside, someone in our building with an impressively loud speaker started blasting Garland's fight song—a frustratingly catchy cacophony of tubas and cymbals and every wind instrument I could name. I rolled over in my bed, checked the time on my phone, and pulled my duvet up over my head with a groan.

The first home football game of the season was usually something I looked forward to. I loved the thrill of being part of a crowd. I loved standing shoulder to shoulder with fifty thousand other people and feeling like we were family as we cheered and chanted and chugged watery beer under the heat of the midday sun. Hanna and I had made a pact freshman year that we'd get to the stadium early, every game, so we'd be somewhere in the first five rows of the student section. That way Andre could always find us in the crowd. I *loved* game day. I probably would've jumped out of bed whistling our fight song if it wasn't for the fact that I'd spent four consecutive nights staring at the ceiling and imagining all the ways this Vaughn story might blow up in my face.

Distantly, and muffled through my duvet, I heard Hanna's mattress creak and groan on the other side of the room. Two footsteps thudded against the floor, and then there was a weight on top of me and my blankets were yanked back from my face.

"Rise and shine!" Hanna bellowed. "It's game day!"

I stared up at her, disgruntled and half-asleep.

"Your breath is heinous," I said.

"Yeah, well, yours isn't too hot either. C'mon. Only five hours until kickoff. Can you help me curl my hair?"

—

I'd never been to Vatican City, but I could only guess that the crowds at Garland University on the morning of a home game must look an awful lot like those at Easter Mass in Saint Peter's Square. Except I don't think anyone would be doing keg stands outside the basilica. Then again, I've never been the best Catholic, so what do I know? The point was, campus was crawling with people, from baby-faced freshmen to wrinkled old alumni, all of them gathered under pop-up tents and shady oaks trees with their coolers and portable grills. As soon as Hanna and I set foot outside our apartment, we became two more specks in the sea of green.

"How is it this hot already?" I demanded, hand shielding my eyes. "It's nine in the morning."

Hanna tugged her tube top up with a frustrated huff.

"I really wish I had boobs."

"No you don't. My boob sweat is unreal right now."

I'd worn my usual game-day outfit—Andre's practice jersey from freshman year, with his last name and number on the back. It stilled smelled vaguely of sweat despite the number of times I'd run it through the wash, but it was comfortable and large enough that I could drink as much beer and eat as many snacks as I wanted without worrying about bloating. Hanna had chosen a black corduroy overall dress and a Garland-green tube top. She looked entirely too trendy to be gallivanting around muddy lawns in search of friends and free alcohol.

We were halfway down the Rodeo, both of us slinking along under the hot sun like animals in search of a watering hole, when Hanna tugged my arm to point out a cluster of fifty or so students gathered under a pop-up tent in the middle of the Baseball House's front lawn, surrounded by rickety beer pong tables and cornhole boards.

"Shit," Hanna said. "I think it's wristbands only."

"Wait here."

While Hanna hovered at the edge of the crowd, I dove headfirst into the chaos, murmuring *excuse me* and *sorry* as I brushed shoulders and sidestepped the crushed beer cans littering the ground. In the middle of the tailgate I found a makeshift plywood bar manned by two baby-faced boys who were trying to field drink orders.

"Have your wristbands ready!" one of them shouted.

"Mine fell off!" a girl whined. "Swear on my life, I already paid!"

While the unlicensed bartenders explained that no wristband

meant no alcohol, I darted around the side of the bar and stepped up to the counter. They had vodka—giant plastic jugs of it, each one larger than my head—and off-brand lemonade, along with several plastic bags of plastic cups. No one was watching me. It took all of fifteen seconds to make one vodka lemonade so strong I could've used it as nail polish remover. Then, with my red cup bounty in hand, I slipped out from behind the bar and darted back into the crowd again, quick as a woodland animal weaving through trees.

When I surfaced on the other side, Hanna slow clapped. I shrugged, feigning nonchalance even as I grinned at her. Invisibility. My favorite party trick. I passed Hanna the cup and she took a long sniff, one eye scrunching shut as a shiver of revulsion rolled down her spine.

"You've outdone yourself, Laurel. This might actually kill me."

She coughed and spluttered after the first sip, then passed me the cup so I could also poison myself before we made our way onto campus.

The Art House had no front lawn to speak of, so they usually set up their tailgate on a shady lawn by the architecture school where the grad students congregated to smoke cigarettes and chug black coffee. But Hanna led me to a tent along the parkway, over near the student union, where a hand-lettered sign that read PATTIES FOR POLLOCK was strung up over a folding table.

Mehri Rajavi stood behind the makeshift counter, the sun glinting off her gold nose ring and the glittery temporary tattoo of Leopold the Lion (Garland's mascot) on her right cheek.

"Five dollar burgers!" she was calling out to passersby. "Help students in need buy art supplies!"

A pair of middle-aged alumni stopped, persuaded by Mehri's sales pitch, and pulled out their wallets. I almost laughed out loud. Mehri wasn't *technically* lying—the Art House *was* going to buy paint. It just so happened to be for Pollock, the black light paint party they hosted in a giant tent in their backyard every October. While the sports-centric houses on the Rodeo were typically known for throwing better, wilder parties, Pollock was the exception. Last year, three people had left the party in ambulances (one for alcohol poisoning, two for crowd surfing–related injuries). Hanna and I already had our all-white outfits picked out.

We waltzed up to the counter just as Mehri was passing a paper plate of hamburgers to the alums. Hanna tugged a crumpled twenty-dollar bill from her pocket and slid it across the table.

"I'd like to make a donation."

Mehri shoved Hanna's money back at her.

"You're helping with setup." She scolded Hanna in a way that told me they'd already had this discussion before. "And you're going to need cash to buy a bottle of water at the game. I can smell whatever's in your cup from here."

Hanna held the drink out in offering.

"Vodka lemonade," she singsonged. "Want some?"

Mehri sighed, like she really had to think about it, then plucked the cup out of Hanna's hand and tossed back a sip.

"Nice," she said with a smack of her lips, then turned her attention to me. "We still on for tonight?"

Mehri and I had a hot date with our shared Google doc.

"Are you guys still drafting?" Hanna asked.

"There's a lot to cover," Mehri said. "And a lot to unpack. I mean, just pulling a decent quote out of St. James's interview took us hours. He's not exactly the brightest bulb in the marquee, is he?" Mehri laughed and launched into a stuttering impression of Bodie's first few responses from my interview with him.

I bristled. "He's actually a smart guy."

"Yeah, sure. Which is why he thinks it's totally normal that his coach says shit that *female reporters shouldn't hear.*"

Hanna sucked in a breath through her teeth. "Yikes."

"Right? We're giving Ellison our final draft tomorrow so she can review it."

"Did Joaquín's cousin ever message you back?" Hanna asked.

I shook my head. "It doesn't look like she's been active on Instagram since August, so she probably hasn't seen mine yet. I sent her a LinkedIn request because that was the only other social media I could find her on."

Hanna's phone buzzed.

"Oh shit," she said. "Thirty minutes until game time. We should go."

"I'll see you tonight, Laurel," Mehri said.

"You're not coming to the game?" Hanna asked.

Mehri threw back her head and laughed as she passed back Hanna's drink. "Me? Voluntarily attend a sporting event? Absolutely not. My dumb ass signed up to cover sports photography freshman year. I went to something like fifteen games in one semester. Torture. I mean, football's not the worst—*baseball*, baseball's definitely the worst—but I'll pass, thanks."

—

Oregon State, our opponent for the afternoon, won the coin toss and gave Garland the chance to play offense first. Hanna and I, both sweating excessively under the blazing California sun, watched player stats cycle on the big screen and sang along to Katy Perry's "Roar," which was blasting over the loudspeakers for what had to be the tenth time that morning—an unfortunate side effect of having a lion for our school's mascot.

We'd managed to grab a pair of seats in the second row of the student section. The trio of girls in front of us, down in the first row, were all wearing knee-high socks and replicas of Kyle Fogarty's jersey (available for purchase at the campus bookstore if you were prepared to pay a hundred bucks for some green mesh with a Nike swoosh on it). When Fogarty's face appeared on the big screen, side by side with his height and weight and other numbers nobody except the diehard fans actually cared about, they erupted in drunken giggles.

"Guys, look, it's our husband!" one of them shouted.

Another cupped her hands around her mouth and called, "Hey, you forgot a stat! He's got a ten-inch dick!"

The three of them dissolved into hysterical laughter.

Hanna shot me an exasperated look.

"Seriously, though," I said. "What is with the penis size fixation?"

"I know," she grumbled in reply. "And he's actually *my* husband, so if they could please stop objectifying him—"

The rest of her sentence was drowned by the roar of the crowd as Bodie St. James appeared on the screen.

Six foot five. Two hundred and thirty pounds. *You should mention how big his dick is.* Kyle Fogarty's voice echoed in my head. I quickly averted my eyes from the big screen and turned to look onto the field, squinting under the shade of my hand. But of course, the second I started searching the crowd of uniforms for Andre, my gaze landed on the very person whose stats I was trying not to think about.

Bodie stood with his back to me, his head bent low to examine the playbook Coach Vaughn was holding in one arm.

Hanna, who misinterpreted my sigh of frustration, nudged my side with her elbow and said, "I know. I can't even look at Vaughn without wanting to punch him in the face."

The song over the loudspeakers shifted to some angsty rap music. The bass shook the concrete under my feet in rhythmic earthquakes.

"What if we're making a huge mistake?" I blurted. "What if the tips are fake? What if Bodie's just really bad at math and the books are fine? What if the women at the country club made a mistake about seeing Vaughn in San Diego? Maybe they ran into someone who just *looked* a lot like him, and—"

Hanna spun on me and clapped a hand on either side of my face, forcing me to look her right in the eyes.

"Laurel," she said very seriously. "Chill."

"I'm *trying.*"

But the stakes were too high. Mehri and I were treading lightly in a minefield. One wrong step and it was mission failed. Game over. The truth—whatever it was—would stay buried.

The student section erupted with noise. Hanna and I abandoned our heart-to-heart and looked at the field, quickly deducing that we'd gotten a first down, and threw our arms in the air and cheered.

The next two downs were far less thrilling—two lousy runs, each eating up only a few yards to the next first down. And then came the third-down play. After the hike, chaos. While the defensive line and the offense crashed together, Bodie leaped back two long strides and surveyed the field. A few seconds passed like some kind of eternity, and then Bodie cocked his elbow back and launched a throw.

It was the cleanest spiral I'd ever seen—and it landed square in the palms of Kyle Fogarty, who'd somehow found a pocket of negative space forty yards down the field, right on the edge of the end zone. The nearest defenders scrambled to catch up to him, but it was already done. He tucked the ball to his chest, turned, and took two steps.

Touchdown.

The stadium exploded with noise. In the row in front of us the three girls in Fogarty jerseys were beside themselves with joy.

"That's my husband!" one of them bellowed.

I suppose Kyle Fogarty was doing some kind of celebratory posing and peacocking for the crowd, but I wouldn't know. I wasn't watching him. I was watching Bodie St. James, who punched a triumphant fist in the air and then turned to chest bump his nearest teammate. His elation was contagious. I found myself clapping along with Garland's fight song.

But my joy dissolved to dust the moment I saw the image on the big screen. It was a close-up of Truman Vaughn on

Garland's sidelines. His headset and mic were resting around his neck, and his baseball cap was pulled low over his eyes, casting them in shadow. He stood with both arms stretched out, palms to the sky, welcoming the roar of the crowd. He looked like a deity. And the crowd was willing to treat him like it, because Truman Vaughn was the kind of mastermind who knew how to orchestrate the perfect play.

Over the loudspeaker came the announcement that the Vaughn Foundation would be donating $5,000 of sports equipment for this touchdown. The Godfather of football had, once again, secured his standing with the community.

The lukewarm vodka lemonade in my stomach was like battery acid as it crept up the back of my throat. I wanted to throw up. I wanted to scream at the top of my lungs that Truman Vaughn might not be the man he'd convinced everyone he was. But I didn't. I just stood in silence and let the crowd cheer, hoping that on Monday, Ellison Michaels would choose a side—our side.

chapter 7

Ellison Michaels was the first female editor in chief the *Daily* had ever had and the recipient of a full-ride to Garland University.

She was smart enough to know that Mehri and I were right.

On Sunday, Mehri and I met with her in her office to deliver our article. It wasn't the charity profile she'd asked for. The first half detailed the university's harassment training program, and the second half outlined the allegations of Vaughn's locker room talk from the mouths of his own players.

"This is solid journalism," Ellison said a bit reluctantly.

"So you'll run it?" Mehri pressed.

Ellison flipped back to the first page and picked at the staple with her fingernail.

"The university won't like it," she said, eyes glazed over in thought. "But they can't point fingers at *us* if we're just calling attention to program failures. They've put a lot of resources into this harassment training. If it's not working—or if someone on their payroll is undermining it—then it's a PR opportunity for them."

"They'll get to make a big show about it," I agreed. "Promote a woman in the athletics department. Print a bunch of pamphlets about consent and sexism. Invite a big-name feminist speaker to campus."

Ellison nodded, like this decided it. "We'll run it."

—

Between the text I received from my mother (*Felicidades on YOUR ARTICLE mi compañera mi amor TE QUIERO so proud!!!*) and the email I received from my Writing 301 professor (*Hi guys, unfortunately I have to cancel class today. Someone stole my car last night*) Monday morning felt eerily like Christmas. Then I slipped out of my bedroom and found my two favorite elves waiting for me.

"Congratulations!" Hanna shouted, tossing a handful of glittery confetti that rained down on my head.

"Oh, come on, I *just* swept in here," Andre protested.

The two of them had hung dark-green streamers on the kitchen window and tied a bouquet of multicolored balloons to the back of our IKEA chair. There was a pink box of donuts on the counter and a newspaper attached to front of the fridge.

"Is that—" I began, tears welling in my eyes.

"Your article," Hanna whispered, steering me to the fridge

with a hand on my shoulder. "I jogged over to campus this morning to grab a hard copy. Took me a while to find one, but I got it. Your article's on the second page."

I ran my fingers over the newsprint, tracing a line between the page number and my own name, printed neatly beside Mehri's.

The second page. We'd done it.

—

I'd be lying if I said I wasn't nervous to see Bodie again. The thought of him having even the slightest bit of resentment toward me made my stomach churn, but I was able to comfort myself with the knowledge that nobody really read the *Daily* anyway.

Besides. I had faith that, once our investigation was done, he'd understand why I'd interviewed him. He'd appreciate the investigation and he'd forgive me for asking him about Vaughn's obsession with *The Godfather*.

The elevator in the biological sciences building was much roomier without a six-and-a-half-foot-tall quarterback crowding the cramped space. Down in the basement, the lecture hall was mostly empty, since only a handful of people had beaten me to class. They were scattered around the auditorium, heads bent over their phones and laptops as if in prayer. I sauntered down the aisle to the pair of seats three rows from the back where Andre and I had been sitting since the first day of class, dropped my backpack to the floor, and plopped into a chair.

Eight minutes until class.

While I scrolled through Instagram, students trickled in and the lecture hall filled. I had just tucked my knees to the side so a pair of guys could slip past me and take the last pair of empty seats farther down the row when my phone buzzed with another pair of texts from my mom.

The first read: *Don't be mad at me!*

"Oh god," I muttered.

The second explained: *I sent your article to your tia. She read it to Mama and forwarded it to Tony and Gloria. She also reminded me Alicia's quince is next month. You should call her. It would mean so much to Alicia to hear from a FAMOUS WRITER. Ay dios SO proud. TQM*

A backpack hit the floor beside my feet, startling me so bad I jumped an inch in my seat. Andre plopped down next to me. He was in a pair of baby-blue shorts that hit just above his knees and a short-sleeved button-down shirt with little pineapples embroidered on it, and his face was freshly shaven. Like he'd had time to kill that morning and had spent every minute of it on looking nice.

"Look at *you!*" I cried. "So did you just come from a photo shoot or—"

"Thanks," he interrupted me, his voice a hurried whisper. "But you should know, this morning the whole team got an email from Coach Vaughn. He canceled practice."

The thinly veiled panic in Andre's voice made me uneasy.

"Did he say why?" I asked.

"Um," Andre drawled, averting his eyes. "Hey, you thirsty? I didn't drink my Gatorade this morning—I usually kill it during practice no problem, but—"

He reached for his backpack. I leveled him with an unamused stare.

"Andre."

He winced.

"He said you and the *Daily* are going to write an article about his sobriety problems. The guys in the team group chat are saying they think next time you're going to try to spin his charity trip this summer to sound like some big binge."

I reared back in stunned disbelief.

"Why do they think that? Does Vaughn have any proof that it was just a charity trip?"

"It's not like that. I'll show you the texts. It's just Fogarty and some of the other guys hyping each other up. I should've said something this morning before it got really bad, but they *just* added me to this group chat last week, after that Baseball House party, and—"

And Andre didn't want to be excommunicated. Not when he'd just managed to wedge his foot in the door with the starters on the team. I gave his hand a tight squeeze.

"It's not your job to stand up to them," I told him.

Andre sighed, seeming equally frustrated and embarrassed. "I should, though. You're my friend, and that's your investigation. And I *know* you. But Fogarty and these guys—they think someone's trying to sabotage their season, or some paranoid shit like that. They're convincing themselves the *Daily*—like, you and Ellison and Mehri—are making something up."

"They think we would just *make something up*?"

Andre's eyes blew wide. He tipped his head pointedly at the other side of the room, and I followed his gaze. Kyle Fogarty, Scott Quinton (the offensive tackle with the thick neck and cherubic face) and a few other first-string players were settling into a cluster of seats on the far end of the center column of seats, two rows down from us. They weren't looking our way, which meant they hadn't noticed my outburst, but they looked on edge. Restless. Agitated.

Fogarty's faux hawk glinted neon green in the auditorium lights as he dropped into his seat with an audible huff, then turned to the others to say something in a low, furious whisper I couldn't make out. I sank lower in my seat, feeling suddenly cold and jittery.

They think you made it all up.

"Why would we make something like this up?" I whisper-hissed to Andre. "We're the fucking school paper. Why would we try to sabotage our own football team?"

Andre ghosted his fingers back and forth over the racing stripes buzzed into the side of his hair, like it calmed him.

"They're scared. They're just scared, is all. It's making them stupid."

One of the two pairs of doors at the top of the lecture hall popped open and our professor, Nick, appeared. He was wearing his usual T-shirt and blazer combo, despite the sweltering heat outside, and he had his laptop bag slung over one shoulder. He stopped two steps into the room, an arm stretched back to hold open the door for someone behind him.

"You can just bring it down to the front," he said over his shoulder.

My stomach dropped when Bodie St. James slipped through the door. He was carrying an old-school projector—a big, heavy hunk of plastic with a light box on the base and a stand mirror that cast an image onto a wall. The thick, corded muscles in his arms strained under the short sleeves of a white Garland University T-shirt, but there was an easy smile on his face, like helping our lanky hipster of a professor was genuinely making his day.

His dark hair was mussed, like he'd slept in that morning and hadn't bothered brushing it. He looked well rested. Happy. Blissfully ignorant.

"Yeah, just right there's perfect," Nick said as Bodie set the projector down next to the podium up on stage. "Thanks so much, Bodie."

"No problem," Bodie said earnestly.

I would've rolled my eyes at the chumminess of it all if I wasn't so busy trembling in ice-cold panic. I watched Bodie's face very carefully as he turned to start up the aisle toward Fogarty and the others, thumbs tucked into the straps of his backpack like a third grader on his way to school. I watched his smile dissolve, ever so slowly, into a confused frown as took in the sight of his teammates, with their dark glares and tensed shoulders.

"Bodie hasn't heard yet," I murmured.

Andre shook his head. "I don't think he read the group chat."

We both watched Bodie shrug off his backpack and lower it slowly in front of the empty seat on the aisle, like he wasn't quite sure if his teammates were going to let him sit there.

"What's up?" Bodie asked, his eyes on Fogarty. "Practice was canceled this morning, right? I thought the email said—"

Fogarty whipped out his phone, tapped the screen harder than totally necessary a few times, and handed it to Bodie wordlessly.

Mierda, I thought.

On stage at front of the lecture hall, Nick clicked open his

PowerPoint and then looked up and surveyed the room. His eyes landed on Bodie, who was still standing in front of the seat on the aisle, eyebrows pinched and mouth half-open as he stared down at Fogarty's phone in stunned silence.

"All right," Nick teased pointedly. "Why don't we all take a seat and we can start."

There was a little titter of snorts and giggles throughout the lecture hall. Bodie blinked at Nick for a moment—like he couldn't seem to remember where he was and didn't understand why people were laughing—before he glanced down at Kyle Fogarty, who tipped his chin to the empty seat. Bodie braced one hand on the back of the chair, like his knees might give out beneath his weight, and sank down into it obediently.

"All right," Nick said, clapping his hands and shooting us all a smile that was perhaps a little too cheery given the subject matter we were about to tackle. "Today we're starting unit three, STIs and STDs."

I wasn't paying attention. I was watching Fogarty put a hand on Bodie's shoulder and lean in close to whisper in that quick, furious way again. I had the sudden urge to chuck my mechanical pencil across the room, like hitting Fogarty in the back of his dumb green faux hawk with a tiny stick of plastic and graphite might keep him from spewing poison into Bodie's ear.

Bodie nodded along halfheartedly as he kept reading. And then, suddenly, his head reared back like he'd been slapped. He turned over his shoulder and narrowed his eyes like he was searching the room. Like he was looking for someone. I watched, with a growing pit in my stomach, as he scanned each row of the lecture hall. There was a girl my shade of brunet three rows down. Bodie paused, craned his neck a little, then continued his search when the girl turned her head and he saw her profile. I propped one elbow on my stupid little swivel desk and braced my hand over my eyes, shielding my face as inconspicuously as I could. But this felt pretty conspicuous, so instead I clasped my hands in my lap and tried my best to pretend I was paying incredibly close attention as Nick read off a PowerPoint slide about genital herpes.

I risked another glance at Bodie, who was twisted around in his seat. His eyes landed on me and stopped.

I was going to throw up. Here, in the middle of lecture, like a freshman who'd hit the boxed wine too hard on Blackout Thursday.

I tried to look away but I wasn't quite quick enough. Our eyes locked and latched for a split second—just long enough that I caught the flicker of recognition that settled over his face. Bodie St. James remembered me. Under other circumstances, this might've been a cause for celebration. Popping open pinot noir with Hanna, blasting a throwback playlist, dancing around our kitchen. "A cute boy noticed me" celebration. Instead, I swallowed the lump in my throat and realized that, for perhaps the first time in my life, my invisibility had failed me.

chapter 8

Ellison lived in an apartment building one block over from the Rodeo—close enough that, on a Saturday morning, you could hear the Baseball House blasting country music. I climbed the stairs to the second floor and found Mehri Rajavi down the outdoor walkway, looking between her phone and the numbers on the doors.

"Did she summon you too?" I called.

Mehri shielded her eyes with one hand. "She sends some really fucking ominous texts."

Together, we found her apartment and knocked. The door swung open and our editor in chief appeared before us, a tiny plastic party cup of champagne in one hand. I'd never seen her in leggings before.

"Hi, ladies," she greeted us. "Thanks for coming."

Her apartment was exactly what I'd expected—impeccably clean and decorated like something out of a Pottery Barn catalogue, down to the chunky knit throw on the couch and the potted succulent on the kitchen counter. There was a mountain of cardboard pizza boxes piled up on her dining table, which was twice as big as the one Hanna and I had at our apartment.

"Come on, Cates," Ellison said, hand on my shoulder to steer me away from the door and into her living room, like she thought I might turn and make a break for it. "Cheese or pepperoni?"

"You could've told me we were having a party," I mumbled.

I'd wasted the morning knee-deep in pessimism when I could've skipped my shitty granola bar breakfast to prepare my body for the onslaught of free carbs.

Ellison shrugged. "I thought it'd be a nice surprise. Here—let me grab you a cup of champagne. You look like you could use it."

She disappeared into the kitchen. I turned and regarded the mountain of pizza boxes. All my worrying that morning had done a real number on my appetite, but I knew better than to turn down free food when it was offered. I stepped up to the table and popped open one of the boxes, letting the scent of hot bread and cheese and tomato sauce waft up to my face. It was hard to choose between cheese and pepperoni, so I took one of each and smacked them together, cheese to cheese. The sandwich of champions.

"What are we celebrating?" Mehri asked, less easily distracted by the culinary offerings.

I cupped a hand under my chin to catch a string of melted cheese.

Ellison twisted her lips and said, "I don't know if I'd call this a *celebration*, per se."

"Vaughn told the whole football team he thinks we're trying to drag up his past with addiction in order to get attention," I piped up. "They're convinced we're running a smear campaign."

"I know," Ellison said. "Owens was furious about the article. I tried to tell him about your original pitch, and he vetoed the shit out of it. Says we're not allowed to touch it with a ten-foot pole."

"Oh." The pizza settled like a rock in my stomach.

"He's forbidding us from investigating?" Mehri demanded.

Ellison nodded. "He confiscated every binder of tips I had in my office."

"You're joking," Mehri said. "Oh my god, this is a nightmare."

"Well, yes, it *would've* been," Ellison corrected, "if I hadn't scanned everything and dropped it into the Google Drive attached to my personal email. But that's not why I called you here. About five seconds after Owens left my office, I ran over to the athletics department and told them Sterling needed a few documents."

"Why?" I asked, frowning.

Ellison forced a shaky smile as she slapped a few sheets of paper on the table.

"Because we're going rogue," she announced. "The girl who sent us that tip about Vaughn groping her during an event filed this report with the athletics department. They were supposed to forward it to the Title IX office, but they didn't."

Mehri gasped in scandalized delight. "You stole this?"

Ellison nodded. "I'm not letting the administration bury this."

"So we're still pursuing the story?" I asked.

"We are. But this has to be top secret now," Ellison said, lowering her voice despite the fact that she was safe in the comfort of her own apartment.

I could appreciate that there was a lot at stake. Ellison was the editor in chief of one of the oldest college papers in California. She had much more to lose than Mehri and I did, even if her perch at the top of the *Daily's* pyramid meant she was more likely to weather a firestorm than two junior writers. I glanced between Ellison and Mehri, a strange warmth blooming in my chest that was equal parts pride and nausea. Ellison must've noticed I looked like I was about to hurl, because she turned on the pep talk.

"I need you on this. Both of you. This could be huge."

"I'm in," Mehri said immediately.

She and Ellison turned to me. I felt like a domino in a chain. Like if I didn't budge, nothing else down the line would. "Me too."

Ellison gave my shoulder a squeeze. It felt like a hug, coming from her.

"Did those women at the country club have any evidence that could confirm Vaughn was in San Diego the weekend this girl was assaulted?" she asked.

"I think one of them said she had a selfie with him."

"See what else they have—videos, pictures, texts. We have to make sure whatever we print is bulletproof. The second this is out we'll have people trying to poke holes in our research to defend Vaughn."

The flare of panic in my chest was almost painful.

"Wait, are you sure you want—I mean, Joaquín's cousin hasn't even messaged me back yet. This could be *nothing*." And Mehri's tips, while damning, were more than five years old and from anonymous sources.

"We're not writing this article today," Ellison insisted, setting her elbows on the table and folding one hand over the other. "We're *investigating*. Don't get ahead of yourself, Cates. All I need you to do right now is wait for the text and track down those women from the country club and interview all of them again. Make sure their stories haven't changed. Record everything."

"I can do that," I said.

"And I need *you*," Ellison continued, turning to Mehri, "to find the girls who sent in those tips. I don't know if any of them checked into the student health center or contacted Title IX services—"

"But I'll find out," Mehri confirmed. "Gotcha, boss."

Ellison nodded tightly. I caught a flicker of fear in her eyes before she tossed back her cup of champagne and reached for the nearest box of pizza.

—

I took two entire pizzas home. Ellison had gone a bit over-board with the order in her excitement (because we were rebels with a cause now) and hunger (because she'd been running off nothing but black tea, trail mix, and anxiety for twenty-four hours), and was more than happy to get rid of a few pies so she wouldn't have to take up every square inch of space in the communal fridge.

My walk home felt like something out of a music video. The sky was a cloudless, unmarred blue, and every manicured lawn and ancient oak tree was vibrant green and bathed in warm sunlight. The afternoon air was warm and filled with the chirps of birds and the laughs of students. I felt light on my feet, despite the weight of the two large pizzas. But that probably had something to do with the two cups of cheap champagne I'd downed.

Back at the apartment, I found Andre and Hanna in the kitchen. Andre was standing in front of the open fridge, forlornly, and Hanna had crawled onto the counter to look through the top shelves of our cupboards. The second I stepped through the front door, she inhaled sharply, like one of those TSA German shepherds when they catch the scent of a fifty-pound bag of cocaine.

"Where'd you get the pizza?" she demanded.

Andre slammed the fridge shut. "Oh, *hell* yes."

I set the boxes on our rickety dining table, then took a step back so I wouldn't be trampled as Hanna and Andre descended on them with giddy laughter and cheers.

"I'm going to go call my mom," I announced, using a paper towel to mop up a bit of grease that'd seeped through the cardboard and stained my fingers. "I'll be quick."

"M-kay," Hanna hummed through a mouthful of pizza.

"Save me a slice," I told them.

"No promises," she and Andre said in unison.

I slipped out the door and headed for the back exit. Our apartment building didn't have a real garage, just a handful of parking spots tucked under the shade of the second floor along a driveway that connected to a side street. There were cars in all six spots that afternoon.

The ugliest of the bunch was mine. On my sixteenth birthday, my parents had gifted me a white 2014 Toyota Corolla with thirty thousand miles on it. They'd bought it from our neighbors—an older couple who were planning to move into a nice old folks' home with a reliable shuttle service. My mom and dad had been nervous that I'd hate it because it wasn't new, it definitely wasn't cute, and it *did* sort of smell like old people, but I'd been so happy I'd bawled my eyes out.

I loved that car. I knew all her quirks too—like how you had to give her to the count of three after you unlocked her because if you opened the door too quick she'd panic and start with the alarms. She also doubled as a great place to have a moment alone. I'd cried in my car. I'd done homework in my car. But calling my parents was always the most fun. I wiggled into the driver's seat, getting comfortable, and then clicked on my phone and went through my starred contacts until I found MADRE.

She answered on the second ring.

"Laurel! Your father's sitting next to me, let me just put you on speaker."

There was a lot of rustling and muttered Spanish before she figured it out.

"Hey, *mija*!" my dad greeted me, chipper as could be.

Me-juh. Patrick Cates couldn't seem to pick up a passable Spanish accent no matter how many telenovelas we watched or how often he spoke to my mom's side of the family. The man's language skills were just nonexistent.

"Hi, Dad," I said. "Is now a good time to talk?"

"Now works," he responded. "Your mother and I just had a business lunch together. Very upscale place."

"We went to Subway," she clarified. "What are you up to, *mi amor*?"

I smiled in disbelief, because I never imagined I'd be calling my parents with this kind of news. "I just wanted to let you know that my editor asked me and another girl to write a special feature. And I *think* we might be on the front page."

"Laurel," Mom said very seriously. "We are *so* proud of you."

I laughed, then blotted my eyes with the sleeve of my jean jacket. "Don't make me cry, okay?"

"You've got your mother's smarts, that's for sure," Dad tossed in, fully ignoring what I'd just said. "I never would've been able to connect the dots like that."

I let out a wet laugh. "Yeah, but which one of us knows how to do an oil change?"

Dad laughed at that. Then, because he's my dad, he said, "How's the car doing? The AC giving you trouble again? I can always drive down on the weekend and give it a quick once-over—"

"Patrick, not now," Mom chided him.

"All right, all right. Text me about the AC, though."

"*Te quiero mucho!*" Mom shouted.

"Yeah!" Dad seconded. "*Te quiero mucho*, kiddo."

Tea-queer-uh-moo-cho.

I smiled and shook my head. "Love you too."

chapter 9

On Thursday morning I convinced myself that I needed to skip Human Sexuality. The carpet in the bedroom was a hair magnet. The fridge smelled a little funky. The bathroom mirror was splattered with water droplet stains. It was therefore justifiable—nay, *imperative*—that I stay home and, in the pursuit of cleanliness, address these very urgent matters. It totally had nothing to do with the fact that I'd heard the entire football team was fuming about our article.

"I can just take notes for you," Andre had told me the night before. "But I really don't think they're going to do anything, Laurel. It's all talk."

I wasn't scared. I just needed to clean the apartment. That was the plan, at least, until Andre texted me fifteen minutes before class: *Okay so Fogarty said Nick warned St. James there's a pop quiz on the reading today.*

I spat out an expletive and tore off my rubber gloves. There was no time to change into something more flattering than the stretched-out leggings and my dad's old XL shirt, which I'd thrown on that morning. I grabbed my backpack and booked it to campus, wishing the whole way that I was one of those kids who didn't care about disappointing their parents.

The auditorium was crowded when I slipped through the double doors behind a pair of blond girls who were bitching loudly about a chem midterm with a bad curve. I scuttled straight to my usual seat—the third row from the back, second in from the aisle—and slapped my notebook and a mechanical pencil onto my desk, then scanned the auditorium for signs of trouble. Nick stood up at the front, shuffling stacks of papers at his podium. Fogarty and a couple of the other starters were sitting in the middle of the room, their voices lowered and significantly less rowdy than I'd grown accustomed to. There was no sign of Bodie.

I pulled out my phone and shot off a quick text to Andre. *Okay made it*

His reply was immediate and overpunctuated.

Typography ran late!! Be there in 5!! Save my seat!!

I flipped up the too-small swivel desk on the aisle seat so people wouldn't throw their stuff down without stopping to ask if it was taken. Then I cradled my phone in my lap and scrolled through Instagram while I waited for Andre to come be my human shield.

I was six months deep in a meme account when I heard

the snap of a swivel desk being shoved back between seats. A backpack hit the floor at my feet. I looked up, fully prepared to warn Andre not to make a single comment about how horrible I looked unless he wanted me telling Mehri about the enormous crush he'd had on her before we learned she was exclusively interested in girls.

But it wasn't him. It was Bodie St. James. In a suit.

He wasn't wearing a tie—just a crisp white shirt with the top button undone—and his dark hair was slicked back into a perfect wave that suggested he'd skipped the tie by choice. He looked like a *Sports Illustrated* cover story. Tall and handsome and perfectly composed, the favorite son of a multimillion-dollar athletics empire.

Bodie stood in the aisle for a moment, blinking down at me like I was a cockroach in a bathroom stall on the first floor of Buchanan. Like he wanted to crush me under his shoe but was sort of hoping I'd just skitter off and he could pretend he'd never seen me. Our stare down lasted either a half a second or twenty-five years. It felt like the latter, given that my entire body was tensed with fear, like a newborn deer in the headlights of a semitruck.

Bodie finally took a bolstering breath, a muscle in his jaw ticking, and dropped into the seat next to mine without a word. And then it got worse. A few rows down from us, Kyle Fogarty twisted around in his seat. When his eyes landed on Bodie, he smirked and raised his eyebrows in question. Bodie nodded once, curtly. Fogarty saluted him with two fingers to his forehead, then tipped his chin up in a way that said, *You got this, bro.*

I did not care for this nonverbal conversation *at all*. I

considered grabbing my backpack and sprinting out of there (screw the pop quiz—I'd email Nick to tell him I had food poisoning and beg for mercy), but Bodie and his ridiculously long legs were blocking the aisle. I wasn't about to ask him to move his knees. And I most definitely wasn't going to try to squeeze around him or crawl over his lap, even though it looked very welcoming in navy-blue dress pants.

Except his hands were shaking. I only noticed it when he leaned forward to fidget with his backpack, and then again when he sat up and reached between our seats to pull his swivel desk back up in one violent tug. The tiny slab of faux wood locked into place with a hollow *thunk* so loud I flinched.

"Sorry," he snapped. Then he exhaled sharply, splotches of pink blooming on his cheeks, and turned to face me. "Hi, Laurel."

"Hi," I croaked.

I braced myself for a follow-up of some kind, but Bodie just pressed his lips into a solemn line and turned back to the front of the lecture hall, seeming suddenly very interested in the bright blue loading message on the projector screen that warned, in blinking letters, that no HDMI input was detected. The tips of his ears were pink.

Is that it? I thought.

In my peripheral, I saw someone very tall pause at the end of the aisle, then keep walking. It was Andre. He darted into a row across the aisle and a few down, muttering apologies as he squeezed past a few people to get to an empty chair. When he was seated, he turned over his shoulder to shoot me a wide-eyed look and mouth the words, *What the fuck?*

Great question. I didn't have time to answer it, because

up at the front of the auditorium, Nick cleared his throat and started his introductory spiel.

"We've got three graduate students sitting in on the class today," he announced, sweeping one hand toward a trio of twentysomethings in the front row who turned in their seats and waved awkwardly. "They're going to help me with a few things. Let's actually kick things off with"—he held a stack of papers aloft—"a quiz on the reading!"

This was met with a chorus of groans and expletive-laden whispers.

"It's only five questions," Nick added, sounding a touch peeved. "One point each. This is really straightforward stuff, guys. We went over most of it in lecture on Tuesday."

The three teaching assistants started up the aisles, handing out stacks of quizzes to each row as they went. When one of them reached ours, Bodie offered her a tight smile, took a sheet off the top, and passed the rest to me without looking up.

"Thanks," I said, my voice reaching an octave higher than was audible to the human ear.

I grabbed my mechanical pencil, tucked my hair behind my ears, and tried to focus on the sheet of paper in front of me—which got a little challenging when Bodie started bouncing his knee so hard it made my chair shake.

The first question was easy. *Name an STD that condoms can help prevent (when used properly).* I cleared my throat and hunched over my desk, hoping that my hair would shield me. Something about having to write the words *genital herpes* while Bodie St. James sat close enough I could smell spearmint on his breath was unspeakably embarrassing.

What contraceptive methods can be used during oral sex to help protect participants from STDs?

I scribbled down my answers in an increasingly small, condensed version of my usual chicken-scratch handwriting. The other three questions were simple enough. I finished the whole thing in less than a minute, then flipped the quiz over and sat back in my chair to twiddle my thumbs.

Beside me, Bodie exhaled in a huff. I shot a discreet glance at his paper. He still hadn't written anything other than his name. I knew it was just a five-point pop quiz, and that it was probably his own fault that he hadn't studied for it even after Nick tipped him off, but Bodie seemed like a nervous wreck. His knee was still bouncing wildly and he'd given up on trying to answer the questions and resorted to staring at his teammates on the other side of the room.

He was probably having a rough week. The whole team was, obviously, but Bodie was the one who'd been named in the article. It was bad luck that, buried in all the well-meaning praise, Bodie had accidentally offered up something damning.

I wondered if Vaughn was mad at him. The thought made me sick.

So it was an unholy combination of empathy and guilt and that drove me to attempt—for the first time in my life— to cheat. I sat up as straight as I could and lifted my paper, just a little, like I needed to double-check my answers but had suddenly become farsighted. Bodie glanced over at my quiz, then averted his eyes.

Come on, you noble moron, I thought. *It's five points. You gave me quotes, I'll give you my answers. We'll be even.*

I set down my quiz, faceup, then faked a stretch and let

my hand accidentally knock the corner of it, so it was better angled for him to read.

He didn't look over again.

But why would he take anything I offered him? Bodie St. James probably thought that I was the kind of girl who closed elevator doors in people's faces. The kind who interviewed people and then used their own words to cut down the people they cared about. The kind who felt comfortable cheating on pop quizzes. I felt a sudden and unrelenting urge to say something. To turn to him and explain myself—that this was about much more than a few sexist jokes.

When one of the TAs came up the aisle to collect our quizzes, I caught another glimpse of Bodie's (blank, save for his name in neat block letters in the upper left corner). I sank lower in my chair and busied myself with picking little torn scraps of paper from the spiral ring of my notebook.

Up at the front of the lecture hall, Nick waited until he had our quizzes to click on the projector. The words *Unit Three: STIs and STDs* appeared on the screens.

"All right, guys," Nick said, tapping the stack of papers against his podium to even them out. "I'd like to start off the lecture today by having you turn to the people around you and talk about what you think some of the common myths are surrounding sexually transmitted diseases."

I'd rather get syphilis and die, thanks was my first thought.

My second was that I should probably identify someone who was not named Bodie St. James to discuss STDs with. The pair next to me—a small, skinny boy with perfectly coifed black hair and a girl with wavy hair and bushy eyebrows—had already started talking, but the sliver of conversation I caught seemed to be a private one that had absolutely nothing to do with class. I wasn't brazen enough to interrupt them, even in such desperate circumstances.

I risked a glance at Bodie. He was still looking at his teammates, so I took half a second to stare shamelessly at his face, tracing the sharp lines of his profile and the tan on his cheeks and forehead. Then I followed his line of sight just in time to catch Kyle Fogarty nod once, firmly, before shooting me a mocking sneer and twisting back around in seat. I glared at the back of his stupid green faux hawk, hating that my eyes prickled. Nobody had ever sneered at me unironically before.

Bodie shifted beside me. I felt the heat of his stare on me—on the hole in my leggings on my right knee, on my oversized T-shirt, on my unbrushed hair—and felt small. But I tipped my chin up and faced him anyway. His hand clenched into a tight fist on his desk, then went slack again as he stretched out his fingers.

"Why are you doing this?" he asked.

"Doing what?"

"Why are you trying to drag up Vaughn's addiction? He's clean now. You have no right to ridicule him for something he battled almost a decade ago."

"It's not about his addiction. We—" I pressed my lips shut and tried to think of a way to tell him everything and nothing simultaneously. "If the *Daily* has cause to believe an investigation is needed into some . . . concerning behavior, we investigate. If we don't find anything, there won't be an article."

Bodie examined me carefully. "Is this about money?"

"No," I snapped. "It's about doing the *right thing*."

He reared back like I'd slapped him.

"You—" he began, then exhaled a harsh breath that was almost a scoff. "Dragging a man's name through the mud so yours can be on the front page is the right thing?"

It shouldn't have cut me like it did, but there was a part of me that worried he was right. I'd always been curious about the spotlight, hadn't I? And I'd sat back and basked in the glory of it all when Ellison had invited me to join a top-secret investigatory team. I'd called my parents to brag. I'd wanted to be heard.

The surge of self-doubt was like a punch to the stomach.

And so my response was, perhaps, a bit rash.

"Eat shit, St. James."

Whatever Bodie had been expecting me to say, it definitely wasn't *that*. To be fair, I also hadn't anticipated my outburst. It was like I'd been spontaneously possessed by the spirit of the spitfire, whiskey-chugging family matriarch in a telenovela— there didn't seem to be any other logical explanation for how I'd suddenly acquired the courage to tell a Division I football player to, and I quote, eat shit.

Bodie flushed red from his hairline to the collar of his shirt.

"Really? That's how this is going?"

I had two friends, the upper body strength of a stale Cheeto, and was dressed like my next class was an intermediate seminar on dumpster diving. I was in no position to start a fight with anybody, least of all a quarterback. But I was determined not to apologize, despite the fact that confrontation made me feel a tiny bit like I might burst into tears, because I wasn't about to let Bodie St. James accuse me of taking a shot at Vaughn just so people would know my name. I hadn't realized this was a metaphorical bruise of mine until he'd prodded it.

"Have you ever read the *Daily*?" I demanded.

"Yeah, I've *read* it," he said, so indignantly you'd think I'd accused him of being illiterate.

"Okay, then you realize we take our work really seriously. When we release an article, everything in it has been fact-checked a hundred times over. Right now, we're investigating. We have a handful of tips and an anonymous source on the football team who's made some serious allegations about sexism in the locker room. If you have a concern, you can email the editor in chief, but I'm not—"

"Bullshit," he snapped. "You took what I said out of context."

I opened my mouth to make a counterargument, then caught the hint of someone's conversation behind us—something about gonorrhea—and remembered that we were sitting in the middle of a lecture hall.

"I'm not doing this right now," I told Bodie.

He leaned over his desk so his eyes were level with mine.

"Laurel, please. I just want to talk."

The twinge of desperation in his voice made me hesitate. It would've been so easy to pretend that Bodie St. James was just some Neanderthal with his privileged head wedged too far up his ass to see the world for what it was. But he looked up to his coach. He'd told me so during our interview.

Bodie had trusted Vaughn to be a good leader and a good man. Of course he'd choose to believe him in the face of accusations.

The alternative was too horrifying.

"Look," I said, reaching out just far enough that my fingertips brushed the sleeve of his jacket over his forearm. His eyes dropped to my hand. "We are researching because we have to, okay? Not because we *want* to."

Bodie's eyes searched mine. And then, all at once, his face went soft with concern.

"Did Notre Dame put you up to it?" he asked, voice lowered. "If they're blackmailing you guys to try and knock us out of the playoffs or something, you can tell me, Laurel. I can help you."

Bodie was looking for an antagonist. Someone who cackled malevolently as they plotted his team's demise, and who'd have a clear motive to lie about Vaughn. He needed me to tell him that person existed—a cardboard cutout villain for him to hate. But I couldn't do that.

"Nobody's forcing us to write this," I said. "And I know because I'm the one who pushed for this story. I'm the one who pitched it, and I'm the one who wrote it. Bodie, we—" I lowered my voice to a whisper. "We think you might be right. About what you said off the record, about the funds. And we think it might be way, way worse than any of us expected."

Bodie tugged his arm out of my reach, the color draining from his face. He turned to the front of the auditorium, the muscle in his jaw ticking again, and clenched his hands into tight fists in his lap. His chest rose and fell in quick, sharp heaves. I thought I saw him squeeze his eyes shut a little too quickly, but then Nick dimmed the lights to play a video clip from the Centers for Disease Control and Prevention, and it was too dark for me to be sure.

"I have to do the right thing," I whispered, trying to get his attention before the video started. "We don't know if it's true or not yet, but we have to investigate. Which is why I'd really appreciate it if you spoke with me again."

He didn't even flinch. It was like he hadn't heard me. And he didn't look at me again for the rest of the lecture. I folded my arms over my chest and returned the favor, feeling a lot like I had after the Art House's Pollock party freshman year, when I'd woken up in my dorm room covered in black light paint and then spent three consecutive hours clutching a toilet in the communal bathroom. It'd been the most disastrous hangover of my young life. I'd been feverish and weak for three whole days.

This adrenaline crash felt a lot like that hangover. Why had I told him? What if he told Vaughn? What if Vaughn told Sterling, and Sterling shut down the paper?

By the time Nick finally clicked on the references slide, signaling the end of the lecture, I was shaking. My notes for the day were pathetically underwhelming. I'd only written down my name, the date, and *Unit Three: STIs and STDs*. A quick glance at Bodie's desk told me he hadn't even gotten that far. There was just a small collection of rudimentary sunflowers scattered across the bottom of an otherwise blank page of his notebook. He let out a heavy sigh and scrubbed a hand over his eyes.

But Nick wasn't quite finished with us.

"Okay, guys, we've got about five minutes left here, so I want to talk about the final project."

All around the auditorium, students paused, then resumed packing up their things, but more slowly—like that somehow made it less rude.

"As I mentioned when we went over the syllabus, the final will consist of a fifteen-page research paper and a thirty-minute in-class presentation. I know some of you have friends in the class you'd like to work with, since this is a project you'll be doing in groups of four—"

I saw it coming a mile away.

Don't do this, Nick, I thought. *Not today.*

"So I'm going to go ahead and partner you guys up with the people sitting next to you. Our lovely grad students will come up the rows to take down your names, just so we can make sure everyone's accounted for!"

It felt like a joke. It had to be a joke.

Beside me, Bodie scrambled to shove his notebook into his backpack and fold his swivel desk back between our seats. He wasn't quick enough.

"Hey, Bodie, right?"

It was the boy two seats to my right. The short one with the perfectly fluffed black hair, like he'd just come from an audition to be in the next inevitable rip-off of One Direction. He'd leaned forward so he could see around the girl between us, who was aggressively typing out a very long text I was glad not to be on the receiving end of.

"You're the, uh—" Boy Band pantomimed throwing a football.

"That's me," Bodie confirmed with a smile.

He tried, once more, to turn and slip out of his seat.

"I'm Ryan! Nice to meet you, bro. I'm a really big fan. This is my friend—" He glanced at the girl between us, who sent off her monologue of a message and then slapped her phone facedown on her desk.

"Hi! Hi, sorry," she said in a flurry. "Olivia."

She reached out to shake my hand.

"Laurel."

Olivia was wearing a long-sleeved bohemian dress and brown ankle boots—something you'd wear to Coachella if it was chilly out. I could tell she was still heated from whatever argument she'd been having on her phone, but she played it off well.

"Great to meet you, Laurel," she said, then reached across me to shake Bodie's hand too. "Sorry, I don't watch football. Which one are you?"

I held back a snort. Just barely, though.

"Quarterback," Bodie replied, perching on the edge of his seat.

"Should we add each other on Insta?" Ryan interjected. "So we can keep in touch and work out when to meet about the project?"

Bodie pursed his lips, like he was trying to think of a good excuse that wouldn't pulverize Ryan's enthusiasm.

"Yeah," he finally ground out. "For sure."

And so we exchanged names and Instagram handles. I knew it was just a formality. Bodie would inevitably go to Nick and demanded to be moved into another group—one without me in it—and some random kid who'd skipped lecture today would take his place. But Ryan didn't know this. He kept asking Bodie questions about their upcoming game that weekend at the University of Washington. Was Quinton's ankle recovered? Did they think he'd be able to play? How was the defensive line looking without Greene and McNeil?

I tapped open Instagram to accept two follow requests from Olivia Novak (@onovakphotography) and Ryan Lansangan (@ryanlasagna).

When people finally started to filter out of the lecture hall, Ryan smiled sheepishly and wished the anxious quarterback beside me good luck at the game. Bodie, who couldn't seem to get away from me fast enough, shot Ryan and Olivia one last smile before he stood, slung his backpack over his shoulder, and stepped into the aisle. Instead of joining the flow of students headed for the doors, Bodie started for the front of the room.

Knew it. I jolted out of my seat and tore after him.

"St. James."

He tossed me a reluctant glance over his shoulder and stopped to let me catch up.

"If you don't want to work with me, I get it," I said. "But that guy's really excited to be grouped up with you, so just— just tell Nick to move me around or something."

Bodie stared down at me, a muscle in his jaw working, and then nodded. I spun on my heel to find Andre standing in the aisle with his arms folded over his chest and worry etched into his face.

"You good?" he asked, giving me a quick once-over.

He'd worn a sweater I hated—this big, bulky one with vertical stripes of gaudy colors like teal and magenta and orange. He looked like the Fresh Prince of Bel-Air. I could've roasted him. I had so much frustration I needed to channel, I'd probably get some kind of sick relief out of it. But Andre didn't deserve the verbal hellfire I could rain.

"Can we just get out of here?" I mumbled instead, marching past him.

"You want to grab some Pepito's?" he asked as he trailed behind me.

I said yes, because I didn't want Andre to worry too much, but the truth was that I'd lost my appetite.

chapter 10

The Garland Country Club was a splotch of green in an endless sea of drought-kissed hills. It boasted two Olympic regulation–sized swimming pools, one water slide, three hot tubs, and a series of tennis, badminton, and basketball courts. In the middle of it all stood the clubhouse, a Mission-style monstrosity of faux stone and white adobe under a terra-cotta tile roof.

It was an oasis playground for the athletically and socially inclined. More importantly, it was a ten-minute drive from campus—just far away enough that I could pretend I didn't have a Writing 301 paper due on Wednesday, and that Ryan and Olivia weren't blowing up my Instagram notifications about finding time to discuss our group project, and that the entire football team didn't hate me.

It was my paradise—and my own personal purgatory.

"Move your fucking feet, Tori!"

The Real Housewives of Garland all had one thing in common: they were stupid rich. The twins had a collective eight million Instagram followers and a swimsuit line. Diana's family owned thousands of acres of farmland in the Central Valley and a majority stake in a line of organic grocery products. Jessica was the specific type of rich that snapped at waiters to get their attention and had been a victim of wine forgery on two separate occasions. Despite their different backgrounds and business ventures, they all liked to set their weekends aside for some physical activity to channel their built-up aggressions in a healthy and productive way. And I respected that. I did. But it was Saturday, and Garland's away game against the University of Washington had kicked off at eleven o'clock in the morning. It was almost two in the afternoon now, and I was still stuck dodging and chasing stray tennis balls.

But I'd miss the whole damn game if it meant they'd give me a sit-down interview.

"Break point!"

Tori grunted as she tossed a ball up and whomped it right into the net. Across the court, Jessica and Diana howled with laughter and high-fived in celebration.

"Don't even start with me, Cheryl!" Tori screeched.

Cheryl and Tori Lasseter were sisters—something I'd guessed the second I met them, but had further been confirmed when I saw the way they seamlessly transitioned from screaming to laughing and back again.

"All right, Laurel," Diana called. "I think we're ready for a little break."

What a lucky coincidence. I was *also* ready for a break. While the Real Housewives collected their color-coordinated gym bags and Hydro Flasks, I corralled the last of the loose tennis balls and wheeled them away. We reconvened on the shaded patio outside the clubhouse, where I sat them at their favorite table and asked what they wanted to drink—because they were the kind of rich that liked to day drink.

The twins ordered spiked seltzers. Diana asked for an IPA. Jessica wanted a glass of her favorite pinot grigio garnished with a single frozen grape.

I ducked inside. The country club's annual charity function—a golf tournament—was still several weeks out, but the event called for an enormous amount of planning and staging and nitpicking. There were boxes of fake candles and massive floral arrangements sitting in the main lobby, and people in club uniforms jogged up and down the hallways and spoke quickly into walkie-talkies. From the depths of the ballroom, I could hear my boss, Rebecca, shouting at someone to tear off all the tablecloths, iron out every crease visible to the human eye, and then burn them in the dumpster outside because they had clearly been selected by someone who wouldn't know *refined semiformal elegance* if they caught it sleeping with their wife.

I darted past the ballroom doors and slipped into the real heart of the clubhouse—the bar. It was empty save for a trio of older men in khaki pants and assorted sweaters who'd each ordered an old-fashioned. They were watching college basketball on one of the TVs mounted over shelves of bottles of liquor that probably cost more than I made in a week of work. Behind the bar stood a tiny redhead—my favorite co-worker.

PJ (short for Parker Jane, a name only her mother was allowed to call her) was a few years older than me. She was a former pageant queen, which meant she was good at applying false eyelashes and even better at smiling cordially while people asked her idiotic questions.

"How are the Real Housewives?" she asked me.

"Cheryl broke up with her boyfriend. The Silicon Valley one. She's taking it out on her sister. They all want their usuals."

PJ saluted me and went to work.

I returned to the table with a full tray of alcohol.

"All right," Diana said after a long pull of her beer. "Ask away."

I scanned the court-facing side of the clubhouse for any sign of my boss before I whipped out my phone. "I'll be recording our conversation," I told the Housewives, flashing them the app. "Can you tell me when and where you saw Truman Vaughn?"

"He was at the Alvarado Resort," Tori said.

"And you said he looked intoxicated?"

"He was *hammered*," Cheryl chimed in. "I'm a hundred percent sure of it."

"And he invited you onto his boat?"

"His yacht," Tori corrected. "Yeah. He was inviting every woman in the place."

"Did you see anyone leave with him?"

"No," Cheryl said. "But he was giving out his number to women left and right. I wouldn't be surprised if someone actually went."

"Did you see him hitting on any young women? Like, my age?"

"Are you calling us *viejo?*" Diana teased.

I laughed. *"Claro que no."*

"How are we doing over here?" a voice sounded from behind me.

I turned over my shoulder just in time to see my boss approaching from the far side of the outdoor patio. Rebecca was only in her early thirties but she'd been working at the country club for almost a decade, and had the sculpted calves and intense tan lines to prove it. She ran a tight ship. PJ and I liked to vent to each other about how demanding and condescending she could be, but a part of me was empathetic. Rebecca had spent years working in a male-dominated space. That had to wear a woman down.

Still, the sight of her approaching always made my fight-or-flight instincts kick in. Even when I was on my best behavior Rebecca used a tone of voice with me that made me feel like a kid who'd been called into the principal's office for skipping class or vandalizing lockers. And today I'd actually broken some of her rules: I had my phone out (strike one) while I was hovering to chat with guests (strike two) in Spanish (strike three).

The fight or flight kicked in. I chose flight.

"Thanks so much, Diana. I'll be right back with those napkins you wanted."

I skittered away before Rebecca could catch me; interview abandoned.

—

Inside the clubhouse bar, I climbed onto one of the stools and propped my elbows on the dark wood counter. PJ slid a crystal glass of Sprite across the counter and popped one of the miniature technically a stir-stick straws I liked into it.

"Rebecca heard me speaking Spanish again," I grumbled. "I'm an idiot."

"How are you an idiot?" PJ countered. "You speak *two* languages."

"Remember the email she sent out last year about speaking English during work hours?"

For the first two weeks after I started working at the club my freshman year, Rebecca had been soft toward me. She'd smile patiently when I came into her office to ask the same questions four times a day, and she'd let me leave early on Sundays so I'd have plenty of time to get my homework done. I could pinpoint the moment our relationship had shifted. It'd been the afternoon she heard me speaking Spanish to a pair of maintenance men. She'd asked me, later that day, how many years of Spanish class I'd taken. I told her I'd picked all of it up from my Mexican mom. Rebecca had frowned and told me she'd thought I was white. I'd laughed and said I was.

I hadn't thought too much of that comment at the time, because a lot of people struggle with the difference between race and culture and nationality.

My dad always maintained that he'd wanted to name me after my maternal grandmother, Maria Fernanda. He loved her name. But my mom had protested. She'd wanted Laurel, a name that could be pronounced two ways. Since she'd been eight months pregnant, she'd won that argument, and as a compromise, Maria was tucked between Laurel and Cates, two names that were entirely palatable to the English-speaking crowd.

It was only later, after Rebecca started berating me for every slipup and sent a staff-wide email reminding us that we were to speak English during operating hours, that I realized Mom knew something Dad didn't.

PJ huffed and wrung out a wet hand towel. "You know, I may only have my GED," she said, "but even I know it's illegal to tell your employees they can't speak a second language."

I sighed and sipped my Sprite.

"On the bright side, at least you got to miss that shit show of a game," PJ joked, then promptly went wide-eyed with mortification. "Shoot. Were you going to watch it? *Shoot.* I'm so sorry, it's been such a long day with all the setup for tonight and—"

I waved her off.

"Hanna would've spoiled it for me anyway," I said. Then I stooped down awkwardly to sip from the tiny straw in my Sprite and asked, "Why was it a shit show?"

Everyone who knew anything about collegiate football knew that Garland would win against Washington. We were simply the better team. Our defense was top five in the country and our offense was the athletic equivalent of a Justin Bieber song—denounced as overrated and annoying by many but celebrated by those of us who could appreciate true genius.

Plus, Washington's quarterback was a freshman with weak ankles and poor depth perception. We had Bodie freaking St. James.

But even the best teams had their off days, and given how upset some of our players probably were about the whole

Vaughn mess, it wouldn't have come as too much of a shock to hear that we'd struggled. But surely we'd won. A loss would've been the upset of the year.

Which is why I nearly choked on my Sprite when PJ said, "Oh, honey, we got crushed."

I pressed a fist to my mouth and coughed, eyes watering and carbonation in places where it had no business being.

"Rebecca's not taking the L too great," PJ stage-whispered behind one hand.

Rebecca had graduated from Garland University a decade ago and made a point of reminding everyone that she'd been good friends with at least four guys on the football team who'd gone on to play in the NFL (like this somehow meant that she had more of a right to root for the school than I, a currently enrolled student, did). PJ hadn't gone to college at all thanks to an abandoned attempt at an acting career after she'd come in fifth place at Miss Iowa Teen, but she'd adopted Garland as her honorary team despite not knowing much about football.

"How did we lose?" I asked, still in disbelief. "Did someone get injured?"

I had the sudden thought that my anger-fueled daydreams about Bodie St. James taking a cleat to the crotch might've become realized, which was simultaneously a thrilling and guilt-inducing prospect.

"No, thank god," PJ said, extinguishing my hopes. "No one was hurt. We just sucked. I mean, I figured we might have trouble when I heard Vaughn wasn't in the stadium, but shit. It was a hot mess to watch. I really wish I followed the news more. Do you know what all this talk is about some student activist group trying to take him down for an alcohol problem? I thought that was over with, like, a decade ago."

For the second time in under a minute, I came uncomfortably close to inhaling a mouthful of soda.

"Here!" PJ said, fumbling for the remote to one of the TVs mounted behind the bar. "Let me check if—there we go! ESPN's doing postgame stuff. Looks like the highlight reel. Maybe they'll say something about Vaughn?"

She turned up the volume. It was less of a highlight reel and more of a montage of misfortune. Each clip was worse than the last. Twice, two members of our offensive line managed to crash into each other because they were so lost. Kyle Fogarty had to dive to make a catch that he should've been able to run with. It was a little hand-off pass, nothing too fancy, but its failure indicated two things: one, that Fogarty was out of position, and two, that Bodie St. James hadn't had enough time after the snap to see that the play wasn't going to plan.

And then there were the sacks. These were broken down in slow-motion replays so viewers could watch the exact moment that Washington's defensive line broke through and tackled Bodie to the ground. I wanted to laugh, like this was all some kind of slapstick comedy routine, but each hit was more brutal than the last—helmet-rattling, bone-bruisingly brutal. And each time he went down, Bodie took a little bit longer to climb back to his feet.

"Garland's quarterback, St. James," came the voiceover of one of the analysts, "issued a statement this week in defense of head coach Truman Vaughn, who's been accused of sexist language in the locker room by a scathing report in the school's newspaper."

Then, before I was ready for it, Bodie appeared on the screen, fresh-faced and arrestingly handsome against a black backdrop patterned with the ESPN logo. It took me a moment to recognize that he was dressed in the same navy suit he'd worn to class on Thursday. He must've filmed it that morning, before he sat next to me.

"As a team," Bodie said into the camera, his voice steady and practiced, "we stand behind our coach one hundred percent. We're appreciative of all he's done for us and how hard he's fought for our combined success. The allegations being made against him are hurtful and untrue, and we won't tolerate slander of his character."

The analyst appeared on-screen again, mouth set in a tight line and eyebrows furrowed seriously. "St. James was quoted in the article as saying of Vaughn: *He definitely says some stuff I don't think female reporters should hear.* A second source, a player who asked to remain anonymous, listed some of those things."

He began to list Andre's comments. The screen shifted to footage of Washington fans rushing the field in celebration of the win they hadn't even thought to hope for. The cameras caught Bodie as he walked against the crush of people and toward the sidelines. He tipped his head up to the scoreboards, the sunlight catching his eyes through the face mask of his helmet for a brief moment before he hung his head.

Later, as I drove back to my apartment with the windows of my Corolla down and music blasting from her janky speakers, I thought about Bodie. I thought about the way he'd looked on the field, limping and grass stained, his shoulders hunched against the roar of a crowd celebrating his failure. I thought about the long flight he'd have back to Garland and the unknown he'd be stepping into when he returned.

And I couldn't help but hate Truman Vaughn a little bit more than I already did.

chapter 11

On Monday, I slept through my alarm. I knew I'd be late for Writing 301 the moment I pulled my eyes open. The room was too bright, too uncomfortably warm from the sunlight streaming in through the window.

By the time I made it to the humanities building, hair still dripping wet from the fastest shower I'd ever taken in my life, it was five minutes past the hour. I tugged out my earphones, still mouthing the lyrics of the song I'd been blasting to make myself hustle, and pushed my sunglasses on top of my head, where they promptly got tangled in my wet hair.

The first-floor hallway was barren save for a pair of girls hovering across the hall from the bathrooms, in front of a glass case of posters for various performance art groups. The two girls were almost comically opposite—one tall and built like a runner, the other short and curvy—but I didn't bother paying that much attention to them until the taller of the two spotted me over her friend's shoulder and, with an exchanged nod, they circled around to stand shoulder to shoulder in the middle of the hall.

I stuttered to a stop in front of the human barricade they'd formed.

"Hi there!" the shorter girl greeted me, metallic red nail polish glinting in the light as she shifted her paper coffee cup from one hand to the other.

"Hi," I parroted, a bit breathless from the brisk walk across campus.

"Are you Laurel Cates?" asked the taller girl.

It took me a second to register that I was, in fact, Laurel Cates. In my defense, I was still preoccupied with trying to free my sunglasses from my hair. But I also wasn't used to people knowing who I was—especially not when I knew absolutely nothing about them—so I was a little thrown off my game.

"Um," I said after far too long a pause. "Yeah, I am."

The girls exchanged a look.

"We have a message for you," the shorter one said. "From St. James."

"A what?"

Maybe if I'd been paying more attention, I would've noticed that they both looked a bit nervous. Jittery, but determined. And if I'd caught onto this earlier, then maybe I would've been suspicious when the shorter of the two popped the white plastic top off her paper coffee cup. But I didn't realize what she was doing until it was too late.

Some instinctual part of my brain told my body to brace

for the sting of scalding-hot liquid against my skin. It was almost a relief when I realized the coffee was lukewarm—like it'd been sitting in the cup for an hour.

And then it sank in. Literally. Because they'd dumped coffee on me.

Two girls I'd never spoken to in my life had paid four bucks at the campus Starbucks and waited for who knows how long outside that specific classroom just to toss a drink down the front of my shirt, like this would somehow inconvenience me more than it had them. It was the pettiest thing I'd ever witness anyone do. Which is probably why, in the tense moment of silence after it happened, I had the strangest urge to laugh.

The shorter girl set the lid back on her coffee cup and smiled at me like we'd just promised to exchange notes for class or something. Like she *hadn't* just assaulted me fifteen feet from the door of my Writing 301 classroom.

"Go Lions," she said.

The two girls turned and took off down the empty hallway, murmuring excitedly in an "I can't believe we pulled that off" kind of way. I stared after them in open-mouthed shock, watching as they disappeared around the corner. I might've believed that I'd imagined the whole thing if it wasn't for the fact that when I looked down, there was a very real puddle of black coffee on the linoleum floor at my feet.

I darted into the women's restroom. The stall doors were all propped open, the off-white toilets dingy and menacing under the harsh fluorescent lights. It was a small consolation that my attackers hadn't cornered me during passing period, when the lines for the bathroom wrapped into the hall and hundreds of students were streaming back and forth to their next classes—there had been no witnesses to my caffeinated assault.

I stood at the sinks and stared myself down in the mirror for a moment. There was coffee from my neck to my toes. It dripped from the ends of my hair and onto my pale-pink shirt and the straps of my backpack. A few rivulets traced the length of my arms, tickling the insides of my elbows and spilling off my fingertips.

Why hadn't she aimed for my face? It seemed like a missed opportunity.

I tore a paper towel out of the dispenser, ran it under the sink, and mopped up the stain down the front of my shirt. When I glanced at my reflection again, a laugh bubbled up in my throat and came out in a sharp burst that echoed off the tiled walls.

"What the fuck?" I asked aloud.

Talking to myself in an empty bathroom seemed a little melodramatic, but really, what the fuck was that? How had they even known where to find me? Had they actually bought a coffee just to throw it at me? I had so many logistical questions.

And then there was the matter of the shorter girl's prefacing statement.

We have a message for you from St. James.

So Bodie had sent them. I hadn't thought he was capable of something so malicious. Wasn't his whole thing supposed to be that he was unwaveringly nice? So much for *that*. He'd wanted me doused in hot coffee and he'd sent a pair of minions to do it—probably so he wouldn't have to get his hands dirty. The coward.

I wet another paper towel and kept rubbing at my shirt, watching the coffee stain bloom like one of Mehri's watercolor flowers. It was only getting bigger, more spread out—a little paler, perhaps, but still undeniably there.

My nose started to run. I sniffled sharply, and pressed harder on my shirt, then had to stop for a second and use the dry corner of the paper towel to blot at my teary eyes. When I tried to laugh again, it was a tiny, hoarse thing.

"What the *fuck*?" I croaked.

I went through three handfuls of paper towels before I finally gave up. There was no saving my shirt—or my morning, since I couldn't walk into Writing 301 without having to explain both my tardiness and my dampness.

Time to go home.

The hallway was still empty, so at least my assailants hadn't been able to make a spectacle of me like they'd intended to. I scurried back to the main doors, my head down and shoulders hunched in case anyone caught a split-second glimpse of me through the windowed panels on every classroom door.

I knew my luck had to run out eventually. I'd just hoped it would last me to the end of the hallway. But fate really was a stone-cold bitch, because just as I thought I might escape my miserable morning without any more witnesses, a walking storm cloud dressed in all black (T-shirt, joggers, Nikes) burst through the main doors, a backpack slung on one shoulder and a Garland football jacket hooked over his elbow.

Bodie.

I stopped twenty feet short of the lobby, every muscle in my body bracing for confrontation. But Bodie didn't look up. He kept his head down, eyes on the ground, and hooked a sharp turn and started up the staircase to the second floor.

My feet moved. Before I could think rationally, I was at the bottom of the stairs, my fight or flight instinct having decided it was a smackdown kind of day. Bodie was already halfway up the steps. There was something wild about his movements—a kind of restlessness that might've given me pause if I wasn't so damp and filled with unbridled rage.

"St. James!" I roared.

It was unspeakably satisfying to watch Bodie flinch so hard he nearly ate shit on the stairs. His arm shot out and grabbed the handrail. To my slight disappointment, he managed to right himself from the missed step. I saw the muscles in his back pinch beneath his T-shirt and remembered, suddenly, that on Saturday I'd watched him get the absolute shit knocked out of him by the University of Washington's defensive line. He was hurting.

I balled my hands into fists at my sides. There would be no mercy.

Bodie turned around to see who had bellowed his name like it was some kind of Viking war cry. He was clearly startled to find *me* standing at the foot of the stairs, glaring up at him with fire in my eyes.

"Laurel," Bodie huffed, his shoulders slumping. Like, *Ugh, it's you again.* Then his eyes dropped to my shirt and the little wrinkle between his brows deepened. "Why are you always wet?"

I was so distracted by the way the sunlight streaming through the window behind him caught his brown hair, casting a halo of gold around his head, that I almost missed the blatant double entendre. *Almost.* But Bodie seemed to realize how his question sounded the second the words left his mouth. His ears went bright red.

"Not like—I meant like in the elevator—"

"I know what you meant," I snarled. "Call off your attack dogs."

His eyebrows furrowed. "What?"

"Your attack dogs. The ones you sent to dump coffee on me. You could've at least done it yourself, you know. You didn't have to be such a little shit about it."

Bodie looked bewildered for a moment before his face sank with sudden realization. He knew exactly who I was talking about.

"I did *not* tell them to do that," he said, pointing an adamant finger at my stained shirt.

"Okay. So you *suggested* it."

"No! I—*fuck*. I was just talking to them about the *Daily* and they said they'd be willing to talk some sense—" He cut himself off abruptly, and pinched his eyes shut like he hadn't realized until now what those words usually connoted.

"Talk some sense into me?" I finished for him, in a tone that added, *Are you serious, you idiot?*

"Yeah, all right," Bodie grumbled. "All right, that's my bad. But I didn't—" he began, then groaned in exasperation and scrubbed one hand down his face. "I didn't want them to do *that*."

I folded my arms over my chest, immediately regretting it when I felt my cold, damp shirt become plastered to my stomach. Bodie's eyes flickered down, then snapped back to my face. I wasn't sure which of us blushed harder. The moment broke when Bodie cleared his throat, his face hardening.

"Look," he said, impatiently. "I'm really late—"

I flinched despite myself. The coffee hadn't scalded me, but his dismissal did.

"Go, then," I snapped, waving him off. "I'm—it's fine. We're done here."

Bodie frowned and, once more, I wanted to chuck something at him. How dare he look at me like he knew I'd just spent ten minutes in the bathroom trying to convince myself that crying would only ruin my makeup.

"Take my jacket." Bodie held it out like an overpriced, waterproof olive branch. More softly, he added: "Please."

I tipped my chin up and jammed my sunglasses back on. We were indoors, so the dark tint made it tough to see and I was sure I looked like a complete tool, but I was determined to make an exit. I left Bodie standing on the stairs and stormed out of the humanities building with what was left of my coffee-stained dignity.

chapter 12

The cherry on top of my morning from hell came in the form of a broken air conditioning unit. By the time I climbed the front steps of our building, the coffee stain on my shirt was dry from the long walk under the scorching sun. Between getting lukewarm coffee dumped on me by a pair of strangers (both of whom cared more about the NCAA Championship than justice for victims of harassment, apparently) and my verbal gun slinging with Bodie, I'd had—and I'm understating this—the worst day.

So when I unlocked our door only to be hit by a wall of hot air, it felt a little like life had come back to kick me in the ribs when I was already sprawled and waving my white flag.

I dropped my backpack and went right to the thermostat. The dial was set to midsixties, as usual, which meant neither

Hanna nor I had accidentally bumped into it and cranked up the heat. I stood on my tiptoes to put a hand in front of the vent over the bedroom door.

Nothing.

I yanked open the kitchen window, hoping to get some kind of ventilation, but the air outside was just as oppressive. There was a heat haze over the asphalt of the gas station outside—the same wobbly distortion I saw over the toaster every time I left a Pop-Tart in for a little bit too long.

Hanna got home ten minutes later, after I'd resigned myself to a life of sitting on the floor in front of the open refrigerator. I heard the clatter of her keys and the creak of our busted-up door, followed by, "What the fuck?"

I leaned back and poked my head around the fridge door. "AC's dead."

Hanna, who was dressed in her usual workout attire (running shorts and a sweat-drenched tank top), tugged out her earphones and flattened back a few stray pin-straight black hairs that'd popped out of her tiny stump of a ponytail.

"Why are you here?" she asked, frowning at me. "I thought you had class."

I sighed. Then I stood, closed the fridge, and put my hands on my hips.

Hanna snorted out a laugh.

"Laurel! You big goof. Is that coffee?"

I wished I could've laughed the whole thing off. Instead, I made a show of scoffing as I recounted the story of the girls who'd waited outside my Writing 301 classroom to dump coffee on me. If Hanna noticed I was feigning nonchalance, she didn't say anything. She just flushed bright red with indignant outrage.

"What'd they look like?" she demanded. "I'm finding them on social media and reporting them to the university. Fuck it—I'm messaging their moms on Facebook. Who even does this shit? That's so—so—"

"Hanna."

She folded her arms over her chest, dark eyes going glassy with tears.

"I'm so mad," she whispered.

I held my arms out. Hanna stepped forward into my embrace and buried her sweaty little head in the crook of my neck.

"I'm okay," I assured her. "It was just room-temperature coffee."

"It's not about the coffee."

She was right. It wasn't about the coffee, and it wasn't about the stain on my shirt, which I could probably coax out with the right kind of detergent. It was about the fact that two strangers had been mad enough about our investigation that they'd tracked me down to serve up their own brand of misguided vigilante justice.

I squeezed Hanna tight.

"Can we go to Andre's?" she asked, her face still pressed against my shoulder. "It's so fucking hot in here. I feel like I'm gonna pass out. Also, this is probably going to sound insensitive, given the circumstances, but can we stop and grab some iced coffee on the way there? I'm sorry. You smell really good."

Hanna and I took turns showering, threw on clothes that weren't stained with coffee or sweat, and climbed into my car (me wincing when my bare thighs pressed down on the hot vinyl upholstery, Hanna letting out a string of curses when her elbow knocked against the blistering metal buckle of her seat belt).

We ordered three large black iced coffees from the drive-thru window of the McDonald's at the end of the Rodeo. Then, at Hanna's request, I stopped at Smart & Final so she could run in and grab a can of sweetened condensed milk—the secret ingredient to Vietnamese coffee. When she came back to the car, she had a can of the stuff in one hand and a jumbo bag of Flamin' Hot Cheetos in the other. The Cheetos, she explained when I shot her a disapproving look, had been in a display at the checkout. What was she supposed to do, ignore them?

With our bountiful harvest secured, we headed to Andre's. He lived with three other second-string players in the Palazzo, the apartment complex most of the football team chose for its proximity to the practice field and the Rodeo—and because it was, in true Garland football fashion, extraordinarily bougie. There were fountains in the central courtyard, three separate gyms, a rock-climbing wall, and a 24-7 café stocked with a selection of premade organic salads, gluten-free sandwiches, and fresh-pressed juices. Whoever had designed the complex had clearly been aiming for the Italian villa aesthetic, but had gone a bit overboard with the friezes and potted palm trees and faux candle chandeliers. The resulting blight of a building looked like it belonged on the Las Vegas strip, not four blocks from one of the best private universities in California.

Andre's mom was a cardiologist and his dad was a San Diego real estate agent. Money had never been an issue for the Shepherds. But I never felt the financial divide between us as keenly as I did standing in the marble-floored lobby, chipped toenail polish on display in a pair of plastic flip-flops as I spelled my name out for the woman behind the security desk so she could print me up a visitor's badge.

Hanna and I didn't come over often, mostly because Andre's roommates were obsessed with video games and always hogged the living room, but also because the Palazzo was such a hassle, between the guest parking and the security check-in.

When Andre came down to the lobby in sweatpants and some Adidas slides to claim us, he found Hanna and me sprawled on the couches in front of the eight foot–tall fake fireplace, basking in the artificial chill of top-notch air conditioning.

"Ugh, finally," Hanna said. "I need your can opener."

Andre frowned for a moment before I held out the large iced coffee we'd brought for him. Then his eyes lit up.

"We having *ca phe sua da*?" he asked, rubbing his palms together.

"A bastardized version," Hanna confirmed, then grunted as she rolled to her feet and stood, jumbo bag of Cheetos tucked under her arm like it was a pillow she'd brought to a sleepover. She cleared her throat. "But we need to have a chat first."

Andre blinked, took a tiny sip of his coffee, and frowned. "What'd I do?"

"Your quarterback," Hanna said, perching on the edge of the couch I was sitting on so she could loop her free arm around my shoulder, "dumped coffee on our girl."

Andre's head jerked back. I sighed and shrugged off Hanna's arm.

"He didn't dump coffee on me," I grumbled, fidgeting

with a corner of my visitor's badge that'd started to peel off my shirt. "He just told some girls to do it. By accident. It's fine—"

"It's not *fine*," Andre said. "Vaughn's mad, so St. James is taking it out on you."

"What do you mean?" I suddenly felt too cold. I set my large iced coffee on the floor at my feet and pulled a tasseled decorative pillow into my lap. "It's because of the article, isn't it? The quotes Bodie gave us."

Andre nodded solemnly. "He's not, like, *blatantly* making him pay for it. You saw our last game—St. James was a mess. He got ten passing yards. Maybe. That's being generous. I think Vaughn must've spoken with him before, but ever since, he's been a total hard-ass. Everything St. James does in practice is wrong. The boy's been in the gym every night this week. I think Gordon's trying to play peacemaker and talk Vaughn down, but it's *not* good."

"Chester Gordon?" I asked. "The assistant coach?"

"Is that the dude Vaughn got into a shouting match with on the sidelines during the Notre Dame game last year?" Hanna asked. "I love that guy. What a king."

Andre looked at me again and shook his head. "It doesn't even matter. St. James shouldn't have messed with you. That was out of pocket."

It wasn't him, I thought to say. But my brain was already tackling a bigger problem: Truman Vaughn was terrorizing my source, and I didn't have the first clue how to stop it.

—

That afternoon, Andre and I sat side by side on his bed—our faces slathered in some kind of detoxifying charcoal goop he swore would do wonders for my pores—to watch a movie we'd seen a hundred times on his laptop. Hanna had been exiled to floor until she finished her jumbo bag of Flamin' Hot Cheetos, because Andre wasn't about to let her get neon-red Cheeto powder on his pristine white sheets.

I almost didn't notice when my phone lit up with an Instagram notification. A follow request from Bodie St. James. My first thought was that it had to be a fan account or something. I didn't believe it was really him until I clicked on the group chat Ryan had started (which he'd named, affectionately, Group Sex) and saw that, just ten minutes ago, Bodie had liked Olivia's message about meeting up in Buchanan sometime next week to brainstorm.

Before I could overthink it, I hit Accept and followed him back. Then I flipped my phone over, trying not to wonder why he hadn't asked Nick to switch me into another group.

"Oops," Hanna muttered from the floor.

"You drop anything, you vacuum," Andre snapped.

"I know, I know!"

When I was sure Andre's full attention was on the movie and Hanna's full attention was on analyzing the carpet for specks of Cheeto dust, I picked up my phone and clicked back onto Bodie's profile. And then I scrolled. And scrolled. And scrolled.

He'd been dorky in high school. Still incredibly popular, judging by the abundance of classmates and friends grinning and making duck lips in almost every photo, but decidedly chubbier and more awkward—at least until the summer before his senior year, when it looked like he'd dropped thirty pounds during football camp (at which all the boys in attendance had shaved their heads in what I guessed was some kind of weird male bonding ritual). Then there was the picture of him sitting at a table, Garland baseball cap on his head, grinning at the camera as he signed his national letter of intent. Coach Vaughn stood behind him, one hand braced on Bodie's shoulder, smiling haughtily.

The hair on the back of my neck prickled.

And then a notification appeared at the top of my screen—a new message. At first I assumed it must be from Ryan or Olivia. Then, with a sudden shot of adrenaline, I wondered if it could be from Bodie. But it wasn't any of my group mates. Instead, I clicked open my messages to find that Gabi de Hostos, Joaquín's cousin, had finally responded to me.

She wrote, concisely:

We don't want to talk to the media. Please don't contact me again

chapter 13

The media center on a Monday morning was about as calm and enjoyable as Disneyland in July. A line of desperate students formed in the hallway outside Ellison's office, each of them clutching pages scattered with red pen marks—our beloved editor in chief's handiwork, no doubt. I shuffled into a spot at the end. Ellison, who stood in the doorway of her office with arms folded over her chest, spotted me and frowned.

"Cates! Get up here."

I felt everyone's eyes on my back as I skittered around the line. Ellison ushered me into her tiny, cramped office and tugged the door closed behind us, letting it shut right in the face of a forlorn freshman.

"Good morning," I said cordially.

"Did you have the transcripts?" Ellison asked, skipping the small talk.

"Right here." I handed her a laminated folder of papers that'd blessedly survived the ride to campus without getting crumpled. "I got statements from all four of the women from the country club. I sent you the audio clips of the recordings in an email this morning, too, along with the transcripts."

"Fantastic."

"I also heard back from Joaquín's cousin," I said, wincing as I pulled open my Instagram messages to show her the ominous response I'd received. "And it wasn't *great*."

"*We don't want to talk to the media*," Ellison read. "Well, that's suspect. Scroll up for a second. What did you originally send her?"

"I didn't use Josefina's name. All I said was that I knew Joaquín and he said she might be open to talking to me about the resort. I mean, for all she knew, I might've been writing an article about spring break spots. But this sounds like she knows what I'm talking about, right? I mean, why shut me down and say something like that if there's nothing to hide?"

Ellison nodded. "Message the other friends. See if anyone will bite."

"But Gabi wasn't just shooting me down. She said *we*. She was speaking on behalf of her friend group. Right? I mean, at the very least, she was speaking for Josefina."

"I can't tell you how many times I've told writers not to run with what a secondary source says until they've tried to get in contact with the primary source," Ellison said. "You have to let Josefina speak for herself."

"It just feels so insensitive to ask about . . ." I trailed off with a wince.

Ellison sighed. "Laurel, you're going to meet so many people who think journalists are nosey, conniving assholes. But I know you. And *you* know you. You're not an asshole. You're not going to send Josefina anything offensive, and you're not going to harass her if she says she doesn't want to talk. But you have to give her the chance to make that decision for herself."

I hated when Ellison was right.

—

It took me a few tries to find a good bench on campus, since all the ones under trees were splattered with bird shit (and the ones *not* in the shade were scalding hot from the sun), but eventually I found a place to park myself for fifteen minutes while I waited for Andre to get out of his typography class so we could walk into Human Sexuality together. I texted to let him know where to find me: a narrow, hedge-lined walkway between two redbrick buildings near the architecture school.

Andre replied, *Be there soon just gotta fix this fucking kerning.*

Confident that I had plenty of time before the perfectionist in Andre would be appeased, I pulled up Instagram and typed in Josefina's name. Her account was still set to private. I could message her, but it would sit in her requested inbox— she might not see it for days, weeks, months. No. I'd contact her another way. Facebook, maybe. Did people our age use Facebook anymore? LinkedIn. Surely she had a LinkedIn.

Her name was excessively common, but with a bit of

hunting, I was able to find the Josefina Rodriguez who was studying communications at the University of California, San Diego. She had her school email listed.

I gave her my cell number, my school email, my personal email, my Instagram, my Snapchat, the address of my editor's office, and the address of my apartment. Then I typed: *Sincerely, Laurel Cates.* I stared at the sign-off, hating how formal it sounded. How impersonal and distant. So, on impulse, I wrote a postscript: *You're not alone.*

With a little *whoosh*, it was out of my hands.

I exhaled and clicked back to my inbox. Sandwiched between two spam emails was an unread message from Diana Cabrera, the subject line of which was a sunglasses emoji followed by a martini emoji. It was the photos from their night out. They'd all been taken in a dark bar with the flash on. I squinted at my screen as I tried to make out the collection of washed-out blurs. Tori and Cheryl grinning over their cocktails. Jessica with shot glasses in both hands. A mirror selfie of Diana in what looked like a crowded women's bathroom. There was a group of younger-looking girls huddled at the sinks, but I didn't recognize any of them from Gabi's social media. I scrolled to the next photo—a group shot of all four women with a man standing in the center of them: Truman Vaughn, pink faced and staring with glazed eyes and a wide grin. There was a wet streak down the front of his blue button-down shirt where he'd spilled something, and sweat beaded on his forehead.

"Yuck," I said aloud.

That was the last of the photos.

I turned my phone off, flipped it over, and counted out

my breaths. When that didn't settle the sudden swell in my chest, I riffled through the emergency snack reserve at the bottom of my backpack, even though I knew food wouldn't ease the ache in my gut. This wasn't hunger. It was anxiety.

I took two bites of my granola bar before I felt nauseated. I sighed and looked out across the pavement in front of me, toward the hedges bordering the other side of the walkway. The leaves rustled. A lone squirrel emerged, his tail twitching and his beady little eyes fixed on me. I snapped off a tiny corner of my granola bar and chucked it at him.

And so, when Andre arrived a few moments later, it was to find me sitting cross-legged on a bench, dutifully distributing granola crumbs to a gang of four squirrels who were circling me like little furry sharks on the hunt.

"What Snow White bullshit is this?" Andre demanded.

"It's not funny! They won't leave me alone."

"Because you fed them, dumbass."

Andre plucked the remaining half of my granola bar out of my hand and took an enormous bite of it, then stomped his feet. The squirrels scattered.

"Has your group figured out your project yet?" he asked as he trailed along beside me toward the biological sciences building, crunching away on my granola bar.

"No. Yours?"

"Pretty sure we're doing something on the sex toy industry."

It was bad enough I had to work with Bodie. I couldn't imagine having to spend the next few months discussing vibrators.

We took the stairs down to the basement of the biological sciences building and shuffled to our usual spot in the third row from the back of the lecture hall, which was buzzing with passing-period chatter. Andre settled into his seat and angled his too-long legs toward me, so his knees weren't wedged against the back of the chair in front of him. I let my backpack slide off my shoulders and hit the floor by Andre's feet.

Before I could plop down beside him, someone called my name.

"Yo, Laurel!"

It was Ryan Lansangan, the man of a thousand inappropriate group project puns. He and Olivia were sitting in the end seats a few rows down. Bodie loomed over them in the aisle, both hands braced on the straps of his backpack and mouth set in a grim line. He wore a black shirt and black joggers—again, moody—and had a beige compression wrap looped around his left wrist. Our eyes met. His face seemed different now that I'd scrolled through pictures of him growing up. I could see traces of the kid in him beneath the sharp features.

Somewhere in the sleepless haze of last night, I'd let myself entertain embarrassingly improbable theories about why Bodie hadn't ditched our group. Theories that I'd usually only come up with after a half a bottle of wine—that from the very first day in the elevator, when we'd both been wet from the rain and late to class, he'd been curious about me. That despite our opposing allegiances, he was *still* curious, and had decided that working on this group project together would give us the chance to talk things through and reconcile our differences.

But those theories all withered under the weight of his obvious discomfort at seeing me again. He didn't look like he wanted to talk things through with me. He didn't look like he wanted to talk to me *at all.*

I turned to Andre, who'd taken it upon himself to stare down Bodie. I'm sure Andre intended to look threatening, but the way he was squinting, he sort of just looked like he'd forgotten to put in his contacts.

"I'll be right back," I murmured.

I marched down to where the rest of my group was gathered. Ryan and Olivia watched me approach but Bodie fixed his eyes somewhere across the lecture hall—which I was sort of glad for, because something about the weight of Bodie's gaze on me made walking very difficult.

Given that Nick had let Bodie enroll in a full class and had also totally been willing to turn a blind eye when he rolled up fifteen minutes late to lecture, I couldn't imagine our professor telling Garland's golden boy that he couldn't switch into another group for the final project. Which left only one possible course of events: Bodie hadn't asked to change groups.

"You look cute today, Laurel," Olivia said as I came to a stop at the end of their row, careful to leave an arm's length of space between Bodie and me. "Love the dress."

"Oh," I said, a bit caught off guard by the compliment. "Thanks! It has pockets."

I shoved my hands into them, like this was a claim I needed to prove, and immediately felt like a moron. A quick glance at Bodie confirmed that he'd been watching my pocket demonstration. He exhaled sharply and looked back across the room to the spot where his teammates were socializing in their usual seats.

I wished he'd smile again.

"What's up?" I asked, tugging my hands back out of my pockets and smoothing down the front of my dress.

"Okay," Olivia said, popping up in her seat like a bottle of champagne that'd been uncorked. "I used to waitress at this Mexican restaurant in Hollywood that does the most *amazing* drag karaoke nights. And I was thinking we could totally do our project on drag culture! You know, like, its history in Los Angeles, and gender performance and identity, and all that stuff. The restaurant's kind of a long drive from here but I could get us interviews with the manager and some of the regular performers. We'd have solid primary sources."

"That's perfect!" I gushed. Really, I was just overjoyed to hear that somebody in this group was going to pull their weight. All Ryan had contributed thus far were inappropriate jokes in our Instagram group chat, and as far as Bodie was concerned—well, at least he was here.

"It's a pretty dope idea, right?" Ryan said, beaming.

"We could go to a drag show at a club or something too," Olivia added excitedly. Then she turned to Bodie and me and asked, "Are you guys twenty-one?"

Bodie nodded. I'm not sure why that surprised me—I knew he'd redshirted his freshman year, so it made sense that he was a year older than me. Still, the sudden mental image I had of him standing in a bar, drinking a legally purchased beverage that wasn't served in a plastic cup, was jarring. Especially since I'd spent a solid hour and a half last night looking at pictures of him from high school.

"I'm only twenty," I admitted.

"That's okay," Olivia said with an easy wave of her hand. "I'm sure we can find over-eighteen places."

The doors on our side of the lecture hall swung open. Nick entered with a "Good morning!" that I could tell meant

Please be quiet, you greasy little heathens, and marched down to the stage. I went to shuffle out of his way at the same moment Bodie stepped forward so a girl could squeeze into Ryan and Olivia's row. We bumped shoulders. Well, my shoulder bumped into his (very solid) biceps. But I wasn't too concerned about that technicality. I was too busy blushing from my collarbone to my hairline.

"Sorry," I blurted.

Bodie cleared his throat and took one comically large step back from me. *Brutal.*

"Let's meet up tomorrow afternoon," Olivia said quickly, so focused on the fact that our professor was starting class that she'd completely missed my horrifically uncomfortable interaction with Bodie. "I can reserve us a study room at Buchanan. Does three o'clock work?"

We all looked at each other, checking if any of us had a conflict or objection. Somehow, this little burst of team spirit resulted in Bodie and me looking each other dead in the eyes and nodding just as he said, "Works for me."

I stifled a grin and said, "Me too."

Tomorrow, Bodie St. James would have to talk to me again whether he wanted to or not.

chapter 14

Ellison Michaels turned from her office windowsill, where she'd been watering a potted purple orchid that did little to brighten up the dingy and outdated room, and regarded me with a frown. It was Wednesday afternoon. The student union was pretty quiet, save for the incessant laughter of a group of boys who were trying to play hacky sack with one of the beanbag chairs out on the floor of the media center.

"I want you in the press box for the next football game," she said.

"Aren't there already people covering football?" I asked, fidgeting with the button on the sleeve of my denim jacket. "I wouldn't want to, like, step on anybody's toes—"

She didn't honestly think that sticking me on a glorified

lawn with eighty-five very large, adrenaline-drunk boys who hated my guts could end well, did she?

"You won't be alone. You'll have Mehri. She's photographed football games before, so she'll know what the rules are for media."

"I really don't think . . ."

Ellison plopped into her university-issued desk chair. She'd pimped it out with a white faux sheepskin cover, but I could tell it was old and sort of janky by the way it creaked under her weight.

"Laurel," she said, "you can handle this."

"They're not going to talk to me. How am I supposed to do a postgame report when the team won't answer any of my questions?"

"They'll talk. They're used to answering questions. And if your interview with St. James is anything to go by, you're pretty damn good at asking them."

"That was—"

Ellison beat me to the punch. "It was *not* luck. You have good instincts. You knew the right questions to ask, and you went off script when you needed to."

I narrowed my eyes.

"This is just because my name is attached to the Vaughn stuff now," I accused. "If I get enough material to write something, it'll get a ton of hits on the website. If I get decked by a linebacker, then Mehri takes a picture of my lifeless body and you still get a ton of hits on the website."

"You're not going to—" Ellison began, then huffed and pinched the bridge of her nose. "Oh my god, Cates. Worst-case scenario, you get snubbed and you have to write a recap of the game without any quotes. But whatever you write is going to get attention from them, whether it's directly about Vaughn or not. And I know you don't *like* attention, but what are you going to do? Just stop writing?"

I ran my tongue over my front teeth, embarrassed to admit that I *had* thought about that. I loved writing. But I already missed the comfort of knowing that nobody would be reading my work. Sure, I hadn't been getting any recognition, but I also hadn't been getting coffee dumped on me in petty retribution.

"The only way for us to make progress on this investigation is to be unapologetically nosey," Ellison continued, her voice gentler, borderline sisterly. "I need someone who can ask the right questions. And you're my girl."

You're my girl. What a cheap shot.

"I can handle it," I said like the sucker I was.

"Good," Ellison said with a triumphant smile. "Because I took the liberty of ordering your field pass for you last week, so it should be ready for you to pick up by Saturday. Just show them your student ID in the communications office at the athletics center. Mehri can fill you in on the protocol for getting into the stadium through the media entrance, and I'll draft a couple of questions for you to ask the players, too, just so you know where to start."

I knew then that Ellison asking me to cover game day had been a formality. She'd made up her mind. The rest was inevitable.

Ellison's cell phone vibrated on her desk, clattering loudly against the wood surface. She glanced down at the screen and sighed, though her smile didn't fade.

"I should take this call. Why don't you swing by tomorrow afternoon?"

I stood, saluted her, and turned to leave.

"And Cates?"

I stopped with one hand on the doorknob.

"Your makeup is amazing today," Ellison said. "Seriously. Your eyebrows are so symmetrical they look photoshopped."

I reached up unthinkingly, then remembered Hanna had told me not to put my grubby little fingers anywhere near her masterpiece because I'd inevitably smudge something. The eyeliner, the eyeshadow, the contour, the brows. There was a lot to be smudged.

"Thanks," I said sheepishly. "My friend did them for me."

Ellison hummed thoughtfully. "Special occasion?"

"Nope. No occasion."

—

The second floor of Buchanan reeked of permanent markers, energy drinks, and despair. At the far end of the sprawling space, separated from the elevators by a maze of study cubbies and tables strewn with books and empty coffee cups, were the study rooms. These were nothing more than glorified closets with glass doors (a feature meant to discourage students from using the rooms for activities that were decidedly *not* academic in nature).

The one Olivia had reserved for our group meeting was barely large enough to house a circular table and a couple of chairs. She sat to my left, her dirty-blond hair pulled back in a choppy ponytail and her bushy eyebrows furrowed as she glared down at the screen of her phone. The stacks of delicate rings on her fingers winked under the fluorescent lights as she typed out a monologue of a text message to someone whose contact name was *CAN GO TO HELL*. On my right was Ryan, who'd worn a floral-patterned silk bomber jacket and white suede Chelsea boots to an entirely casual after-noon meeting.

I had no room to judge. I'd asked Hanna to do my makeup like I was competing in Miss Universe at four.

And so it was with winged eyeliner, glittery champagne and chocolate brown eyeshadow, and a set of false lashes (a strange and alien weight Hanna had promised I'd get used to eventually) that I glared at the empty chair on the opposite side of the table.

"It's three fifteen," Olivia murmured, setting her phone facedown on the table.

Bodie wasn't coming. I didn't have to say it. We were all thinking it. This was why he hadn't asked to switch groups— he was trying to get back at me. He was going to sabotage our group project by leaving us a man down and forcing us to drag his apathetic ass across the finish line for a passing grade.

To be clear, I was upset because he'd slighted our whole group.

Not because I'd wasted the day's makeup. Definitely not that.

"He probably got caught up with team stuff," Ryan said with an easy shrug.

It was Ryan giving Bodie the benefit of the doubt that really set me off. What was it about St. James that made every-one want to forgive him? He showed up fifteen minutes late to lecture, and Nick was ready to burn the entire attendance sheet to erase any evidence of his tardiness. He stood up our group project meeting, and Ryan was happy to shrug it off. He accused me of fabricating accusations to destroy a man's life and then (accidentally) approved two girls' plan to dump coffee on me, and all I could think about was how I hoped the wrist he'd had wrapped up didn't hurt because the guy was having a hard enough time as it was.

Was it the understated confidence? The biceps? The boyish, charming smile that made you feel like he could read you with one look and liked every bit of you, from opening line to closing chapter?

"Whatever," I snapped. "Let's just go over the rubric and divide up the work without him."

If my teammates noticed that I slammed my notebook down with a bit too much force and immediately snapped the lead on my mechanical pencil when I went to jot down the date, they didn't comment on it.

But Olivia did say, "I like your eyeliner, Laurel."

—

After we were done in Buchanan, I figured while I was on campus I might as well pick up the field pass Ellison had so kindly ordered for me. My makeup was nice. I needed to maximize the number of people who saw me.

The athletics center was a palatial shrine of overrated prestige. The whole compound was made up of three floors of administrative offices, two practice fields, and one brand-new training facility. This part of the building was closed off to those who weren't student athletes, barricaded behind a row of turnstiles you had to swipe an ID card to get through. Commoners were expected to use the main gym, where the combination of crowds and poorly maintained equipment meant half-hour lines just to use a squeaky elliptical.

The gatekeeper of this elite portion of the fifty million–dollar shrine to athletic achievement was a polo shirt–clad student with chlorine-bleached hair and an enormous pimple on his chin. I marched across the lobby, my sneakers squeaking on black marble as I passed gilded portraits of old white men and glass cases of assorted trophies, ribbons, and medals, and stopped at the front desk.

"Hi, I'm with the *Daily*. I'm here to get a field pass."

The kid behind the desk smacked a button on the keyboard and the nearest turnstile swung open. I barreled forward into the unknown.

The architect who'd designed Garland's training facility had to have been big on space movies, because the whole complex looked straight out of *Star Wars*. The walls were smooth, dark concrete. The floors were a black marble so polished they reflected everything as clearly as mirrors. It felt like a fun house. A really, really overpriced fun house. The deeper I wandered into the labyrinth of hallways and workout rooms, the more idiotic I felt. Eventually, I found myself in a hallway lined on one side with floor-to-ceiling windows. They overlooked a full-sized indoor football field nestled one story below. The turf glowed neon green under the rafter lights. There were two assistant coaches and a handful of players out on the field running drills. Bodie wasn't among them.

I continued down the hall to a juncture next to an alcove

with a pair of water fountains tucked in it, and wondered why there weren't maps posted all over this maze of a building.

A man's voice carried through the walls of the office next to the water fountains. The plaque on the door read GORDON. The assistant coach. Still not the communications office, so I wasn't all that interested—until I heard a second voice. Bodie's.

"Well, obviously, you guys don't think so."

I knew that, ethically speaking, I shouldn't eavesdrop on a conversation that was so clearly personal and contentious. And then there was the matter of expectation of privacy, which meant that I couldn't legally report on anything I overheard Gordon talking about in his private office with the door shut. There was really no reason for me to linger. It would be best if I walked away. At the very least, I should've turned on the water fountain or dropped my backpack or something, so they knew someone was within earshot (and that Gordon should really get a thicker door or learn to use his inside voice). But I've never exactly been a shining example of great decision making.

I ducked into the alcove with the water fountains, so I'd at least be hidden if someone came out of the office, and leaned one shoulder against the wall of the head coach's office.

"That's not what we're saying," came Gordon's voice again. "I just think you're spreading yourself thin, all right? You're all over the place in practice. You couldn't make a solid throw to save your life against the University of *Washington*—"

"I had a bad day," Bodie said. "Since when am I not allowed to have a bad day?"

A third voice spoke up: "You're failing that general ed class I got you in."

It was Vaughn. A sharp chill rolled up my spine. There

was silence. Drawn out, horribly uncomfortable silence. It was almost a relief when Bodie finally spoke again.

"We haven't even had the midterm yet. I can't be failing."

"Oh really?" Vaughn said. "Because your professor emailed the entire coaching staff about it. You got a zero on a reading quiz. He says he's concerned you might land yourself on academic probation."

Gordon sighed wearily. Bodie remained silent.

"I'm done with this discussion," Vaughn said.

Gordon's door swung open and heavy footsteps thudded out. I froze, horrified that Vaughn might turn and see me hidden in the alcove, but he marched off in the opposite direction.

A long moment after he was gone and my heartbeat had slowed back down, I heard Bodie say, "I didn't want to take that class."

"Then why the hell are you in it?" Gordon asked.

"Vaughn heard the professor graded easy."

Gordon sighed. Something rustled—it sounded like that stiff, water-resistant material the team jackets were made out of—as he shifted in his seat. His desk chair was definitely nicer than Ellison's, because instead of the terrible groaning of rusty metal, there was just a muted creak of leather against leather.

"If you're serious about changing your major," Gordon said, voice gentler now, "you've got to get your grades up. Look, we can get you hooked up with a tutor, but I really think you should consider getting—"

"I'm not changing my major," Bodie interrupted.

"Really?" Gordon sounded surprised.

"I talked about it with Vaughn. He thinks it's a bad idea."

"And what do *you* think?"

There was a pause.

"I think he's right," Bodie said at last. "You're both right. I can't handle any more on my plate right now."

Another long silence. Then, "Bodie, if you've heard anything—"

"I'd tell you." The reply was immediate. Decisive.

"No," Gordon said. "If you've heard anything, you don't come to me. You don't come to anyone in this department. You take it right to the police. Do you understand me? Don't be stupid, St. James."

This was, on Gordon's part, a horrible choice of words.

"I am *not* stupid."

"I know you aren't. That's not what I'm saying here."

"You guys can't bench me because I failed one fucking reading quiz, all right? I'm *fine*. I've got this. I just—*fuck*. I want everything to go back to normal."

I wished I hadn't stopped to eavesdrop. I wanted to give it all back—to rewind and unhear the frustration and embarrassment and desperate insistence that everything was fine.

Bodie stepped out of the office and slammed the door behind himself so hard that the wall I was leaning against shuddered. I held my breath, listening closely for any indication that he might come around the corner to use the water fountain. There was an outraged grunt of frustration. Then, so quietly I almost didn't catch it, a solitary sniffle. I waited a long time after the sound of his stomping footsteps had disappeared before I scurried out of the alcove and resumed my search for the communications office.

chapter 15

"I love you," Hanna said, "but if you don't stop moving your pinkie, I'm going to snap it in half."

Being a hand model was difficult. I hadn't realized this when I'd volunteered. I'd just wanted to shut Hanna up about how she was going to fail this figure drawing class and let down her parents, who'd always supported her pursuing her art despite the less-than-abundant job prospects waiting for her on the other side of graduation. Five minutes into me holding still while Hanna ripped out pages of her sketchbook and brushed eraser dustings all over our bedroom carpet, Andre had shown up (still bleary eyed and yawning from a postdinner nap) and asked if he could join in. Hanna lent him a pack of charcoal sticks and one of her giant pads of newsprint paper, then scooted over so all three of us could fit on the floor between the beds.

"I'm fine if you want to take a break soon," Andre told me, using the back of his hand to push his glasses up on the bridge of his nose. "Just got to do some shading."

"Good for you," Hanna muttered, reaching for her eraser again.

She was about to start attempt number seven on my left pinkie finger when Andre's phone buzzed where it sat on the carpet. He looked down at his charcoal-stained hands, then at me. I looked down at my carefully posed hands, then at Hanna. She groaned, smacked down her sketchbook, and reached across Andre's lap to check his phone for him.

"There's a party at the Baseball House tonight," she said.

"Can't go," Andre said without looking up. "Fogarty said he was going out tonight. If he's too hungover tomorrow, Coach might put me in."

"What about tomorrow night?" Hanna asked.

"Oh, the after party's still happening," Andre said. "Me and the boys are hosting at the Palazzo. We got, like, twenty-five handles of Svedka. If we win, we're celebrating. And if we lose . . . we've got *twenty-five* handles of Svedka."

Hanna turned to me, an eyebrow raised. I didn't like her smile.

"What is it?" I asked.

"You wanted to talk to Bodie, right?"

—

Hanna's corduroy overall dress made me feel like I'd accidentally ordered something online from the kids' department. It was snug around the hips and hit me well above midthigh no matter how much I tugged it down. But it was black. And if I was going to borrow Hanna's clothing for the night, I was going to wear something stain resistant, in case anyone decided to dump their drink on me. Because apparently that was a thing I had to prepare for now.

The Baseball House sat in the middle of the street, wide and imposing with its wraparound porch and speaker system so loud I felt the bass in the sidewalk under my feet. A pair of enormous freshman hockey players stood at the front door, gatekeeping like two baby-faced bouncers. For a split second I imagined them spotting me among the line of people waiting to get into the party and telling me to screw off. But when we got to the top of the porch steps, both of them greeted the reigning beer pong champion with high fives.

And just like that, we were in. I'd never felt so cool.

All the houses on the Rodeo were old Victorians, but the Baseball House looked like someone had taken an ice-cream scoop and hollowed it out room by room, then poured a catalogue's worth of modern furniture, fresh paint, and brand-new hardwood flooring into each shell. Hanna steered me through the crowded living room, with its black leather couches and dimmed lights, and into the modern kitchen I'd gotten a glimpse of in the blurry Snapchat Andre had sent me the night he'd gotten the party invite from Bodie. I stopped in the archway between the two rooms. Through the sea of beautiful people and student athletes stood a granite-slab kitchen island lined with at least forty bottles of wine. Glass bottles. And not even twist tops. *Corked.*

"Oh my god," I whispered reverently. "Okay, let's do a lap."

"I don't see him," Hanna said. "I don't see any of the football players, actually."

A quick scan told me she was right.

"Fuck," I said. What a waste of an outfit. "All right. Let's go home."

Hanna folded her arms over her chest and tipped her chin up. "No."

"What do you mean, no?"

"We're already here, Laurel. You've been working nonstop on this investigation. You deserve a night off."

I reluctantly agreed. Not because I genuinely thought I deserved the break, but because, selfishly, I wanted to spend a few hours thinking about anything other than Vaughn.

"I'm going to find some suckers to challenge to a round of beer pong," Hanna told me.

While she did that, I made my way over to the extensive wine selection. I grabbed a red cup and poured myself a splash of the nearest open bottle: a white wine. It was sour and pungent. I chugged it anyway. After I'd drained my cup, I hummed thoughtfully (like I had even the slightest idea what I was supposed to be looking for in a wine other than a price tag under five bucks) and then moved on to a peachy pink bottle with cursive on the label. Rosé.

I swished it around in my mouth. Considered gargling it. Remembered I was in public. Restrained myself.

Next were the reds. The first one I poured into my plastic cup was a deep, dark burgundy that sent a little shiver of anticipation up my spine. I stuck my nose in the cup and inhaled deeply a few times before I drank.

Dios mío. They were all pretty bad. But they were free, and they'd get the job done. I put another splash of red wine in my cup, then picked up two more bottles and added a bit of each into the mix, swishing everything together.

"*Wine* not?" I murmured under my breath, borrowing the phrase from a T-shirt I'd seen at Target, and tossed back a sip of my improvised jungle juice. How many drinks was that? I wasn't having full servings—just, like, shots. Wine shots. I tried to count them on one hand, then gave up when I figured I'd had a tough week and deserved to turn off my brain.

I found Hanna in the living room, at one end of a collapsible beer pong table beside a stone fireplace with a glass mantel. At the other end of the table stood two very tall, very relaxed young men (swimmers, judging by their wide shoulders and well-developed lats) who were clearly underestimating the BP powerhouse that was my best friend.

"Team meeting," I said. "What's our strategy?"

"I'll do the shooting," Hanna said. "You be cute. Enjoy yourself."

These were mutually exclusive things. I chose the latter and started swaying side to side to the pounding beat of the music, working myself up to more of a hula-hooping motion. Clearly, our opponents didn't think the pair of us were much of a threat since Hanna barely came up to their elbows, even in her platform sneakers, and I was dancing like my dad fresh out of his knee replacement surgery. The two swimmers across the table laughed with each other as they readied their Ping-Pong balls and straightened their cups, looking like they couldn't wait to make two drunk girls chug lukewarm beer.

It was deeply satisfying when Hanna singlehandedly took them out in just four turns. While the two of us hooted obnoxiously and high-fived over our untouched triangle of cups, the taller of the two losers came around the side of the table and held out his hand in concession.

"Good game," he told Hanna.

"Nice effort," she replied.

The swimmer was cute, and I was definitely in favor of Hanna replacing her Art House stoner booty call, Danny, with Mr. Good Sport—which meant it was time for me to excuse myself for a moment and let the two of them talk.

"I'm going to top up my wine," I whispered, clapping Hanna on the shoulder and then winking far too conspicuously. Hanna reached out to pinch my side. I dodged her, cackling, and darted into the crowd.

Back at the kitchen island, I plucked another bottle of wine and scanned the label like it even mattered. As I poured myself another cup, I thought that perhaps it wasn't so bad that my plans had been derailed. It'd turned into the perfect night. Hanna and I were kicking ass and taking names at beer pong, she was totally going to bag a hot swimmer, and in spite of the too-short overall dress, I felt comfortably invisible again—a welcome relief after the two weeks of paranoia since Vaughn had told the football team we were out for blood.

This, I thought, *was exactly what I needed.*

And then, from the living room, came the war cry of someone who had clearly pregamed way too aggressively.

"What's up, bitches?"

I nearly snorted out my wine.

From the cover of the archway between the kitchen and the living room, I watched as Kyle Fogarty stumbled into the party. His hair—an admittedly pretty shade of pastel green now that the semipermanent dye was fading—was suspiciously damp, along with the left side of his shirt. Like he'd shotgunned a beer and missed his mouth completely. But I was less concerned about Fogarty's coordination than the guy who'd walked in behind him.

Bodie St. James followed Fogarty into the party with his arms folded over his chest and an air of stoic responsibility, like a bodyguard—or the exhausted single mother of a toddler who'd decided to throw a tantrum in the grocery store. Between the flannel pajama pants, ratty off-white T-shirt, and the signature scowl of sobriety, I deduced that Bodie hadn't come to the Baseball House to drink and be merry. He was chaperoning.

As Fogarty chest bumped a hockey player in greeting, both of them landing on their feet so hard the living room walls trembled, I saw Bodie tuck his keys into the pocket of his pajama pants in resigned acceptance. They weren't planning on leaving any time soon.

Hanna appeared in the archway and grabbed me by the front strap of my black corduroy overall dress to tow me around the corner and into the kitchen, out of sight.

"Bodie's here," I said way too loudly.

"I saw. We got to go."

"Are you kidding? We can't leave. This is my chance to talk to him."

Maybe it was the wine, or maybe it was the knowledge that Ellison Michaels would be proud of me, but I was determined to follow through on the night's original plan.

"Do *not* do that," Hanna begged.

"I'm definitely going to do it."

Hanna sighed, then pressed herself flush against the wall

and peeked around the corner and into the living room with secret agent–like discretion.

"Do you see them?" I asked. "What are they doing?"

"Just high-fiving people." Hanna scrunched her nose in obvious disgust. "Fogarty is such a dumpster fire of a human being. I can't believe I thought he was hot."

"We all make mistakes."

"Yeah, but look at his *hair*. I should've known."

I took another sip from my red cup and smacked my lips together. "If it makes you feel any better, he's probably getting benched tomorrow for being here."

Which reminded me. I set my red cup on the counter and fumbled for my phone, figuring I should at least let Andre know Garland's starting tight end was going to have the hangover of a lifetime tomorrow morning. My thumbs tippy-tapped across the screen in slow motion.

You're r going ton get playing tomes!!! Kyle is super duck!!! Congrats

He'd know what I meant.

"Fogarty's definitely not going to be fresh as a daisy tomorrow," Hanna agreed. "But St. James seems sober. Guess he's got to stay sharp the night before a game."

"Yeah, except he's—" I began, then stopped myself when I remembered that I only knew Vaughn was already planning to cut Bodie's playing time because I'd eavesdropped on their conversation in his office.

"Except what?" Hanna asked.

I hummed noncommittally.

"Never mind," she said with a shake of her head. "Let's get out of here."

She started across kitchen toward the second exit—a doorway that spilled out into the hall that ran the length of the house, from front door to back. I stopped her with a tug on her arm.

"I'm serious, Hanna. I'm going to talk to him. Can you, like, distract Kyle?"

Hanna gave me this look, like *What has gotten into you?*

The answer was alcohol. A lot of it.

"You owe me," Hanna grumbled as she dove into the crowd.

I poked my head around the corner, far less stealthy than Hanna had, to watch her. Luckily, our targets were too distracted to notice our plan of attack unfolding. Bodie was talking to a trio of girls from the soccer team while, behind his back, Fogarty was down on one knee with his head tipped back so a pair of baseball players could pour a third of a bottle of Grey Goose down his throat. When Bodie turned and saw this gross demonstration of collegiate binge-drinking, he snapped into action before Hanna could reach him.

It happened so fast. One moment, Bodie had ducked into the hallway, disappearing from sight, and then the next, he had appeared across the kitchen from me and plucked a fresh red cup off the counter, and went to fill it with tap water. I marched up to the sink.

My opening line was, regrettably, "Hey, fucker."

Bodie didn't startle. He just pinched his eyes shut, exhaled wearily, and—when his cup was full—turned to blink down at me with resigned vexation.

"Laurel," he said, monotone. Done with my shit.

Don't let him know you're drunk, I thought.

"That's my name," I said, failing spectacularly.

He dropped his hands to his sides. I cleared my throat and tried to flatten back my rumpled hair, almost dropping my phone into my cup of wine in the process.

"What are you doing here?" Bodie asked.

"Wine tasting," I said, tapping a fingernail against the red cup in my hand. "Good stuff. Napa Valley cabernet—"

Bodie pinched the bridge of his nose.

"Look, Kyle's really fucked up right now. You should go. Before he sees you."

Something about the way he said *you should go*—like I was a mosquito ruining the family barbecue—made me prickle.

"You're *kicking me out*?" I asked, cocking one eyebrow in a way I hoped look incredulous and not like I'd just had a wine-induced stroke. "You don't have the authority. You don't even live here."

Bodie held up one finger.

"Okay, first off, that's *not* what I'm doing. I'm just trying to keep—"

"You didn't show up to our group meeting."

Bodie jerked back, whiplashed by the sudden conversational shift, and then pressed his tongue to the inside of his cheek.

"Something came up," he said, much quieter than before.

I had the impulse to say something nasty, since I knew exactly what'd come up and where he'd been, and felt immediately guilty for it. Bodie's academic struggles were not something I wanted to wield against him. It was a cheap shot, and I knew it.

I glared at him over the rim of my cup, wishing I wasn't so soft.

"St. James!" Fogarty bellowed from the living room.

Bodie scrubbed his hand over his eyes. He had very nice hands. Enormous and tan, with long fingers a bit banged up at the knuckles but otherwise—

Oh, I am drunk, I thought. *I am so, so drunk.*

"Seriously, you should go," Bodie told me. "I don't want Kyle to see you."

"Fine," I snapped. "Just let me finish my—"

"St. James!" Fogarty called again, his voice suddenly much closer.

Bodie shot into action. He plucked my red cup out of my hand, set it on top of the fridge, and turned back to face me, all before I managed to scoff in outrage.

"*Tu tienes* the fucking nerve—*pinche pendejo*—"

Undeterred by my protests, Bodie put one hand between my shoulder blades and shepherded me through the doorway and into the hall, which felt narrower and darker than I remembered it being when Hanna and I had first entered the house. When he tried to steer me to the right, toward the front door, I dug my heels into the floor. Bodie sighed and let his hand drop from my back. I turned to glare up at him and roll my shoulders, trying to get rid of the weird little tingle where his hand had been.

"Don't manhandle me," I snapped.

"St. James! What the *fuck*?" came Fogarty's voice from the kitchen.

Bodie looked to the ceiling. "Like herding fucking cats."

He slapped one hand on the wall, caging me in place so I couldn't make a run for it, and leaned to the side to poke his head around the kitchen doorway. He was so close I caught a whiff of his deodorant.

174

"Kyle! Give me a minute, okay? I'll be right there."

There was a long beat of silence.

Then Fogarty said, "Are you hooking up with someone?"

I expected Bodie to blush—because that seemed like the on-brand thing for him to do—so it caught me off guard when he replied, without missing a beat, "That would take longer than a minute, asshole."

I tried to bite back a laugh and ended up snorting. Bodie glanced sideways at me, cutting me with a half-startled look that said *Pull yourself together*. I cleared my throat and ducked my head. My nose bumped against Bodie's very warm, very solid chest.

"Sorry," I whispered.

"Seriously," Bodie called to his drunk teammate. "Go set up beer pong."

"If you're not out in five, I'm coming to find you!" Kyle threatened.

"I'll be there." Bodie let his hand drop from the wall beside my shoulder and sighed. "Yeah, you've got to go, Laurel."

I tilted my head up at him.

"Why?" I demanded. "Worried your best friend—"

"He's not my best friend."

"—will say something incriminating? Or hurt me?"

"He wouldn't hurt you," Bodie said immediately, but he didn't sound fully convinced.

"I don't know," I said, looking him dead in the eye. "People can do terrible things when they're drunk. Even someone you think you know really well can turn into a total stranger."

Bodie's face pinched.

"You should go," he said again. It sounded like a plea.

"Well, we were here first. And you're not even supposed to be out tonight. So."

Bodie's eyebrows furrowed. "How do you—" he began, then sighed. "I keep forgetting you and Shepherd are tight."

I straightened my spine.

"Who—who's *Shepherd*?"

I don't know why I even attempted lying, but the thought that anyone on the football team might hold my friendship against Andre made me sick.

"The guy you sit with in class," Bodie deadpanned. Then he added, a bit hesitantly, "He's your anonymous source, isn't he? The football player who told you Vaughn was saying sexist shit in the locker room."

My stomach twisted into a sailor's knot.

"Andre didn't talk," I began, my voice tight with panic.

"It's fine," Bodie cut me off. "Shepherd's a good guy. I'm not mad at him, or anything."

"Because he told the truth?"

A muscle in Bodie's jaw ticked. "I'm not doing this with you right now."

"Yes, you are," I spat, my frustration made worse by the fact that my voice came out a bit slurred. "I don't give a shit if Vaughn was serious or joking. It doesn't matter. Words are *not* harmless. Thoughts become words become actions. Somebody said that. Margaret Thatcher! No. Fuck. Kanye? I don't remember right now. But it's *true*."

"Look," Bodie said with a heavy sigh, "I get that it's awful. Okay? I'm not disagreeing with you. But we're not all these big idiots who sit around shitting on women."

"I know that," I snapped. "You realize I'm friends with Andre, right? I *know* not everyone on the team is an asshole. Not all—I am *not* going to say *not all men*, because I absolutely despise that argument—but not every individual guy on the team is a raging sexist. I know that. But your head coach says sexist shit, which means you all either agree with it or are too scared to call it out. That's a problem. A problem you need to *fix*."

Bodie shoved his fingers through his dark hair.

"What do you want me to do?" he asked. "That's how Vaughn talks. That's how *his* coaches talked to *him*. What am I supposed to do when there are a hundred guys in the locker room and they're all laughing? I can't just stand up and—"

"You can," I told him. "You're the fucking quarterback."

"It's not that easy," he insisted.

"Because you're a *coward*." In the brief silence that followed, I realized both of us were breathing too hard. I had to clamp my lips against the urge to apologize. To mend. To back down. "You don't have to do it on your own, you know? We—the *Daily*"—I gestured vaguely at myself and the empty air around me—"are here."

Bodie sighed like the weight of the world had settled on his shoulders.

"What do you want me to do?" he asked.

"You can start by telling me what you know about the Vaughn Foundation."

"That was off the record," Bodie said, his cheeks flushing. "And it might be nothing."

"But it might *not* be nothing," I said. I could blame the wine for the less than poetic phrasing. "You told me about the books for a reason. There's something rotten there. You feel it.

You can be a whistleblower, Bodie. I'll protect you. And you have no idea how many women you could be helping."

Fuck.

Too much. I'd said too much.

Bodie narrowed his eyes. "What women?"

"I can't tell you the details of our investigation. It would, um, compromise . . . the integrity of everything."

"Then this is pointless. This—this *arguing.* I get it, okay? You hate me, and you think I'm a horrible person because I'm not pulling out the fucking pitchforks on Vaughn. I'm telling you right now, I'm not doing that. I *can't* do it."

"Getting benched isn't the worst thing in the world," I said lowly.

Bodie looked back and forth between my eyes, like he was half hoping he'd see the flames of hell reflected in them so he'd known I'd been sent to earth just to torment him. I stared back, into thundercloud gray, and wondered if it'd make me strong or weak to give him the patience he was asking for. I folded my arms over my chest and tucked my hands in my armpits, feeling very miserable and very intoxicated.

"St. James!"

Bodie and I flinched and turned in unison to find Hanna storming down the hallway.

She wedged herself between us, looking me over from head to toe before she spun around and glared up at St. James, who stood more than a foot taller than her (even in her platform sneakers) and was twice as wide.

"Hanna," Bodie said with a cordial nod.

Right. They'd met before, at the last Baseball House party. She'd beaten him at beer pong.

"Leave my friend alone," Hanna warned.

Bodie sighed. "I'm *trying*. You need to get her out of here before Fogarty sees her. I'm just making sure he doesn't start shit."

Hanna's shoulders deflated. She'd been primed and ready for a fight.

"All right," she grumbled. Then she asked me, "You good?"

I was not good, but I nodded anyway. Hanna held her hand out. I took it and let her lead me to the front door. Bodie walked along with us, his body like a wall between me and the living room. The three of us squeezed past the freshman hockey players manning the door and stepped out onto the porch. The night air was cool and sharp as a slap across my face. There were still a few clusters of people scattered across the front yard, but the line to get into the party had thinned. Without the sensory overload of thumping rap music, low lighting, and the stench of alcohol, I felt hollow and wobbly.

I was too drunk. The porch was moving.

"I'm sorry, Hanna," I whispered, the words all jumbled in my mouth.

"Shut up," she murmured, giving my hand a squeeze. Then she looked over her shoulder and said, "Watch yourself, St. James."

I thought I saw Bodie nod.

Hanna hooked her arm around mine and led me down the porch steps and out to the sidewalk. I stumbled along beside her, too drunk to think of anything except that I hoped Bodie St. James was still watching us, because Hanna's stupidly short overall dress made my ass look like a million bucks.

—

Later, with my knees on the cold tiles of our bathroom floor and my arms braced against the toilet seat, Hanna's fingers brushing against my scalp as she gathered my hair into a scrunchie, I remembered that there was a football game tomorrow. I was going to have to face Bodie St. James again in the locker room.

chapter 16

My Saturday morning began with Advil, half a bottle of Gatorade, and half a slice of untoasted white bread.

I'd never been so hungover before. While Hanna headed to the Art House to pregame with a girl from her figure drawing class, to whom I'd transferred my student ticket so my beloved roommate wouldn't be alone in the stands, I tried to pull myself together. Ellison Michaels was expecting ESPN-grade coverage of this game and, by god, I was going to deliver. Even if it killed me. Which, as I marched across campus, I thought it might.

I'd never realized how bright the sun was (blinding, even through sunglasses) or how loud thousands of people could be when they'd all started drinking at ten o'clock in the morning (deafening). I was on the parkway when Garland's marching band started their prekickoff rally outside the student union. I decided, on the spot, that our fight song was the most obnoxious harmony ever composed.

I hated this school. I hated everyone in it. I was never drinking ever again.

Mehri was waiting for me outside the media entrance on the far side of the stadium, an enormous Nikon camera in her hands and a lanyard bearing her media pass slung over her neck. I marched up to Mehri, knowing full well that I looked like something that ought to be plunged out of a public toilet, and pushed my sunglasses on top of my head.

"Hey, Mehri."

She gave me a once-over and asked, "Did you bring your media pass?"

I'd shoved all my crap into a reusable tote from Target. I now regretted this, seeing as our opponent for the day was Stanford, whose colors were also red and white. My glorified shopping bag also provided no organizational benefits, which meant it took me several long, uncomfortable moments of digging around to find my media pass.

"Gotcha," I grumbled in triumph.

I looped my pass over my neck. The lanyard caught on my ponytail. I grumbled an expletive under my breath.

"You good?" Mehri asked.

"I'm fine," I snapped. Then I admitted, "No. I'm really nervous. And hungover."

"This," Mehri said with a dry smile, "is why I smoke."

I was both jealous of and glad for Mehri's clearheadedness as she led me through the security line and explained what kind of notes I should take during the game and when we'd be allowed to walk down to the field and approach the players and coaching staff for interviews.

We took an elevator up past the concourse and the luxury suites, all the way to the long, windowed room perched high over the stadium—the press box. I'd never been inside it before. Most home games, I was somewhere in the student section with Hanna, so all I knew was that I loved the press box because it cast a pleasant shadow across the field during brutally hot afternoon games. Mehri informed me that things worked a little differently up here, high above the commoners.

There was no favoritism and no cheering allowed in the press box (which I wasn't complaining about, considering my throbbing hangover headache).

Mehri and I had to display our passes at the door, and then we were in.

The press box was almost two stories tall, with floor-to-ceiling windows looking out over the stadium and three rows of solid desk space to house laptops, clipboards, and paper cups of coffee. Each row was twice as wide and twice as tall as traditional stadium seating; you could walk behind the lines of desk chairs without blocking the view of anyone in the next row up.

All around us were journalists and broadcasters from the *Los Angeles Times*, Bleacher Report, *Sports Illustrated*, CBS, NBC, Badger Sports—every major media outlet in the collegiate sports scene. It was a journalism major's networking heaven.

I felt suddenly and unshakably inadequate. Everybody in the room had résumés that made mine look like I'd written it in crayon. Even the other writers from the *Daily*—four seniors and two juniors who, like Mehri, had been sports-beat reporting since their first semesters at Garland—made me feel like two children stacked under a trench coat, just masquerading as a real adult.

As Mehri and I shuffled down to the second row and took our seats alongside the other *Daily* writers, I felt eyes on my back. People were staring at me.

"Do I look, like, aggressively hungover?" I whispered, wiping my palms on the front of the dark-green blouse I'd worn in substitute of my usual game day outfit (I'd figured a sweat-stained practice jersey didn't exactly exude professionalism).

Mehri glanced over her shoulder and must've caught more than a few people watching us.

"Don't worry about it. They're just curious about the Vaughn investigation."

I couldn't figure out if I wanted to throw up because I was hungover or because I felt like a bug pinned under a microscope.

I turned my attention to the field. It took me an embarrassingly short measure of time to spot Bodie in the sea of uniformed players stretching and warming up. Just seeing his jersey number made me sink lower in my seat.

I had, perhaps, gotten too drunk last night. It was so embarrassing to think about. As soon as I'd heard Fogarty walk into the Baseball House, I'd *known* that I should cut my losses and call it a night. I'd known, and still—when I'd seen Bodie, I'd looked for reasons to hover. I'd wanted to talk to him even though I'd known it would only lead to another dead end and additional outrage. Because I'd been drunk. And wine-drunk Laurel had categorically no chill to speak of.

WHISTLEBLOWER

I'd stuck around for a fight.

It shouldn't have mattered so much that he didn't believe me—most of the football team didn't—and I certainly shouldn't have been spending mental energy thinking of ways to convince him I was sincere when I said I just wanted to do the right thing. He just made me so *frustrated.*

"It's go time," Mehri said.

They were clearing the field. It was almost time for kick-off. I hunched over my clipboard and finished labeling the columns on my stats chart. Since my experience as a sports-beat writer was lacking, I could at least fake my way through today with an almost asinine dedication to organization. I'd take note of every play. No detail would slip by me.

A murmur of confusion rolled through the press box. Fuck. I'd missed something already.

"What happened?" I asked, looking between Joey's wide-eyed expression and the field, where one of our starters and a Stanford player were at the fifty-yard line for the coin toss.

Joey shook his head, his eyes focused on the field.

"Fogarty isn't starting," he murmured. "And neither is St. James."

Instead, Gordon had put in Andre (my darling boy) and the second-string quarterback, Copeland—a sophomore I'd only ever seen play when Bodie was injured or completely worn out. The kid was quick on his feet but his passing wasn't nearly as sharp as Bodie's.

Gordon's benching him because his grades are tanking.

The words were on the tip of my tongue but I swallowed them back down in the name of journalistic integrity. Bodie's

185

academic failings weren't mine to share—not when he and Gordon had discussed them privately.

Besides, right now we needed to focus on what was happening *on* the field.

Stanford won the coin toss. We went on the offensive.

On the first play Andre caught a half-decent pass for a twelve-yard run and I had to remind myself there was no cheering allowed in the press box. On the second play, Copeland was sacked. And then, on the third play, Stanford scored a pick and six off Copeland's pass, and I could see the trajectory of the game laid out before me like a movie for which I'd already read the plot summary on Wikipedia.

Stanford was going to slaughter us.

—

Vaughn finally put Bodie in the game at the beginning of the fourth quarter. He took the field like a hurricane. His first few passing attempts sailed clear over the grasping hands of his receivers and into the sidelines. He was too hopped up on adrenaline to rein in his arm. Fourth down came and went. While Stanford worked on scoring another touchdown on us, I saw Gordon grab Andre by the shoulder pad on our sideline.

I didn't realize what he was up to until we were back on offense.

After the hike, Andre took off like a shot. Bodie's pass was just as much of an overshoot as the ones before it—but this time, Andre was there. He caught it and carried it home to the end zone. It was his first touchdown in a regular season game.

I made a strangled noise at the back of my throat that I tried to disguise as a cough.

Unfortunately, despite the heroics, it was too late. The game was practically over. Even with Andre's touchdown, Garland was still down by more than thirty points. I heard a broadcaster from ESPN say to his colleague that, if the score held, it would be the biggest margin of a loss our team had experienced in over seven years.

Mehri tapped me on the shoulder. "C'mon. Let's head down so we're first at the gate when they let the media into the locker room."

Ellison had given me two sheets of postgame questions, one entitled *If we win* and the other *If we lose*. She'd further divided up the questions into a few categories—offense specific, defense specific, and for the coaches. I quietly shuffled to the *If we lose* document.

Mehri and I packed into the elevator with a few other journalists, including a young female reporter wearing Stanford-red lipstick. She kept staring at me and my media pass in the reflection of the doors. I ducked my head and tried to hide behind Mehri.

"So, I just, like, walk up to them?" I asked him in a low whisper. "And what do I say? *Hey, I'm Laurel for the* Daily?"

"I think they'll know who you are," Mehri said.

I let out a distressed huff.

"What do I do if they won't talk to me?"

I wasn't a beat reporter, so I hadn't built up a rapport with any of the players the same way Joey and the other sports writers had. Even if one of them managed not to recognize that I was one of the girls Vaughn claimed was trying to topple his career, it wasn't like they'd be comfortable giving me great sound bites.

Mehri seemed to know exactly what I was thinking.

"Apparently, Vaughn's got the whole team trained to be tight-lipped," she said. "They're all really rehearsed—when you ask them about what's going on behind the scenes, they've got this mentality, like what happens on the team stays on the team. But you're controversial. Yeah, okay, some of the guys *probably* won't look at you twice—but you'll crack one of them."

I snorted. That seemed unlikely.

"You cracked St. James," Mehri pointed out. "He gave you more in that Vaughn interview than anybody else has managed to get out of him."

I blushed. I don't know why I blushed.

"Here's your tape recorder," Mehri said, handing me a rectangular hunk of plastic that looked like it'd come straight out of the '90s. "For the interviews. You'll want audio clips of the players just in case you need to transcribe something later."

"Can't I just use my phone?"

"The sound quality won't be any good. It can get *really* loud in the locker room."

Fantastic. Not like I had a raging headache, or anything.

—

Hanna had once shown me a YouTube compilation of Black Friday stampedes. I don't know why she found humor in the complete degradation of human composure and empathy, or why so many of them had taken place in Walmarts. But those videos were all I could think about as Mehri and I waited among the herd of journalists and photographers and cameramen itching to get in the locker room first. The door swung open, and we were off, a hundred A-type personalities shoving their way forward in pursuit of the players and coaches.

I spotted Bodie through the crowd. There was a giant grass stain down back of his right thigh and sweat beaded on his bare arms. The red-lipped student reporter from Stanford stood at his side, grinning wickedly into a microphone as a guy with a video camera propped on his shoulder filmed their interaction.

As Mehri and I pushed toward them, I caught the tail end of whatever Bodie was saying to her.

"—two years from now, he'll be a great leader for this team."

"Bodie?"

I'm not sure how he managed to hear me over the tumult, but the moment his name was out of my mouth, his head whipped around. His eyes were dark as storm clouds, and his lips pinched into a flat line. I knew he wanted to bolt.

"Can I ask you a few questions for the *Daily*?" I asked in a tone that made it clear I would sooner tackle him to the ground—in full view of the team, coaching staff, and a veritable sea of media personnel—than let him get away without an interview.

His eyes slid down to my chest. It took me a split second to remember I was wearing my press pass around my neck, which meant the only thing he was checking out was my credentials.

"Fine," he relented. His voice was hoarse, like he'd spent the last three hours shouting at the top of his lungs.

"How would you describe Copeland's performance?" The question was drowned out by a burst of shouting from the other end of the locker room.

"What?" Bodie shouted, ducking his head and offering me his ear.

I rolled onto my tiptoes and tried to ignore the scent of grass and sweat lingering on him. Something about it made my face feel too warm.

"How did Copeland do?" I asked, voice cracking.

"He's a true freshman," Bodie replied, stepping back from me, his eyes straying to the crowd around us like he was bored. "He played hard out there. I'm proud of his effort. Two years from now, he'll be a great leader for the team."

He was giving me the same canned answer he'd given the Stanford reporter.

"What about Gordon's coaching?" I pressed. "Do you think his offensive strategies work against a team as strong defensively as Stanford?"

Of course he didn't think Gordon's offensive strategies were working—he'd spent most of the game on the bench, unable to do anything but watch the team's miserable train wreck of a performance unfold. That was exactly why I'd chosen the question. I caught the spark in Bodie's eyes before he managed to tamp it down.

"Our coaching staff always gives a hundred percent," he said.

The reply was so rehearsed it made me grind my teeth. I looked down at the list of questions on my clipboard, scanning them for one that might trip him up and get him to drop the robot act. But I couldn't do it. I couldn't grill him. He'd had a shitty game on top of a shitty month, and there was no reason for me to prod him other than my own wicked satisfaction at seeing him twitch.

So instead I lied and said, "You looked really good out there."

Bodie went very still.

"I mean—like, you *played* well. You made smart passes." It was categorically untrue. He'd played horribly, except for that pass Andre had caught.

To my surprise, Bodie barked out a stunned laugh. "I *sucked.*"

"Look, I'm not going to lie and say you were perfect out there, but if you'd had more than one quarter of playing time you guys might've been able to pull out a win."

I meant this to sound consolatory. Instead, Bodie bristled.

"It's not my fault Gordon's being passive-aggressive about—"

Chester Gordon, the assistant coach, appeared as if summoned. He was badly sunburned on the bridge of his freckled nose. Wisps of his copper hair had gone nearly white from all the afternoon practices.

"You guys are with the *Daily?*" he asked, brazenly interrupting my interview. It wasn't a question, but I felt the need to nod in confirmation regardless. "Jeez. Okay, uh—" Gordon sighed and scratched at the nape of his neck. "I don't think it's a good idea for you to be here."

"I have a media pass," I said, lifting it as proof.

Gordon's eyebrows pinched and he looked up and down the hall. "I know, I know. I'm not kicking you out. If I could just get the three of you to relocate to a private room—"

His idea was cut short, because the next person to come around the corner toward us was Truman Vaughn. What he lacked in stature he made up for in sharp features and an unflinching stare. I'd forgotten how intense the weight of his full attention was. I felt like a gazelle staring eye to eye with a panther. I felt like prey.

"Am I interrupting?" Vaughn asked as he approached. The question was punctuated with a smile that was far too relaxed.

Gordon rolled back his shoulders. "Just pointing the *Daily's* team to the exit."

"Actually," I snapped, leveling Vaughn with an unflinching glare, "I'm interviewing your quarterback."

"Ah, jeez," Gordon said under his breath.

But Vaughn didn't look bothered. He laughed.

"That's a journalist for you," he said. The way he said it was slightly condescending—not enough that I was sure he was being a dick on purpose, but enough that it was impossible to ignore. He chuckled again and clapped a hand on Bodie's shoulder. "What'd you think of his performance out there, huh? Give us your review."

"I was just telling Bodie I thought it was unfortunate that he only had a quarter of playing time."

"Got to rest those muscles. Kid's been doing a lot of weight training lately. I need him trimmed down. He's a brilliant young player but he's gotten a little distracted with academics this semester. We've got to get him focused on polishing what shines."

Polishing what shines. He meant prioritizing football over school—prioritizing Bodie's strengths over his shortcomings. Vaughn had convinced a young man that his only worth came from his strength, speed, and stamina. That he was stupid.

But Vaughn was wrong.

"St. James is a brilliant player," I agreed. "He's also a good person."

I caught the tiniest flicker in Vaughn's eyes.

"We've got a great team here," he said. "Wonderful coaching staff."

"Would your female employees agree with that assessment?"

Vaughn stared at me for a long moment, unflinching. And then he tipped his head toward Gordon, his smile still in place, and said, "Call security."

And just like that, my heart rate was off to the fucking races.

"I have a media pass," I said through clenched teeth. "I'm allowed to be here."

Vaughn sighed, like my existence was the worst kind of inconvenience for him. "This is my locker room. If you're going to act like a brat, I'm going to throw you out like one."

"You don't have to *call security*," Bodie spoke up, snorting at the absurdity of his head coach suggesting such extreme measures to combat someone who posed as little a physical threat as I did. "She's just doing her job."

"You can get back to your other interviews," Vaughn told Bodie. "We're calling security. The *Daily* is sending their spies in here now, and none of you boys needs that."

"I'm not a *spy*," I said, more exasperated than panicked. "I'm a fucking journalist."

Vaughn cleared his throat and put a hand on my shoulder. It sat heavy. "There's no good reason for you to be harassing my quarterback right now," he told me. "If you can't be a serious reporter, then you can't be in my locker room. This isn't a fuckin' sorority house."

I shot one last look over my shoulder as Mehri and I were ushered to the exit by a locker room staff member. Bodie's face was red, his eyes wide and wild, his hands clenched at his sides. We locked gazes. For a split second, I had the strangest sense that he was going to march after me and Mehri—to join us. But then Vaughn clapped a hand to the back of Bodie's neck and twisted him around to face an ESPN journalist.

Security slammed the door shut on our backs.

Mehri turned to me and said, "I'm going to burn this stadium down one day."

chapter 17

I made the executive decision to skip the after party. Hanna, who'd volunteered to help with setup, sent me several Snapchats from Andre's apartment but didn't try to talk me into coming. I think she understood that my absence was a necessary thing.

Besides. I was still recovering from the thralls of my hangover and therefore neither mentally nor physically prepared to smell alcohol again. This left me with two options: I could either sit in the apartment all night rewatching old Spanish shows on Netflix (and inevitably dive four years deep into Yon González's Instagram) or I could get in my car and do something productive with my night, like restocking my granola bar stash and buying nail polish I'd use once and then forget I owned.

I chose door number two. Dressed to impress in my cleaning-the-apartment leggings and a white sweater that had shed so many tufts of fuzz on my pants it looked like I'd wrestled a polar bear and won, I grabbed my car keys and hopped in my white Corolla. The old Ariana Grande CD I'd had in the player since I was sixteen came on automatically.

I rolled down the windows and headed to my usual destination for time killing and snack perusing: Target.

It was starting to get dark when I arrived and maneuvered into a spot on the far side of the crowded parking lot, positioning my Corolla nose to nose with a black Tesla Model X crammed door to door with guys wearing various forms of athletic wear.

Kyle Fogarty sat in the driver's seat. We locked eyes.

"Fuck," I said out loud.

There was no way he heard me through our cars and over the bass of the music he was blasting, but he probably read my lips. I ducked my head and pretended to be searching for something in my center console. Napkins. My ziplock bag of nickels and dimes. A melted ChapStick. Actually, I *had* been looking for that. Bummer.

The music went silent. Car doors opened, then slammed shut. Part of me expected to hear someone tap on the driver's-side window of my Corolla. Instead, I heard chatter and laughter fade into the distance. I looked up just in time to see the pack of muscular bodies shuffle through the sliding glass doors and into the store.

My hand moved to jam my keys back in the ignition, but I caught myself. I'd already compromised to keep out of the football team's way tonight. I wasn't going to keep making myself smaller so they could have more room—especially not when Target was the size of an independent city-state. No. I was getting my errands done. I climbed out of my car, retrieved three reusable tote bags from my trunk, and grabbed a cart someone had left in the designated return space. And then I marched into the store with my chin held high.

I wasn't an idiot, though. Given that there were football players in the building, I stuck to the departments they probably wouldn't touch with a ten-foot pole: skincare and bath products. I stocked up on makeup-removing wipes, then took the time to pop open the caps of no fewer than eight different bottles of shampoo before deciding on a chamomile-scented one that reminded me of the kind my abuelita kept in her bathroom.

My phone buzzed in my crossbody bag as I swung my cart around to the next aisle. The number on the screen was one I didn't recognize, which meant it was either a telemarketer or one of my idiot friends was in trouble and borrowing someone else's phone.

"Hello?" I answered, plucking a box of tampons off the shelf.

"Hi, is this Laurel Cates?" a young woman asked.

"This is she." Should I get two boxes? Hanna always forgot to stock up for herself.

"My name's Josie Rodriguez. You emailed me like a week ago?"

The tampons tumbled out of my hand.

"Josefina! Oh my gosh. Hi." When I'd daydreamed about landing a primary source on my first major story, I certainly hadn't pictured myself stooping over to pick a box of feminine hygiene products up off a dusty linoleum floor. "Thanks so much for calling. I'm sorry if my email was, like, superaggressive."

"No! No, actually, it was—" Josefina paused. "I'm glad you reached out."

"Okay, good. I was a little worried. Your friend Gabi made it sound like you didn't want to talk to any journalists. Which, like, I totally get. But I just wanted to check with you."

The other end of the line was quiet.

"How are you doing?" I blurted. "Are you—are you okay?"

"Um," Josefina replied, her voice a little watery. "No, I don't think so."

Guilt smacked me thump in the nose. I'd gotten so excited about making contact with a primary source that I'd let myself forget why I wanted to find her in the first place—why there was research to do and a story to chase.

"Josie," I croaked. "I'm so sorry. If you don't want to—"

"I want to talk," Josefina said determinedly.

"Okay, then," I said, combing my fingers through my hair and gazing up at the wall of pink and purple packages on the shelves in front of me. "Look, I'm in Target right now, and I've got a cart full of shampoo and tampons, and this is *not* how we're going to have this conversation. We should do this face-to-face. Maybe over coffee? I have a car. I can come to you!" I was speaking way too quickly. "Are you free tomorrow? In the afternoon? I have work in the morning but I can make it down to San Diego by—"

"I don't know how much help I'm going to be," Josefina blurted.

I treaded carefully. "What do you mean?"

"I don't remember everything. I was—I had a lot to drink."

"That's *not* an issue," I insisted. "Seriously. I'm not a lawyer, and you're not on trial. And, full disclosure, I drank about two bottles of wine last night and browned out, so there's literally no judgment from my end. Okay? All we're doing is sitting down to talk. That's all I'm asking. I promise."

Josefina sniffled. "If we talk, is it like—are you going to write about it?"

"Only if you give me permission."

She was quiet for a long moment. All I could do was grip my phone in one hand and white knuckle my cart in the other and hope that she and I could help each other.

"Okay," Josefina said. "I'll text you my address."

I exhaled in relief. "Perfect. I'll see you tomorrow."

Josefina hung up first. I held my phone to my ear for another moment, collecting my thoughts, before I dialed Ellison's number to relay the news.

"Cates," she answered before I could speak. "Rajavi told me what happened today in the locker room. Are you okay?"

"Yeah, yeah, I'm fine. I mean, I've been having vivid fantasies about punching Truman Vaughn in the face"—Ellison hummed in acknowledgment—"but otherwise, I'm okay. And I have good news! Josefina Rodriguez just called me. She said she'll meet me tomorrow to talk."

Ellison and I brainstormed strategies for my meeting with Josefina while I wandered up and down the aisles of Target. By the time we hung up, it was getting truly late. I had several missed Snapchats from Hanna, the most recent of which had come in almost an hour ago—a close-up of what looked like Andre's left eyebrow captioned with a single poop emoji. I sent back a selfie from the checkout line, where my cashier told me, through a yawn, that my total was approximately five and a half hours of my paycheck.

When I emerged into the parking lot, the night air was cool and sweet. Most of the other cars had cleared out; my Corolla was alone at the far edge of the lot. I pushed my cart along, the plastic wheels loud enough against the asphalt to drown out my off-pitch humming.

Josefina Rodriguez wanted to talk. I had a primary source. We were going to do it—we were going to help each other. Journalist and source, teaming up to make the world a better and brighter place. I briefly considered stepping onto the back of my cart and surfing it to my car.

But, abruptly, I stopped walking.

It was dark in the far corner of the parking lot, the nearest lamppost a bit too far to reach my car with its fluorescent orange glow, but my Corolla was white, so the letters across the hood looked like they'd been drawn on with a big, black Sharpie. Only it wasn't marker. The word was etched deep into the metal, four enormous and sharp-angled letters.

LIAR.

I was still for a long moment, my brain a blank loading screen. And then I swung my cart around to the back of my car, tucked my bags safely in the trunk, and tugged out my phone to google: *what to do if your car is keyed.* Step one. Document the damage. That made sense—Garland PD would need to see evidence. Some with flash, some without, maybe a video panning from Target to the place where I'd parked. I could probably email the store about security footage.

And I'm not sure why *that* was the thought that made terror surge up my throat, strangling me. Someone did this. Someone singled out my car. Someone singled out *me*. I whipped around in a circle, scanning the parking lot, but found only abandoned carts and one crushed coffee cup a few spaces over.

In the quiet of my car, with a phone loaded full of pictures and all the doors locked, I squeezed my eyes shut and tried to think coherently again. Someone had done this. Who were my suspects? Well, Fogarty had seen me. He knew this was my car. He was a green-haired moron, but was he capable of something as awful as this?

"Fuck," I said aloud.

I fumbled with my key, trying and failing twice to jam it in the ignition. My hands were shaking too hard. When I finally got the engine on, the dashboard lit up and my Ariana Grande CD started blasting through the speakers again, the familiar opening chords of what I knew to be the sixth track both comforting and eerily out of place.

Through my windshield, I could see jagged lines on the hood. My parents would know how to fix this. They'd know how to file the police report, how to make an insurance claim. But then I'd have to tell them that someone had tracked down their daughter's car in an empty Target parking lot and carved the word *liar* into the hood. No. I wouldn't tell them. I'd handle this myself. But first, I was going to cry like a baby. I felt it coming—the prickle behind my eyes and the catch in my breath. So when my phone vibrated in the front pocket of my hoodie, it was a welcome distraction. Andre's name stretched across the top of the screen. I reached for the volume dial on the dashboard, sniffling furiously and clearing my throat as I silenced the music.

"Hello?" I answered.

"Yo," came Andre's voice a half second later, like he'd gotten distracted right after he dialed my number.

"What's up?" I asked, my voice high-pitched and squeaky.

Luckily, Andre was drunk, so he didn't pick up on my distress.

"Can you—" he began, then said something I couldn't catch that seemed directed at someone else. "Are you home yet?"

"No," I said. "No, I'm—I'm just about to leave Target. I'm in my car."

"Perfect. Can you come over?"

"What? Why?"

"Hanna's not doing too hot. She's been in the bathroom for like an hour now, and I told her she could take my bed, but she says she wants to go home. I can't find her key."

I squeezed my eyes shut and pressed my forehead to the top of my steering wheel.

"Did you ask her to check her bra?" I mumbled.

"Yeah. She took it off. Key ain't in there. Can you pick her up? My roommates already went to bed. There are like three or four guys sleeping over. Fogarty's not here. St. James is, but he's just making sure Quinton and Torres drink some water before they pass out. He'll probably leave in the next five, ten minutes. I just need you to drive her home."

Hanna *never* overdid it. The last time I could remember her getting sick after a night out had been freshman year, and that'd been after we binged Pepito's and then taken an Uber home because we were too tired to walk. She was going to feel rotten tomorrow morning, no matter what. But waking up at Andre's with a bunch of football players everywhere would add insult to injury—or, rather, mortification to hangover. Hanna had carried me home when I was a drunk mess. It was my turn to do the same for her.

"Hold tight," I told Andre, buckling my seat belt. "I'm on the way."

———

I didn't want Hanna or Andre to see my car so I left it on the third floor of a university-owned parking garage across the street. It was spillover for the Palazzo, so there were security cameras and plenty of cars much more alluring to potential thieves and carjackers than my shitty white Corolla. Especially now that she had the word *liar* carved into her hood.

There was nothing I could do about it tonight. I had to get Hanna home, put my bag of groceries away, and get some sleep. And there was no use crying about it until I knew how much it'd cost to fix. Still, as I clambered down the winding steps to ground level, my eyes started to sting and my vision went blurry.

I stopped on the sidewalk outside the parking garage and pinched the bridge of my nose.

"*No llores, no llores*," I chanted under my breath.

There was no time to feel sorry for myself. Hanna needed me.

The lobby of the Palazzo was more hectic than Target at eight o'clock on a Saturday night. It was far too easy to blend in with the residents and slip past security. I got into the elevator with a group of four girls who looked like they'd had a great night, judging by their tangled hair and smudged makeup. One of them carried a cardboard box of pizza that made the whole elevator smell like melted cheese. Another girl had her high-heeled booties in her hands; on her feet was a pair of beige socks with pink-nosed pug faces on them. I listened to them chatter and giggle softly about the bar they'd been to (somewhere halfway to Los Angeles, it sounded like, judging by the way they complained about the disgustingly expensive Uber) and all the boys and girls they'd danced with and given fake numbers to.

When the doors slid open on Andre's floor, I darted out and made my way through the maze of plush-carpeted hallways until I arrived at apartment 352. I pounded on the door twice before it swung open, revealing a bleary-eyed Andre. His button-down party shirt (the one with little pineapples embroidered all over it) was thrown open, abs on full display, and he wore a string of green plastic Mardi Gras beads around his neck.

"I love you," he said earnestly. "You're a goddamned saint."

"I know," I said, shouldering past him. "Where is she?"

The party had ended but wasn't completely cleared out yet.

An expensive set of speakers in the corner of the living room was still playing music—though the volume was barely a whisper—and there was a small army of empty glass bottles on the coffee table in front of the black leather couch, where Scott Quinton, the offensive tackle with the wide neck, was snoring.

There was a bra hooked over the corner of the flat screen TV. I had a split second of terrible panic before I realized the cup size was too big for it to belong to my roommate.

"Classy," I said, nodding at the new decor. "Where's Hanna?"

"Bathroom," Andre answered.

I turned toward the hallway.

At the very same moment, Bodie St. James appeared, a half-empty bottle tucked under one arm. He wasn't in flannel pajama pants this time. Instead, he wore dark-wash jeans that hugged his thighs and a black Henley that did wonderful things for his shoulders.

He stopped short when he saw me.

Then, like he'd suddenly remembered he and I weren't the only people in the room, he turned to Andre and said, "I got Torres in bed. He's all set with a trash bag, in case he gets sick again."

"Thanks, man," Andre told him.

Bodie's eyes slid back to me. The last time we'd come face-to-face he'd taken his coach's side. But that'd been eight hours ago. A lot had happened in eight hours.

"Excuse me," I murmured as I inched around him.

Halfway down the hall, the bathroom door was cracked open, a single sliver of light beaming across the wood floors.

"Hanna?" I called, aiming for the same tone of voice I'd have used if she was sober. "You good, babe?"

She was not good. This became clear when I eased open the door to find her on the floor beside the toilet, one tiny fist clutching a handful of the plastic curtain on the bathtub-shower combo for stability. Her winged eyeliner was smudged and there was, inexplicably, a streak of mascara halfway up her forehead. She cracked one eye open and grumbled unintelligibly at me.

Andre appeared at my side with a towel. I thanked him,

then dropped to my knees to take care of Hanna's rogue makeup and dab the vomit on her chin.

"I tried to put her hair back," Andre said. That explained the poorly centered ponytail gathered in what looked like black prewrap—the stuff athletes use when they have to tape up sprained wrists and ankles.

"You did good," I told him.

Andre shook his head. "This is my fault. We were celebrating my touchdown."

"Because it was fucking awesome," I said. "And we're going to keep celebrating it for the rest of the semester, okay? This is *not* your fault. You both overdid it. Happens to the best of us. Do you think we're safe to move her now? When did she last throw up?"

"She stopped puking like fifteen minutes ago. I think we're okay. I can carry her down to your car—"

Fuck.

"Um," I said, trying to think on my feet. "I can handle it."

I could probably piggyback her home. She was small— packed solid with muscle, but still small. I was always saying I needed a good workout. Here was my chance. Leg day.

"Hanna, darling," I murmured, "it's time to go."

She let out a low whine, then picked up her head and met my eyes. "M'sorry, Laurel."

"Shut up," I said, stroking her hair. "Let's get you home."

I motioned for Andre to come around and help me get her to her feet. He stepped out of the doorway, and I realized Bodie had been hovering behind him, out in the hallway. I wasn't sure how long he'd been standing there, but his eyebrows were pinched with concern.

Andre and I tugged Hanna to her feet. She could barely stand—and Andre wasn't much help, considering he was a little unsteady on his feet too.

Bodie cleared his throat. "Do you want some help?"

"We're good," I snapped. Then, to Hanna, I said, "C'mon. You're going to jump on my back, okay? One, two—*oof*. Shit. Okay. We're good. We're good."

We were not good. My quads were screaming, and I had to brace one hand against the wall as I made my way back into the living room with Hanna's arms wound tight around my neck and her legs around my hips.

Bodie came around us to hold open the front door, his face tight like he badly wanted to help us. I marched past him and into the hallway.

"Text me when you get home!" Andre called after me.

I was too focused on not falling over to give a verbal response, so I just chucked up a peace sign over one shoulder. In an unprecedented feat of lower body strength, I managed to stand upright the whole elevator ride down. But as soon as the doors opened and I saw the lobby stretched out before us, I knew I was doomed. We made it halfway to the sliding glass doors before I had to stop.

"Hanna," I grunted, quads spasming. "I need to—I'm just—going to set you—"

She slid down off my back. Her bare feet hit the floor and she tilted to the side, her shoulder rustling the plastic leaves of a faux fiddle leaf tree before thudding against the wall. She kept sliding until she was on the marble floor in the fetal position.

The two security guards at the front desk were printing

up a visitor's badge for one half of a couple who were being obnoxiously touchy with each other, so they hadn't noticed yet that my friend was trying to take a nap on the floor of the lobby.

"Hanna!" I whisper-hissed.

"No."

"Come on. It's just a few blocks. It'll be over before you know it."

Hanna leaned her head back against the wall and snapped her eyes shut.

"M'so tired," she slurred. "Just—just leave me."

"*Hanna.*"

I blinked furiously. I was *not* going to cry in the Palazzo's tacky fake plant and faux adobe hell of a lobby. That was a rock bottom I was determined not to hit.

But what was I supposed to do? Drag her home by her ankles?

Across the lobby, the elevator doors slid open. I was only a little surprised when Bodie St. James stepped out. For a moment I held on to the hope that he was on his way home and that he'd somehow march straight past us and out the sliding glass doors. Worst-case scenario, he'd stop just long enough to wish me good luck. But when his eyes fell on me, I knew at once that he'd come down expecting to find us here, like this. Me, helpless. My best friend, in the fetal position. I folded my arms over my chest and chewed on one of my cheeks, hoping I looked more like I was done with Hanna's shit than two seconds from tears.

"Hey," Bodie said.

"Hey," I croaked. "She's just taking a little break."

Bodie nodded, and I had the sense that he could see right through me.

I stepped back and watched as he crouched beside Hanna.

"Hey, champ," he said. "You ready to go home?"

Oh, don't do that, I felt like saying. *I'm trying to hate you.*

Hanna grunted out what sounded like a reluctant concession. As Bodie stood again, he scooped her up, one hand tucked behind her knees and the other braced on her back. Hanna's arms went immediately around his neck, like a weary princess holding tight to her savior. I wondered if Bodie was strong enough to carry *me* like that.

It was a stupid thought. I don't know why it came to me.

"Lead the way," Bodie told me.

"I don't have my car. I could call an Uber, though."

"How far do you live?"

"Four blocks."

"We can walk."

"Are you sure?"

The corners of Bodie's lips twitched like he was charmed that I'd even ask if he, a Division I athlete with biceps as wide as my neck, could handle my very small, very floppy-limbed friend.

"I'm sure," he said with a gentle nod of his head.

I chewed on the inside of my cheek for a moment.

"Okay. Fine. Let's go."

The four blocks between Andre's place and ours had never felt so long. It didn't help that it was late at night, so there was nobody else walking around and no traffic to speak of. We were submerged in eerie silence, save for our footsteps, our breathing, and Hanna's gentle snores. Every thirty seconds I looked over my shoulder to check on Bodie. He was fine, of course. He didn't even break a sweat. I don't know why I kept checking.

It wasn't until I tugged my keys out of my pocket and jammed them in the door of our building that the embarrassment hit. Our apartment building was the antithesis of the Palazzo. I wondered if Bodie noticed it all—the wrought iron bars on the first-floor windows, the stained carpets, the creaky doors and lingering stench of rubber that billowed over from the gas station next door. I'd never been ashamed of where Hanna and I lived, but as I led Bodie up the stairs to the second floor, a pernicious little voice in my head whispered that I should be.

"We're on the second floor," I said, wiping my palms on the front of my leggings. "First door on the left."

"Right behind you," he said.

I marched up the stairs, telling myself that Bodie would be too focused on his own feet—and too much a gentleman—to stare at my ass, even if it was in his face. At the top of the stairs, I unlocked our apartment door and slipped inside, smacking on the lights in the kitchen and cringing at the mess on the counters before I pushed open the bedroom door.

"Her bed's in here, on the right," I directed.

And it was a mess. I gathered what I could—a pair of jeans turned inside out, a bag of Hot Cheetos, an enormous textbook entitled *Introduction to Abstract Expressionism*—and tossed them onto my desk, knocking over a stack of poorly folded laundry I'd been meaning to put away for the better part of a week.

A pair of my underwear (seamless beige hip-huggers)

fluttered to the floor. I grumbled out a frantic curse and kicked them under my bed. When I turned back around, Bodie was standing in the doorway. If he'd seen me punt my underwear, he didn't comment on it. He was reverently silent as he shuffled into the room—sideways, so as not to smack Hanna's head or feet on the door frame—and deposited her gently on her mattress. The box spring creaked as she sprawled flat on her back. I stepped forward to pull her onto her side.

Beside me, Bodie flexed his wrists back and forth. It was the only outward indication he gave that carrying Hanna four blocks had taken even the smallest measure of physical exertion.

And now he was in my bedroom. What a wild turn of events. Andre was the only boy Hanna and I had ever had over at the apartment, and he'd never seemed to fill the space up quite like Bodie did. It was like standing next to a bonfire— the warmth of him was nice, but, if we were really pressing the metaphor, I felt like just brushing up against him by accident might give me third-degree burns.

I glanced up at him. My eyes traced the hard line of his eyebrows and the slope of his nose. I stopped myself before I got to his mouth, which was lucky, because he chose that moment to turn to me for further direction. I nodded toward the door wordlessly.

Together, we migrated back into the kitchen. Hanna might've been passed out, but her snoring reminded me that I wasn't totally alone with Bodie—and I needed that kind of hands-off chaperoning, so I left the bedroom door propped open behind us. I didn't trust myself not to say something stupid.

When I turned, Bodie was examining the gallery of Post-it

Notes taped on the fridge—little, scribbled messages Hanna and I left for each other when something in the apartment needed fixing or replacing or if one of us needed words of encouragement. This somehow felt more intimate than the underwear on my floor.

"So," I blurted, a bit too loudly.

Bodie spun on his heel, the tips of his ears pink. I pulled the sleeves of my sweater down over my hands and shoved them under my armpits.

"Thank you," I said. "For carrying her."

"Of course."

"I'm sorry," Bodie blurted, reaching across his chest to scratch at his shoulder, "for the way I behaved at the Baseball House last night."

The last thing I'd been expecting was an apology.

"It's okay," I mumbled instinctively.

"No, it's *not*," Bodie said. "You work with the *Daily*. I don't know why I expected—" He broke off. Shook his head. "I just—sometimes I hate that you're a journalist."

For someone whose life I'd inadvertently flipped upside down, Bodie was being remarkably empathetic. It didn't feel like he hated me. At least, not the way that whoever'd keyed my car hated me. But someone he was friends with had done it. Someone he laughed with in the locker room, and went to Chipotle for lunch with, and sat with on flights to out-of-state games had seen me park my car and decided to take the time to carve four sharp letters across the hood.

"I get it," I said. "You can go home. I've got Hanna."

I nodded to the front door. But Bodie didn't leave. He lingered, looking unsettled.

"Vaughn shouldn't have kicked you out like that."

"No. He shouldn't have. But we already know he doesn't like women in his locker room."

Bodie nodded. And then he said, "I'll talk."

"What?"

"I'll talk to you about the foundation. But I want to stay anonymous, like Andre did."

I waited for Bodie to take it back—to laugh in my face— but his stare was unwavering. He meant it.

"You seriously want to be a whistleblower?" I asked.

"Yes. I know the risks. I still want to do the right thing. If there's something fucked up happening with the Vaughn Foundation, it's not fair to the kids. Or the donors, or the volunteers, or anybody involved. If you still want me to"—he paused to swallow—"I'll talk. Just give me a few days to pull together all my screenshots."

I regarded him through narrowed eyes. Bodie's cheeks flushed pink, but he didn't squirm and he didn't backtrack. So, at last, I held out one hand.

"If we shake on it," I warned, "you can't back out."

Bodie lifted his hand to meet mine. He really had no business being the size he was—an absolute unit of a boy with hands that made mine look like a travel-sized version—but his grip was gentler than I'd expected of someone who could launch a football seventy yards.

Somewhere in my chest, a knot unwound. My shoulders slumped with relief.

"Is this a bad time to point out that a handshake isn't legally binding?" Bodie quipped.

"*Horrible* time."

"Sorry. Can't help it. Business major."

I didn't want to smile. I really didn't. I'd had a miserable roller coaster of an evening, and according to Google, I had a police report to file. But Bodie St. James was in my kitchen, and for the first time since my interview with him, it felt like we were on the same team.

"Good night, Laurel," he murmured.

"Night."

Bodie left, closing the front door behind himself. In his absence, the kitchen was an empty kind of quiet that made my smile dissolve. I slumped back against the kitchen counter and pressed the heels of my palms to my eyes, kaleidoscopes of light dancing under my eyelids.

In the span of a little over two hours I'd landed myself interviews with two primary sources—an impressive feat. One I'm sure I would've been more willing to celebrate if someone hadn't vandalized my car.

chapter 18

When I opened my eyes the next morning, my first thought was that I really needed to shut off the bell tower alarm on my phone before it woke up Hanna. This triggered an avalanche of memories. Hanna slumped over Andre's toilet, hair askew and eyes heavy lidded. Bodie St. James carrying her home, the muscles in his arms flexing elegantly in that black Henley shirt under her weight. Him agreeing to finally, *finally*, speak to me about what he knew.

Me kicking him out of the apartment so I could have a moment alone to mourn my—*my car.*

I pulled my duvet up over my face, burrowing deep in the detergent-scented darkness beneath the covers. I wanted to scream but there was no time for emotional breakdowns in modern capitalist society. My Garland Country Club uniform was in a clump on the floor of the closet. After I'd patted out most of the wrinkles, brushed my teeth, and braided my hair, I fired off a text to PJ asking if she'd be able to swing by and give me a ride to work.

My car has a flat tire, I lied, adding a frowny emoji to keep it casual.

Her reply appeared a few seconds later.

Sure thing girl! Be there in fifteen

She'd punctuated this with a shooting star and a thumbs-up. With my ride sorted, I pulled on my sneakers and padded out to the kitchen, tugging the bedroom door shut behind me. I was shoving granola bars into both front pockets of my jean jacket when the door flew open. Hanna appeared, like a tiny hungover goblin emerging from her cave, one hand raised to shield her eyes from the kitchen light.

"Good morning," I whispered.

"How bad was I?" she demanded, her voice a gravelly croak. Half her hair was still tied up in a prewrap ponytail. The other half was matted to the side of her neck in one enormous thicket.

"Andre was the only one who noticed you got sick," I said. I didn't know if that was true, but I figured I'd rather lie and save her the embarrassment than let her spend all morning panicked and picturing the entire Garland football team listening to her hurl.

"Did he carry me home?" she asked. "I remember somebody carrying me."

"Actually, Bodie did."

"Bodie *St. James?*"

"PJ's here, got to go, talk later." I dashed out the door. "Stay hydrated!"

—

On Sundays, the Garland Country Club was dominated by the retirement crowd, which meant PJ had to cruise cautiously through the parking lot, and stop for a solid three minutes while a very elderly man tried to navigate his Audi into a spot big enough to house a doublewide trailer. We ended up sliding into an employee space right next to Rebecca's car—a pretty Lexus (black and sleek as a river rock) with a Garland University decal on the rear window. Just the sight of it made me slump in my seat.

"I hope you're serving today," PJ said, using her rearview mirror to check her lipstick and fluff her hair. "I had the *worst* blind date on Friday. You would not believe the kind of guys I attract on Tinder."

Hearing the trials and tribulations of PJ's dating app activity sounded like the best kind of distraction to keep me from wallowing in sorrow about my car, but I had other things to think about—like what I was going to ask Josefina this afternoon.

"I think Rebecca wants to fire me," I admitted. "She keeps giving me the dumbest jobs."

"Girl, she wants to fire *everyone*," PJ said with a laugh. "I heard her on the phone with the owner last week. Bitchin' about the fact that I don't have a degree. Like I need to know shit about international relations to bartend."

"International relations?"

"That was her major. I looked her up on LinkedIn. I'm petty, Laurel. You *know* this. Look, Rebecca's just high strung. She's not going to fire you unless you genuinely fuck up."

I sighed. "I feel like today's a fuck-up kind of day for me."

"Then I'll just hide you under the bar," PJ said.

This was precisely what she did three hours later, after Rebecca had given me luxurious duties such as scrubbing the toilets in the men's locker room and cleaning mud splatters off the golf carts. I was in desperate need of a fifteen-minute break, so while PJ cleaned glasses, I sat on the floor behind the bar, basking in the air conditioning and munching on toasted almonds.

"I think I'm getting Bermuda-short tan lines," I said, scrunching up my shorts to show her the distinctly paler upper half of my thighs.

"I've got some self-tanner if you need it," PJ offered. "And, babe, you need it."

I scoffed in outrage and chucked a toasted almond at her. PJ laughed as she dodged it, but almost as quickly, dropped her smile and cleared her throat.

"Hi, Rebecca," she said, voice theatrically loud. "How are you?"

I stilled.

"Fine," Rebecca answered curtly. "Have you seen Laurel?"

"No, ma'am," PJ answered smoothly. "Think she went on break."

I still had an almond in my mouth. I was too afraid to chew it—the crunch might betray my hiding spot.

"When you see her, could you let her know the front windshields on the carts are all streaky."

Bullshit. I'd scrubbed them dry with plush monogrammed Garland Country Club towels. Rebecca was, for someone who claimed to be low maintenance, very much *not*. She was looking for things to pick apart. She was looking to fire me.

"I'll let her know," PJ said generously.

There was a pause. I didn't hear footsteps.

"Is there—uh, is there anything else I can help you with?"

"I'm just watching the TV," Rebecca replied. My eyes flickered up to the screen mounted over the bar, which—given the sharp angle at which I was viewing it—was populated by very distorted figures against seas of green. "Have they talked about football at all this morning? I hear ESPN's still going after Vaughn. It's a damned travesty what they're doing to that man. They should be ashamed."

I opened my mouth as if to argue, then bit down hard on my almond.

"Didn't he say a bunch of derogatory stuff?" PJ asked, nudging me with the side of her foot in a way that said *Don't you dare make a sound.* "I think they're right to call out sexism like that. Must make it a hostile environment for all the female reporters and anchors. And if his players are complaining about it, doesn't that mean it's hurting the team?"

Rebecca sighed the way she did at every question that came out of PJ's mouth.

"All I'm saying is, he should be allowed to coach however he wants. The locker room should be a safe space for men. Some people don't like that—that kind of strong, traditional, masculine personality. But that's Vaughn. He says what he thinks and he gets the job done. They should let the man handle his business."

PJ just smiled and nodded.

"Anyway. I need to jump on a call with the florist for the charity tournament. If you see Laurel—*golf carts*."

I knew Rebecca had left when PJ scoffed and declared, "I hate her."

"I *told you* she wants to fire me," I whispered.

PJ snatched the Costco-sized bag of almonds out of my hands and set them on the bar, out of my reach. "Go do the golf carts," she told me. "I can't survive this place without you."

I had never turned my nose up at an honest paycheck for the sake of my pride. I could complain about the day-to-day frustrations of my job—the majority of which revolved around the stick wedged firmly up Rebecca's rear end—but when it came down to it, the positives outweighed the negatives. I liked the club. I liked PJ. I even liked the Real Housewives. And I *definitely* liked my paychecks. So Rebecca could pry this job from my cold, dead hands. I wasn't going anywhere until I had enough cash to fix my car.

—

Despite the number of times I refreshed and reworded my Google searches, there was no direct bus route from Garland to San Diego, which meant I had no other choice: I hopped in my car and mapped a route to the address Josefina had sent me. Driving the newly christened LIAR-mobile in broad daylight was about a hundred times worse than the night it'd happened. Andre's sunglasses were my security blanket. I knew, of course, that people could still see my face—and they could *definitely* still see the word on my hood—but the tinted lenses felt like a shield against both public humiliation and UV rays.

An hour and a half of Ariana Grande songs later, I was in San Diego, navigating blocks upon blocks of off-campus student housing.

Josefina lived in a compact gray apartment building with two stories of enormous sliding glass doors that let out onto balconies shaded by towering palm trees. It was smaller in person than it'd looked in the brochure that'd popped up when I researched her address. The main entrance was a set of simple glass doors and a paved patio.

Gabi de Hostos sat perched on a retaining wall dotted with grassy plants. She was wearing a striped T-shirt dress I'd seen in one of her Instagram pictures and she bore a striking resemblance to her cousin Joaquín. As I parked in the little lot and climbed out of my car, she watched me through narrowed eyes.

"You're the journalist?" she called, no-nonsense.

I nodded. "Are you Gabi?"

She ignored the question and tipped her chin toward my car. "What happened there?"

"Someone didn't like my article. Too many adverbs, I guess."

Gabi didn't laugh. I didn't blame her.

When I reached the patio steps, she hopped off the retaining wall and swiped us into the building with her student ID. We marched through a small lobby, up a set of fire stairs, and down a short hallway to an unlocked door that Gabi pushed open with her hip.

"She's here," Gabi called into the apartment.

I trailed in after her, my eyes bouncing from the sleek cabinets and spotless floor of the kitchen to the enormous L-shaped couch in the living room. The building itself had the vacuous feeling of a new construction—everything was a little too plain, a little too cold—but the girls who lived here had thrown together an eclectic mix of decor. Empty alcohol bottles were stacked on top of the kitchen cabinets like trophies. There was a guitar propped against the couch, and on the wall above the TV were two movie posters (one for *Pride & Prejudice*, the other for *Deadpool 2*). There was a Hydro Flask in the kitchen sink with three Greek letters on it. The same three Greek letters were embroidered across the front of a sweatshirt tossed over the back of one of the kitchen island stools.

"Laurel?"

I turned just as Josefina Rodriguez emerged from her bedroom. She was taller than I'd expected—almost my height. Her dark hair was pulled up in a ponytail and her bare legs were tan and toned under baggy running shorts.

"Hi, Josie," I said. "Thanks for having me."

We shook hands.

"We can sit down here," she told me, setting her phone on the kitchen island and gesturing to the stools. "I'm just going to fill up my water. Do you want anything to drink? Coffee? Tea?"

"Water's fine."

While Josefina filled up the Hydro Flask in the sink and grabbed a glass from the cupboard, Gabi stood with her arms folded over her chest like a bouncer.

"Thanks for showing her up, Gabs," Josefina told her friend in a tone that said *You can go now.*

"*Si me necessitas*," Gabi whispered and tapped Josefina's phone.

"*Puedo manejarlo*," Josefina said, straight faced.

Gabi shot me one last look before collecting the knit blanket and sweatshirt from the stool beside mine and padding into a second bedroom, shutting the door tight behind herself.

"She didn't interrogate you, did she?" Josefina asked.

"Maybe a little. But I get it. I live with my best friend too. We look out for each other."

Josefina nodded.

"Your Spanish is beautiful," I added, hoping it didn't sound as jealous as I felt. "You have the same accent as my mom. She's from Mexico City."

"Oh," Josefina said, visibly recalculating her assessment of me. She looked me up and down as she came around the kitchen island and grabbed the stool next to mine. "Yeah, I was born in Mexico City, actually. Lived there until I was eight."

"What part?"

"Polanco."

"So, the bougie part," I said. Josefina laughed. "I visited this summer. My cousins like to hang out at Chapultepec Park."

"Oh god, I love that area," Josefina said. "Like—oh my god, okay, we had this place on the corner of our street that put out these huge trays of fresh *bunuelos* in the window every morning. I can still smell them. I mean, I know there's really good shit here, because we're so close to the boarder, but damn. The food in Mexico just hits different."

We smiled at each other for a moment, our feet firmly on common ground.

"Thank you for meeting with me," I said quietly.

Josefina stood a little straighter and a little more rigid. "I guess you want to talk about what happened," she said, her smile going tight as she fidgeted with her water bottle. "How much did Gab's cousin tell you?"

"That on Friday night you were at the Alvarado Resort, and on Saturday morning you were in the hospital."

"Yeah, that's—" She laughed weakly. "That's about it. Um. One of Gab's friends from work said that the resort is always packed with guys who'll buy women drinks, so me, Gab, and a few of our friends decided to go before the semester started. We pregamed here. Took an Uber. Got to the resort, went straight to the bar, ordered a round of shots. And then, you know, ten minutes in, guys started coming up to us and asking us if we wanted something to drink."

"Were they young guys? Or, like, older?"

"Older, mostly. There's was one guy who was hitting on Gab hard-core, and said he was at San Diego State, but for the most part, it was guys in their thirties, forties, fifties. So we keep getting hit on, and we keep drinking, and eventually this guy comes up to me and is like, *Hey, have you ever been on a yacht?*"

"Oh god."

"I know. I shouldn't have gone—it's like the first rule they teach you, you know? If a guy offers you candy, don't get into the unmarked white van with him. But I was drunk. And stupid. And I didn't even realize that none of the other girls who came with us were my friends."

"There were other girls on the boat with you?"

"Yeah. No idea who they were. But I only remember them

being there in the beginning. At some point I went inside to sit down. It was a really fucking big boat. There was like a living room area with a big-ass couch and a flatscreen TV, and I remember being on the couch and just realizing, all of a sudden, that it was really quiet."

"Were you the only people on the boat?" I asked very quietly.

"I don't know. I don't remember all of it. But I know I made noise, and no one helped. So."

"How'd you get out of there?"

"I don't remember. We were on the boat, and then it goes black, and then I woke up on a bench near the docks at like four in the morning. I had my purse and all my clothes on, but my belt and my shoes were missing. I called Gabi. She picked me up and drove me to the hospital. They did a rape kit and put me on an IV because I was so dehydrated."

"Did you file a police report, or anything?"

"Fuck no." She laughed. It was a sharp, bitter thing.

I frowned. "Do you have any idea who this guy was?"

"Oh, I know who he was," Josefina said. "That's why I didn't file a report. He's not the kind of person I want to stand up against." She hesitated, eyes dancing over my face. "You would know, Laurel. You wrote an article about him."

A chill crawled up my spine.

"Vaughn?" I said. "You—you're absolutely sure it was him?"

She nodded again. "Positive."

"Could you tell me what he was wearing that night?" I ask, thinking of the group picture Diana Cabrera had emailed to me.

"Blue button-up. Sleeves rolled up."

Breath left my body in a rush. *"Fuck."*

"I know. Total douche bag," Josefina said with a smile and an eye roll that I saw right through. She was trying to laugh it off. To minimize what'd happened so it didn't feel so big and scary. I could empathize, because when I'd first stepped out of Target to find my car had been vandalized, I'd just wanted to squeeze my eyes shut and pretend it hadn't happened.

But it had. The report I'd filed with Garland PD was proof.

"Josie," I said, "we have to go to the police."

She laughed again. "No, we don't."

"But you—"

"Laurel, I don't know if you've noticed," Josefina said, holding the back of her hand up beside her face, "but I don't look like you. I'm *brown*. I'm not going to the fucking police."

I winced.

"And I'm in a sorority, so there are messy pictures of me all over social media," Josefina added. "Like, pictures of me shotgunning beers and wearing tight little dresses and—"

"Most college kids party," I argued.

"But you *know* those pictures get dragged out when girls say they—" Her voice wavered. Josefina sat back in her stool and reached for her water. Her fingers trembled. "Look, I'm talking to you in case anything I have to say can help other girls. But I'm not going to set myself up to be knocked down. I won't do it. This semester has already been hell, okay? Gabi's the only reason I'm not failing my classes or dropping out or jumping off the library or something."

I swallowed hard, because that last bit only felt like half a joke.

"I can't ask you to come forward if you don't want to," I said.

"I *do* want to," Josefina groaned, rubbing a hand over her face. "That's the *problem*. If I didn't want to say something—to do something—I would've deleted your email. I almost did. Gabi thinks I should've. But I—" She clenched and unclenched her hands.

"I want to help you. I want you to come forward."

"I'm sorry, Laurel," she said. "I can't."

———

I drove back to Garland in silence, stopping once to buy gas and a packet of peanut M&M's. The woman filling up her car at the pump next to me kept sneaking furtive glances at the letters carved into my hood. I watched her, bizarrely amused at the clash between being polite and being morbidly curious.

When my tank was half full and my M&M's were gone, I texted Ellison and Mehri to let them know I wanted to meet.

We congregated in Ellison's office.

"How'd it go with Josefina?" she asked from her chair. "Did she share anything worthwhile?"

"Is this resort as shady as we thought?" Mehri added, perched on the corner of the desk.

I wrung my hands.

"Vaughn raped her."

There was a horrible silence as Ellison and Mehri registered what I'd said, both of them stone still and open mouthed.

"Oh god," Ellison whispered.

"She was drunk," I continued, "but she remembers bits

and pieces. She has a few Snapchats she took on his boat. I asked what her attacker was wearing, and she described the same shirt Vaughn was wearing in the picture the Real Housewives took with him. I'm going to try to get more confirmation from Bodie."

Mehri's eyebrows pinched. "St. James?"

"We talked last night. He agreed to speak with me on the record. Anonymously, though."

"What do you think he knows?" Ellison asked.

"I think he suspects someone's embezzling from Vaughn's charity. But that's all."

"That's all?" Mehri repeated dubiously.

I nodded. "I trust him."

"Oh, fuck me," she said, burying her face in her hands. "You *trust* him."

"I'm serious. He's scared but he's being cooperative. He wants to help—"

"Because he thinks you're pretty!" Mehri exclaimed. "He wants to get in your pants, Laurel. Why are we trusting white boys now? And when did we decide that one of the dudes who benefits the most from Vaughn being head coach is a reliable source of information?"

"Just because he benefits doesn't mean he's complacent with how things work," I argued. "He's willing to come forward and be a whistleblower for us."

Mehri ran her tongue over her teeth, her fingers tapping out an anxious rhythm on the arm of Ellison's chair. "I don't like it."

"Well, we need him, okay? Josie doesn't want to speak right now. If she comes forward now, people are going to make this about the sexism shit. They're going to say she's a liar, or that she's exaggerating—"

"And uncovering embezzlement in Vaughn's charity is going to help?"

"Josie was assaulted on the same yacht Vaughn partied on when he told everybody he was doing charity work. Any evidence that ties Vaughn to that trip—to that resort, to that stupid boat—is going to help her case. This isn't about us. This is about her, and every other woman Vaughn's ever put a hand on. The more evidence we have, the safer they are."

Even as I said it, I knew it wasn't true. We couldn't promise any of them safety.

But we could at least try to make them feel heard.

chapter 19

On Tuesday, about fifteen seconds before Nick started a *riveting* lecture on pornographic Peruvian pottery and Greek brothel murals, Bodie arrived to class. I expected him to make his way down to the spot where most of the football team was sitting together, but instead, he dropped his backpack and sank down into a seat three rows from the back—directly across the aisle from where Andre and I were.

It felt like a brilliant stroke of good luck that he settled for a seat at the back of the classroom. I needed to talk to him about scheduling our interview. Unfortunately, Bodie's proximity—and what I knew now about his coach—made it downright impossible to focus on the lecture. By the time Nick powered off the projector and closed his laptop with a reminder to finish reading chapter eighteen before Thursday's lecture, I felt as if I'd just chugged three cups of black coffee: on edge, jittery, and needing to pee, just a bit.

"Damn it," Andre mumbled beside me. "What was the last slide? I was doing calligraphy."

I glanced over at his notebook, where he'd written, in devastatingly beautiful penmanship: *This class can kiss my ass.*

"Sorry. I totally zoned out." I slid my own notes into my backpack before Andre could see that I hadn't written down anything substantial in the last hour and a half.

In the same moment, Bodie stepped into the aisle, blocking my escape route. My heartbeat said, *It's go time.*

"Hey, Bodie, can we talk for a sec?" I asked.

Andre cleared his throat behind me. I scooted to the side so he and everyone else in our row could get around me, but he stopped at my side to glance pointedly at Bodie, then back at me. I didn't like his smile. It was the smile of someone who was reading too much into things.

"Catch you later, Cates," Andre called over his shoulder as he left.

"I'll see you—see you soon," I flubbed.

"How's Hanna doing?" Bodie asked me.

"Huh? Oh, she survived. Just had the worst hangover of her life. Do you want to schedule a time to do the follow-up interview?"

Ryan and Olivia came up the aisle behind us.

"Yo!" Ryan said. "Squad's all here!"

"Hey, man," Bodie greeted him, indulging him in a fist bump. "I'm sorry I didn't show up last week. I had this meeting with my coach and—"

"Don't worry about it," Ryan said.

This did nothing to ease the pinched guilt on Bodie's face. "Can we meet tomorrow? Maybe five, if that's not too late?"

"Works for me," Olivia said. Ryan nodded in agreement.

Bodie looked at me, eyes bright with hope. "And we can talk after?"

I agreed. "We'll talk after."

———

It was midterm season, the frustratingly long and fuzzy-edged stretch of the semester that, as far as I could tell, ran from the end of syllabus week to the beginning of final exams. Consequently, Buchanan resembled an outlet mall three days before Christmas. In other words, a living hell. When I got there, I was hit with a double whammy of mildly unpleasant surprises—first, that I was the last of the group to arrive (everyone already had their notes laid out and everything), and second, that the minuscule workspace we planned on hunkering down in for the evening was disconcertingly warm.

"Is it really hot in here?" I asked, shedding my backpack and jean jacket in a move I suppose made the question rhetorical.

Olivia looked up from her notebook and nodded in solidarity.

"Hot as *balls*," Ryan concurred.

"I'm sorry," Olivia said. "It was the only study room left."

I dropped into the seat between Ryan and Bodie, who I was sure I felt watching me as I set out my own notebook and pens. The study rooms were small to begin with, but he dwarfed them. I reached up to brush back my hair, a bit self-consciously, and discovered the spaghetti strap of my sundress had slipped off my bare shoulder when I'd tugged my arms out of my jean jacket.

"So I'm thinking," I began as I righted my rogue strap discreetly, "we should start by going over the outline?"

I glanced at Bodie. He stared unwaveringly at his notebook. Maybe I'd been mistaken about him watching me— although his cheeks *did* look flushed, but that was probably due to the heat. He was wearing a charcoal gray long-sleeved shirt. He'd rolled the sleeves up to his elbows, but he still had to be baking in it.

"I read through it last night," he said. "Looks really good. I'm happy to cover the sections you guys don't want."

It was the response of a true people pleaser.

"Oh," Olivia said, unable to hide her surprise. "That makes it easy. I guess we can get right to prepping for La Ventana."

La Ventana was a Mexican restaurant in east Los Angeles whose reputation had been built on their table-side guacamole and thriving lineup of drag queens who performed karaoke there on weekends.

"All right, so, we should try to get there before six," I said, reading from my notes. "The acts start at eight, and I want to have plenty of time to talk to Carla Asada. She said she's down for an interview, so she'll come an hour early to meet with us."

"Should we uber?" Ryan asked.

"It's like an hour away," Olivia pointed out. "It'd be way better if one of us drove. I mean, I don't have a car, but if someone *does*—"

I thought of my car, still tucked on the third floor of the overflow parking garage across from the Palazzo, and sank lower in my chair.

"I'll drive," Bodie volunteered. "I can borrow my roommate's car."

That was it. I'd never bitch about him being a people pleaser again. With our method of transportation decided upon, we turned to the next bullet point on our agenda: brainstorming questions.

"Okay, so, Carla started doing drag about ten years ago, and they're from—" Olivia flipped back through her notes.

Bodie interrupted. "What pronouns does Carla use?"

"She, her when she's Carla and they, them when they're not in drag," she said.

Bodie jotted this down and underlined it twice. As Olivia kept reading through the bio I'd pulled off Carla's Facebook page, I watched Bodie out of the corner of my eye. He made another note of something she said. Then, in the margins, he started drawing little looping designs before he caught himself, dropped his pen, and propped his elbows on the table, focusing his undivided attention on Olivia.

"Do you think we can ask what their parents think of them doing drag?" Ryan said. "I don't know if they're, like, conservative and shit."

"Yeah, that could be a sticky one," Olivia said, scrunching her nose.

"I think Laurel should ask it," Bodie piped up. When I shot him a wide-eyed look, he added, "She's a journalist. She's really good at that stuff."

It didn't sound backhanded. It sounded like he meant it.

"All right," Olivia said. "I'll mark Laurel down for that one."

While Ryan and Olivia launched into a debate about the pros and cons of bringing up religion—a topic Olivia argued would end up leading us into the mouth of a whole different beast that we didn't have space to tackle in a fifteen-page paper—I made a note to myself to draft some questions. I needed to ask about Carla's family anyway. This was the perfect lead-in. And Bodie had handed it to me.

Beside me, he started to bounce his knee so hard it shook the whole table. I cleared my throat. When he didn't get the message, I reached out—without considering how intimate the gesture might be—to cup my hand over his kneecap. Bodie stilled.

"Thanks," he murmured sheepishly.

I pulled my hand back into my lap, balling it into a tight fist. *I should tell him about Josefina.* I brushed the thought off and tried to refocus, but Ryan and Olivia were arguing about her ex. I'd overheard enough in the weeks since we'd been grouped together to know that his name was Lewis, and that he was an asshole. He also had an enormous penis, which seemed to be why Olivia had been unable to permanently delete his number.

"You can't just bone your way through problems—" Ryan was saying.

Bodie nudged me with his elbow.

"You want a carrot?" he offered.

The plastic baggie of baby carrots looked so tiny in his hand that it made something in my chest twist. Affection, maybe. With a little pinch of heartbreak. "No, thanks."

"Are you good? You're quiet."

I made a face like *Who, me?* that couldn't have been very convincing. Bodie quirked an eyebrow in question. The thought came again—I should warn him about the article. He'd asked me to keep him in the loop. To warn him.

Instead I said, "I'll take a carrot, actually."

—

We decided to call it a night after three hours of discussion. Olivia, who had redevoted herself to leading our group in an attempt to forget about CAN GO TO HELL Lewis and his massive dick, talked us through the major points of our presentation while we migrated to the elevator bank. She tore out three pages from her notebook and distributed them to us. The one she handed me had my name written across the top in purple gel pen; beneath was a numbered list of our slides, highlighted and underlined and circled.

When the elevator finally came, we all shuffled in together. The doors opened on the third floor. A crowd of students stood outside, waiting impatiently. I slid to the side, toward Bodie, and flattened myself against the wall. The horizontal handrail was cold where it pressed into the small of my back, but Bodie's arm was warm against mine. I couldn't help but think about the fact that the last time we'd been in an elevator together we'd been strangers.

It was dark outside when we emerged from Buchanan. The four of us walked down the front steps together, groaning and stumbling as our eyes adjusted to the sudden absence of harsh fluorescent lighting. When we reached the sidewalk, we lingered.

"See you guys tomorrow?" I said.

"Tomorrow," Olivia confirmed.

"Dope," Ryan declared. Then, to Olivia, he added, "Let's roll."

He dropped his longboard on the sidewalk, stepped onto it, and pushed off the pavement with the toe of his cheetah-print sneaker in one fluid movement. Olivia scoffed in mock outrage and started after him. He slowed himself to an easy roll, and when Olivia caught up, she gave Ryan's shoulder a shove that nearly knocked him backward off his board. His arms windmilled and he wobbled for a moment before he managed to steady himself by latching on to her shoulder with one hand.

I watched Olivia tow Ryan along across the quad, acutely aware of the fact that Bodie and I were now alone together on the front steps of Buchanan.

"I guess we should head somewhere private," Bodie said.

"We can do it at my place," I offered. "I mean we can talk. At my apartment."

With my foot wedged firmly in my mouth, we turned and started off to my apartment, the silence punctuated by our footsteps (three of mine for every two of Bodie's) and the distant whir of sprinklers dousing the rosebushes along the side of Buchanan.

Walking home alone at night always necessitated a certain degree of alertness—valuables tucked away, no headphones in case someone tried to sneak up behind me, key wedged between my knuckles in case I had to get scrappy. Garland was a relatively safe town, but my freshman year there'd been a string of incidents involving a man dubbed the Booty Bandit.

The name was only really funny until Hanna came to my dorm room in tears because a thirty-year-old man on a bicycle had slapped her on the ass as he rode past.

Ever since, I'd been on high alert every time I had to walk across campus after dark. The only time I ever really relaxed was if Andre was with me. Big softy that he was, being six foot four and a Division I athlete was usually enough to dissuade potential muggers and ass-slapping assailants.

Bodie had a similar effect. It was like having a bodyguard.

He'd carried my drunk best friend home and scheduled a group meeting to which he'd come excruciatingly prepared to do his part. And he'd agreed to talk.

"Thanks," I said as we walked, "for getting the group together. It was good to go over all that stuff before we do the drag show thing."

Bodie shrugged.

"I didn't do anything," he said. "Olivia booked us the study room, Ryan made all those slides, you wrote that kick-ass outline—"

"It's not that great."

"Better than I could do."

He smiled in that self-deprecating way of his. The business administration program at Garland was notoriously packed full of student athletes and wealthy kids who were only getting a degree so that when their company-owning parents got them cushy jobs right after graduation their diplomas could mask the nepotism. I thought of the conversation I'd overheard between Bodie and Gordon at the athletics center and wondered how many football players Vaughn had singlehandedly funneled into the major.

Bodie seemed to take my silence as judgment. "I'm thinking of switching to kinesiology, though."

I knew, from the way he pulled his hands out of his pockets and stuffed them under his arms, that this was not something he told a lot of people. Gordon knew, obviously, and Vaughn had shot down the idea. Why he was telling *me*, I didn't know.

"Kinesiology," I repeated.

"It's the mechanics of body movement. I've always kind of wanted to be a physical therapist. I probably won't have time for grad school and residency if I want to keep playing football after college. It's just something I've thought about."

Of course Bodie wanted to be a physical therapist. Of course he wanted to professionally help other people feel better.

"You could always go back to school after a few years in the NFL," I mused. "Pull a Hannah Montana."

"Best of both worlds," he said without missing a beat.

My smile was automatic. For a very long moment, we were quiet.

"Thank you," I whispered finally. "For talking to me."

When we reached my apartment building, I jogged ahead up the three steps to the front stoop. The halogen lamp in the ceiling overhead hummed like a wasp's nest in the still night air. With a sharp twist of my key and a little brute force, I got the front door open.

Inside my apartment, Bodie and I sat in the little IKEA chairs at my rickety dining table. I set my phone between us and began a recording.

"This is just for my records," I told him. "You won't be named unless you give me permission. Maybe you can start by telling me what your role was at the Vaughn Foundation?"

"I was an administrative intern over the summer. I helped with the calendar and bookkeeping."

"And what did you see during your time there that led you to suspect funds might be being used in a way that wasn't conducive to business?"

Bodie reached into his backpack and withdrew a Garland University folder—the one they sold at the bookstore for twice the cost of any off-brand ten pack you could find at Office Depot—that was stuffed with loose sheets of printer paper. As he laid them out across my dining room table, I realized they were his evidence—spreadsheets, bank statements, screenshots of online donation portals.

"This one," Bodie said, handing me an invoice, "I noticed first. It's a thirty-grand charge to some consulting company I can't find any info about online—other than the fact that they've got a PO box in LA."

"Can I borrow your phone for a sec?"

I typed *Thomas Hagen Consulting Garland CA* into Google and scrolled through the first page of results.

"Nothing. Wait, hold on. There's a *Tom* Hagen."

"Who is he?" Bodie asked, scooting his chair up against mine so he could read over my shoulder.

The page I clicked brought me to a blog article. "He's . . . a character?"

"From what?"

I scrolled and scrolled, and then I stopped.

"*The Godfather*," I croaked. "Tom Hagen, consigliere to the Corleone family." Bodie and I exchanged a look in which we both silently agreed that neither of us knew what *consigliere* meant. When I had the definition pulled up, I wasn't sure whether to laugh or chuck Bodie's phone across the kitchen. "This—this *bold* motherfucker! It's an advisor. 'The right-hand man to the boss of an organized crime syndicate.' Jesus Christ. Vaughn isn't even being subtle about it!"

Bodie looked pale. "You think Vaughn's the one stealing money from the foundation?"

"How else do we explain this? A consultation firm with no online presence that just so happens to have the same name as a character from his favorite movies?"

"It doesn't make any sense," Bodie said, shaking his head. "Vaughn's got money. *Everyone* on the board at the foundation has money. Why would any of them need to steal from a charity?"

My impulse was to say, *Because Vaughn's just that kind of asshole.* But Bodie raised a good point.

"Maybe they weren't stealing," I murmured. "Maybe they were just moving it around. The Vaughn Foundation has a lot of big donors, right? People who give tens of thousands of dollars at a time for the tax write-offs. Maybe somebody at the foundation is helping somebody fuck with the IRS."

Bodie sat back and looked at me, the oddest smile on his face.

"What?" I demanded, cheeks burning.

He shook his head. "You're just so fucking good at this. This is, like, James Bond shit."

"Shut up," I said, scrubbing my face for an excuse to shield my blush. I scanned the papers splayed out before us, looking for anything else out of the ordinary. My eyes landed on a Wells Fargo statement for the month of August. "What about these charges?"

"Those are legit. That's all for the networking trip to San Diego."

"Do you know anything about that trip?"

"I think they stayed at some yacht club—hold on." Bodie riffled through his notes and pulled out an invoice stapled to a bank statement. "Yeah. The Alvarado Resort. He had three rooms booked for four nights. I think he spent a few nights on his boat too."

"Who went with him? Coaching staff?"

"I think one of our trainers may have gone with him. He does a lot of the outreach to the schools they donate to. Other than that, it was probably some of the foundation staff."

"What are these? Two seventy-five, two ninety . . . what were they spending like three hundred dollars a night on at this resort?"

Bodie shrugged. "Dinner, maybe? Maybe there was a restaurant."

And a bar, I thought. "Is Vaughn still sober?"

"Yeah. For the last seven or eight years," Bodie said. He watched me for a moment before adding, more quietly, "Why?"

I tapped my fingernails against the kitchen table, weighing my options, and then reached for my phone to retrieve Diana Cabrera's email.

"I interviewed a few women who were in San Diego the same weekend as Vaughn." I pulled up the group shot she'd sent me and zoomed in, so the Real Housewives were out of view and Vaughn, in all his shiny-faced, sweat-stained glory, was on full display.

When I flipped my phone around, Bodie leaned in.

"Holy shit," he said, his face twisting up like he'd just watched an oblivious freshman crash their bike on the parkway and eat pavement. "He looks . . ."

"Drunk," I finished.

"*Wasted*," Bodie corrected. "This was over the summer? *This* summer?"

I nodded. "At the Alvarado Resort. The women I talked to said they ran into him at the bar and he invited them onto his boat. Apparently, he was throwing a party." I tried to phrase the next bit delicately, because I knew this was all difficult for Bodie. "They said he was really drunk. They think he might've been on something too."

Bodie sat back in my tiny IKEA chair and rubbed his hands over his eyes. When he leaned forward again, elbows on his knees and head hung, the defeated look on his face made my hand twitch to reach out for him.

"I think he needs help," he said, resolved.

He needs to be in jail, I corrected in my head. But Bodie saw the best in Vaughn—in people. And Bodie didn't know what I knew, and it wasn't my place to tell him. But when Bodie met my eyes, for one horrifying moment, I felt that he could read my thoughts like they were written across my cheeks in permanent marker.

"What else do you have on him, Laurel?" he asked quietly.

"I can't tell you," I said, shaking my head. "Not yet. I'm sorry. Our job—the media's job—is to relay the *facts*. Not to sensationalize. Not to skew. And I can't present the facts to you just yet. You're not the only person I need to protect, okay?"

He exhaled a shaky breath and, with a nod, said, "Okay. I trust you."

I trust you.

It was not the time to get emotional. If anything, it was the time to channel Ellison Michaels, queen regnant of competence and composure. But tears were prickling in my eyes and a lump was lodged in my throat that made it very, very difficult to stay cool. I hadn't known how big of a relief—how big of a comfort—it would be to have Bodie St. James on our side.

chapter 20

I assumed Bodie St. James would take us to La Ventana in a truck. I don't know why. I guess I just figured that white guys from Texas who played football were precisely the demographic to drive around in a mud-splattered Ford F-150 with the windows down and country music blasting. So it came as a real slap in the face when I spotted a familiar black Tesla.

We'd agreed to meet in a little parking lot outside of one of the older and grungier freshmen dorms. The asphalt was littered with cigarette butts and—poetically—one old, used glow-stick bracelet. I'd run into Ryan on my way to campus. He was telling me about the time he'd broken his wrist attempting to skateboard along the edge of the fountain outside the student union, but I was a little preoccupied with eyeing our method of transportation for the evening.

Bodie stood with his back against the driver's-side door, his head down as he scrolled through his phone. He'd had practice that afternoon (I knew this because Andre had complained about all the conditioning, not because I was, like, a stalker). His hair was damp from the shower and the bridge of his nose was sunburned.

It took me a solid four seconds to notice that Olivia was standing next to him, flipping through her notebook and jotting down last-minute notes.

Ryan announced our arrival with a loud and drawn out, "Let's gooo!"

Olivia looked up.

Bodie smiled and said, "So, whose funeral is it?"

We'd all somehow worn black. Olivia looked, as she always did, like she was on her way to an outdoor music festival—just a somber one. Ryan was in jeans so tight I wondered if he had any feeling at all in his feet, which were encased in a pair of faux alligator sneakers. I'd just borrowed Hanna's black corduroy overall dress again (lame) and Bodie was in black jeans and a denim jacket. A perfectly unremarkable outfit. There was absolutely no reason for me to stare at him. None at all.

Olivia sighed. "At least we're coordinated."

"Go team," I quipped.

"Shotgun!" Ryan hollered.

There was also no good reason for me to want to elbow Ryan out of the way as he jogged around the car, but I tried not to think about that as Olivia and I climbed into the back seat together through the stupid falcon-wing doors.

"Nice car," I muttered.

"It's Kyle's," Bodie said, his eyes meeting mine in the rearview mirror.

I know, I thought as the engine turned on with a low, eco-friendly rumble. The fact that Fogarty drove an electric car made him no less of an asshole. The vegan leather seats were soft as butter. I wanted to cut right through them with my fingernails.

—

The closer we got to Los Angeles, the worse the traffic on the I-10 became. Ryan was in charge of navigation and music selection, to the detriment of everyone's happiness. He had a flare for incredibly grating techno music and 1960s throwbacks.

It was a small relief when we finally pulled off the freeway and navigated into a more upscale neighborhood dotted with boutiques and furniture stores. We passed two burger places and a BBQ joint before we spotted La Ventana—a saturated sunset-orange building with a roof made of arched clay tiles, like russet scales, and an outdoor patio in the front that was partially hidden behind several thick-trunked palm trees.

Parking was a nightmare, naturally. We eventually settled for a spot along the narrow sidewalk bordering a soccer pitch almost five blocks from the restaurant. The field was a sharp neon green—turf, probably—and corralled by a high chain-link fence coated in black rubber. We climbed out of the car. Out on the field, a pair of teenage boys were passing a ball around.

"Kick with your left foot, coward!" one shouted to the other in Spanish.

I snorted. Bodie glanced at me sideways.

Ryan ducked his head to read the meter and announced that it was two hours max.

"Someone can come back out and top it up later," Olivia said, already inching down the sidewalk. "Let's just go, I don't want Carla to get there before us."

Ryan jammed in a handful of quarters, and then we were off. I glanced over my shoulder before we turned the corner. Something about the sight of Fogarty's Tesla parked against the curb spurred in me the sudden and violent urge to march back up to it and smash my fist down on the hood. But I didn't.

La Ventana was comfortably buzzing—not too empty, not too packed. The square terra-cotta tiles on the floor were polished to a glossy shine. Painted ceramic plates and sombreros hung on the textured walls alongside a collection of framed and autographed photos of performers in drag—towering wigs, false eyelashes, sequined minidresses, lipsticked smiles, and fierce pouts. Brightly colored *papel picado* banners were strung from the ceiling above us. They swayed and fluttered in the air conditioning.

The hostess tucked four menus under her arm and led us through the main dining area, down a narrow hall lined with bathroom doors, and into a back room dominated by a low stage with a projector screen and an elaborate speaker system. It was darker than the main dining area, the windows shuttered and fake candles flickering on the tables.

I knew we were close to the kitchen because the scent of roasting chiles and jalapeños made my mouth and eyes water. Our booth sat on the far side of the room from the stage. Olivia and I slid onto the padded bench against the wall while the boys took the distressed wooden chairs. As Bodie scooted forward, his knee knocked mine under the table. I pretended to suddenly be very intrigued by the drinks menu, despite the fact that I couldn't legally order anything from it.

"Ooh," Olivia said, "they do sangria by the pitcher, if we're all in the mood to get shit-faced."

Boy, did that sound tempting. Something about Bodie St. James in artificial candlelight made me want to chug alcoholic beverages. The football team had been practicing in the afternoons recently, and it showed—the hair on top of his head was kissed the color of whiskey and his face was developing a tan beneath the traces of sunburn. He looked like he'd shaved a few hours ago too. I wondered if his skin felt as smooth as it looked.

It was a small blessing when the fresh guacamole and tortilla chips arrived, giving me something to occupy my thoughts (and hands) with that *wasn't* Bodie's jawline. All conversation at the table died as we shoveled God's chosen condiment into our mouths. Even Olivia relented and put down her extensive prep notes and indulged.

It took us all of sixty seconds to empty the basket. Bodie flagged down our waiter and asked for two more. We killed those too.

"Oh, this is them!" Olivia said.

I think I'd been expecting Carla Asada to show up in drag, which was dumb, because it wasn't like potters constantly walked around in clay-splattered smocks. Also, I'd seen pictures of Carla both in and out of drag. But they were somehow more beautiful in person—all perfectly manicured eyebrows and skin glowing under the warm light of the restaurant.

We introduced ourselves and shook hands, the pleasantries walking an awkward line between formal (because this was an academic excursion) and casual (because it wasn't every day you got to go to a drag show for research). Carla pulled up a chair from the empty table beside ours. I noticed, for the first time, that there was a peach emoji patch ironed onto the lapel of their army-green jacket.

"Thank you *so* much for this," Olivia gushed.

"Don't mention it," Carla said, reaching out to pluck a chip from the basket (our fourth now) in the middle of the table. "Do you mind if I steal some guac? I had an audition out in Santa Monica. Got stuck in traffic. All I had in my car were some raw almonds."

"Go for it," I said, pushing the stone mortar down the table.

Carla shoveled guacamole in their mouth while Olivia gave them a brief recap of our class and the requirements for our project—the thirty-minute presentation and the fifteen-page paper. After this rundown, Carla sat forward and dusted tortilla chip crumbs off their hands, turning their attention to Ryan, Bodie, and me.

"All right, so, first things first. How familiar are you with drag?" they asked us. "I don't want to treat you like a bunch of first graders, but I also don't want you to be totally lost."

I had no experience with drag, other than the time sophomore year Hanna and I had gotten the flu at the same time and had spent an entire week bingeing *RuPaul's Drag Race* and chugging DayQuil. And given the number of Spanish telenovelas I watched, I knew one show was far from a comprehensive representation of the community. It was tricky to try to appreciate a larger culture through the filter of visual media.

"We've been doing a lot of research," Bodie said.

"Have you been to any shows, though?" Carla asked. "Or met anyone who performs?"

"I saw *The Rocky Picture Horror Show*," Ryan said. "Does that count?"

Carla opened their mouth to answer.

"Wait!" Olivia interrupted, then turned to me and said solemnly, "The recordy thingy."

"We'll be taking an audio recording of this conversation," I explained to Carla, setting my phone on the table and tipping the screen toward them so they could see the app I was using. "It's just to be sure we don't misquote you."

Carla smiled. "I know the drill."

"Oh, perfect." I tapped open the settings on the app and toggled the volume. "Do you do interviews often?"

"Only really in the last few months," Carla admitted sheepishly. "I *just* started doing performances full-time. This year's been sort of crazy for me—I got invited to do a panel at DragCon, I was featured in a piece for the *LA Times*, did a little interview for *Variety*. I mean, there were like eight other performers in the article, but still. *Variety*."

"Holy shit," I said. "Congratulations."

"Thank you. I mean, it's still brutal trying to make a living as an artist, but at least when you search my name on Google, my Instagram's the first hit under *Did you mean* carne asada?"

I laughed. "Well, I'm definitely going to need you to sign something for me."

Beside me, Olivia was flipping frantically through her notebook. She'd come to dinner with a detailed game plan. I respected her need to steer our conversation to get the information we needed rather than let it all unfold organically, so I decided to let her take the wheel.

"All right. We're recording," I announced, then turned to Olivia. "Start us off?"

She nodded and consulted the numbered list in her notebook. "Could you introduce yourself?"

"I'm Carla Asada, and I am drag artist born and raised in Irvine, California."

"How'd you choose your name?"

"Because I'm packing the meat, baby." Carla winked. "And, in all honesty, your name is a big part of your brand as a performer. I'm Latine, and I'm a little raunchy. My name lets you know what you're getting."

"When did you start doing drag?"

Carla propped their elbows on the table, tapping fingernails painted a brilliant sunflower yellow against their cheeks.

"I mean, unofficially? As soon as I could walk." Carla laughed as they turned over a memory in their head. "My mom used to let me wear her costume jewelry and stomp around in her shoes. I think that's how a lot of us start out—you're not even thinking of it as drag. It's just—I don't know. *Creative expression.*"

"You knew you wanted to be a drag queen when you were little?" Ryan asked.

"Drag artist," Carla corrected, sitting upright again. "I know a lot of performers call themselves queens, and that's totally fine, but it definitely gives this impression that we're all gay men. And the community's a lot bigger than that. I mean, I know the term *drag* has that connotation. I guess it supposedly comes from an abbreviation for one of Shakespeare's stage directions—*dressed as girl*. And William Dorsey Swann was the person to call himself a *queen of drag*, and he was a pioneer of drag in the US. But it feels a little narrow to me. I think drag is really just any performance of gender. Calling myself an artist feels more accurate."

Olivia nodded. "That makes *so* much sense."

"You're really in touch with the history of drag," I commented.

Carla shrugged. "I feel like I know less than I should. I mean, you guys have been doing your research, so you know that drag has been around for fucking ever. Ancient Egypt. Greek and Hindu mythology. Kabuki. Vaudeville. There's so much to cover. But it's pretty hard to ignore history when you're doing drag in West Hollywood. I mean, it's *LA*. We had the Cooper Do-nuts Riot in—oh, god. I forget the year. The late '50s? I just know it was ten years before Stonewall. Literally, before Stonewall! The LGBTQ community has such history here—and so much of it is linked to the performing arts. So you follow that trail, and you eventually get *The Rocky Horror Picture Show*—like you mentioned," they said to Ryan, "and *RuPaul's Drag Race*, and bam, it's today, and I'm getting paid to sing Cher at a Mexican restaurant. Living the dream."

Olivia frowned down at her bullet points, frantically trying to find the ones she could cross off. When she'd reoriented herself, she asked another round of basic questions about Carla's performance background.

"Mostly public-school theater stuff. I didn't start doing

shows until I was in my twenties, and even then, it was still super low-budget stuff. Drag gets *expensive*. The travel, the makeup, the wigs. And I hand make all my own outfits, so that's the cost of the materials *and* the hundreds of hours it takes to put a piece together. My mother used to do most of the sewing for me but her eyesight's getting bad, so I told her she has to cut back."

I saw an opening for the question Olivia had delegated to me. As I reached for the chip basket, I said, "Do either of your parents have a background in the arts? I mean, it sounds like your mom knows how to put together a costume."

Bodie propped his elbow on the table and rested his hand over his mouth, like he was covering a smile. I tried not to let it go to my head.

"Well, I definitely got my voice from my mother, but she only sings in church or when she's cooking. And she learned how to sew because she had to. My parents are *really* traditional. Mama handles the housework; Papa goes out and makes the money. Classic Mexican Catholic couple shit. My father sort of ignores what I'm doing—he's got that *machismo*, you know, can't talk about his feelings—but my mother really likes all the music and the dressing up."

"So she's . . . supportive?" Olivia asked tentatively.

"Oh, she *loves* it," Carla said. "She comes out to my shows whenever she can."

I glanced across the table at Bodie. He was listening to Carla, so he didn't seem to notice that I was staring. I waited for him to bounce his knee or fidget with his hands, but he was perfectly still, his attention as sharp as it was on the field during a football game.

Ryan had asked another question, but I'd missed it completely.

"My goal isn't to *pass* as a woman," Carla answered. "I don't really mind what pronouns people use with me while I'm in drag—it's actually sort of fun to walk the line. Because then people realize there's only a line because someone came along and drew one. It's pretty arbitrary, what we deem *feminine* or *masculine*. It's not as biological as people assume."

"Do you think that makes people uncomfortable?" Olivia asked, following my lead and skipping past several questions on her list to ask a more relevant one. "The walking the line stuff?"

"Oh, absolutely," Carla replied. "For some people—you know, it just makes them feel weird. Because they've got this idea of what gender is supposed to be. I'm a six-foot-four, plus-sized brown person, and then I get up there and I'm singing love ballads by Dolly Parton and Etta James. Some people can't reconcile it. They start guessing, you know? *Well, are you a guy or a girl?* And sometimes I say neither, and sometimes I tell them to guess."

Bodie cleared his throat.

"When you're dressed up—when you're Carla," he said, pausing for a moment to consider his words, "do you feel like you're, I guess, a different person?"

Carla thought about this for a moment.

"You know, I don't," they said at last. "Who someone is on stage is never exactly who they are off it. It's always performative. I mean—Olivia said you play football, right?"

Bodie looked startled. "Yeah."

"That's a performance too. It's not that different. I put on

255

a dress and sing, you put on your big shoulder pads and thump your chest and act tough. But we're still ourselves under that performance. I do feel like Carla is—she's part of me. She's an alter ego. I think that's the beauty of drag. The freedom you have to explore all the little corners of yourself."

"You *find yourself* through drag," Ryan concluded.

"You can, yeah. And I'm not saying you have to get up on stage in a dress and sing Cher. I know that's not for everybody. I'm saying, you got to do *you*. You got to do what makes you happy, even if you think people will see you as less masculine—or less feminine—or *whatever*."

"So true," Olivia whispered reverently.

"As soon as you do it, you understand how much all of it is performance. Every single day. You wake up, and you're thinking about what other people think of you. If you're attractive or ugly. If you seem friendly or weird. If you're taking up too much room. It's hard to do, but drag has taught me a lot about just—letting that shit go."

We sat in silence.

Ryan finally let out a low whistle and said, "Damn."

It wasn't eloquent, but it did sum up exactly what I was thinking.

"That wasn't too *inspirational quote on a novelty T-shirt*, was it?" Carla asked.

"It was beautiful," Olivia insisted, eyes tracing her notebook one last time before she shut it. "And I'm totally out of questions. That was *amazing*. Thank you so much again. You're such a superstar."

Carla put their hands down on the table, palms to the wood, and pushed their chair back.

"Perfect timing," they announced. "I've got to start getting ready. It takes forever and a half to beat this face. It was great meeting you three. And *you*." They turned to Olivia. "Tell me you dumped the deadweight."

"I did," Olivia said proudly.

"And you deleted his number?"

Her smile deflated.

Carla sighed. "Just do it, sis. Thank me later." They turned to the rest of us and said, "It was wonderful meeting you all. Hope you enjoy the show."

Bodie nodded and said very earnestly, "Thank you."

"Yeah, thanks so much," I added at the same moment Ryan went, "Break a leg, or whatever, if they even say that in real life."

Carla snorted, snatched one last chip, and left us.

I grabbed my phone from the center of the table and switched off the recording. Ryan, Olivia, and I immediately launched into discussion. What quotes were we sure we'd use? How would we integrate what Carla had said into the preexisting structure of our project without compromising context or content?

Our waiter appeared, took our orders, and—what seemed like sixty seconds later—swung back around with four plates of food. Olivia, the vegetarian of the group, kept talking through her list of bullet points while she stabbed at her cheese enchiladas with a fork. Ryan and I mumbled out our thoughts through mouthfuls of carne asada tacos.

Bodie, who had ordered a burrito the size of my head, ate in silence. He had the stares. I was considering nudging him under the table with my foot, just to tug him out of his thoughts before he became hopelessly lost in them, when our waiter materialized again with an enormous pitcher of sangria and announced that Carla Asada had bought it for our table.

My elation at being provided free alcohol was almost immediately crushed when our waiter asked to see our IDs. While Ryan and Olivia handed over their driver's licenses, I propped my chin on my palm and watched perfect wheels of sliced orange float among ice cubes in a sea of deep burgundy. La Ventana wasn't legally allowed to provide me a cup with which to consume the free sangria, but, when our waiter had left and no one was looking, Olivia slid hers across the table so I could try it. It tasted like summertime in Mexico City.

We ate and we talked and we laughed—even Bodie, who didn't say much but chuckled at Ryan's jokes. The back room filled up steadily until, all at once, there wasn't an empty table in the house.

I kept stealing tiny sips of Olivia's sangria. I was sure I'd never felt the effects of alcohol so fast. My smiles were coming easier and I kept laughing too loud and meeting eyes with the football player across the table. Given that the last time I'd gotten drunk I'd spent the night trying to fight Bodie St. James and puking—in that order, not simultaneously, *thank god*—it seemed wise to take it easy. So when Olivia offered the last of the glass to me, I shook my head.

"You sure? You had, like, three sips. We haven't even made a dent in the pitcher."

"I'm good," I said.

She poured herself a refill and kept drinking.

"What kind of music do you think they play here?" Ryan asked through a mouthful of chips.

As if to answer his question, the lights came on, brilliant magenta and cyan blue, and Carla appeared on stage.

Except Carla was a new woman.

She wore a black bolero jacket and matching wide-brimmed sombrero, both intricately embroidered with gold thread. Her lipstick and dress were the red of a matador's cape, and her false eyelashes cast shadows like raven's wings.

There was a beat of awestruck silence before the room erupted with whistling and cheers.

"*Bienvenidos a La Ventana,*" Carla bellowed into a microphone. "We begin tonight with a tribute to the Queen of Tejano!"

The opening chords of a song I hadn't heard in years poured from the speakers.

My heart lodged in my throat. It was Selena Quintanilla. My mom's favorite singer. I didn't realize I remembered the lyrics until I caught my mouth shaping out the words. I hadn't heard the song in years—not since elementary school, it felt like—but my brain had filed the lyrics away for safekeeping, like I'd somehow known I would need them later. Like I could've possibly known that, one day, I'd be at a Mexican restaurant and a drag artist would take the stage and reach right into my chest to hold my heart.

When the set ended, I couldn't stop smiling. The low hum of conversation filled the room as the performers slipped off stage for a costume change.

"I should go put more money in the meter," Bodie said.

I watched him disappear down the narrow hallway between the bathrooms. As soon as he was out of sight, Olivia leaned across the table, fingers folded together like she'd summoned me to a board meeting.

"So," she said. "What's the deal with you and St. James?"

A tortilla chip lodged sideways in my throat. I spluttered and washed it down with her sangria. "What?" I croaked.

"There's weird—I don't know. *Tension*."

"She wrote that article," Ryan said, startling me. "The one about Vaughn."

"That was you?" she demanded, then slumped with disappointment. "Ugh. Well, first off, I love you, because that article was so fantastic. But what a freakin' letdown! I was hoping there was something more romantic going on between you two."

I snorted. "Ha! *Romantic*. Um, no. Definitely not."

Olivia tilted her head to the side.

"He *looks* at you, Laurel."

She said this like I was supposed to know what it meant. And maybe I did. But instinctively—the way your hand snaps away from a hot pan if your skin so much as brushes it—I opened my mouth to tell her she was wrong.

"Honestly, we're just—"

I couldn't finish the sentence. We weren't even friends, were we? Just a journalist and her whistleblower. Her whistleblower with a soft, squishy, loyal-to-a-fault heart and thundercloud eyes. My identity crisis was drowned out by the opening bars of a Cher song. While my group mates turned to watch the action on stage, I glanced at Olivia's glass.

How much sangria had I had? I felt lightheaded.

He looks at you.

I turned Olivia's words over in my head until they didn't sound like English anymore. The Cher song ended. I didn't notice the music had gone quiet until Ryan set down his glass of sangria a little too hard and declared, "What the fuck? St. James has been gone, like, ten minutes."

It'd been thirteen and a half minutes, actually. But Ryan had a point. It couldn't take this long to shove a couple quarters into the meter. I doubted anything dramatic had happened—Bodie wasn't exactly the kind of target you tried to mug, unless you wanted to be body-slammed into the sidewalk—but I still couldn't shake my concern.

Maybe something Carla had said had gotten to him. I pushed back my chair and stood before I could overthink what I was doing.

"I'm going to check on him," I announced, wadding up my napkin and setting it on the table beside my empty plate. "I'll be right back."

Neither of my remaining group mates said anything, but I caught Olivia grinning against the rim of her glass before I headed to the entrance, and I couldn't help but think that I was getting real tired of everyone smiling like they knew something.

chapter 21

Night had snuck up on us while we were inside sipping sangria. The heat of the afternoon lingered, but the sky was dark when I slipped through the front doors of the restaurant and started down the steps. Light pollution from the city blotted out all but a handful of stars.

I sighed and hugged my arms over my chest. He couldn't have gone far.

I turned the corner around the front patio and stopped short. Bodie was heading down the sidewalk toward me with one hand in the front pocket of his jean jacket and the other braced around a paper-wrapped cone of soft serve ice cream.

And here I'd thought he was off having an emotional breakdown.

"Hey," he called from the end of the block. He looked at the restaurant, then back at me, clearly confused. "What's up?"

An excuse. I needed an excuse.

Instead, I blurted, "You ditched us."

Bodie stopped a few feet short of me, lifted his soft serve to his mouth and licked around the side of the cone, just barely catching a drip before it hit the side of his thumb. I was absolutely not staring at his hands. There was nothing remotely interesting about the way they made the cone look cute and miniature.

"Sorry," Bodie said, oblivious to my pink cheeks. "I went to put some more money in the meter. It's nice out. Thought I could use a walk to clear my head a little."

"Where'd you get the ice cream?"

"I took a shortcut on the way back and passed a Fosters Freeze. I had a few quarters left over, so I figured, you know, why not?"

I was jealous. Of Bodie—not the cone. Fosters Freeze sounded delicious right now, and he'd gotten the best kind: chocolate-dipped vanilla.

"Did I miss any good ones?" he asked.

"Pardon?"

I managed to tear my eyes off his soft serve. Bodie nodded to the restaurant, from which the muffled sound of a Beyoncé single drifted into the warm night air.

"Oh," I said. "Um. Carla sang some Cher."

Bodie hummed and leaned back against the low retaining wall. He just wanted some alone time to think. So what was I doing? What did I think I could accomplish by hovering like this? Why did I feel like I was waiting for something? I tried to step back and be a voice of reason for myself. *Go back inside, Laurel.*

I didn't budge. But neither did Bodie. We just stood there, staring at each other, while his ice cream melted.

"How do you know all the words to that song?" he asked out of nowhere. "The Spanish one."

It took me a second to realize what he was talking about, and another second to get over the embarrassment of knowing he'd seen me mouthing the lyrics.

"Oh. My mom's from Mexico. She *loves* Selena." At Bodie's narrowed eyes, I clarified: "Quintanilla. Not Gomez."

"I know," he said in a bashful tone that told me he hadn't.

My mom was born in Mexico City in the mid-1970s, so Selena had been her Ariana Grande—the music she listened to when she did homework and when she drove around in my *abuelito's* car with the radio blaring. She and her sister had known all the words. She'd moved to the US for college the same year Selena was killed, but that didn't feel like the kind of thing you shared when someone was trying to enjoy their ice cream.

"That's why your Spanish is so good, then," Bodie said, smiling like he'd finally found the missing corner piece of a jigsaw puzzle.

I tilted my head at him. First, because it wasn't true. My Spanish was basic at best, and unintelligible Spanglish at worst. Second, "When have you heard me speak Spanish?"

Bodie ducked his head, bashful. His eyelashes had no business being so thick.

"You called me a dumbass at the Baseball House. I google translated it."

I opened my mouth to protest and was immediately thunked over the head with the memory of the word *pendejo* spilling out of my mouth when he'd taken my glass of wine and put it up on the fridge, out of my reach.

"Oh my god," I said. "I'm sorry. I had so much *wine*—"

Bodie laughed, the sound bright and clear over the hum of LA traffic.

"You were mad. I learned some Spanish. It's a win-win."

He took another lick of his ice cream. I caught a glimpse of his tongue, all pink and bathed in melting white ice cream, and imagined his hair tickling the insides of my thighs. The thought came so abruptly I didn't know where it'd come from or what to do with it. It had to be the sangria. Beneath the sweet, punchy aftertaste lay dangerous volumes of alcohol. A few sips and my head was lodged in the gutter.

Definitely the sangria.

Luckily, Bodie completely misinterpreted the way I was looking at him. "Nuh-uh," he said, keeping his cone out of my reach. "Get your own ice cream."

I rolled my eyes and leaned back against the white-washed adobe wall that encircled the outdoor patio. Then, because I was desperate to steer my thoughts away from his tongue and what it could theoretically do, I asked, "How do *you* know the words to that Beach Boys song Ryan played in the car?"

"First off," Bodie said very seriously, appearing not at all ashamed that I'd caught him mouthing the lyrics, "it's a classic. But also, I grew up with"—he paused and squinted a little—"*outdated* pop culture. My sister's ten years older than me. And my parents are *old*."

I snorted. "Well, they're parents. Isn't being old part of the job description?"

"I mean my dad's seventy."

"Oh shit," I said, completely sidestepping tact.

Bodie laughed it off.

"Yeah, I know. I was his midlife crisis."

He said it like it was a joke he'd told a hundred times before. Like it was something he always peppered in when he talked about his dad, to ease other people's discomfort. To ward off the uncomfortable silence as you tried to think about something to say that wasn't *So does he have dentures yet or . . . ?*

All at once, I wanted to tell Bodie everything. I wanted to tell him about my parents, and my hometown in the Central Valley that smelled of methane (because of the cows at the agricultural college—you got used to it) but had night skies so heavy with stars it felt like you could jump up and grab handfuls of them at a time. I wanted to tell him that I lived off of granola bars and Mexican food and had Ariana Grande's third studio album in my car and that, when he smiled at me, I felt the opposite of invisible.

Instead, I popped off the wall, nudged Bodie with my elbow and said, "You know ice cream tastes better if you share it, right?"

He studied me carefully over the cone. "Sounds like an urban legend."

I shook my head. "Scientific fact."

"I'm going to need to see a peer-reviewed study."

It took me a solid three seconds to realize that he'd cracked a joke. My laugh came out as a delighted snort. Bodie hid a proud smile behind another lick of ice cream.

"Thanks for driving, by the way," I said, scuffing the toe of my sneaker against the sidewalk and trying not to think about the green-haired owner of the car we'd come in. "And for—I don't know. *Doing shit.* For this project. I know you've got a lot going on right now."

This last bit came out mumbled. Bodie heard me anyway.

"Don't mention it," he said tightly. "I'm sorry I was the world's worst group member for a few weeks there."

The guilt in his voice bothered me. "Bodie?"

He hummed. His mouth was full of ice cream. It was my chance to monologue.

"Whatever happens with our article, I think—" The words were coming out all mushed together. I was horrible at this. "Whatever Vaughn did—just hear me out—whatever he did, it's okay to be upset about it. It's okay to step back from everything to figure out how you feel. You're allowed to not be okay."

Bodie stared down at his ice-cream cone and pulled a face like he'd lost his appetite.

"Can we talk about something else?" he asked. "I—I'm really sorry, Laurel. I just don't want to bring this up tonight."

I did. I wanted to press it. To press *him*. But I could tell I was prodding a bruise, and tonight had been too nice to ruin with another receptive, predictable argument. Besides, getting away from campus made it so much easier to forget about everything. Our classes, our responsibilities, the investigation that'd upturned both our lives. Maybe we both deserved a night off from being ourselves.

I folded my arms over my chest, relieved I'd gotten the words out but kind of hating that I'd made things awkward again, and said, "Okay. You're right."

Should've gone back inside. Dumbass.

The worst kind of silence stretched out before us. Bodie broke it when he sighed, turned to face me square on, and extended his ice-cream cone like a chocolate-dipped olive branch.

"One lick," he said, a warning in his tone and a smile on his face.

I'm not sure what possessed me to wrap both of my hands around Bodie's wrist, anchoring him and his cone in place and using his solidly muscled arms to leverage myself up onto my toes. The bite of ice cream I took was massive, and the rush of cold made my front teeth sting like a bitch, but it was worth it to see Bodie's eyes light up with delighted outrage.

"You did *not*," he said.

I held my hand over the bottom half of my face, on the off chance that my laughter would send ice cream out of my nose, until I'd swallowed.

"Sorry." I was not at all sorry.

Bodie narrowed his eyes. And then he said, in a mediocre Spanish accent, "*Pendejo.*"

I knew then that I couldn't blame the sangria. I wasn't drunk. Not even a little bit. With a surge of wild and chaotic bravery I imagine skydivers feel before they launch themselves out of airplanes, I reached up and pressed my fingertips to the top of Bodie's shoulder just firmly enough to keep my balance. I rolled up onto my toes again like I was going in for seconds. My lips made contact with his jaw—an accident, not a strategic step in my poorly thought out plan to kiss his cheek.

Bodie froze. The regret was instant. I'd fucked up more monumentally than previously thought possible. I pulled back, an apology forming at the back of my throat even as our faces were still so close that I could've held him there and counted his eyelashes.

But then I heard the wet splat of ice cream on the pavement, and Bodie's hands were on either side of my face, his fingers brushing across my cheekbones and knotting into my hair.

His chin dipped. His mouth caught mine.

His lips were still cold from the ice cream but his mouth was *hot*, and he tasted like chocolate-dipped vanilla. He was so much taller than me that I had to stand on my tiptoes. A muscle in the arch of my left foot was cramping. I didn't care. I looped one arm around his neck for leverage and pressed my other hand flat to his chest, fingers splayed over his T-shirt. His heartbeat hammered against my palm. I had the most inappropriate urge to bust out laughing.

Somewhere behind us—what felt like miles off—the front door of the restaurant opened again and a burst of music spilled out onto the sidewalk. Footsteps plodded down the steps.

And then, with all the subtlety of an airhorn: "Yo!"

Bodie and I broke apart with a wet smack. For one long moment, we stared at each other in bemused shock. And then it hit me.

I'd kissed my source.

Bodie cleared his throat. "Hey, Ryan," he said, voice low and rough and deeply annoyed.

"I thought you guys got jumped or something!" Ryan said with a laugh. "Show's over. You missed the big finale. It was so good, yo. They did a fuckin' Beyoncé tribute. Olivia covered the bill, so we just got to Venmo her like twenty bucks each. Cool?"

"Yep. Sure. Good. After you," Bodie told me, with a rather formal sweep of his hand.

My sneaker caught the lip of the top step and I stumbled. Ryan snorted.

"No more sangria for you," he teased.

It had nothing to do with the sangria.

He kissed me. I kissed him. We kissed.

In the dark hallway between the dining rooms, just outside the door to the men's bathroom, the three of us had to pause to let a pair of women and a waiter carrying a steaming plate of fajitas pass each other. I knew Bodie was right behind me. Half of me wanted to turn and apologize for mauling him so hard his ice cream had become a casualty. The other half of me wanted to do it again. I tried to think about the feel of his lips against mine so I'd remember it right. I should've been handsier while I'd had the chance. I should've combed my fingers through his hair—my nails on his scalp would've felt nice to him. Had whatever I'd done with my hands felt nice to him? I wished I'd been paying more attention. I hated that I hadn't had the time to catalogue every little feeling, every little point of contact. I wanted to remember it.

I wanted to do it again.

But he was my source. This was a major conflict of interest.

Olivia watched me as I slid back onto the bench beside her. I cleared my throat and asked casually, "'Sup?"

The corner of her mouth twitched.

"Your lipstick is smudged, babe," she said.

I lunged for a napkin. When Bodie sank into his seat

across the table from me, our knees bumped. We apologized simultaneously.

Olivia beamed at us.

"Well, kiddos," she said, tucking her notebook under her arm. "It's almost eleven, and I've got a pure barre class at seven. I think we should head out."

I refused to meet Bodie's eyes.

I'd just broken rule number one of protecting your whistleblower.

—

The cool night air roared through the open windows of Fogarty's Tesla, tangling our hair in our faces and drowning out Olivia's voice as she shouted along to Ryan's '90s playlist.

The closer we got to campus, the tighter the knot in the pit of my stomach became. I didn't want to go back to reality. I wanted to sleep on the terra-cotta tiled floor of La Ventana and live off guacamole and sangria while drag queens sang for me. More than anything, I wanted to stand outside the restaurant with Bodie and pretend none of this existed—not Vaughn, not Josefina, not our school. None of it.

We dropped off Olivia first. When Bodie turned to Ryan and asked where he lived, I realized he was going to save me until last to drop off. He wanted to talk too. I wasn't sure whether I was relieved or disappointed when Ryan insisted that his place was farther, and that it'd make more sense for Bodie to drop me off first.

"I'm *hella* tired," Ryan exclaimed as we turned onto my street.

The second we stopped in front of my building, I climbed out through the stupid falcon-wing door and made a run for it.

Idiot, idiot, idiot.

This was my mantra as I darted up the front steps and onto the stoop, where I fumbled with my key. It was only after I'd shouldered open the front door of the building that I heard quick footsteps on the sidewalk behind me. I thought someone who lived in my building was jogging to catch the door, so I held it open behind me.

Bodie appeared on the stoop.

"Hey," he said, a bit breathless.

It would only dawn on me later that he was an athlete and had much better stamina than that. I stepped back, as if to get out of his way, and he slipped into the building along with me. The hall was dimly lit and smelled of Thai food. One of my neighbors was listening to John Mayer at a volume that John Mayer did not necessarily warrant, but other than that, it was just me and a heavy-breathing Bodie St. James. I don't think I should've found it so romantic.

When I spoke, my voice was small. "Did you need something, or . . ."

"I am," Bodie said, "so, *so* sorry."

I blinked. "What?"

"I don't know how to do this," Bodie blurted, one arm braced out as he held the door open behind us, letting the cool night air drift in. "I'm so, so bad at this stuff, Laurel. I like you. I'm sorry I kissed you, but I—" He huffed. "I'm sorry. I should've asked you first."

I heard Mehri's voice in my head. *Because he thinks you're pretty. He wants to get in your pants, Laurel.*

"Did you agree to give me the interview because you wanted to kiss me?" My voice was quiet and croaky and miserable.

Bodie reared back like I'd smacked him dead on the nose.

"No," he said. "It wasn't like that at all."

"Bodie, you're my *source*. It's my job to protect you, and your anonymity, and it's my job to"—I tossed my hands up helplessly—"to *not* kiss you. I wanted to, okay? Obviously, I wanted to, but I can't—"

Bodie's face split with a grin. "You did?"

I sighed. "Of course, that's what you got from that. Look, I do like you. But we can't do . . . this."

"Can we still be seen together?"

I took a deep breath and said, "I'll save you a seat on Tuesday."

He exhaled in a *whoosh*, the tension in his shoulders dissolving. He glanced down at my lips again, and I was sure I saw his fingers twitch against the front door he was still holding open, but he didn't move.

"Good night, Laurel," he whispered.

Bodie slipped back out into the night. The door swung shut behind him. I turned and jogged up the stairs. I wasn't even halfway up the flight before laughter bubbled up in my throat—wild, reckless laughter.

I could still taste his soft serve on my lips.

chapter 22

Hanna was slouched in bed, her face bathed in the multi-colored glow of her laptop screen, when I slipped into our darkened room. She sat upright and flicked on her bedside lamp. I braced myself against my desk to toe off my shoes.

"How'd your group project go?" she asked.

I paused, one shoe on and one shoe off. Where did I even begin? There was almost too much to cover. Ryan's horrible taste in music. Carla's set list and outfit changes. The food, the sangria, the way Bodie's hand cupped the back of my neck when he kissed me?

I kicked off my other shoe and perched on the end of Hanna's bed.

"Do you promise not to judge me?" I asked.

"You washed vomit out of my hair last weekend, Laurel.

My high horse is a miniature pony. Was drag karaoke fun? You guys got back later than I thought you would. Shit. Did St. James give you any trouble?"

"No." I let out a burst of laughter. "Well, yeah. He kissed me."

"He what?"

"Or I kissed him. Actually, I think it was mutual."

Hanna looked stunned. I laughed again and covered my face with my hands, half in disbelief. But when I dropped my hands, Hanna's expression didn't mirror my excitement. Instead, her face was pinched with something suspiciously like concern.

"What?" I asked.

"I really want to be your number one hype woman right now," Hanna said gently, "but . . . is this entirely *ethical*?"

"God no," I said with a scoff. "But—"

But I like him. It sounded insignificant when I put it that way. Immature. Like I was a middle schooler with a crush on a boy from science class or something, instead of a college-aged woman who'd mauled one of her most important sources. It wasn't ethical. It was shortsighted and selfish. If anyone found out that Bodie and I were running around Southern California kissing outside Mexican restaurants, it could leave cracks in the credibility of everything Ellison, Mehri, and I were trying to do.

"But?" Hanna repeated.

"But it won't happen again."

I couldn't tell whether she believed me or not.

Neither of us spoke again as I pulled on pajamas, washed my face, and brushed my teeth. Hanna decided she was done with her movie and tucked her laptop away. Once I'd crawled into bed, she flicked off her lamp, engulfing the room in darkness. The silence felt solemn and stretched out. I squirmed under my blankets and chewed on my bottom lip to keep myself from saying something stupid. Something about Bodie's smile, or his hands, or the ice-cream cone that'd been the first casualty of whatever had ignited between us.

I wished Hanna could ask me about it. I wished we could stay up late into the night breaking down every single detail. But I had a responsibility not to fuck this up.

For Josefina. For Ellison and Mehri. For Bodie. For myself.

So I rolled over and tried to sleep.

—

On Tuesday, in a turn of events that surprised absolutely no one who knew me, I was late to Human Sexuality. With the lightning-quick agony of ripping off a DIY waxing strip, I shoved open the first set of double doors.

It was something out of a stress-induced nightmare. Up on the stage, Nick went silent. An entire lecture hall of my peers twisted around in their seats to see what the interruption was. It was me. Wide-eyed, stone-faced, wearing light-wash jeans that may or may not have had five tiny smudges of Cheeto dust on the right thigh where I'd accidentally wiped my hand after Hanna and I had shared a nutritionally disastrous breakfast.

"Hey there," Nick called from the stage.

Oh god. He was doing this.

"Hi," I said, my voice suddenly very high-pitched.

"We're ten minutes into the lecture," Nick said, not looking remotely remorseful for the public humiliation he was subjecting me to. His hair wasn't in its usual ponytail today but the rest of his hipster aesthetic remained intact: grandpa glasses, *Star Wars* T-shirt, tweed blazer.

"Sorry," I said. At least, I *tried* to say it. Terror had frozen my vocal cords. I'm pretty sure I just mouthed the word.

Nick took a breath, shot me one last withering glare so the whole class knew he wouldn't tolerate being interrupted, and resumed the lecture. I briefly considered turning on my heel and leaving. It wasn't too late to drop a class. I could take the incomplete. Drop out of college entirely. Change my name. Become Carla's assistant and tour the drag circuit.

"Laurel," I thought I heard someone whisper.

Like a pair of magnets, my gaze snapped together with Bodie's. He was sitting in the third row from the back. My row. The seat on the aisle was occupied by his backpack. He'd saved it for me. I could've cried with relief, but I was a little too focused on not tripping over my own feet as I darted down the aisle. Bodie lifted his backpack half a second before I threw myself into the seat. I tugged on the swivel desk with a tad too much enthusiasm, and it snapped into place with a loud *thunk* that caused a few heads to turn again.

What specific brand of asshole called out his students in a one hundred–person lecture? Honestly. Four years of tuition at Garland was enough to buy a starter home in most states. You'd think Nick could respect that my being late to class came at a far greater cost to me than to him.

It wasn't until I leaned back in my seat and exhaled a shaky breath that I noticed the paper coffee cup that'd appeared on my desk. Across the side, scribbled in black marker, was BUDDY. (I guessed, statistically speaking, there had to be at least one barista in Garland, California, who didn't follow football.)

"Is this for me?" I whispered.

Bodie shrugged. "Figure you need it more than I do."

"Guess I owe you my firstborn now, huh?"

Bodie cleared his throat. I realized, belatedly, that this saying held significantly more sexual connotation when uttered while the dual projector screens up at the front of the room read *Unit Seven: Fertility, Pregnancy, and Childbirth.* I had a jarring flashback to Friday night, when our mouths had been on each other's, and promptly choked on my first sip of hot coffee.

"That paint party the Art House does is coming up, right?" Bodie said, guiding us into a new topic of conversation like a pro.

Fuck. I'd forgotten about Pollock. I needed to find my white shorts—the ones I'd picked up at Goodwill freshman year exclusively for the one paint party I attended annually—and make sure they still fit. I'd been hitting the tacos a little too hard this semester.

"Yeah, it's two weeks from Friday," I said in answer to Bodie's question. "I need to get my hands on a white T-shirt. I like your sweater, by the way."

I wasn't just trying to flatter him. Bodie looked nice in sweaters. But, predictably, the compliment made his cheeks go pink.

"Are you going to go?"

"Of course," I said. "Are—are you going? Because Hanna and I are throwing a pregame at ours, so you—you and Andre, could, like, walk over together?"

Bodie's smile made warmth bloom in my chest.

"I'd like that," he said.

"Cool," I said.

"Cool," Bodie parroted.

And then I took another gulp of coffee, because I really needed something to keep another dumb word from coming out of my mouth. I wasn't supposed to be inviting him to things. *Not ethical.*

Nick announced it was time for the first group presentation of the day. On the other side of the aisle, Andre and three significantly shorter girls stood from their seats and started down to the stage. The girls had index cards in hand. Andre carried a reusable Target tote he'd borrowed (stolen) from my collection.

"Do you know what Shepherd's presenting on?" Bodie whispered.

"Yeah," I replied absentmindedly. "They're doing—"

Oh god.

The first slide of a PowerPoint entitled *The History of Sex Toys* appeared across the screen. *Dildos. They're presenting on dildos.* I clutched Bodie's coffee cup in my hands and sank low in my seat, wondering if it was too late to pack up my things and take a nice five-point deduction from my already-abysmal attendance grade.

"Today," said one of Andre's group members, "we're going to be walking you through a brief history of sex toys."

Beside me, Bodie started bouncing his knee.

—

Purgatory ended with the final PowerPoint slide—a tastefully done black-and-white illustration of the world's first vibrator, originally used in a nineteenth century Paris hospital on *hysterical* women, whose wombs tended to wander about their bodies like lost Disneyland tourists searching for the entrance to Indiana Jones Adventure.

Just kidding. They were women with perfectly normal sexual frustrations, anxieties, and premenstrual symptoms.

Men just didn't know shit.

"We hope this is a very happy ending to the presentation," one of Andre's group members quipped boldly.

Giggles and chortles swept through the crowd.

I was pretty sure I hadn't taken a breath during the last half an hour.

Beside me, Bodie was still as a rock.

Another of the three girls in Andre's group grabbed the mic and held up a baseball hat full of shreds of paper.

"We wanted to thank everyone in this class who answered the survey we sent out," she said. "As a token of our appreciation, we put the email addresses of everyone who responded in this hat, and we're going to draw three lucky names to win some prizes!"

I was suddenly very relieved that I hadn't bothered taking that survey, despite the initial guilt I'd felt when Andre kept asking me about it, because it meant that my name wasn't even in the running.

The first prize was a tiny purple bullet vibrator.

They had to draw four different email addresses before a boy on the other side of the lecture hall—to the amusement of his friends—jogged down to claim his prize. He held it aloft like baby Simba over the animal kingdom.

His friends absolutely lost it.

The second prize was even worse—an enormous cheetah-print dildo, seemingly too large to be in any way practical. Despite the wave of laughter that rolled through the lecture hall, I saw people sink down in their chairs and fidget nervously.

A girl in the fourth row whooped with celebration when her email was read out.

The third and final raffle prize came in a hot-pink box.

"This," proclaimed one of Andre's group members, "is the Casanova V4."

She read the specs like she was auctioning off a luxury sports car. *Ten speeds. Waterproof silicone casing. Smooth ride.* I glanced at Bodie out of the corner of my eye. I wish I hadn't. I'd never seen him so red-faced.

"Aight, let's do it," Andre said, rubbing his hands together.

He pinched his eyes shut and reached into the hat. He pulled out a single slip of paper, unfolded it, and then looked up into the crowd. His eyes fell on me, and I knew, with striking clarity, that Andre was about to pull a bitch move.

"Lcates@garland.edu?" he called out.

He furrowed his eyebrows like he'd never heard this email address in his life, which I knew was bullshit, because he'd sent me several papers for a quick proofread over the years.

And now this. Betrayal.

Beside me, Bodie ducked his head. His shoulders shook with laughter. I slumped lower in my seat. I was *not* about to stand up and claim a vibrator in front of a lecture hall full of people. I'd had enough public humiliation for one day. Any more and I risked the complete dismantlement of my precarious self-confidence.

"Do we got an L. Cates here today?" Andre repeated.

He was holding back a smile. I was going to *throttle* him. My mind was so busy imagining all the ways I could get back at him, I didn't put up enough of a fight when Bodie reached out, suddenly, and caught my wrist.

"No, wait—"

Too late. He held my arm aloft, his grip unyielding even when I wriggled.

"She's here!" Bodie called.

Andre started up the aisle, his grin a mile wide.

People turned in their seats, craning their necks to see the girl who'd won *Cosmopolitan*'s top vibrator of the year.

"No, no, no," I chanted, still fighting to free my hand.

Andre arrived at our row and dropped to one knee, bestowing me with the boxed vibrator in a sweeping gesture.

"Enjoy," he told me, and had the nerve to wink.

People laughed. *He's not that funny*, I wanted to yell. But Andre was already jogging back down to the stage. I glared at the back of his fade and thought about chucking something at him.

I looked down at the box in my hands.

Across the side, in atrocious cursive, was *The Casanova V4. Ten speeds!* it proclaimed.

Somebody please end my suffering, I thought.

Bodie suppressed a snort. He'd leaned over to inspect the box in my hands. I lurched forward to shove it into my backpack, out of sight, and turned to glower at Bodie for his role in my well-orchestrated humiliation.

He smiled and held out his hand like he wanted me to shake it.

"Congratulations," he said. "I'm so happy for y—"

I bit back a smile, without much success.

"Eat shit, St. James," I grumbled.

Bodie laughed again.

His hand was still reached out toward me. I smacked it away with the back of mine, but he caught my fingers in his and held them, just for a moment, before he let my hand drop.

——

After class, I noticed I had a voice mail from Ellison Michaels. I'd missed her call by four minutes. The message she'd left was cursory and ominous, in true Ellison fashion: "Cates. Text me when you get this. There's someone in my office right now I think you want to meet."

Her name was Sarah.

She was twenty-six and a Garland University alumna. An economics major. Uselessly good at Ping-Pong, frustratingly bad at all forms of creative expression. Two dogs. A nine-month-old son and a wife at home watching him. Sarah lived in Michigan now, and she did not watch football. Not anymore.

Seven years ago she'd been an athletics department intern getting paid minimum wage to work at a charity event when Truman Vaughn had grabbed her ass. A few days later she'd submitted a tip to the *Daily*. She hadn't known what else to do. But nobody had answered her. And now she was sitting in Ellison Michaels's office, hands braced around a ceramic mug of chamomile tea, dark eyes tracing over the student events posters tacked up on the walls with a bittersweet blend of pride and nostalgia.

"You're Laurel," she said when I arrived, breathing heavy because I'd jogged from class.

"Yeah. Yeah, that's me."

I apologized for the delay. Sarah assured me she didn't mind.

"I was a little shaken when you emailed me," she told Mehri, steeling herself with a sip of tea. "I'm sorry I didn't come out here sooner. I was going to lie to my wife and say it was some kind of alumni thing, but—" She shrugged helplessly. "I had to tell her. I tell her everything."

Except for this. She'd held on to this for seven years. Kept it tucked away, so it wouldn't bother anyone she loved. So it wouldn't hurt them the way it hurt her.

"Thank you," Mehri told her. "Thank you so much."

Sarah nodded.

"I want to help," she said. "Whatever you need . . ."

"Is whatever you're comfortable giving," Mehri finished.

Sarah's face scrunched up. I plucked the tissue box off Ellison's file cabinet and passed it to her without a word.

"My memory isn't great," said Sarah, fingers shaking as she fumbled for a tissue with one hand so she could keep hold of her mug. "I don't know if I can get all the details right. I know—" She inhaled, and it caught in her chest, but she pushed on. "I know the event was on a Saturday, and I think it was March, but I—I can't remember who they were honoring—a water polo coach? I don't—"

Sarah's voice broke off with another tight inhale.

Mehri leaned forward so she was eye to eye with her.

"Sarah," she said, "nobody expects you to remember everything."

"But isn't that how this goes?" Sarah asked, breathing faster now. "They put you up on the stand and they ask where you were and when and why and what shade of lipstick you had on and what color shirt the guy was wearing and—and if you say I don't know then they—they—and it's not even a big deal. He just—he grabbed my ass! And maybe his fingers were—*I don't know*—wedged in—and maybe he ground himself against me, and I felt—" Sarah's face shuttered, so quickly I could've blinked and missed it. When she continued, I had the strangest sense that she was telling us exactly what she'd told herself for seven years: "But I feel like that's *nothing*. There are women out there who get *assaulted*, you know?"

"What he did *is* assault," Ellison said. "And if it's a big deal to you, it's a big deal. Period."

Sarah set her mug down on the desk so she could blow her nose properly.

"I thought nobody read the tips," she admitted after wiping the first nostril. "I thought I was just, I don't know"—she paused to tackle the other—"shouting into the void."

Ellison waited until Sarah had finished wiping her nose to say, "If you don't want to come forward publicly, you don't have to. But know you aren't alone. Not in any part of this."

Sarah looked from Ellison to Mehri to me and back again. Then she took a shaky breath and tossed her clump of used tissues in Ellison's trash can.

"Okay," she said. "Okay. Let's do it."

Ellison nodded.

"Sarah, if you're ready, Mehri can formally interview you right now. Cates, come with me. I need more caffeine if we're going to get this article done in the next five days."

—

Ellison Michaels had the keys, codes, and all required credentials to get us into the media center after hours. We'd decided, as a team of three, that putting our article in print meant the *Daily*'s faculty advisor would have a chance to catch it and warn Vaughn and everyone at his foundation.

At midnight on a Monday we went to the media center to post our article—detailing our anonymous whistleblower's evidence of embezzlement within the Vaughn Foundation, the Real Housewives' firsthand accounts of Vaughn's weeklong partying binge, and the testimony of Sarah. A face popped into my head—thundercloud eyes, a boyish smile, hair stubbornly rumpled. I hoped that when Bodie St. James woke up in the morning he would see just how important his words had been. How many people he'd helped.

"Ladies," Mehri said. "We're live."

I sent Hanna the link first. She texted back immediately.

I'm opening the Fireball come get drunk with me after u post it u journalistic powerhouse we r popping bottles tonight!!!

Then I sent the link to Josefina Rodriguez.

Remember, I captioned it, *you're not alone.*

chapter 23

I'd always been warned that Garland was a dry place, and that just one ember was enough to spark a wildfire capable of destroying everything in its path. You had to stomp them out quick if you wanted to stop the whole state from going up in flames.

"Laurel. *Laurel*. Answer your phone."

Hazily, I became aware of Hanna's pillow-muffled voice and the rumble of a phone vibrating on my bedside table. I slapped blindly at my nightstand until my fingers found the battered plastic of my phone case.

"Hello?" I croaked.

"Laurel," Mehri said, her voice small and pinched. "They killed the website."

I sat up and tried to scrub the sleep from my eyes. "What website?"

"The *Daily*'s. It's gone."

"Wait," I said, my brain still working at half speed. "Our article got taken down?"

"Laurel," she said lowly, "the whole *site* got taken down."

—

I was halfway across the quad in front of the student union when a middle-aged white guy in charcoal slacks and a neatly pressed button-down shirt stood from where he'd been perched on the ledge around the fountain and called my name.

"Excuse me, Miss Cates?"

I ducked my head and tried to pretend I hadn't heard him, but he was quick. Just before I made it to the doors of the student union, he launched himself in front of me, blocking my path with one outstretched arm. In his other hand was a cell phone. It took me a moment to realize why the angle he was holding it at looked so awkward. He was recording me.

"Sorry," I rasped, my voice betraying my panic at the intrusion. "I've really got to get to—"

"Adam Whittaker for Badger Sports," the man interrupted me. "I was wondering if I could ask you a few questions about the Vaughn profile."

Ellison had prepped me for this kind of thing. She'd given me some long statement packed with legal jargon and told me to recite it—verbatim—if anyone tried to ambush me with an interview.

What came out was, "Lawyer. I get a lawyer. It's the rule."

"This won't take long," Whittaker continued, unfazed by the fact that I sounded like a child playing a board game. "Did you or anyone at the *Daily* receive money from another university to sabotage Garland's team?"

"We didn't—" I began, then remembered I wasn't supposed to engage and huffed in annoyance. "If you'll excuse me, I really need to—"

I tried to sidestep Whittaker. He mirrored my movements, blocking the doors.

"Who made the executive call to weaponize the Me Too movement?" he asked. "Was it you, or your editor in chief?"

One of the glass double doors behind Whittaker flew open. Ellison Michaels appeared as if the fact he'd spoken her title was enough to summon her from thin air. Her platinum-blond hair was slicked back into a tight French braid, and her glare was cold as ice.

"This is private property," Ellison said, so quietly and calmly that a prickle of unease rolled down my spine. "If I see you harassing my writers again, I'm calling the police."

"And telling them what? That I'm *trespassing*?" Whittaker asked, eyes narrowing and the corners of his mouth twisting up in a self-satisfied smile. "The university offers public access to this campus between the hours of six a.m. and ten p.m. I'm not breaking any laws."

"I have the number for President Sterling's direct line," Ellison countered. "He has the authority to kick you out of here. You have five minutes before I make the call."

Whittaker's lips pressed into a thin, grim line.

Ellison looked at me and tipped her head, motioning for me to get inside. I scrambled around Whittaker and into the lobby of the student union. I heard the glass door thud shut behind me, and then Ellison was at my side, shepherding me past the curious looks of students who'd stopped to watch the confrontation and into the elevator. When those doors slid shut and she and I were alone, I went to tuck my hair behind my ears and realized my arms were shaking.

"Deep breath," Ellison instructed.

I didn't understand how she could be so unruffled, but then I noticed that she was moving without her usual strength and sureness. There was a hesitance to her steps, a slowness when she lifted her hand to press back a piece of hair that'd fallen in her face. As we marched across the media center floor together, students looked up from their computers and bean-bag chairs to watch us with shameless curiosity.

There were three cardboard boxes stacked outside Ellison's office door.

She waited until we were tucked inside, door closed, to say, "Owens has removed me from my post, effective tomorrow. He's giving me the day to pack up my things and write a statement congratulating my replacement."

"What?"

Ellison motioned to the chair across from her desk. I sank into it, swinging my backpack around and into my lap and hugging my arms around it.

"Why didn't you text me?" I asked, hating that I sounded clingy.

"I've been trying to chase down President Sterling all morning," Ellison explained. "He's not returning my calls, and his assistant won't tell me where he is or how to contact him. He's avoiding me."

She swept a shriveled flower that'd fallen from her potted orchid into the palm of her hand and deposited it gently in the trash can beside her desk. I watched her and saw traces of anger glinting in her eyes—a ferocious outrage that'd burned hot and bright but had, at some point between the time she'd found out and now, smoldered to ashes.

I couldn't say she looked defeated, because Ellison Michaels was never defeated. But she looked tired. She looked like she wanted to take off her battle armor and rest, just for a few minutes. But we didn't have that luxury.

"How did this happen?" I asked softly.

Ellison shook her head. "One of the women you quoted—the ones from the country club—came out and said you'd misquoted her and her friends. The others haven't said anything, but given that they're all Garland elite, I wouldn't be surprised if they've decided to step back. And the university is claiming Sarah was never employed by the athletics department, so her story isn't plausible. They can't disprove that she was a student, and they won't say if the event she described is something they ever held, but they're adamant they don't have any trace of her in the student employment records."

"How is that possible? Did she—" I cut myself off. I couldn't ask that. Wouldn't.

"Seven million dollars," Ellison said.

"What?"

"That's how much revenue football brings in for the university, after you factor in the cost of keeping the team up and running and in brand-new Nike jackets. It's far from the most lucrative program in the country, but Vaughn's grown it a lot in the last decade. Which is why his salary is in the ballpark of three million a year."

The university didn't want to sack him. Ticket sales might drop. Merchandise might sit on shelves. Investors and sponsors would start reconsidering their partnerships with the school's athletic program. Vaughn was just a man, but he'd become an icon for our school. Of course the university wouldn't dig deep for dirt. They'd probably been the ones to sweep it under the rug.

My anger was a riptide. It swallowed me whole. I wanted to take a baseball bat to the Leopold the Lion statue in the center of campus. I wanted to set Buchanan on fire and watch millions of dollars in university-owned property burn. I wanted to march into President Sterling's office and tell him that I was angry, and that I was not going to let him silence us.

"Ellison," I croaked. "I need—"

I dropped my backpack to the floor and replaced it on my lap with the trash can she handed me with a panicked expression. I stared down at the shriveled orchid and tried to keep the granola bar I'd had for breakfast where it belonged.

"What about Josefina?" I asked miserably, my voice echoing in the belly of her plastic trash can.

Ellison was quiet. When I lifted my head, she was watching me with startlingly gentle eyes.

"You're a good journalist, Cates," she said. "Owens will probably email you and Mehri later today to kick you off the *Daily*, but I want you to know we don't have to have an institution behind us to do important work."

Somehow what my brain caught on was "*kick you off* the

Daily." Like all great female journalists who'd sunk their teeth into a forbidden story about a wealthy and well-connected man behaving badly, we were being shot down. Reprimanded. Exiled.

I hung my head over the trash can and counted backward from one hundred.

—

I got to lecture ten minutes early, on the off chance Bodie was similarly anxious to see me and had already gotten there, but there was no sign of him. I headed straight for the third row from the back and put my backpack down in the seat to my right to reserve it for him.

The lecture hall filled. There was still no Bodie. When someone dropped into the chair to my left, I lifted my head with his name on my lips, but it was only Andre. I deflated.

"Um, hi to you too," Andre mumbled.

"Hi," I said. "Sorry. I'm just—sorry."

The doors swung open again. I spotted a Garland football T-shirt among the pack of students who trudged in, but it wasn't Bodie. It was Scott Quinton, the thick-necked offensive tackle. I sank back into my seat, simultaneously disappointed and relieved. This was *torture*. Halfheartedly, I watched Quinton lumber down the aisle to the spot where his teammates sat, their legs and arms sprawled and backpacks everywhere, like they'd rented the place.

"Laurel!"

I turned and saw Bodie standing in the doorway of the auditorium, hair stubbornly rumpled and headphones looped around his neck. He wore a sleeveless black Under Armour shirt and a pair of gray mesh shorts. His arms were beaded with sweat, his hair slicked back with it, and cheeks so flushed they were nearly purple.

He smiled at me. Just like that, the knot in my chest dissolved. I shoved my swivel desk back between the seats and leaned over to set my notebook on the floor. In my haste, I dropped a mechanical pencil; it rolled off into oblivion under the seats in front of me. Screw it. I'd order another pack of them online. I stood, leaving my backpack behind.

"What're you doing?" Andre asked.

"I need to talk to Bodie," I said. "I'll be right back."

The second I stepped out into the hall, Bodie said, "I'm sorry I didn't text you."

"Did you just go on a run?"

"Yeah. Just a quick one."

"Class is starting in, like, two minutes. You're going to sit through it all sweaty and gross?"

"I can't stay," he said. "I've got to go meet with Gordon."

My stomach gave a weird twist. "What about class?"

"Football's more important right now. I've got a whole team behind me, and I've been playing like shit. I'm letting them all down."

Frustratingly enough, I understood where he was coming from. Despite my extensive athletic failures, I knew what it was to be part of a team: the *Daily*. I'd prioritized the school paper over my own mental and physical health more than a few times. I'd skipped class to write articles before. How was Bodie skipping class to work out any different?

"Do you need a copy of the notes?" I offered, rather than

insisting on dragging him to Human Sexuality by the cord of his headphones. "Because I can send you mine."

"That'd be great, yeah. How are you holding up?"

So we were ready to talk about the article, then. Oh boy. I took a deep, bolstering breath and tried to plaster on a smile.

"I've been better," I admitted.

"I know this morning was really tough for you," Bodie said. "You know I'm not mad at you, right? I don't think you made all that stuff up. I know you wouldn't lie."

The relief I felt was the hug of a best friend, the smell of fresh tortillas, the sunshine on your face after you walked out of your last final. *I know you wouldn't lie.* It was the best thing he could've said.

"And, seriously," Bodie pressed on, "you're still the best journalist I know. It's not your fault that girl came to you and lied. You couldn't have known—"

"I'm sorry," I croaked, shaking my head. "What?"

Relief turned to ice in my veins.

Please don't do this, I thought. *Please.*

"It's not your fault that girl sent in a fake tip," Bodie repeated.

"There's nothing wrong with Sarah's tip. There's nothing wrong with any of our tips."

Bodie's eyebrows pinched. His smile looked uneasy now.

"She never worked for the athletics department," he told me, repeating what'd been in Sterling's statement.

I ripped my hand out of his like he'd electrocuted me.

"And you think the school's telling the truth?" I demanded. "Garland makes *millions* off Vaughn. They'd want him back as soon as they can, don't you think?"

"Sterling wouldn't *lie*, though," Bodie insisted. "The school could get in huge trouble for that kind of thing. He wouldn't risk jail time."

"Unless he knows he can get away with it."

Bodie shook his head in disbelief. It stung like lime juice on a paper cut.

"Vaughn's a dick to you, you know," I added bitterly.

Bodie winced. "He's my *coach*, not my dad. He's supposed to be tough on his players. It's an entirely different relationship."

"That doesn't excuse the way he treats you."

"You don't *know* how he treats me," Bodie shot back in a tone that was snappy, for him. "How many times have you actually spoken to the guy? You've seen the absolute worst in him, and I get that, okay? But you didn't see him drive me to the airport at two in the morning so I could fly home when my dad had a stroke, and you don't see him helping me schedule my classes and find tutors—"

"Of course he's going to help you with your grades! That's not for you. That's for *him*. He needs a quarterback."

"He's important to me, and I'm important to him."

"You're an *investment* for him."

"And what am I to *you*?" Bodie demanded. "You realize that the *Daily* is getting a ton of clout for this, right? Every single person involved gets to put *I helped with the Vaughn article* on their résumé. You're all going to get jobs wherever the fuck you want them. How many times have you quoted me now? How am I not an investment to you too?"

It was a blow I hadn't anticipated. I'd never once considered Bodie St. James might think that I was using him, but, in an instant, I could see it the way he did. Because he didn't know that I cared about him. That I really, *really* cared him— the kind of care that made a nest in my brain and haunted my thoughts while I was in lecture or driving to the grocery store with Hanna or caddying for retired couples or shampooing my hair.

I cared about him so hopelessly it *hurt*. And he thought the worst of me.

"You caught me," I deadpanned. "It was all about my *résumé*. Definitely not about the girls and what they went through. Who gives a shit, right? I just *really* wanted people to throw coffee on me and—"

Key my car. I almost said it. But the humiliation was so fresh it made my eyes wet. I tried to blink them back, because I refused to let Bodie think I was playing the tears card, but it was too late.

Bodie's face went slack. "Laurel—"

"Don't you *dare*," I interrupted with a jab of my finger in the center of his sweat-soaked chest, "try to make me feel *guilty*. Your coach is a horrible human being. That's *not* my fault. It's his. And yours, for not picking up on all the signs. People who think horrible things and say those horrible things also *do* horrible things. It's not fucking rocket science."

Bodie scrubbed a hand over his eyes.

"How would you feel if—if *Hanna* was accused of doing something awful?" he asked, searching for more level ground to have this conversation on. "Wouldn't you defend her?"

"Well, first off, that would never even happen," I said, sniffling despite myself. "Because Hanna treats everyone on the planet the same way she treats her friends. But if somebody accused her of something *this* awful, I definitely wouldn't jump on TV two days later to tell the world the people who exposed her were full of shit."

Bodie's jaw ticked as he ground his teeth.

I turned on my heel.

"Laurel," he called after me.

I stepped into the elevator and smacked the button to close the doors. Bodie stepped forward like he might come after me.

"Don't," I snapped.

The doors shut.

I wished I hadn't left class. I wished I'd known, at La Ventana, that this was all going to happen—that the university would claim there was no proof a man who was situated to bring in millions of dollars of revenue for the athletics program had done anything to warrant his removal. If I'd known on Thursday, I would've done things differently.

I would've kissed Bodie a little bit longer.

I shouldn't have kissed him at all.

chapter 24

On Friday morning—approximately twenty-four hours before the first tee time for the Garland Country Club's charity golf tournament—Rebecca sent me in search of a missing box of fake flowers that she thought were somewhere in the windowless storage rooms in the basement of the clubhouse. I spent the first hour of my shift alone, covered in dust, with a framed and autographed photo of decorated Olympic swimmer Ryan Lochte watching over me as I riffled through boxes and giant plastic storage tubs.

It was a relief when I located the flowers just in time to head upstairs and watch kickoff. Garland had an away game against Arizona State, who'd been struggling harder than we had this season but would probably still kick our collective ass.

I found PJ unloading fresh bottles of alcohol onto the

shelves behind the bar. The retired population of Garland, California, consumed an absurd amount of top-shelf tequila—mainly due to the fact that the Real Housewives of Garland were obsessed with post-tennis frozen margs.

"Yo," I greeted her, sounding a bit too much like Ryan (my group member, not the Olympian) for my liking. "How's it going?"

"Hi," PJ croaked. "I'm thriving."

"Yikes. What's wrong with your voice?"

PJ tried—and failed—to suppress a hacking cough. "It's nothing. My throat's a little sore. I think I'm just dehydrated." I wasn't sure if this meant she was hungover or getting sick. For both our sakes, I hoped it was the former—working at the club when PJ wasn't there was like cannonballing into a swimming pool without any water. In other words: not even a little bit enjoyable. I couldn't make it through this weekend without her.

"Morning, ladies!"

Speaking of unbearable, Rebecca bustled into the bar with a smile on her face. She wore her long, dark hair in twin French braids and had a white streak of sunscreen across one cheek. She never wore makeup, since she considered it *false advertising*—a fact she brought up every time someone made a remark about how strong PJ's eyelash game was.

I'd never had the balls to ask Rebecca who, exactly, she thought she was selling herself to. *False advertising.* Fuck off. Women weren't Big Macs. Just because I looked better on Instagram than I did during Writing 301 on a Monday morning didn't mean I was any less delicious.

"I found the flowers," I announced.

"Oh. You can put them in the back room. I think we have enough for now."

"Son of a bitch," I muttered under my breath.

"Did you hear the news?" Rebecca asked, pushing her Ray-Bans onto the top of her head. "I'm sure you've heard, Laurel. I guess all those tips were fake after all. What a relief, right?"

No. It was not.

"I *knew* they'd clear Vaughn," Rebecca continued. "I *knew* he was being scapegoated."

I was good at biting my tongue. Every once in a while my anger (or a few too many alcoholic beverages) led to a slipup—like the time I'd told Bodie St. James to eat shit. And the time I'd called him a coward. And a dumbass, *en Español*. But, for the most part, I prided myself on knowing when something wasn't worth my harshest words. So I kept my mouth shut.

But PJ, ever a real one, combed her fingers through her hair and said, in her best impersonation of the airhead former pageant girl Rebecca thought she was, "Don't you think it's suspicious that they never passed on that Title IX claim the way they were supposed to?"

Rebecca's eyes flashed but she shrugged it off. "Doesn't matter, does it? The girl's a liar."

"Oh look!" PJ cried. "The game's starting."

She grabbed the remote and turned the volume up so loud that Rebecca had no choice but to abandon the conversation.

—

"Well, fuck me," PJ said two and a half hours later, a wry smile tugging at her lips as she gazed up at the TV screen mounted over the bar. "We're actually going to win one."

Garland was up by fourteen points in the third quarter. I wish I could say I was enjoying our first real triumph since the first game of the season, but it was hard to see any silver lining when Vaughn's face kept popping up on screen. I hated his face. His empty, glaring eyes. His wicked-witch nose. His graying stubble, his baseball-cap tan and pale half-moon of a forehead that poked out whenever he tried to adjust his headset. But worse than his face was the fact that the commentators hadn't said a word about the *Daily* or our article.

It was like our article had never happened—like nobody gave a shit that the man on the field had groped a student, siphoned off charity funds, and said ragingly sexist things. All they cared about was the game he was going to win for them.

Bodie, for his part, was the driving force of our success. Four touchdowns, one two-point conversion, so many passing yards that I'd stopped being impressed when they read off the count. It was the best game Garland had managed in months. And, like, good for him. So glad one of us had escaped this whole debacle unscathed. I totally wasn't bitter and absolutely did not want to angry vomit having to watch Bodie conquer the field like some kind of warrior of old.

And then, less than a minute into the fourth quarter, Bodie had a little hiccup.

After the snap, chaos. Both tackles—the guys in charge of protecting Bodie's blind side—seemed to disappear, taking the defense with them. Bodie faked left and took off right. At the very same moment, the opposition's broadest and heaviest linebacker appeared in a gap left by the scattered offensive line, charging like a bull aiming to skewer a matador on its horns.

It was a brutal hit. A head-on collision with a semitruck hit. But for the split second after Bodie was knocked back, it felt *good*. I wanted him to hurt the way I hurt. Selfishly, I thought it was something that could be balanced out. Like a linebacker to the chest for not believing in me, for not standing by me, was a fair trade-off.

But after that initial wave of bitter hurt passed, my stomach knotted tight with guilt. When Bodie sat up, there was blood trickling out of his nose. It was already swelling— broken, probably. His helmet had been knocked clean off.

It was a small relief to see him get to his feet and jog off the field, instead of being loaded onto a stretcher like I'd briefly worried he might be, but his head was down, his sweat-soaked bangs hanging over his forehead and casting his face in shadow. We won the game by twenty-one points. I didn't celebrate.

———

On Saturday morning I texted PJ in an attempt to mooch a ride to Rebecca's charity golf tournament, but her sore throat had turned into a full-blown case of the flu, which meant that—not for lack of trying—she was unable to get out of bed. The bus would've taken hours, so I was left with no alternative: I walked to the parking garage across the street from the Palazzo, where she was still hidden, climbed three flights of stairs, and got into my vandalized car.

I told myself I'd be all right. I would get through today. If

I swung around the side of the clubhouse and parked in the very back corner of the employee lot, under that awful tree that perspired sap, then nobody would even see me.

It was a solid plan. And it totally went to shit when, on the freeway, I glanced down at my dashboard and realized my engine was running on fumes.

"Fuck, fuck, fuck," I chanted as I took the next exit and pulled into the first gas station I could find. "Fuck"—I climbed out of the car—"fuck"—I jammed my card into the machine—"fuck!"

I only had the patience for half a tank. Rebecca was going to have my head on a gold platter.

It was a full ten minutes into my shift when I pulled up to the clubhouse. The parking lot was packed. As I maneuvered into the corner-most spot under the sappy tree (a tricky feat, considering Rebecca had parked her black Lexus in the adjacent spot with its wheel halfway over the white line) my phone buzzed twice in my cup holder. I cut my engine, ripped my phone off the charging cord, and found a pair of texts from my boss.

where are you?

laurel if your sick get someone to cover for you. their are already tons of people here ok today is very important

I uttered my twenty-seventh *fuck* of the morning, pocketed my car keys, and booked it to the workers' entrance by the kitchen, where the catering staff was wheeling carts of supplies into the clubhouse. I was all of two steps into the building when Rebecca materialized before me like a polo shirt–clad poltergeist. Her hair was slicked back into a tight ponytail and she had mascara on. I'd never seen her in mascara.

"Laurel," she said, followed by a phrase I never thought I'd hear come out of her mouth: "Thank *god* you're here."

"What happened?"

"PJ was going to be my cart girl for the back nine today but she's got allergies or something—"

"She has the *flu*."

"—so I need you to step up."

The cart girls always made more in tips in an hour than I made in a whole weekend of work. PJ was good at the job, since golfers preferred being served drinks out on the course by girls who laughed at their jokes and twirled their hair and made a mean cocktail. But I didn't have the patience for it. And, also: "I'm not twenty-one. All I can serve is beer."

Rebecca waved me off. "We have enough beer to fill the swimming pool. Come on."

I followed her through the bar and into the lobby. The clubhouse looked vaguely like the set of a Real Housewives reunion, with its ostentatious flower arrangements and hors d'oeuvre platters on crisp white tablecloths. Through open double doors, the main ballroom was set up for the evening's silent auction. Some of the reps and sponsors from the participating charities were snacking away, mimosas in hand and conversations loud and boisterous.

"Now, before you get out there," Rebecca said abruptly, "we need to have a quick chat about professionalism."

I jerked to a stop in the middle of the lobby. Rebecca didn't need to say more. Through the floor-to-ceiling windows overlooking the course, I could see a pair of men on the practice putting green beside the first tee, golf bags propped up on the cart path and a pair of caddies hovering on standby.

One of the men was President Sterling, Garland University's long-standing head of school. The other man had his back to me, but it didn't matter. I recognized him anyway.

"Truman Vaughn is here to represent the foundation," Rebecca said.

"I'm not—I can't—" I spluttered.

"I know," she interrupted, huffing in impatience. "I'm not asking you to apologize to him. I don't want you anywhere *near* him. But we've got two hundred people here, half my staff is out sick, and I'm out of options. If Vaughn asks you to serve him something, do it with a smile, okay?"

I wanted to put my foot down. I wanted to tell her I probably had the flu, too, and that I should really go home and get back in bed before I smeared my germs all over these rich people. But if Rebecca thought for a second that I was going to pass up the chance to look Truman Vaughn in the eye and make him squirm, she was a moron.

"Okay," I said, doing my best impression of PJ's pageant smile. "Whatever you need."

The drink carts were, in essence, regular golf carts that were weighed down by approximately a thousand cans of beer and one heaping spoonful of misogyny. Normally the cart girls wore skintight tops and little tennis skirts ("The shorter the hem," PJ had once informed me, "the better the tips.") but I'd worn my usual hideous khaki Bermuda shorts and shapeless polyester uniform polo, in which my own parents probably could've mistaken me for a pudgy twelve-year-old boy. Didn't matter. People were here for a charity tournament—the social pressure to tip me would more than make up for the lack of eye candy.

When I pulled the drink cart around to the front of the clubhouse, Vaughn had disappeared, but James Sterling, the president of Garland University and one of the most successful private fundraisers in California, stood on the practice green with a putter in one hand and an honest-to-god cigar in the other, like some kind of mob boss. There was a no-smoking rule at the club, but clearly Rebecca wasn't enforcing it today.

Beside him stood Jessica Kaufman and Diana Cabrera—two of the Real Housewives.

I stomped on the brake. The drink cart lurched to a stop, wheels creaking.

Sterling and the two women turned abruptly. Jessica stared at me, eyes vacant of any and all recognition, before turning back to Sterling and picking up whatever conversation I'd interrupted. Diana, at least, had the decency to look nervous as I hopped out of the cart.

"Ms. Cabrera?" I called. Then, in Spanish: "Can I talk to you for a second?"

"Good morning, Laurel," she replied in English. Her smile was toothy and bright, but she was wringing the grip of her putter like it owed her money. "You wouldn't happen to have a frozen marg machine in that cart of yours?"

I stopped at the edge of the putting green. "You read our article."

Her smile dropped. "I did, yes."

"And you've heard the university's rebuttal?"

Diana exhaled and cast a glance over her shoulder at Jessica.

"Which one of you went back on what you said to me?" I asked.

"Laurel, this whole thing is a lot more complicated than we realized—"

"You said he was falling over drunk," I said, trying and failing to keep my voice low enough that it wouldn't carry across the green. "You said he was hammered, and that he invited you onto his boat. Right? All four of you confirmed that. *Twice.* So either you guys have a *seriously* distorted sense of sarcasm that I can't read or you got scared."

Diana met my eyes.

"Jessica called the media," she murmured. "The twins and I haven't said anything."

I nodded. "Are you going to?"

"We stand by what we told you, Laurel—"

"I mean, are you going to speak up?" I asked. "Are you going to let people know I quoted you correctly?"

Diana pressed her lips shut, and I had my answer. I wanted to call her one of the words my cousins had taught me—something wicked. Something dirty. Something that would convey just how little I thought of her right now.

Instead I asked, "Can I get you anything to drink, ma'am?"

Diana had the grace to wince. "No, thank you."

I climbed back in my cart and floored it to the eighteenth hole.

—

I had none of the grace and none of the patience of a good cart girl. Twice, I grabbed the wrong brand of beer and handed it over with the unjustified confidence of a blissful idiot. Once, on a particularly narrow stretch of the cart path by the sixteenth fairway, I nearly took off the front bumper of my cart on a rocky outcropping. I was a hot mess. This became a far more literal self-reflection as the morning sun climbed higher in the sky. The back of my hideous polyester uniform polo soaked through with sweat. My cheeks were hot as frying pans to the touch. A single drop of perspiration rolled from my underarm to my elbow, unimpeded, and I shivered with my full body.

And if feeling like the human equivalent of an enchilada (steaming hot and floppy) wasn't bad enough, I pulled up to the shady patch of the course between the tenth and eleventh holes to find three men on foot coming down the fairway toward the putting green, a caddy in a cart trailing behind them.

Truman Vaughn and James Sterling walked side by side, heads down as they spoke.

Behind them, lurking like a shadow, was a tall, broad-shouldered boy with a green baseball hat pulled low over his eyes. My heart hiccupped at the sight of him. *Bodie.* His nose was still swollen and dark bruises bloomed under his eyes, spreading out from the bridge of his nose like moth's wings. He looked miserable. He looked beautiful. He looked, inexplicably, like Troy Bolton about to launch into an angsty musical number across the fairway.

Neither Vaughn nor Sterling noticed the arrival of a sweaty drink-cart girl, but from across the rolling grass, Bodie's eyes locked on me and the toe of his shoe caught a clump of grass. He stumbled forward a step.

"I'm playing like shit," Sterling said with a barking laugh. "You know what, I'll write a check out to the foundation for twenty grand just to apologize for singlehandedly dragging down our team score."

"Don't worry about it. We've got our secret weapon," Vaughn said, thumping a hand on Bodie's shoulder and jostling him so hard he winced. "Look at the size of this kid! He can hit a driver better than some of the pros."

I was so mad I didn't know what to do with myself. Mad at Vaughn for being so rough with a boy whose broken nose he was responsible for. Mad at Bodie for existing. Mad at myself for being so relieved to see him alive and well after last weekend's game that I *almost* forgave the fact that he'd come to the country club with the very man I'd warned him he should steer clear of.

Bodie was first up to putt. It was an easy enough shot, since his ball was only a few yards from the hole—a quick swing of his club, a round of hearty applause from the others in his party, and a humble tip of his baseball cap.

"I'm going to grab some water," he announced.

He started toward my drink cart. I kept my hands tight on the steering wheel, refusing to fuss with my hair.

"Hey," he said gently. Uncertainly. Something about the broken nose made him look like a brutal mythological warrior or a cologne model. I hated it. "I didn't know you worked here. It's really good to see you, Laur—"

"Bottled water's three bucks."

Bodie winced but fished his wallet out of his back pocket anyway.

I averted my eyes from his hands—his hands that'd looked so beautiful wrapped around a Fosters Freeze cone and had been so warm against the back of my neck—and took some consolation in the knowledge that Truman Vaughn was perhaps the worst golfer I'd ever witnessed, and I'd once watched an elderly club member send her putter flying into the man-made pond on the second hole.

"Goddamn it," he shouted as his ball skated past the hole and over the lip of a sand trap.

Vaughn turned, saw that I was closer to his cart than their caddy, and snapped his fingers to get my attention.

"Get me my chipping wedge," he said. It wasn't a request, nor a question. It was a demand. "Actually, you know what, just bring the whole damn bag."

I wasn't sure what was worse: that he thought all staff should be at his beck and call, regardless of our job titles and responsibilities, or that he didn't recognize me.

I slipped out of the drink cart, shouldered my way around Bodie, and marched over to their abandoned cart. Vaughn's bag was enormous and dark green, with the Garland school crest on one side and the Titleist logo on the other. It pained me to think that this hideous display of school pride had probably cost him more than I made in a week of work. I hooked my hand under the strap and tried to lift it with all the strength of one biceps.

Bodie appeared at my side. I braced one foot on the back bumper for leverage and hauled Vaughn's bag up and over the barrier. The bottom end of it hit the pavement with a thunderous clanking of clubs.

"You got it?" Bodie asked.

"Yep," I grunted. "Keep walking."

But Bodie was, well, Bodie. "Here, let me help."

He didn't even give me a chance to wield the attitude.

Before I could manage a single word of protest, he'd slung the strap of Vaughn's Titleist bag over his shoulder.

"I can carry it," I snapped.

"I know you can," Bodie said, meeting my eyes. "I just want to help."

"Shouldn't you be resting or something? Isn't your head fucked up?"

"That's an understatement," he muttered under his breath.

Vaughn's eyes narrowed a fraction when he saw Bodie was the one who'd brought over his bag, but he didn't comment on it. He took three mediocre practice swings before attempting to chip his ball out. It ricocheted off the lip of the grass and tumbled back into almost exactly the same position it'd started. It took Herculean effort not to scoff. Bodie seemed to notice. He jogged back to the drink cart and ducked his head, as if to adjust his baseball hat.

"Laurel, can we—"

"I'm not talking to you with them around," I snapped, tipping my chin discreetly at his head coach, who was cursing under his breath as he lined up his second shot out of the bunker. It was a solid excuse. Much better than *I'm not talking to you because if I do I'm probably going to cry about your stupid broken nose again.*

Bodie handed me three one-dollar bills. I reached into the cooler strapped to the passenger's seat and dug out a bottle of water so cold it was clouded and speckled with condensation. I shoved it at him, then shook out the front of my shirt, trying to dry up the river of sweat between my boobs. What I really wanted was to slip away unnoticed to the women's bathroom and blot my armpits with paper towels. But I wasn't going to look Bodie in the eyes and tell him that. I peeled my hair off the back of my neck and bunched it up in one hand, longing for PJ and her infinite supply of hair ties.

I let out an embarrassing squeak when Bodie lifted his bottle of water and pressed it to the back of my bared neck. My shoulders pinched up to my ears against the cold, and then I slumped over the steering wheel, sighing in relief against my will.

"Too cold?" Bodie asked.

"No, s'perfect."

It dawned on me after several long, euphorically cooling seconds that, should Vaughn look over, he'd see his beloved quarterback attending to the girl who'd done everything to try to take him down. I reached back, fumbling for hold of the bottle. If I happened to grab Bodie's wrist first, and then trace my fingers over his knuckles, it was entirely accidental.

"I got it," I told him.

"I don't mind," he said. Then, more quietly: "Look, ESPN's doing a series of player interviews with their top ten collegiate prospects. I'm here because Vaughn said he'd pull some strings if I came out and participated in the charity thing."

I scoffed out a laugh and rubbed hard at the back of my neck.

Unbelievable. He'd chosen landing a TV interview over being a decent human being.

"How generous of him," I drawled bitterly. "And good for you—"

"Do you remember what you said to me right after the

article came out?" Bodie interrupted, lightning in his thunder-cloud eyes. "That day I sat next to you in class and asked you why you wrote it. Do you remember?"

"Not—not verbatim. Why? What—"

"You told me you had to do the right thing."

Bodie was half blocking me and the drink cart shaded my face, but I could've sworn Truman Vaughn was staring straight across the putting green at me. My spine prickled with nerves.

"Can you just make your point?" I asked.

"My point," Bodie said, "is that I believe you."

A hot breeze whistled through the trees along the cart path and out over the fairway, lifting strands of my hair and rippling the thin fabric of Bodie's shirt. I stared hard at him—at his open, honest face—and felt the simmering anger in the pit of my stomach come to a rolling boil.

"You don't get to have me *and* Vaughn," I snapped. "It's one or the other. Staying out of things and not picking sides means you're just standing out of the way and letting the big guy stomp all over the little guy. If people like you"—I jabbed a finger into his sternum—"don't *pick a side*, then what you're really doing is siding with the big guy."

"I don't want to be a pawn," Bodie said.

I winced. "When I quoted you, it—you're not an *investment* to me."

He shook his head. "I shouldn't have said that. It was selfish of me. You're a journalist. You weren't trying to get information out of me so you could fuck me over. You were trying to figure out the facts because it was the right thing to do. I know that. And you were right."

I stared up at him. At his angular, boyish face and thundercloud eyes and that big, charming freckle on his right cheek and his bruised, swollen nose.

"So you think he's guilty?"

I had to ask. Brutal as the question was, I needed the answer.

I could tell, from the agony in Bodie's eyes, that he did. He knew Vaughn had created a fake consulting firm, and he knew Vaughn had said enough sexist bullshit in the locker room that fondling the ass of a student worker wasn't entirely out of left field for his character.

"I choose you," Bodie said. "I choose the *Daily*."

When I spoke again, my voice was low and my eyes were wet.

"Don't say that if you don't mean it, Bodie. And don't say that if you're just going to back down again when shit gets ugly. Because it's not just sexist jokes in the locker room, and it's not just moving money around for tax breaks. It's grabbing the ass of a nineteen-year-old girl who was serving him at a school event." My breath caught in my chest. "It's— fuck, Bodie. It's luring drunk girls onto his boat to have sex with them while they can't consent and telling everyone it was a charity trip. So—so *don't* say you're on my side if you don't mean it."

I'd meant to tell Bodie about Josefina somewhere private, where we could talk things out and he could process things at his own pace. But there was no privacy here—just wide, open expanses of green. There was nowhere for Bodie to hide. I saw everything written across his face as he registered what I'd said, connected the dots, and came to the conclusion.

"Wait," he rasped.

Then he pressed his lips shut, turned his back on me abruptly, walked forward three steps, and bent over at the waist to heave up his breakfast onto the grass.

"Fuck," I said, hopping out of the cart. "I didn't mean to tell you like this. Do you need a towel? Some water? I won't charge you, obviously—"

Bodie waved me off.

"I just—I need a minute," he croaked.

"Bodie!" Vaughn called. He and Sterling were coming across the green toward us, startled and clearly dismayed to find the strongest link in their team doubled over and tinted green in the face.

"I'm fine," Bodie said, standing to his full height and shuffling to one side in a way I belatedly realized was meant to conceal me.

But it was too late. Truman Vaughn had already seen me, and those hawkish eyes had narrowed.

"Laurel Cates."

—

Whatever cooling effects Bodie's bottle of water had provided were grossly overshadowed by the shot of ice that rolled down my spine when I found Rebecca waiting on the back steps of the clubhouse, her expression eerily blank. She came down to meet me as I pulled the cart up.

"Laurel, can we chat for a second?"

I left the cart keys in the ignition and followed her into the lobby, where we were alone except for the potted ferns rustling in the air conditioning. The midafternoon sun poured in through the glass doors, bouncing off the freshly waxed tile floor and blinding me.

"What's up?" I croaked, dusting off my khaki shorts.

Rebecca watched bits of grass land on her impeccably clean floors for a moment before she cleared her throat. "Actually, let's do this outside."

My stomach twisted with unease as we slipped through the glass doors together. The front steps of the clubhouse were shaded but the hot breeze was suffocating.

"We've had a client complain about you, Laurel."

"Who complained?" I asked, even though I knew the answer.

"That's confidential information. But there was a complaint, and it was quite serious. I don't want any troublemakers on my staff—"

Once, when I was fifteen and my dad was first teaching me how to drive, I'd lost control of the wheel just before a sharp turn. We'd been in an empty parking lot and I'd been going about five miles an hour, but in that split second of untrained panic, my body had clammed up and my foot had come down on the gas pedal instead of the brake.

I quit, I thought.

We'd hit the curb so hard my dad had shouted.

I quit, I quit, I quit.

Why wasn't my mouth opening?

"—so I'm going to have to ask you to leave."

My overheated brain was lagging. It was the only explanation for how long it took me to open my mouth and respond.

"And come back next weekend?"

I wasn't delusional. I'd just never been fired before. I wasn't exactly a shining example of unwavering work ethic, but I'd never made any major mistakes. I'd always straddled the line between model employee and the co-worker you complained about in the break room every day. I'd always been comfortably in the middle. But that didn't matter, because Rebecca was the kind of woman who didn't like other women. Not ones who wore makeup. Not ones who spoke languages other than English. Certainly not ones who dared to speak out against men. Somewhere along the way, someone had told Rebecca that only one kind of woman was a good woman, and she'd believed it.

"I'm sorry, Laurel," she said.

But she wasn't. I saw straight through her.

Rebecca had made the decision to get rid of me a long time ago. Maybe the day the article had broken, maybe the day she'd overheard me speaking Spanish with the groundskeepers. Today had been the perfect storm she'd been waiting for—PJ, my biggest ally, was out sick, and Truman Vaughn, my worst adversary, was there to serve as witness.

The fatigue was gone. In its place came the flood of fury.

My hands shook as I tore across the parking lot. I was so desperate to get the hell out of there I almost forgot to give my car the extra two seconds she needed to switch her locks off.

When I tugged the driver's-side door shut, I made sure to let it slam.

I imagined myself revving my engine, or rolling down the windows and turning the radio to a Spanish music station and just *blasting* it. I thought about flipping her off too. Maybe with both hands. Driver safety be damned, I could go out with my middle fingers in the air and my mouth shaping the words *fuck you.*

But when I drove around to the front of the clubhouse, Rebecca was gone.

In her place stood Bodie.

He was looking for me. I could tell because he had my half-empty water bottle in one hand, the other shielding his eyes from the sun as he peered across the parking lot. He turned when he heard my engine. I'd never wanted to be invisible in the literal sense as much as I did in that moment. And I couldn't stop. If I stopped, I'd break. So the last thing I saw before I floored it out of the Garland Country Club parking lot was Bodie St. James in my rearview mirror. Between the shadowy bruises under his eyes and the horror-stricken expression, he looked like a Halloween lawn decoration. His face haunted me the whole way home.

chapter 25

Since my pride had already been smashed to pieces, I figured there was no use hiding my car in the garage across the street from the Palazzo anymore. I drove straight home and parked in our building's lot. Between the blast of my car's air conditioning and the shock of my confrontation with Rebecca, I felt cold and shivery. I dug my emergency cardigan out of my trunk, shaking sand off it and trying to remember when I'd last been to a beach.

I found Hanna sitting cross-legged on the kitchen floor, hunched over a large pad of newsprint and wielding a stick of conte charcoal with violent passion. She sat upright when she heard me come in and drop my bag to the floor.

"Hey," she greeted me. "How was the tournament? I thought that was supposed to go all afternoon."

I hummed noncommittally, because I didn't trust myself to tell her I'd been fired without completely dissolving into tears.

Then I asked, "What're you drawing?"

"Nike of Samothrace," Hanna said, pushing a chunk of loose hair out of her eyes and smudging her forehead with charcoal in the process. "We've been practicing using sculpture as reference."

I reached out and buffed the charcoal off her forehead with the sleeve of my cardigan.

"Sounds fancy."

"It's the opposite, actually," she said. "The fine arts budget got cut again. We can't afford any more live models this semester."

I wish I could say I was surprised Garland University was prioritizing their athletics department and STEM majors over the arts, but which universities in the United States weren't? Hanna's parents loved her art. They did. But they were also terrified that, after graduation, she'd face the same uphill battle they'd faced after moving to the US—that she'd constantly feel like she was climbing upstream on a recently soaped Slip 'N Slide to pay her rent, put food on her table, and earn respect.

Once, very late at night and after a little bit of beer, Hanna had asked me if I thought she should transfer into a more *useful* major. I hadn't known what to say. Because it wasn't that having a fine arts degree was a kiss of socioeconomic death—last summer, Andre had done a graphic design internship at a high-profile marketing firm in Huntington Beach. It'd been unpaid, but his parents had covered the cost of an apartment and all his public transportation for two and a half months. I didn't want to ask how much that bill had been. I doubted Andre even knew. Maybe he didn't even think about it.

But Hanna and I did. We always did. Art wasn't the problem—it was money. Always, always money.

"I got fired."

The words spurted out and hung there, suspended, for a moment.

Hanna blinked in shock. "You what?"

"Rebecca fired me. I'm fired."

I felt like a broken vase a guilty child had patched together with Elmer's glue. Like I could sneeze and fall apart. But I managed to get the whole story out, from the reappearance of Bodie to Rebecca's less-than-warm send-off, and then it felt so good to let someone in on my misery that I scratched my nose on the sleeve of my cardigan and sighed wearily.

"I need to show you something, Hanna."

Together, we walked outside to the little lot tucked halfway under our building. I didn't want her to see it. Each step was like trudging through knee-deep mud, but I knew I needed to show her—to let someone I loved shoulder this burden with me instead of trying to take it all on my own shoulders. Because it wasn't my fault. None of this was my fault. And I was tired of letting myself believe that I was somehow responsible for how horrible people had been to me.

Hanna's sharp inhale was followed by a strangled cry of disbelief. For a long moment, we stared at my car in silence. Hanna tugged the sleeve of her sweatshirt down over one hand, stepped forward, and rubbed tentatively on the tail of the *L*. I'd already tried this myself, but I didn't bother telling her it wouldn't buff out. I just appreciated the thought.

"When?" Hanna finally asked. "When did this happen?"

"The night you blacked out while I was at Target. Somebody keyed it in the parking lot."

"Did you see who?"

"No," I said. "But I—I did see Kyle Fogarty before I went inside the store. And he saw me. So. It's fine."

"Please tell me you filed a police report."

I nod. "They'll get back to me eventually. I think. Maybe not. I'm sure they've got bigger fires to fight."

Hanna turned to face me squarely. "You know this isn't just bullying, right?"

"What do you mean?"

"Those girls dumping coffee on you. Your boss firing you. *This*." Hanna pressed a fingertip to the hood of my car for emphasis. "This is *illegal*. It's harassment. It's vandalism. It's targeted crime—"

I laughed before I could stop myself.

"Nothing about this is funny," Hanna cried, incredulous.

"I know! I know. It's just—you made a pun." At her blank stare, I added sheepishly: "*Targeted* crime. Get it? Because it happened in the Target parking lot."

Hanna's lips pressed into a flat, trembling line. I think she couldn't decide whether to laugh or throttle me. But when she spoke again, she was calm.

"Get in," she told me, nodding at the driver's-side door.

"What?"

"Get in. We're driving to Ralph's and I'm buying you whatever wine you want. I've got my fake in my wallet. Let's go."

"Hanna. I'm not going out in public in my car again. Everybody will see—"

"Everybody's going to see that you were harassed," she cut me off. "Everybody will see, and everybody will know that you don't give a flying shit what they do to you."

I'd had coffee dumped on me. I'd had my car vandalized. I'd been fired.

"But I *do* give a shit," I admitted.

And then my throat was tight, and the corners of my lips tugged back as I tried to hold back a sob I'd been stamping down for the last month. I buried my face in my hands and pinched my shoulders up to my ears, burrowing into my cardigan like a turtle hiding in its shell. Like maybe, if I squeezed every muscle in my body, I could hold it together.

I didn't see Hanna come toward me but I felt her when she threw her arms around me and hugged me tight.

"I hate this," I sobbed. "I hate this. I can't do it."

"You can," Hanna whispered fiercely. "You *are*."

I hated that Hanna was seeing me cry. I never liked crying in front of the people I loved—her, Andre, my parents—because I didn't want them to be the sponges that mopped up my anxieties. I hated Truman Vaughn for all he'd caused. I hated Rebecca for firing me to impress a man. I hated Fogarty for what he'd done to the car my parents had worked so hard to buy me for my sixteenth birthday. But most of all, I hated the seed of regret growing in the pit of my stomach. I hated that I wanted to imagine what my junior year would've been if I'd never heard about Josefina Rodriguez. If I hadn't known.

I just wanted things to be normal again. I understood why Bodie had hated when that had been taken from him now.

Horrible truths could eat you from the inside out, and you wouldn't realize what'd gone wrong—couldn't take action to stop it—until it was too late. But at least it wouldn't hurt.

With all the courage I could muster, I drew back from Hanna and wiped my face with the sleeves of my cardigan.

"You good?" Hanna asked.

"No," I said on a shaky exhale. "But can I maybe get a rain check on the free wine?"

—

For the second time in a row, I skipped Human Sexuality. I didn't want to make a habit of it, but I also didn't want my unemployment to hang over my head. I went to the coffee shops and fast food joints around campus first, to see if they needed waitresses or baristas or someone to mop floors at four o'clock in the morning, before opening. Panda Express had a sign in the front window proclaiming that they were HIRING NOW, but the guy behind the counter wrote down my name and number and then smiled in a way that told me he didn't plan on telling his manager that the girl who'd written the Vaughn article wanted to scoop orange chicken to pay her rent.

My next stop was the student union. There was a corkboard in the lobby where people tacked up posters and pamphlets for everything from job fairs to hip-hop ballet classes. I sighed and tore a strip of paper off the bottom of a flyer declaring proofreaders were needed. The wording of it was sketchy—I was pretty sure some freshman was just looking for someone they could pay fifty bucks to author a Writing 101 paper for them—but my standards were basement level at the moment. I'd started to dream up strange business ideas, as desperately broke college students are prone to do. Worst-case scenario, I always had a spare kidney to auction off.

And that was kind of a joke, but also not, because what if I didn't find another job? What if I was doomed to let the car my parents had bought me for my sixteenth birthday sit and rust?

I didn't have the money to cover our insurance deductible—and I wasn't even sure I could claim insurance, since I hadn't heard anything back from the police about the report I'd filed and I was too chicken to call them. I didn't want to cause any more trouble or draw any more attention to myself. I just wanted my car back.

As I was shoving the tear-off phone number from the flyer into my backpack, my phone buzzed with a text from Andre.

Um??? Explain yourself???

A moment later, a second message came through: *I had to sit through a lecture on childbirth without you.*

I hadn't told Andre I'd lost my job yet. I started to type out a response, but then my screen went dark with an incoming call.

"Hi, Andre, sorry I—"

"*Childbirth*," he interrupted me, shock palpable through the phone. "The second time in a row you leave me to tackle this shit on my own, and this motherfucker puts an entire vulva on the screen and makes us watch a kid pop out of it."

I waited until I heard him exhale.

"Are you d—"

"No, I am not *done*."

"Do you want to come over?"

"Yes. I need to vent."

Back at the apartment Hanna was in our room working on a sketch of *David*. She popped one earphone out when we came in. Andre launched himself onto my bed, landing with a hard creak of the mattress and sending one of my pillows tumbling to the floor. I stooped to pick it up and whacked him on the back of the legs with it.

"How was class?" Hanna asked me. "Did you talk to Bodie?"

"No." I sighed. "I skipped. I just went to the student union to see about writing tutor openings."

"Well, that's good," Hanna said, unplugging her earphones entirely.

"*No*," Andre said, lifting his head. "It's not good. Do you know what today's lecture was about? Tell her, Laurel. Go ahead. Tell her what the lecture was about."

I ignored him. "I mean, they took down my info, but there's no telling if anyone will actually want to work with me—"

"Miracle of life, my ass," Andre muttered.

"Somebody will hire you," Hanna told me. "Seriously. You have a solid GPA, you have lots of experience, you have—"

"No references," I finished for her.

"At least you don't have a kid," Andre said.

I was tempted to whack him with my pillow again.

"I need a break," Hanna announced, grabbing her phone before she rolled off her bed and stretched her arms out over her head, elbows and wrists cracking. "I've been working on this stupid drawing for *hours*. I'm so stupid. I thought picking a statue with big hands would help, like, disguise the fact that I always draw my hands big. But he looks like he's wearing fucking baseball mitts."

"It looks great, Han."

"Don't even," she grumbled as she whipped out her phone.

I turned to Andre. He, too, was on his phone. I was about to clear my throat and point out that baby boomers had a little bit of a point about our generation and technology when Andre suddenly shot up in bed.

"Holy shit," he said, blinking down at his phone.

"What?" I asked. "Did Nick change the reading? I swear to god, if that dirty little fake-feminist hipster makes me read another two hundred pages before Thursday, I'm *rioting*."

Andre shook his head. "St. James landed the ESPN interview."

"What interview?" Hanna asked.

"The ESPN spot. They picked him as one of their top ten most promising college players of the year."

"Good for him," I snapped.

"Hey," Hanna said, giving my shoulder a nudge. "We should go get some nachos or something. Want to walk to Pepito's? I'm buying."

My annoyance, already at a simmer, came to a rolling boil. "I don't want you to pay for me just because I got fired."

"Hold up," Andre said. "When did you get fired?"

"Over the weekend. At the golf tournament."

"Why didn't you tell me?"

"Because I don't want you to pay for my food either!" I cried. "You always pay, Andre, and it's wonderful and I love you, but it makes me feel like shit."

"I didn't—"

"I know you didn't. It's not about you. It's about *me*. I don't like owing you."

"You don't need to owe me," Andre said.

"Can you guys just go," I snapped. "I don't want to eat anyway."

Andre winced. "Laurel—"

"Please. I'm not mad at you, okay? I just need to be alone."

The second I heard the apartment door shut, I tugged my duvet over my head. How was this fair? How was any of this fair? Ellison, Mehri, and I were off the paper, the *Daily* was practically dead, and the entire football team—from Bodie St. James to Truman Vaughn—had walked away unscathed.

I stuck one arm out from under my duvet and smacked at my bedside table until my fingers found the edge of my phone, then smuggled it back into my blanket cave and clicked open my contacts.

"Hi, *mi amor*," Mom greeted me after two rings.

I didn't trust myself to speak. If I opened my mouth, I was going to cry.

"What's wrong?" Mom asked, because of course she knew.

"I had a really bad day," I managed to croak.

"Do you want to talk about it?"

I sniffled. "No."

I wasn't religious, and I was probably a bit too old for bedtime prayers, but my mom seemed to know that what I needed more than anything was the sound of her voice, so she started shushing me and reciting words I hadn't heard since she'd tucked me into bed as a little girl—little cantations about angels in the corners of my bed to watch over me.

I squeezed my eyes tight and pulled my knees up to my chest—like, maybe, if I made myself small enough, I could vanish. Maybe I could become invisible again.

chapter 26

When I opened my eyes, my bedroom was cast in dim morning light. I was still curled in on myself, my stomach sore where the waistband of my jeans had cut into my skin and the underwire of my bra was stabbing me in the tender skin under my arm.

Across the room, Hanna snored under her covers.

I rolled onto my back and stared up at the ceiling. A part of me wanted to stay in bed forever. But that was exactly what Vaughn wanted. Fear. *Silence.* I scrambled up and plucked my laptop off my desk. Out in the kitchen, I pulled our too-small IKEA chair up to the dining table. The university might've pulled our platform, but I was going to post our article on every social media account I had.

It took no fewer than ten minutes for the first comments to roll in.

This is such a load of bullshit

In this house we believe women!!!

Are these bitches still going after Vaughn? Fuck off and kill yourselves

At the beginning of the semester, I might've let those words crush me. But I could never make everyone happy. That was the nature of being a journalist, of being a writer. There would always be people who didn't want to hear what I had to say, even if I'd fact-checked it and sugarcoated it.

When the article was everywhere I could think to post it, I closed my laptop and called Josefina's number. It went right to voice mail. I took it on the chin.

"Hey, Josie. It's me. It's Laurel. I'm going to assume you've heard about Garland shutting down the *Daily*. I don't know where your head's at. I wouldn't blame you if you don't want to come forward this way, or right now. But if you still want to talk, I'm here. I don't care how we do it. If you want me to write your story, I will. If you just want someone to come to the police station with you, I will. If you—if you just want someone to talk to, privately, I—"

The line clicked. My time was up.

——

It was cruel fate that Bodie's ESPN interview would be televised live the afternoon before Pollock, the party I'd looked forward to most of the semester and had now chosen to skip in order to hide from everyone and everything. What was meant to be a day of celebration and collegiate debauchery had become a day I faced with reluctance and dread.

"I found a livestream!" Hanna announced. "Nobody touch my laptop, okay? This website is a minefield of viruses."

"Here tonight with us is Bodie St. James, starting quarterback of the Garland University Lions. Originally from Arlington, Texas, Bodie became a hot recruit in high school and chose to commit to Garland over several top programs, including Clemson and the University of Florida. Bodie asked to kick things off with a statement regarding recent allegations about his head coach, Truman Vaughn."

Bodie appeared on the right half of the screen. He had on the same suit he'd worn for the first interview he'd done for them—navy blue, no tie—and someone had smothered concealer under his eyes to try to mask the severity of his bruised nose. The Los Angeles skyline was superimposed on the green screen behind him. I wondered if anybody had bothered to mention to the video editing team that Garland, California, was over an hour's drive from the city.

"Several weeks ago," he began, in the steady voice of someone who spoke with absolute conviction, "I made a statement on behalf of my team. I said that the accusations made against Vaughn were untrue. I would like to apologize for that statement."

"What the fuck," Andre murmured.

I shushed him.

"My quote from our school paper—the *Daily*—is something I have to stand behind. Truman Vaughn has displayed sexist, misogynistic behavior in the locker room. I've heard him speak. I've seen him kick a pair of female reporters out and tell them that they needed to leave because the locker room isn't a sorority house."

"Was that you?" Hanna whispered.

It was her turn to be shushed.

"The *Daily* recently published a follow-up article. I know there's been speculation about the validity of their sources. Earlier today, I was in contact with Diana Cabrera, one of the women who identified Truman Vaughn at a San Diego resort this summer. She's doubling down on her claims. And as for the unnamed source who divulged information about the Vaughn Foundation—"

Oh my god. He wasn't?

"—it was me."

Hanna inhaled sharply.

"I stand behind what I've said," Bodie pressed on, his voice wobbling so slightly that I might've been the only person on earth who caught it. "More importantly, I want to thank the writers and editors at the *Daily* for their dedication and bravery in bringing these accusations forward. We ask that fans of the team, and fans of Vaughn, treat them with respect and listen to what they're saying. Because it's true. So. Yeah. Thank you for your time."

The open-mouthed ESPN reporter took a second to recover his wits.

"Well, thank you, Bodie. That was—um . . ."

Mehri, Ellison, and I could've spent the rest of the school year protesting on the parkway every single weekday. We could've written a long, vibrantly worded emails and social media posts. And, chances were, our words would've bounced off ears that didn't want to hear from us. But Bodie? Bodie was the star quarterback of a multimillion-dollar collegiate program. His words held weight. His actions held even more weight.

It wasn't fair. I knew that. But so did Bodie.

And that's why he'd spoken up for us.

—

Miraculously, my white shorts still fit. There was no logical explanation for it, but I'd learned not to question miracles when they landed in my lap—or squeezed over my hips. Hanna and I turned on some pregame tunes and pulled open the kitchen window, letting cool evening air drift in while we readied ourselves for the evening's festivities. The flat iron was hot, our faces were primed, and every article of white clothing we owned was laid out on our beds.

And all I could think about was Bodie St. James. I sat with my phone in my lap, our text messages pulled up but my mind totally blank as to what I should say.

Thanks didn't seem to cut it. *Come to my apartment* seemed too forward.

Pollock was always a wild night. Freshman year, when Andre, Hanna, and I were bright-eyed and naive, we'd chugged so much Bacardi that we'd woken up in Hanna's dorm room with five stolen traffic cones and an unmarked Styrofoam box of waffle fries, the origins of which haunted us to this day (none of the restaurants near campus did waffle fries, and there were no Uber receipts indicating we'd ventured off campus to find them—not that an Uber driver would've taken us anywhere, drenched in black light paint as we'd been).

"Han?" I asked. "Can you help me with hair and makeup?"

I pulled one of our dinky IKEA chairs into the bathroom so I could sit in front of the mirror while Hanna fluttered around me, using whatever clips and scrunchies we could find to aid her in the battle to tame my hair.

"You smell like a toothpaste factory," Hanna mumbled as she worked.

"Thank you?"

"No, no. It's good. Bodie will appreciate it."

I pulled back my hair tie and let it fly. It ricocheted off the mirror and hit Hanna in the forehead. Our laughter was interrupted when my phone buzzed on the cluttered bathroom counter, momentarily muting our pregame tunes.

Andre had texted: *I'm outside! Got the goods!*

"Andre's back," I announced.

The thundering of footsteps up the stairs through the paper-thin walls of the apartment heralded his return. Andre had opted for white compression leggings under athletic shorts, a white T-shirt, and a pair of white sweatbands on his wrists to tie the whole look together. He came bearing a plastic bag of sodas and mixers and a jumbo bag of Hot Cheetos, which Hanna immediately snatched from his arms and cradled tenderly like a sleeping newborn.

"And your lemonade," Andre announced as he passed a plastic bottle to Hanna, who immediately unscrewed the top, took a swig, and topped it off with a generous splash of Fireball.

She saw my grimace and said, "Well, since I don't have anyone to impress tonight . . ."

Then she tossed back another long sip.

"Heathens," I said. "You're both *heathens*."

Andre held out my car keys.

"Did you get—"

"I got your wine, yeah," he said. "It's in your trunk."

I frowned again, but harder. "Why didn't you bring it?"

"I forgot," Andre said. "You should go get it. I parked in the garage across the street from the Palazzo. It's close. It'll take you five minutes, tops."

My friends had many artistic talents, but acting was not one of them. I just couldn't figure out why they wanted to send me out to the parking lot. I looked at Hanna, hoping I might catch a glimpse of something on her face, but she was staring fixedly at the nutritional chart on back of the Cheetos bag, which had to be a depressing sight.

"So are you guys mad at me," I asked, "or—"

"Laurel," Hanna said, exasperated. *"Go."*

—

He'd parked on the top floor. Now I was absolutely certain they were mad at me.

I stopped on the landing, panting like an overheated dog from the steep climb up the stairs, and looked out across the street. It was golden hour. The Palazzo's windows sparkled peach and gold against blue and lavender skies. From the east side, the parking garage was a monolith of shadow and concrete, but when I shouldered open the door and stepped out onto the roof level, I was momentarily blinded by sunlight.

I lifted one hand to shield my eyes. And then I saw it.

My Corolla was one of maybe fifteen cars parked on the

top floor. She sat alone along the north wall, her windows and mirrors glittering. There wasn't a single spot of dust or dirt on the body. But that wasn't what made me stop in my tracks. It was her hood—smooth and white as a field of untrodden snow—and the boy in a fitted navy suit sitting on the wheel stop in the empty space next to her, elbows on his knees and a bottle of wine on the ground between his feet.

Bodie picked up his head when he heard me wheezing toward him.

"Hey," he called.

"Hi," I replied, my voice small and watery.

I stopped at the edge of the empty parking space, unable to decide which sight had me tearing up—my repaired car or Bodie in his suit. He wiped his hands on his pants and stood, leaving the bottle of wine behind as he stepped forward to meet me.

"You skipped class," he said. "Twice."

"Did you miss me?" I quipped.

"Yeah," Bodie said with a sincerity I hadn't prepared myself for. "Yeah, I really did."

I tried to laugh, but there was a lump lodged in my throat. I fidgeted with my keys instead. I couldn't stop looking at my car. My beautiful, unmarred car.

"How?" I asked, unable to articulate a more specific question.

"Shepherd helped," Bodie said. "I hope that's okay. I didn't want to invade your privacy, or anything, but I thought—"

I waved him off and sniffled. "How'd you—did *you* paint it?"

"I watched a YouTube tutorial," he said with a shrug. "And Quinton's uncle is a mechanic. I might've called in a favor."

As charming and affable as Bodie was, there was no way he'd allowed his teammate's relative to do that much work for free. And Bodie wouldn't have asked for special treatment. I had a good ballpark idea of what he'd paid. I'd done my research. I knew exactly how much I needed to save up. Except the numbers didn't matter anymore. Bodie had taken care of it. I couldn't think of a single good way to express myself that wasn't straight out of the midseason finale of a telenovela—crying, throwing myself to my knees, slapping him across the cheek, and then kissing him in the same well-choreographed motion.

I settled on "Thank you." I was proud of my restraint. "I hate that you paid for it, though. I really don't like people paying for my shit."

"Yeah, about that," Bodie said, clearing his throat uncomfortably. "Andre and I didn't pay for it. Kyle did. He's the one who keyed it. I asked him about your car before my interview with ESPN, and he couldn't shut up about how he fucked with it in the Target parking lot. I took an audio recording with that app you're always using. Told him if he didn't pay up I'd show it to Gordon. He paid. I sent the recording to Gordon about an hour ago."

I gasped with scandalized delight. "You sneaky little bastard."

Bodie bit back a smile. "I try."

"Fogarty deserves it, though," I told him.

He nodded. "I think I need some new friends."

"Well, I can't help you there. I've only got two. And they're *huge* dorks."

"Shepherd's pretty cool." Bodie's smile slipped a little as he added, "He told me you got fired. I'm sorry. I can reach out to your boss at the country club and—"

"No," I cut him off. "I don't want to work there anymore."

"Are you sure? Because I'll make noise. I will."

"Nah. Rebecca isn't worth the trouble."

"But you are."

I wanted to hug him. I wanted to put my hands on either side of his face and just hold him there, for a few hours, so I could soak up the warmth of his smile. I sniffled again and rubbed my nose on my sleeve. I was sure I looked like some disgusting, puffy-eyed gremlin, but I was too relieved to sink into self-consciousness.

And Bodie was smiling at me. It was so hard to feel bad when he did that.

"I saw your interview," I whispered.

"I'm sorry," he whispered back.

"Why are you apologizing? You were—you were *perfect*."

Bodie winced. "If I was perfect I would've said all that the first time they interviewed me instead of accusing you of dragging his name through the mud."

"You didn't know," I murmured.

"I knew enough," Bodie said. Then he smiled and said, "I was going to quit."

"What?"

"I was going to quit football today. I had a whole second half of the speech planned. It was going to be this big mic-drop moment. Just. I *quit*. But before I went on, the team group chat started sharing your article, so we could all post it on social media at the same time, and I just . . . I realized that if I quit—if I walk away from football—then I won't be around to make sure things actually change. Because all the harassment training and those resources the school throws at us every year won't mean shit if guys like Vaughn and Fogarty treat it like a joke."

I nodded. "They need you. The team needs you."

Bodie looked at the ground between us and swallowed hard.

"What?" I pressed.

"Vaughn was such a big part of my life for the last two and a half years. I know what he's done is awful, and I know—I *know* I can't go back. But what do I do with all the good?"

"Bodie," I croaked.

"He was there for me when I needed someone to be there for me. I was a mess freshman year. I could never have gone on ESPN like that and done a live interview. Vaughn's the one who taught me how to be a leader. So what am I supposed to do with everything he taught me? About public speaking, the game, life? How do I pick apart the good from the bad? Because I can't—" His voice broke. "I can't be like him, Laurel. I can't turn into him."

"You won't," I said, the words coming easy because I meant them. "You won't become him if you choose not to. There was a reason you told me about the foundation during our first interview, Bodie. You chose to do that. No one coached you. No one held your hand and made you. You *chose* to do the right thing. Because you're a good person."

It happened very quickly. Bodie stepped forward, and before I had time to worry that my tearstained face and snotty nose might smear on his shirt, his arms were around me.

I hadn't realized how much I needed a hug. His body

was big and warm and solid. The comfort of it brought on a fresh round of tears that left me completely unable to breathe through my nose.

The duration of a polite embrace came and went. Shamelessly, we held on to each other.

Finally I sniffled and said, "Want a drink?"

I was used to wine that came in bottles with twist tops and tasted like someone had poured nail polish remover into some expired Welch's grape juice. But Andre, bless his heart, had splurged on the good stuff tonight. It was corked.

"Damn it," I exclaimed, stomping my foot in frustration. "Why would Andre do this? He knows I'm not bougie. I don't have a freaking corkscrew in my—"

"Here," Bodie said, holding out a hand.

I passed him the bottle of wine and folded my arms over my chest, glancing over my shoulder just to check that there weren't any university security guards lurking behind concrete columns to catch a pair of rowdy delinquents like us.

"And your keys."

I turned and frowned at him. Bodie just smiled and held out an open palm. I dropped them obligingly into his waiting hand. In one easy move he wedged the key to my apartment into the cork, gave it a twist, and tugged it clear out of the bottle with a satisfying smack of suction. It was the hottest thing I'd ever seen a boy do.

"It's all upper body strength," Bodie said, looking far too proud of himself.

My gaze flickered to the sleeves of his suit jacket where they stretched across his biceps.

"Do you have cups?" Bodie asked.

I did not. But I did have an extensive collection of reusable grocery bags, a loose bottle of Cholula hot sauce, and a rosary my abuelita had given me to hang on my rearview mirror (the constant clattering of plastic had been too distracting, so I figured the Lord wouldn't mind if I kept it in the glovebox with emergency tools I didn't know how to use).

"We can waterfall it," I said.

"Great idea. Do you want to get wine all over your shirt first, or should I?"

The smartass let me take the first swig.

I decided backwash wasn't the worst thing in the world, considering we were already drinking poison, so I let the bottle touch my lips. Then I passed it back. Bodie took a short pull, wiped his mouth on the back of his hand, and shivered like a kid downing cough syrup.

"Oh, come on," I scolded. "It's good stuff."

"I don't drink much," Bodie admitted with a grimace.

While he braced himself for another sip of wine, I tugged my phone out of my back pocket to text Andre. I couldn't decide if I should thank him for helping Bodie or curse him out for not at least warning me.

"Hold on," Bodie interrupted, his smile far too pleased when I lifted my head. "I'm sorry, what's your lock screen?"

I fought the sudden urge to hurl my phone off the third floor of the parking garage.

"Just something from Pinterest."

Bodie's mouth twitched. "I'll show you mine if you show me yours."

Curiosity won out.

"You first," I told him.

Bodie tugged his phone out of his back pocket and held it up.

"Is that your sister's baby?" I asked, squinting at the screen.

He nodded. "Your turn."

I ground my teeth together. Bodie raised his eyebrows pointedly. With monumental reluctance, I handed over my phone and tipped my chin up, holding on to pride even as I melted with embarrassment.

"Is that—" He squinted. "One Direction?"

"Ah, so you're familiar with them."

"Why do you have a picture of One Direction from, like, 2011 as your lock screen?"

"Because they have a very compelling discography."

He snorted. "So are you a Harry or a Niall girl?"

"I'm not answering that."

"Don't tell me you're a Louis—"

"I like their *music*."

"Sounds like something a Louis girl would say."

"Honest to god, Bodie! I have one of their CDs in my car. It goes hard as—"

He was laughing too loudly to hear my review. I folded my arms over my chest and waited, one eyebrow raised with impatience, for him to get his shit together. Bodie eventually composed himself enough to look apologetic.

"All right, all right. I'm sorry," he said. "Here. I'll give it a chance."

He shuffled to the driver's-side door of my car and jammed the key in the lock.

"You have to wait a second after—"

Too late. He'd tugged the handle. The alarm blared. Bodie

stumbled backward, my keys slipping through his fingers and clattering to the ground. It was my turn to howl with laughter.

"What'd I do?" Bodie yelled over the alarm, the terror in his wide eyes sinking into embarrassment as I cackled at his expense.

"She's *sensitive*," I scolded. "You can't just stick it in her and go."

"That's what she said."

"All right, get out."

"It's a public parking garage, Laurel."

I tugged open the driver's-side door, sat back with my legs hanging out of the car, and jammed my key in the ignition. The engine roared to life, followed by the crackle of the stereo system and the opening notes of an Ariana Grande song. I huffed and jammed the Skip button until it shuffled to the next CD: One Direction's first studio album.

Between the fading tail end of one song and the beginning of the next—when Bodie and I had stopped jumping around and were doing nothing but laughing with our arms slung around each other—I let my lips press to his shoulder. Just once. Quickly, so if he noticed, he could think it'd been an accident.

chapter 27

The Art House had used chain-link fences and black trash bag–like tarps to create a tunnel down the driveway to the enormous tent in the parking lot out back. Music was already blasting when the four of us arrived. The cool night air was sweet with marijuana and sharp with the chemical stench of black light paint, which was laid out on folding tables in the front yard. Pink, blue, green, orange, and yellow had been rationed into individual plastic squeeze tubes—the kind restaurants put off-brand condiments in.

Hanna grabbed a tube of blue and immediately drew a crooked phallic symbol on Andre's shirt. Bodie plucked up a bottle of green paint and turned to me. I half expected him to squirt me in the face, like everyone else on the front yard was doing to each other, but instead, he dabbed a little on his finger.

"Hold still," he told me, grabbing my chin between his thumb and index finger.

"You're not gonna draw a dick on my face, are you?" I asked, doing my best not to squirm.

"Definitely not," Bodie replied unconvincingly. I felt him press dots along my cheekbones.

"Let me see!" Hanna said, hauling me around by the shoulder. Her face sank with disappointment. "What the fuck? Where's your creativity, St. James?"

"You realize people have been drawing dicks on shit for literal centuries," Andre said. This earned him another dousing.

With bottles of paint in hand (and two tucked into the pockets of Andre's athletic shorts), the four of us joined the steady stream of students heading into the tunnel. It was my favorite part every year—the first plunge into the dark, before your eyes adjusted and before you got deep enough into the tent that the glow of the black lights could touch you. I ventured forward into the darkness. And then, suddenly, the world was blue. I glowed from my sneakers to my shirt. I laughed and spun around. Bodie stood just behind me, his button-down shirt and teeth all electric blue under the black lights.

I lifted my bottle of pink paint. He caught on a split second too late. I had the front of his shirt covered in erratic zigzag stripes before he lifted a bottle of orange paint and did the same to me.

We disappeared into the colorful crowd in the tent. The music was so loud it shook the asphalt under our feet. Darkness paired with the whiskey lemonade made dancing easy as we pushed forward into the chaos.

Hanna grabbed my hand and shouted, "I think I want another drink."

"I'll come with you," I shouted back. I turned to let the boys know. Andre was scanning the crowd but Bodie's eyes were already on me. "We're going to run to the bar," I told him.

Bodie frowned. I realized he couldn't hear me over the music.

When he leaned down and offered me his ear, I put my hands on his shoulders and rolled up on my toes. The déjà vu was like a flick to the forehead. This was how I'd kissed him the first time around, when he'd chosen my mouth over Fosters Freeze.

The crowd shifted around us. Somebody bumped me as they brushed past us and I had to step to the side to keep my balance. Bodie's hand caught my hip, anchoring me to him. I loved big parties like Pollock for the same reason that I liked sitting in the stands during football games—the crowd swallowed you whole. You were a part of something. You were one tiny, vibrating atom in a big, wonderful universe. I liked that. But right now, I kind of wanted the world to fuck off.

"What'd you say?" he asked over the music.

I didn't remember. Bodie drew back and looked at me again. I thought I saw stars reflected in his eyes. It took me a moment to realize they were the dots he'd painted across my cheeks.

"Bar!" I shouted. "We're going to the bar! Hanna wants a drink!"

I found Hanna's arm, striped with blue paint where Andre

had doused her in retaliation for the dick on his shirt, and grabbed hold. Together, we pushed through the crowd.

One of the best parts of Pollock was running into everyone you'd ever had class with. I saw Ryan Lansangan in a white snapback hat and white button-up romper, his short but well-defined legs bare. I also briefly brushed arms with Mehri, who had a Four Loko in hand and lifted it in cheers as we passed each other. Hanna and I surfaced again at the bar, a rickety plywood construction that'd been relegated to the far corner of the tent opposite the DJ's stand. Given that Hanna was small and I was not, it was my job to crane my neck and see over the people in line ahead of us. Danny—Hanna's stoner ex–booty call—was behind the bar pouring Natty Light into red cups.

"So do you want room-temperature beer or—"

"Are you going to let St. James kiss you or not?" Hanna demanded.

"What are you talking about?"

"That boy is so soft for you. He was *leaning in*, Laurel. Oh my god, I need more whiskey. *You* need more whiskey."

"He leaned in because we were *talking*."

"Laurel."

"Look, the last time we kissed, it blew up in my face."

"Because he was your whistleblower," Hanna said. "You're not protecting him anymore. You're allowed to kiss the boy."

I shook my head. "Just because Bodie spoke up doesn't mean we're done. Vaughn's still walking free. Josefina's still—I don't even know—"

"You can't fix the world tonight, okay? You've done so much, Laurel. Please. For the sake of your own sanity. Have a drink, and kiss your boy."

The trio of freshman girls ahead of us in line fluttered off with their drinks. I stepped up to the bar. Danny smiled at me, his eyes fixed on Hanna, whom I was doing my best to shield from him. Tonight could be wild, but not so wild that I let my best friend hook up with a boy who looked like he'd shunned all forms of modern plumbing.

"Two beers," I called, holding up a pair of fingers.

Danny shuffled over to rip open another rack of Natty Light. Hanna thumped me on the arm to get my attention. It was clearly important, because I was going to have a massive bruise come morning. I turned to see what was up. Bodie was pushing toward us through the crowd. He was easy to spot since he was a head taller than almost everyone else at the party, save for a trio of basketball players who were off to the side passing a joint between themselves. It helped, of course, that Bodie had black light paint dripping off his chin. He was a beacon of neon blue above the crowd.

"What happened?" Hanna shouted over the music when he reached us.

"Andre got paint in my eye," he said, trying and failing to open it through the thick coating of paint that clung to his lashes.

Hanna barked out a laugh. "Fuckin' Andre."

"Does it sting?" I asked, a bit more sympathetic than my roommate.

"Like a bitch, actually."

Andre popped out of the crowd, looking guilty. "You sure you don't want to use my shirt?" he offered, despite the fact that his shirt was also soaked in paint.

"I'm okay," Bodie replied, even though he obviously was not.

"Hey," I said, "do you want to go try to clean up?"

"That'd be great."

I turned to Hanna and said, "I'm going to help Bodie find some water, or a towel or something, and don't you dare smile at me like that."

She ignored the warning and leaned past me to clap Bodie on the shoulder. "You're in good hands."

"Lead the way," Bodie told me.

I grabbed his hand, weaving our fingers so we wouldn't lose each other in the crowd, and tried to keep my fluttering heart in check. Together, we dove into the hot crush of bodies and headed back out through the tunnel. The front door of the Art House was blocked off by a few guys who were in charge of redirecting the constant stream of drunks looking for a place to pee.

"Porta Potties to your left, ladies," one of them called to a trio of girls who had their arms linked for structural stability.

I led Bodie around to the far side of the house instead. The back door was locked, which meant nothing to me, because Mehri Rajavi had told me she and her roommate kept an emergency key (and, apparently, an emergency bong) behind one of the potted plants on the screened-in porch. One twist in the lock, and we were in.

The harsh white glare of the lighting inside was far less flattering than the gentle blue glow of the black light. Bodie and I looked a mess, our hair ruffled and clothes covered in smudged paint. Under any other circumstance, I might've taken a moment to be horrified by how I probably looked, but Bodie was half blind and in distress.

"C'mon," I said, taking his hand again despite the fact that there was no longer a crowd to separate us.

The first floor of the house was empty, save for a few people in pristine white clothes who seemed to be having trouble
deciding when to end their pregame. They were gathered on
the stairs, yelling up and down at each other as they debated
the pros and cons of joining the festivities outside or downing
a few more shots, and didn't even blink when I treaded past,
leaving wet footsteps on the warped wood floor and tugging a
half-blind, six-foot-five quarterback behind me. We made our
way through the kitchen, where the peeling paisley wallpaper
gave way to tiled backsplash and banged-up cabinets, and
down a small set of stairs to the basement (which had been
converted to a bright and cozy theater room, thanks to a stolen
projector from some poorly guarded lecture hall on campus).

"I think this is it," I murmured before I pushed open the
first door along the wall.

Laundry room. Bingo.

It was a small, dim room with two washers and two
dryers. Music carried in through the open window over the
washing machines, which were top-loading and thus sat side
by side. There was a sink in the corner with an enormous
basin and a bucket of miscellaneous cleaning supplies jammed
under the U-bend pipe. Someone had left a laundry basket
of folded clothes on the folding table against the far wall. A
salmon-colored towel sat on top of the pile. I snatched it up
and turned to face Bodie.

"Where do you want me?" he asked.

I snorted before I could stop myself.

"Literally any other time, Laurel, I would be all over you,
but I'm actually starting to worry I might lose vision."

My cheeks heated. "Okay, okay, all right."

I ran the corner of the towel under the faucet, wrung it out, and then hopped up on the washing machine next to the sink and beckoned Bodie forward. He stood between my knees patiently as I mopped up the blue black light paint.

Bodie was stone still until I rubbed the towel over his eye. He winced. His hand shot out, searching for something to brace himself against, and landed on my hip.

"Sorry, sorry, sorry," I said.

"S'okay," he grunted. "Just my nose. It's still a little sore."

Now that it wasn't bruised and swollen, I kept forgetting he'd broken it. When I brought the towel to his face again to get the last clumps of blue out of his thick eyelashes, I was gentler.

I leaned back and gave him a final once-over.

"Ta-da!" I said proudly.

His eyes fluttered open. Bodie and I stared at each other. He started to lean forward. And then his hand slid right off my paint-soaked hip and slammed down on the top of the washing machine with a loud, echoey *thunk*.

I burst out laughing. "So *smooth*."

"Not my fault you're—"

"Wet?" I had to slap a hand over my mouth to keep from snorting at my own joke. I'd just wanted to make Bodie laugh, but it wasn't humor that burned in his eyes when he drew back to look at me. He caught my wrist, tugged it to the side, and covered my mouth with his.

And I couldn't believe I'd been nervous. Our first kiss had been all adrenaline, but this felt more frantic. Like it was all either of us had been thinking about—in class, in bed at night, in cars or team buses—since that night at La Ventana, and we half expected Ryan Lansangan to pop out from inside the front-loading dryer next to us and shout, "Yo!"

Bodie's hands were in my hair. Lips pressing, noses bumping cheeks, tongues touching. I didn't want to come up for air, but eventually, it was either pull away or pass out.

I was embarrassingly winded. Bodie had the whole Division I athlete thing going for him, so he wasn't panting nearly as hard as I was, but I took some comfort in the splotchy blush on his cheeks and the thundering beat of his heart where my hand was braced against the side of his rib cage. I noticed, for the first time, that I liked the Post Malone song playing out in the tent.

I tugged on Bodie's shirt.

He ducked his head again, but didn't go for my mouth. Instead, his lips landed on my collarbone, trailing a slow path up the column of my throat. I tipped my chin up and sighed as he kissed my pulse point.

"I have a request," I croaked.

"Say the word," he murmured against my skin. "I'll do whatever you want."

Heat flooded my face. I laughed breathlessly.

"You don't even know what my request is," I pointed out.

"Doesn't matter."

Behind him, the laundry room door flew open.

"Oh shit! Sorry," someone cried. They were gone before I could catch anything other than the delighted laughter of friends who were several drinks in and found everything adventurous.

Bodie and I looked at each other.

His cheeks were flushed, his eyes bright. I'd made a mess

of his hair. It stood on end, paint clinging to chunks in a way that vaguely resembled frosted tips.

"Can we go dance?" I asked.

"Are you sure you want to subject other people to that?"

"I don't know what you're talking about. I'm a *great* dancer."

"I was talking about me."

"C'mon. I'll teach you."

Bodie took my hand and helped me slide off the washing machine, on which I left streaks of pink and orange and green paint that Bodie hastily mopped away with the towel I'd used on his face. We made our way back into the tent. It wasn't hard to find friends in the crowd, since Hanna had climbed onto Andre's shoulders. When she spotted us, she clambered off of him to throw her arms around my neck and rock from side to side.

"You're back!" she cried, delighted, and then frowned. "You're back."

"Did you find Mehri?" I asked, figuring we should try to say hi.

"Oh, hell yeah, I did."

Hanna grabbed my shoulders, spun me, and pointed across the tent to the place where Mehri Rajavi stood on the risers, her arms wrapped around a girl as they made out like lovers in some kind of artsy zombie apocalypse movie. A pair of pale hands were buried deep in the mass of tight black coils on Mehri's head. Hands that belonged to Olivia Novak. My group member, Olivia. It was such a clashing of worlds that for a moment I just stared, open-mouthed, in delighted shock.

"So I take it you and St. James had a good time," Hanna bellowed into my ear.

"What? We didn't—I just helped him clean up."

Hanna's smirk was far too pleased.

"You have a green handprint on your ass, Cates."

"Are you serious?"

Hanna threw back her head and cackled. And then we danced. Andre and I tried, in vain, to help Bodie find some sense of rhythm. Hanna managed to wrangle three more tubes of paint, the contents of which were immediately dispensed onto my face.

And then, abruptly, the assault ended.

"Hold on, my phone is going crazy," Hanna said, unzipping her fanny pack. She tugged out the plastic bag with our cell phones, turned it over in her hands, and frowned. "Oh shit. Laurel. Laurel, I think it's your phone. Someone's been calling you."

Hanna held up the bag. My phone's screen was bright with two notifications—the first, six missed calls. The second, a text.

I read the message once. Then again. Then a third time.

"What is it?" Hanna asked.

"I have to go."

—

It was midnight, I was covered in black light paint, and I held a plastic bag with two phones in it as I sprinted down a quiet street in Garland. My left calf was cramping and a pair of dog walkers I passed gave me a funny look, but I wasn't about to slow down. I *couldn't*. Because up ahead, on the front stoop of my apartment building, was a cluster of six people congregated around a girl in an oversized UCSD sweatshirt who was blotting at her face with the too-long sleeve. She spotted me through the crowd and knew me at once, despite the layer of paint. And I knew her.

I stopped, panting, on the sidewalk and said, "Josie."

The people around her turned. I recognized Gabi. I also recognized some of the Greek letters on the sweatshirts other girls were wearing and a UCSD soccer logo on the shirt of a short boy with buzzed hair and a hoop earring.

Josefina and I stared at each other for a moment. Me, panting. Her, with tear tracks down her face and her friends surrounding her.

At last she clapped her hands and said, "Laurel, these are my friends. Sorority sisters, classmates. Um. Can you come to the police station with us? I think"—her breath caught, and she laughed self-deprecatingly—"I want all the backup I can get."

I nodded. "Yeah. Yeah, I can do backup."

—

Garland, California, was not a town known for its crime. Other than the occasional rowdy house party that needed breaking up or the clueless freshman who'd chained their bike to someone else's instead of the bike racks, the Garland PD didn't get much action. The station was a small, flat brick building on Cerezo Street, just a few blocks from campus. Their waiting room was not equipped for us.

Josefina, Gabi, three of their sorority sisters, and two boys from her pass-no-pass fitness class. Me, Hanna, Andre, Bodie, Mehri, Olivia, and Ellison. Half of us covered in black light paint. One of us (Ellison) in a pink silk pajama set and running shoes. All of us made the pilgrimage together.

Bodie stepped forward first to hold open the door. Josefina paused, chewed on her lip, and eyed him carefully.

"I saw your interview on ESPN," she said.

"I hope I did all right," Bodie told her, a bit sheepishly.

Josefina shrugged. "Could've used a mic drop."

The pair of officers behind the front desk stood from their swiveling chairs as the fourteen of us piled into the small, clean lobby.

Josefina marched up to the front desk, Gabi on her left arm and me on her right.

"I'm here to report a rape."

"You'll need to write and sign an affidavit, under penalty of perjury," the police officer explained.

"I know," Josefina said with a nod. "I did my research."

The officer gathered the necessary paperwork. "If you'll come this way."

Josefina shot one last look over her shoulder, her eyes wet with tears but a smile on her face, and blew a kiss back at us as we called out our support.

The door shut behind them. Breath left my body like a ghost. Like I'd been haunted. Like something awful and heavy had been occupying the space in my chest where my lungs should've been allowed to expand. And then Ellison Michaels—the unmovable, unshakable force of nature who'd kept her chin high through hell and high water—buried her face in her hands and sobbed in the lobby of the Garland Police Station. I sat down next to her. Gabi de Hostos joined us. We cried until we were done—until the reserves behind the dams we'd built had run dry and we were left shaky but finally free of the pressure that'd built up. Then relief and celebration gave way to the realization of what was to come. We'd climbed a hill only to find an entire mountain range sprawled ahead of us on the other side.

"She's going to have it worse than we did," I whispered.

Ellison gritted her teeth and nodded sharply. "If fucking Adam Whittaker from Badger Sports so much as *types* her name," she said, "the paramedics are going to have to surgically remove my foot from his ass."

A burst of laughter tore from my lungs. It felt so good. And I felt so useless suddenly. So utterly small, so utterly powerless against what would come next.

It must've been another half an hour before Josefina reappeared with the officer at her side, eyes puffy and pink but chin held high. The rest of us stood to meet her.

"Well," Josefina said, voice shaking, "that's done. Um. What now?"

I looked at Hanna and Andre, Mehri and Ellison, Bodie, and all of Josefina's friends, and I knew that all of us were in agreement. She wouldn't be alone. No matter what. This was Josefina's story to tell. It was our job to make sure people listened. To make sure she was heard.

"We make noise," I said. Everyone turned to look at me. My face burned but I powered on. "We get loud. Make a scene. We *make* them listen."

"How?" Josefina croaked.

"We could march onto campus," Mehri said. "That's what happens at other schools when shit like this happens. People get mad, and if you let them know they're not alone in that, you can get a crowd going." She shot me a nod. "Make some noise. Make a scene."

"A march?" Gabi repeated, audibly skeptical but intrigued. "Like, right now?"

We all looked to Josefina.

She swallowed hard and said, "All right. I guess I'm glad I wore sneakers."

chapter 28

The Art House, the *Daily*, and Garland University's football team all had group chats, and all three received the same message. I figured it would take a while for anyone at Pollock to see it (since almost everyone kept their phones tucked away in plastic bags to save them from paint), and that we'd be lucky if one or two people ditched the party for ten minutes to walk onto campus with the girl Truman Vaughn had sexually assaulted.

By the time we got to the Rodeo, there was a small crowd of people in paint-splattered white clothes waiting to join us.

By the time we reached the edge of campus, half of Pollock seemed to be trailing us, and kids in pajamas and jeans and oversized sweatshirts poured out of their off-campus apartments to join in on the commotion.

By the time we reached the football stadium, I had to hold Bodie's and Hanna's hands on either side of me to keep from being separated from them in the crowd.

Our voices went raw.

Still, we shouted.

Justice for Josefina.

We weren't breaking new ground. Other schools had seen this kind of uprising, this kind of student mobilization. Sit-ins. Walkouts. Marches, protests, and, occasionally, scathing social media hashtags full of hard truths and long-kept secrets.

Still, it felt surreal to see something I'd only ever watched happen on the news unfold on my campus. In the days that followed Josefina Rodriguez's trip to the police station, students made signs and T-shirts. Someone brought a microphone and a set of speakers into the courtyard outside the campus center, and kids took turns speaking for themselves and for friends who were too nervous to speak up. Classes were postponed. News helicopters circled and journalists swarmed campus. The police tried to corral us and were promptly met with Garland-green streamers and the kind of humiliating chants that only college kids who felt they had nothing to lose could come up with.

The protests came to an end on a bright and crisp October morning, a perfectly unremarkable day save for the roar of cheers and relieved sobs that erupted on campus when Truman Vaughn, head coach of the Garland University football team, was arrested at his home in Garland, California.

—

I've lived in California my whole life. I know that when a wildfire is finally extinguished, the brief moment of celebration—of relief—is quickly followed by the bone-deep ache when you're finally able to think about all the destruction, all the hurt, all that's been lost.

The immediate danger is gone but recovery and rebuilding can take months. Years.

The work has only just begun.

—

The marquee sign on the roof of Pepito's glinted in the midday sunshine.

"Good afternoon," Oscar greeted me from behind the register as my group members and I huddled under the shade of the stand's red terra-cotta roof. He shot me a smile under his wiry mustache but didn't outwardly show I was a regular, since I was with people he didn't recognize.

Olivia and Ryan ordered first. Bodie insisted I go ahead of him.

"The usual?" Oscar asked me with a smile. He meant, of course, three carne asada tacos with extra pico de gallo and pickled jalapeños and carrots.

"*Si*," I said. "*Y estoy pagando por el chico alto.*"

I beckoned Bodie up to the counter beside me. He ordered a super burrito with extra everything. When he pulled out his debit card to pay, I hip-checked him out of the way and slid a twenty-dollar bill onto the counter.

"You don't have to do that," he protested.

"It's a burrito, not a paint job."

Bodie sighed, like he knew this was a fair point but still wanted me to know he wasn't happy about it, and shuffled over to the plastic cutlery and napkin dispensers, grabbing two of everything for us.

Oscar watched this interaction with unapologetic intrigue.

"*Su novio?*" he asked me in a voice that seemed far too loud despite the language barrier that offered us privacy.

"*Todavía no,*" I blurted. "*Casi. Trabajando en eso.*"

Oscar's laugh drifted after me as I followed Bodie over to the metal picnic table Ryan had claimed. The four of us ate like a family of raccoons who'd found an overturned dumpster, shoveling Mexican food in our mouths with such frenzied ardor that we barely paused to speak. It was only after we were stuffed that Olivia, our beloved group leader, took it upon herself to give each of us a personalized pep talk while she picked at the last few bites of her quesadilla.

"Laurel," she said when it was my turn, "you're going to look very sharp—"

I bowed my head. "Glad I can contribute to the group aesthetic."

Bodie looked up from his phone. He'd been typing away at it for a while now, the last few bites of his burrito abandoned on the foil wrapper he'd flattened into a make-shift plate. I caught a glimpse of his screen. He had Google Translate open.

"I'm not done!" Olivia protested, shooting me an annoyed look even as she bit back a smile. "You're going to look cute, and you're going to do the whole thing without having to look at your note cards, and you're going to make that really good point about diversity and everyone's going to give you a standing ovation."

I rolled my eyes to hide the fact that I was embarrassingly touched. Bodie's foot nudged mine under the table. The teasing lilt of his smile was so familiar to me now.

"What?" I demanded.

"Nothing," he murmured. "Just—I'm working on it too."

It took me a second to realize that he was only repeating back what I'd said at the order window, when Oscar had asked me if Bodie was my boyfriend. I'd thought I was slick. I'd underestimated Bodie's Google Translate skills.

While Ryan and Olivia gossiped, I swallowed my nerves.

"So, what are you doing for Thanksgiving?" I asked as I held my churro up like a cinnamon-sugar rolled cigar. "Are you going home?"

Bodie shook his head and swallowed the bite of burrito he was chewing.

"I have football practice. I'll probably just stay in Garland."

"You know," I said, eyes on my half-eaten churro as a defense mechanism. "My house is an hour and a half north of LA. Pretty easy drive. It'll be super low-key. You don't have to come, if you've got other plans with the team—"

"I'd love to," Bodie said before I was done.

"Really?"

He beamed at me. "Yes, really."

I took another bite of my churro.

"What are your parents like?" Bodie asked.

It took me a moment to recognize the hesitance in his voice. He was nervous. Bodie St. James, Garland's golden boy, who could bench-press twice my weight and had survived the clutches of a man who'd done everything in his power to hold him under his thumb, was *nervous* to meet my monolingual softie of a father and my kick-ass mother.

KATE MARCHANT

"They'll love you," I told Bodie. "You took care of my car."

And me, I added in my head as his knee pressed against mine under the table. *You took care of me too.*

—

Ellison seemed to be expecting me when I marched into her office two weeks before Thanksgiving break. She also seemed to be expecting what I had to say.

"I'd like to keep covering football," I told her.

Ellison smiled and leaned back in her desk chair. She'd gotten a new one—one that didn't creak. In the wake of President Sterling stepping down—which had been less of a voluntary bowing out and more of him being nudged off the cliff by the prongs of pitchforks against his ass—the university had scrambled to do some damage control. This included a public statement in support of the *Daily* and a hefty donation to our facilities.

There were new beanbag chairs out in the media center, which smelled of fresh paint and soft serve. The desks were lined with new computers. Ellison's office was still dingy as ever, since she'd made sure the bulk of the funds were allocated to communal spaces.

But she'd gotten her chair.

She nodded and said, "Good. We need to keep eyes on the program. And I need someone to keep an eye on Mehri. She came in here half an hour ago and said she wants to keep covering the games too."

"Really?"

"Mm-hmm. Something about *keeping those assholes accountable.*"

"Sounds like her. Well. I look forward to continuing to represent the *Daily*."

Ellison smiled. "I look forward to ripping apart your first draft."

"I'll try to start it before the deadline. But no promises."

I was halfway out the door when she called, "Try not to flirt with your boyfriend too much during those postgame interviews."

—

Almost every collegiate sports network in the country had predicted that Notre Dame would crush Garland. In the absence of Truman Vaughn's explosive coaching and ruthlessly bold plays, our team was nothing. This is what people told us. And the first quarter seemed to confirm the theories—but Chester Gordon was a smart man. He knew he had Andre, who wasn't as physically dominant as Fogarty but was far quicker on his feet, and he knew he had Bodie, whose arm meant he could rack up passing yards if he had a target who could get down the field fast enough.

So by the end of the third quarter, the game was tied.

A strange and wonderful buzz of energy bloomed in the stadium. Even in the press box, I felt the crackling hum of excitement. The student section was going to rush the field. It might not even matter if we won or lost. The closer the clock ticked to the end of the game, the more we all seemed to realize that the blowout everyone had predicted was not coming.

"C'mon," Mehri said. "They're letting press on the field."

With less than twenty seconds on the clock, Garland

managed to get within twenty-five yards of our opponent's end zone. If Truman Vaughn had been in the stadium, he would've tried something slick. Some big, over-the-top play that ended in twisted ankles, sprained wrists, and a heroic touchdown. But Chester Gordon was a very different coach. He called out the field kicker.

And so, at the final whistle, Garland had won by three points.

The student section erupted. It didn't surprise me when the first row of celebrating kids hopped over the retaining wall and onto the grass. The press rushed forward too. Out on the field, the crowd was a hot crush of bodies, everyone cheering and laughing and accepting high fives from people we'd never met and bouncing along to Garland's fight song.

Then Katy Perry's "Roar" came on over the loudspeakers. We went wild.

And through the forest of singing, cheering people, I locked eyes with the quarterback.

I towed Mehri forward. Bodie met us halfway, tearing off his helmet and beaming at me.

He caught my hand and pulled me through the crowd until we were chest to chest. He was damp with sweat and he smelled like grass and salt and all kinds of body odor. In truth, I wanted to fling my arms around him and press my nose into the crook of his neck. But both of us had a job to do.

"Bodie, can you tell me what it means to pull out this win?" I asked.

"Everything," he said. "It means everything."

———

Later, we'd see our school's celebration covered on every sports network and media outlet. We'd listen to videos taken in the parking lot, where you could hear the low hum of noise suddenly blow out into an earth-shaking rumble of cheers when the final whistle sounded. We'd hear about the $25,000 fine the conference had slapped our school with, in accordance with their anti–field rushing policies.

Adam Whittaker at Badger Sports would call us the dumbest collegiate sports fans he'd ever seen, but that was because he didn't get it. This wasn't just a win. This was a middle finger in the face of Truman Vaughn and everyone who'd told us we needed him.

chapter 29

The week before Thanksgiving break, the drizzly Southern California rain made a reappearance. I tried to angle my umbrella to shield my backpack as I bounded up the front steps of the biological sciences building. Bodie looked up from his phone when I burst into the lobby.

"Finally," he huffed.

"I know, I know, I know," I chanted.

He started down the hall to the dimly lit alcove where the elevator sat framed by a potted shrub in the corner and a corkboard on the wall. I followed him, falling a little behind as I wrestled my umbrella closed and shoved it back into its protective case.

I barely noticed when Bodie stepped into the elevator without me.

The doors were a half a second from closed when I stuck my arm out. The safety mechanism kicked in and they bounced open.

Bodie's smile was the picture of innocence.

"Sorry," he said. "Are you going down?"

I grabbed a fistful of the front of his shirt and tugged him down so I could cover his mouth with mine. Bodie humored me by stumbling backward until he was flat against the elevator wall.

It was a frustratingly short ride to the basement.

The lecture hall was empty aside from the other half of our group. All four of us had arrived to class fifteen minutes early and were nervous wrecks, vibrating with adrenaline and (at least in my case) far too much caffeine. Olivia was texting. For a moment I worried the contact name on the top of her screen would be CAN GO TO HELL, but it was Mehri Rajavi. Ryan was uncharacteristically quiet. Bodie's knee was bouncing so seismically the entire front row of seats shook. I was absolutely positive I was about to throw up the Starbucks latte Hanna had gifted me as a token of good luck.

Slowly, the lecture hall filled. I spotted Andre sitting on the other side of the room with Scott Quinton, the offensive tackle with the thick neck, and some other football players before Nick—the pony-tailed horseman of the academic apocalypse—arrived and began class with a *quick reminder* about our final exam schedule that did not feel quick at all.

And then he said, "Let's get to our first presentation of the day."

I'm pretty sure I blacked out. Here's what I do remember: the exact shade of scuffed-up yellow caution strips on the edges of the two little steps onto the stage, because I was *not* going to eat shit in front of the whole class. The heat of the lights. The gold coiled snake ring on Olivia's right index finger when she reached out to pass me the mic. My first voice crack (*shit*) and also my second voice crack (*double shit*). Bodie's easy, reassuring smile when I shoved the mic into his chest.

And as quickly as it'd begun, our thirty minutes was over. Ryan clicked to the last slide of our presentation—an image of Carla Asada in full drag, mid–dance number. A wave of tentative applause swept across the sleepy lecture hall.

Olivia lifted the mic to her lips and said, "Thank you, guys!"

We were done. It was over.

I still felt like peeing my pants, standing up there with so many eyes peering at me, but the relief outweighed my anxiety. Nick returned to the stage, a clipboard of notes tucked under his arm, and congratulated us on a job well done. We were allowed to shuffle back to our seats and celebrate privately with silent thumbs-up and relieved grins.

"My voice cracked," I whispered to Olivia. "Did you hear my voice crack?"

"No, no," she said unconvincingly, "you sounded fine."

Bodie nudged me with his elbow.

"I totally heard it," he whispered.

I gave his shoulder—his very solid, well-defined shoulder—a shove.

"All right, next up!"

Three guys and a girl in the second row stood and made their way to the podium. Kyle Fogarty was the last of them. The green in his hair was gone, leaving behind a blond that was pale and dull. The first slide of their presentation appeared on the twin projector screens: *Sexual Assault on College Campus*.

Unease twisted my stomach.

The girl took the lead for their group, walking us through their introduction. Their PowerPoint slides were poorly designed. The font choices were so atrocious that I was sure I felt Andre's soul leave his mortal body on the other side of the room. By slide three, I realized they were just dumping information—statistics and data points and dictionary definitions—in an attempt to prove they deserved a passing grade.

It wasn't going well to begin with. But then Fogarty grabbed the mic.

"Of course, we should take those numbers with a grain of salt," he said. "Girls *do* accuse men falsely, like, all the time."

Beside me, Bodie bristled and tensed in his seat. I set my hand on his wrist.

"For instance," Fogarty began, and I knew some bullshit was about to come out of his mouth. "Let's take the Vaughn case."

His eyes landed on me, and paused. I realized he wanted a fight. He wanted me to crack, to make a spectacle of myself, to shout at him until he could pick apart something I said and twist it around to stab me right through the heart.

I closed my notebook, swung my swivel desk into place at the side of my seat, and leaned forward to tuck my belongings into my backpack. A few heads turned at the sound of my rustling papers, but nobody said a word.

"The girls who accused Vaughn—" Kyle continued, louder now.

I tugged all my zippers shut.

"—ruined his career over *nothing*—"

In the middle of a lecture hall packed with a hundred people, I pushed myself to my feet.

Fogarty stopped midsentence, eyes sparking with satisfaction. The lecture hall was dead silent. I'd never thought I was capable of commanding a room of a hundred people. I wasn't the kind of girl who did theatrics and spotlights. I thrived on invisibility. On making myself smaller, quieter, more docile. Fogarty looked tensed and ready for me to shout at him. To fight him.

"Laurel," Nick called, voice wobbling with uncertainty. "Could you take a seat and let this group finish their presentation? Please?"

I looked Nick dead in the eye as I reached down to grab my backpack then slid both straps over my shoulders. No, I was not going to take my seat. I wasn't going to sit down and give Fogarty his captive audience, and I wasn't going to dignify his utterly idiotic arguments by getting into some rhetorical battle of wits. I was going to do the one thing that would make Fogarty the angriest: leave.

I looked down, prepared to ask Bodie to shift his knees to the side so I could get through, but Bodie pushed his swivel desk out of the way and grabbed his backpack too. I'd turned plenty of heads in the room, but the moment Bodie got to his feet, the whole lecture hall was watching us.

I waited for him to snap and say something to Fogarty— his ex-teammate, his ex-roommate, his ex-friend.

Instead he turned to me and said very calmly, "Lead the way."

He gave me that look again—the one that told me he'd follow wherever I led.

Down on the stage, Fogarty's smile had vanished.

"St. James," he called, his face pinched like *What the fuck, man?*

Bodie kept his eyes on me.

"Are you serious?" Fogarty demanded, voice rising a little bit louder. "It's called freedom of speech! I'm allowed to fucking talk."

I looked down at the stage and let myself feel one moment of empathy. One solid moment to acknowledge that Kyle Fogarty had been hurt, just like Bodie, and that maybe some part of him was just a boy who was lost and scared. But I'd hold boys responsible for their actions. Also, he'd trashed my car, which meant I had every right to stay bitter until the day I died. I didn't owe him my time and my energy to explain why he was wrong. I didn't owe him forgiveness either. I didn't owe him a damned thing.

Together, Bodie and I shuffled into the aisle. Olivia flipped her desk down, grabbed her bag, and came after us. Ryan picked his skateboard up off the floor and joined her. Across the lecture hall, where he sat with his group, Andre rose from his seat too. I met his eyes across the room. He raised his hand to his forehead, saluting me, and started up the aisle toward us. Scott Quinton stood too. I'd never looked him in the eye before. It was a strange feeling to finally have your existence acknowledged by someone you'd seen around campus for more than two years. Quinton was a pleasant surprise. I was sure that he'd be it. The six of us would make our statement, Nick would dock us all participation points, and that would be the end of it.

And then, a few rows down, a girl I had never really seen or spoken to before in my life rose from her seat. I didn't know her name. I didn't know a thing about her.

But she stood for me too.

Fogarty watched, with tight lips and a grim pallor to his face, as more of our classmates vacated their seats. Nick called out, in a voice tight with uncertainty, and begged us to sit down, to listen, to not blow this out of proportion. But the avalanche had started. The dominoes were falling, and neither a boy with fists balled at his sides or the man in charge of our grades for the semester could stop it. One by one, then in pairs and clusters and entire rows of the lecture hall at a time, my classmates stood, gathered their belongings, and followed me.

No looking back.

Acknowledgments

I began outlining this book—much like Laurel began her article—thinking it would be a fluff piece. Something slow burn and enemies to lovers. Lighthearted. Escapist. A little nostalgic, because I was only a year out of college and I missed academic validation, living within walking distance of all my friends, and house parties. And then—like Laurel—I realized I'd accidentally stumbled upon the tip of an iceberg.

As it turned out, I had a lot of residual frustration and anger from four years of feeling like a little fish in a big pond. Especially since some of the other fish seemed to play life by an entirely different set of rules. There were times when I felt invisible and voiceless and overwhelmingly, aimlessly angry. And so, I wrote this book.

A book about finding your voice. A book about acknowledging your privilege and then actually using it. A book about the little fish finding strength in numbers.

True to theme, it really did take a village on this one. To my editor, Deanna McFadden: thank you for believing in me.

This book would not be here without your hard work, your vision, and your unwavering ability to always say exactly what I need to hear. To I-Yana and Monica, my talent managers, and to Daphne Gordon, Shay Bravo, Athena, and Whitney French, who all provided invaluable editorial feedback and authenticity reads: it's been an honor and privilege to have so many wonderful, talented people contribute to this book. And to all the Wattpad readers: your comments and private messages made me feel seen and heard when I felt small. You have changed my life. Thank you.

A special shout-out to the writers in the group chat—especially Ivey Choi, who singlehandedly talked me out of stress-quitting my manuscript no fewer than five times (my Virgo queen); Natalie Walton and Simone Shirazi, who taught me about the joys of impulsive international travel (asking the age-old question, who's going to stop us?); and Anne Zou, who hand embroidered a Garland University sweatshirt for me (no one will ever crush Secret Santa as hard as you did).

Last but never least: thank you, Mom, for being my sounding board and for letting me weave bits and pieces of you into my main character. (I'm sorry my Spanish is so terrible. You tried!) Thank you, Dad, for being a kind, gentle soul who has always made me feel like my opinions, emotions, and dreams matter. Thank you, Chris, for being exactly like your father and also the only person who can routinely make me laugh even when I'm trying my hardest to be an anxious mess. And Elizabeth—you knew I'd save you for last, because this book is for you. My little nugget. My big squish. I love you, and I'm proud of you, and I will happily let you bankrupt me with all the iced coffees and bookstore runs you want forever, because that's what sisters are for. Your heart is gold and your temper is magnificent. So give 'em hell, kiddo.

About the Author

Kate Marchant is an American author of Young Adult and New Adult contemporary fiction. Born and raised in Oakland, California, she began writing on the serialization fiction platform Wattpad when she was just fifteen. In 2017, she graduated magna cum laude from the University of Southern California with a degree in Creative Writing and a minor in Art. After a brief stint at a startup and a few years working at a private school, she now lives and writes in San Francisco.

Her debut novel, *Float*, is being adapted for the big screen and will star Robbie Amell and Andrea Bang.

Chapter 1

The scorching midafternoon Florida sunshine battered my bare shoulders.

If I didn't find some air conditioning soon I was going to pass out and end up sprawled across the concrete pickup platform outside Jacksonville International Airport, where eventually some poor security officer might stumble upon my unconscious body and have the unfortunate duty of reviving me.

I knew I was overthinking it—my mom always said my best talent was working myself up over nothing—but I was the only person who'd been stupid enough to step out of the cool airport terminal and head to the parking lot, where temperatures had to be in the hundreds. And I was way too stubborn to turn around and admit my mistake, so instead I stood in the narrow shadow of a lamppost and squinted along the heat-baked road for any sign of my aunt, Rachel, feeling like an idiot. A damp, sticky idiot.

Would I *ever* stop sweating?

Jeans really hadn't been the right move. When I'd boarded my flight back in Alaska, I'd tried to wear clothes that were understated and aggressively normal—which was probably my first mistake. My family was hardly normal. Jeffery Lyons and Lauren Fitzgerald, both professors of environmental science at the University of Alaska, were well known in Fairbanks for their opposing stances on climate change, their torrid affair (the products of which were numerous inconclusive research papers and, tragically, me) and their cataclysmic divorce. Every summer since I'd turned eight they'd taken turns dragging me along on expeditions up to the Arctic. If my time zone math was right, both of my parents should've been arriving at the research station right about now, unpacking their equipment and counting out rations for the long month ahead.

Normal wasn't exactly in my repertoire.

But I had dressed like *someone* from Fairbanks, land of the aurora borealis and the midnight sun, would. This meant at least three layers and, for good measure, a lightweight raincoat.

I hadn't realized anything was wrong with my choice of outfit until noticing I was the only one on the flight who wasn't dressed like they belonged on a promotional pamphlet for a tropical resort. While I'd managed to strip off most of my upper layers in the cramped airplane bathroom, leaving just a spaghetti-strap tank top, I didn't exactly feel like peeling off my jeans and parading around in my underpants. Airport security wouldn't have appreciated that. Three separate guards had already given me the stink eye when they'd heard the stuttering wheels of my suitcase screech against the terminal's linoleum floor.

Turns out, lugging one tiny roller bag back and forth between my mom's place and my dad's place for nine years really wears down the wheels. Go figure.

I'd started to really hate that abomination of a suitcase. It was small, black, and had given me absolute hell to find at the baggage claim. Maybe I could paint it. Something neon, or striped, or animal print. Anything to help me find it when I returned to Alaska at the end of the summer.

Aunt Rachel probably had some art supplies to spare. She was a freelance painter and graphic designer. My dad, who cared too much about equations and predictability to be anything other than a researcher, had never wanted to accept the fact that his younger sister was a creative spirit. She moved from state to state whenever she felt like a change of scenery. She'd ended up in Florida when she'd dated an amusement park engineer. He'd dumped her while at Disney World, of all places, and she'd settled down in Holden to collect herself.

After staring down at my crummy little suitcase for a minute or two, trying to decide whether to go for stripes or polka dots, I looked up and was practically blinded by the sight of the neon-green Volkswagen Beetle barreling toward me.

My hand flew up to shield my eyes from the reflection of the sunlight off the car's exterior. The Beetle, once I thought about it, would make a pretty good model for my suitcase renovations. How could you possibly miss something that color?

The car drew closer and slowed to a slightly more legal speed. The front tire rolled up onto the curb at my feet, and the car finally came to a stop.

A woman smiled sheepishly at me through the open passenger's side window. I only had to take one look at her to know who it was—the tangled brown hair and scattered freckles were familiar from all the family pictures dad had strung up on the walls of his apartment.

"I hit the curb, didn't I?" Rachel asked.

"You might've tapped it."

"Oh shit," she hissed, then hurried to say, "I mean *shoot*."

"Aunt Rachel. I'm seventeen. I've heard it all."

Rachel looked up from the evidence of her horrible parking job and gave me a once-over. I figured I'd probably changed a lot since she'd last seen me. I was taller now, obviously, and I'd like to think I'd started to look less like a splotchy-faced, braces-clad adolescent and more like a worldly young woman with an expansive knowledge of curse words.

Rachel seemed to agree, because she nodded and said, "Well, then, shit."

By the time I managed to pop out the retractable handle on my rickety little suitcase, my aunt had jumped out of the driver's seat of the car and wrapped her freckled arms around me in a quick hug so tight it made me wheeze.

"Oh, Waverly, you're so tall!" she cried, holding me at arm's length to look me up and down. "The last time I saw you, I don't think you were over four feet. Look at you! You're like—like a *real person*. Practically an adult."

Practically felt like the key word. Rachel and I were both on the taller end of the female spectrum, but she was in her thirties and had learned how to carry herself. I was still recovering from my freshman growth spurt. You'd think by the summer after my junior year I'd have gotten used to being nearly six feet, but the bruises that dotted my shins could attest to the fact that I hadn't quite figured out what to do with so much body.

But I'd take her assessment as a compliment.

"Well, my darling little polar bear, let's get you in some air conditioning," Rachel said, grabbing the handle of my suitcase before I could tell her that my arms were working just fine. "I want to get you settled in before dinner. I'd like to take you out to my favorite place, if you're up for some seafood."

The thought of going out to a restaurant in this heat, after being wedged in a tiny airplane seat for the last twelve hours surrounded by people, sounded like inhumane torture. But this was no time for cowardice. Back in Alaska, I was Waverly Lyons, the aggressively untalented and anxious offspring of two brilliant, bickering minds. The quiet kid with no best friend, only a small collection of people she traded notes with. The dead weight. The kid whose parents had finally cracked and called up a distant relative to play babysitter.

But for the next twenty-eight days, I was four thousand miles from that girl.

I could be *anybody*.

So as Rachel and I rolled back over the curb and pulled away from the platform to begin the hour-long drive south to my home for the month, I tried to do what I'd never managed to do before: not overthink it.

O

Holden was right at the edge of the Atlantic Ocean. And I'd never seen it before, so I couldn't help but roll down my window, lean out, and crane my neck in hopes of spotting the water as we drove past strip malls and suburbs. Eventually, the streets became narrower and greener and palm-tree lined, and then, all at once, we turned a corner and there it was: a gently sloped beach and a perfect expanse of blue-green straight out of a travel commercial. I took a deep breath and tasted salt at the back of my mouth.

"Not bad, huh?" Rachel asked from the driver's seat.

"It looks like a postcard," I said.

"You might want to get your head back in here, though. We're about to hit downtown traffic, and I'd hate to have to explain to your father how exactly you got decapitated within an hour of being in my care."

I almost laughed, but considering Rachel's earlier display of general lack of regard for curbs, maybe her remark was a little bit less of a joke and more of a serious warning.

The downtown area of Holden was small and sand dusted, but brimming with color. The shops were all painted in bold primary colors and pretty pastels, the windows and doors trimmed in brilliant white. I spotted an ice cream parlor, a bookstore, and a long boardwalk perched over white sand where sunbathers lounged on beach towels and a small crowd of teenagers made use of a volleyball net. Out in the water, surfers waited patiently for the next big wave.

"You won't stay inside and read the whole time, will you?" Rachel teased. "That's what your dad always did when we came out here on vacation. The rest of us would be at the beach for hours, but he'd coop himself up in the motel with his little science books."

"I don't know. Sounds like a nice vacation to me."

Rachel laughed, thinking it was a joke. But what else was

I going to do to pass the time? I had no friends here, I wasn't artistic enough to shadow Rachel, and the only thing I could do at the beach was burn.

I couldn't swim. I'd never even set foot in a body of water that wasn't a bathtub. While the ocean might've been at my fingertips, it was still decidedly off limits.

"Have you texted your mom and dad to let them know you landed okay?" Rachel asked.

I went rigid in my seat. I'd been hoping to avoid the topic for as long as possible—maybe even the whole trip—but that'd been naively optimistic of me.

"I actually left my phone in Fairbanks," I said in a very small voice.

"You're kidding. You forgot your phone?" I expected Rachel to simmer for a while in anger and disappointment before she snapped and told me, in a misleadingly calm voice, that my disorganization was unacceptable. That was what my dad would've done. But instead, she laughed. "Oh, honey, I'm so sorry. You got the short end of the gene stick. Your grandmother? Wonderful woman. *Horrible* memory. She left me and your dad at a Kroger once. We were there for four hours before she noticed she hadn't gotten us home with all the groceries. Here. My phone should be at the bottom of my purse. Go ahead and text your dad so he doesn't panic."

I scrambled in her bag. No need to tell her that I hadn't left my phone behind by accident—or that I doubted my parents would care if I'd landed safely or had died in a fiery wreck somewhere over the middle of the country.

The text I sent was short and utilitarian: *This is Waverly. Landed and with Aunt Rachel.*

Rachel's phone vibrated with a response a minute later.

At base camp, Dad wrote back. *Just sent you an email about a marine biology internship for high schoolers. Something to do while you're in Holden? Would look great on your college applications. Let me know if you want me to email the director of the program.*

The last thing I wanted to do was spend my summer vacation voluntarily subjecting myself to more academia. I shoved Rachel's phone back in her purse. I'd figure out an excuse later. Or maybe I'd just get bold and wait until Dad came to Holden to pick me up so I could tell him, to his face, that I hated science and math in all their forms. But that idea was more anxiety inducing than empowering.

"Here we are!" Rachel announced, giving me a split second to brace my hand against the car door before she pulled up to the curb and hit the brakes. "Casa de Lyons."

Her house was bigger than I'd expected for a single woman surviving on an artist's salary—two floors, wrap-around porch, modest front yard with a pair of plastic flamingos hidden in the front flower beds. And here I'd been thinking I'd spend the summer in a beach shack with buckets of paint stacked into makeshift furniture. The houses on either side of it were nearly identical, aside from being gentle pastel shades of blue and green. Rachel clearly wasn't one for muted color palettes. Hers was a brilliant sunset orange.

"We'll drop your stuff off and I'll show you your room," she said as we climbed out of her car. "Then you can change and I'll take you out to dinner."

"I'm good to go now."

Rachel's gaze dropped to my legs. Her nose scrunched.

8

Float

"What?" I asked, worried that one of those giant Florida mosquitoes I'd heard legends about had attached itself to my leg.

"Are you sure you're okay in jeans?"

"I don't have any shorts."

"You didn't pack any shorts?"

"No, I don't *own* shorts."

"Right. You usually go up north with your parents on their trips," Rachel said. "I guess you guys must be in snowsuits all summer. You know what, I'm sure I have some old shorts you could try on."

The inside of Rachel's house was just as colorful as the outside. Nothing in the living room matched—not the blue and white gingham couch or the green velvet armchair or the paisley wallpaper. The shelves on the far wall were cluttered with books stacked sideways between pieces of pottery and clay figurines. It was chaotic, bright, and unabashedly cheerful.

"Kitchen's through there," Rachel said, pointing at the narrow archway leading into the next room. I caught a glimpse of nonstick pans and irregularly shaped mugs on an island counter before she started up the staircase in the front hall.

"This'll be your room," Rachel said as she dragged my suitcase to the room at the end of the second-floor hall. It was, thankfully, more muted than the living room, and held only a single bed, a small desk, a chest of drawers, and one very kitschy seashell alarm clock.

"Is this all mine?" I asked.

"Yeah. Sorry it's so small—"

"It's *perfect.*"

"Here. I've got a few boxes of my old clothes in the closet."

9

Rachel rummaged until she found a pair of denim shorts with a rhinestone-speckled butterfly embroidered on one of the back pockets. She held them up for my approval. I'd never been on the cutting edge of fashion, but I knew it'd been a solid two decades since bedazzled back pockets had been a thing. Still, I didn't want to be a burden.

"I had some good times in these," Rachel said.

I took the shorts without asking for the backstory. She left me to change, closing the bedroom door—*my* bedroom door—as she went. The space felt too big, somehow. Cavernous. I'd never really had a room that was totally and completely my own. Dad used the second bedroom at his place as an office when I wasn't around, and Mom just had a studio apartment, so I slept on a pull-out couch in the dining nook. And the majority of my summers were spent in communal bunks, so this was sheer luxury in comparison.

The bedroom might've been too big, but Rachel's shorts proved to be a near-perfect fit—which was good, because accidentally flashing my underwear wouldn't exactly be the best first impression to make on the good people of Holden. Especially while they were eating dinner. I walked into the bathroom—*my* bathroom—and stared at myself in the mirror for several seconds before groaning. Everything was wrong. I did not look like the mysterious, cool, jet-setting newcomer I wanted to be. I had bags under my eyes from the long flight, a butterfly on my butt, and not a tan line to be seen.

I was the same loser I'd always been, just in a different climate.

"You ready?" Rachel called from somewhere out in the hall.

No, I was *not* ready. But I went downstairs anyway.

Rachel and I were halfway out her front door when I noticed a white couple standing on the porch next door: a man who looked to be in his early fifties, and who was sweating through his golf shirt, and a platinum-blond woman wearing five-inch heels. She looked young—Rachel's age, maybe. I frowned, trying to figure out how they might be related, when the guy in the golf shirt leaned over and kissed her on the mouth. Okay, so *not* his daughter.

"Howdy, neighbors!" Rachel called. "You two look all dressed up. What's the occasion?"

"Date night!" the blond woman called back. "His treat."

A voice in my head whispered, *Sugar daddy.* That's what my mom would say. But it seemed unfair to make any judgment calls on someone else's life choices when I was the one in bedazzled loaner shorts.

"Chloe's joking, of course," the man told Rachel. "She got another promotion, so dinner's on her. I think she said she's treating me to lobster tails and a margarita?"

"Like hell," Chloe said, swatting at his arm. "George is the designated driver tonight. If anyone needs a margarita, it's *me*. What are you up to, Rach? Don't tell me you're headed out to Marlin Bay this late. You're going to ruin your eyes if you keep painting in the dark."

"Don't worry, I'm taking the weekend off. My niece—oh gosh! How rude of me. This is my niece, Waverly." To me, she said, "These are my neighbors, George and Chloe Hamilton." She turned back to the Hamiltons. "I picked Waverly up at the airport about an hour ago, so I'm taking the kid to dinner out at Holden Point before she starves."

"That's where we were headed," Chloe said. "Why don't we eat together?"

"We wouldn't want to barge in on your date—"

"You're not barging," George said.

"I could *really* use some social interaction," Chloe seconded. "Between this new client who can't make up his damn mind about the way he wants his living room to look and Isabel's obsession with *Dora the Explorer* reruns, I don't think I've had a real conversation in weeks. I don't even care what we talk about, as long as it's not carpet samples or Swiper the Fox."

"You could tell us about Waverly's trip," George suggested. "Where'd you get in from?"

"Alaska."

George let out a low whistle. "How are you taking the change in temperature?"

"I'm managing." A complete lie. I felt like I was about to pass out.

"What grade are you going into next year, Waverly?" Chloe asked.

"I'll be a senior."

"Oh, you're Blake's age! George's son."

"Where is he tonight?" Rachel asked. "The kids having another beach bash?"

"I'm sure they are," George said, "but Blake is babysitting."

Chloe opened her mouth to add something but was interrupted by a high-pitched screech of mischievous delight. A toddler dressed in tiny pink overalls waddled onto the porch and made a break for it. Chloe lunged and caught the kid before she could launch herself off the steps.

"Blake," George hollered. "I think you're missing something!"

I glanced at my aunt to see if she was concerned about the fact that this Blake guy was obviously a mediocre babysitter, but Rachel was just chuckling to herself as she rummaged through her purse in search of her car keys.

And then a boy appeared in the Hamiltons' front doorway, his arms folded over his chest and his expression a mask of brooding teenage apathy. He was tall, broad shouldered, and dark haired—a true triple threat—and he was easily the most beautiful boy I'd ever seen in person, which I knew wasn't a very impressive statement given that there was a grand total of 228 kids enrolled in my private high school back in Fairbanks. But I hardly knew how else to quantify just how much the sight of him struck me. The air left my lungs, the world stopped turning, the stars fell. Every awful metaphor I'd ever heard seemed applicable.

"Could you at least *try* to keep an eye on Isabel?" George asked in the trademark disappointed dad voice I recognized from sitcoms.

"I told you, I don't want to watch her," Blake said. "I have to go to the beach."

"No, you don't," Chloe snapped. "Hand over your phone."

She transferred the toddler, Isabel, into one arm and, with her free hand, reached for the phone in question. Chloe sounded shockingly authoritative, given that she was about six inches shorter than Blake, even in her five-inch heels. Rachel, who was studiously giving the Hamiltons some privacy by riffling through her purse, didn't seem surprised.

"No way."

"Blake. Phone." He didn't hand it over. "Now," Chloe snapped.

Blake shoved his hand into the pocket of his shorts and pulled out his cell phone. He slapped it into Chloe's waiting palm. Triumphant, she passed the phone to George, then held out Isabel until Blake reluctantly accepted the toddler into his arms.

"Bubby!" Isabel cried in a happy baby gurgle.

"You've got to be kidding me," he muttered, jerking his head back so she couldn't grab his hair. Isabel, unperturbed, batted at his nose instead.

Rachel laughed and called out, "You're making me miss my big brother."

Blake, who apparently hadn't spotted Rachel and me yet, startled and looked our way. He grimaced. I'm fairly certain I grimaced back. This was *not* how I wanted to make my social debut in Holden.

"Blake," Rachel said, "this is my niece, Waverly. She's visiting through August. I think the two of you are the same age! You'll have lots to talk about, with your college apps and your—I don't know. What do kids your age do now? Are you still on Facebook? I can't keep up."

Blake smiled tightly—almost mockingly. Chloe thumped him across the shoulder.

"Nice to meet you," he ground out.

Too afraid to say anything, I bobbed my head in response. I'd never been good at making conversation with anyone, let alone boys with perfectly symmetrical faces whose tone of voice could best be described as *hostile*.

"All right, Blake. We're heading out to dinner with Rachel and Waverly," George said, turning to his son, "so keep an eye on Isabel. We'll be back in an hour or two, and if you want me to even consider letting you go to the party tonight, you'd better behave."

"Fine."

"We'll meet you at the grill?" Rachel asked, at last extracting her car keys from the depths of her paint-stained purse.

"You lead the way!" George said, taking Chloe's hand in his.

As Rachel and I pulled out of the driveway, the couple next door hopped into the front of a cute little silver sedan parked in front of their house. I watched in the rearview mirror as their son stood on the front porch, sighing in annoyance as Isabel tried to climb on top of his shoulders and grab a fistful of his dark hair.

I might've gotten off on the wrong foot, but at least I was going to have more fun tonight than Blake Hamilton was.